OF MIST AND MURDER

OF MIST AND MURDER

CHANDA HAHN

Of Mist and Murder

Copyright © 2021 by Chanda Hahn

Neverwood Press

Editor: A.L.D Editing

Proof Readers: Corrine Doxey, Laura Martinez & Brandy Michele Barber

Cover Design Covers by Combs

Map Illustration by Hanna Sandvig www.bookcoverbakey.com

www.chandahahn.com

(Hardcover) 978-1950440290

(Paperback) 978-1-950440313

(Ingram) 978-1950440306

All rights reserved.

No part of this book may be reproduced in any form or by any electronic or mechanical means, including information storage and retrieval systems, without written permission from the author, except for the use of brief quotations in a book review.

This is a work of fiction. Names, characters, places and incidents are either the product of the author's imagination or are used fictitiously, and any resemblance to actual persons, living or dead, business establishments, events or locales is entirely coincidental.

Also By Chanda Hahn

The Unfortunate Fairy Tales
UnEnchanted
Fairest
Fable
Reign
Forever

The Neverwood Chronicles
Lost Girl
Lost Boy
Lost Shadow

The Underland Duology
Underland
Underlord

The Iron Butterfly Series
The Iron Butterfly
The Steele Wolf
The Silver Siren

The Seven Kingdoms
KILN
RYA
BAIST
CANDOR
FLORIN
ISLA
TOWN OF NIHILL
EVILLE'S TOWER
SION
N
W E
S

For Ashley
because villains are awesome!

CHAPTER ONE

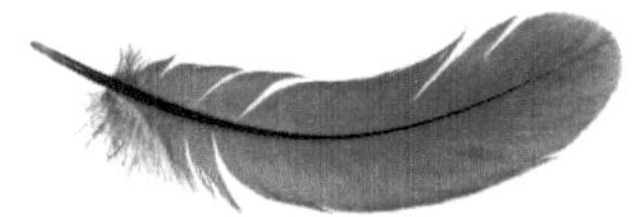

"You can't play with us," Randall spat, his face filled with revulsion. "You're the spawn of a demon. My mother said so."

Two other boys looked on in fear, one tall and knock-kneed, the other stocky and freckled. I didn't learn their names right away. For it was Randall who had caught my eye; the one with the charming, confident smile. It was his good looks that had tempted me to leave Rosalie's side at the market and ask to play stones with them. When I came before, escorted by the oldest of my adoptive sisters, I marveled at the small farmer's market—and a particularly handsome boy.

The other times I came by air, hiding among the trees and the rooftops until I learned everything there was to know about him.

His name, Randall. Favorite color, green. Favorite game, stones. I was young, stupid, and in love.

I begged to go with Rosalie the following week, putting on my nicest green dress and braiding my hair using Rhea's blue silk ribbons. Rosalie's keen eye noticed how I paid attention to my grooming habits and she gave me a smile. We lived on the outskirts of town, in an old, converted guard tower—me, my six sisters, and our adoptive mother—all sheltered from the outside world. I never understood why. Until that day.

"Go crawl back to your tower. Your mother never should have let you leave," Randall called out.

Frozen in place, my hand curled around my set of stones that I had fished out of the creek bed in hopes of joining them.

"I-I only wish to play with you." My voice trembled, but despite my nerves, I put on my brightest smile, hoping to charm them.

"Play with us? Are you mad?"

"You'd probably curse us if you lost," the tall boy said, finally finding his courage.

"We don't want your kind here," Randall sneered, his lip curling, causing his once attractive features to turn ugly.

How did I ever think he was handsome?

"My kind?" I said, my heart breaking at the rejection.

"Witch!" the stout boy shouted. "Go away!"

I shook my head. *Witch . . . really?* They did not know what I could do. I was no mere witch, but a sorceress. Even at my current age of ten, I was more powerful than any mere hedge witch.

Still befuddled at the name calling and the hate directed my way, I never saw Randall's arm rear back, releasing the clump of mud that flew until it hit me in the cheek.

Pain and shock followed. Raising my hand, I touched my face. My fingers came away coated with blood. It wasn't just mud that he had thrown, but a rock as well.

"We said go away, you mud licker!" Randall kneeled to grab another missile.

The river stones in my hand grew warm as I unintentionally created a fire spell, but I quickly released them, dropping the stones to the ground, lest I did something stupid and hurt them. Encouraged by Randall's action, the two other boys quickly followed his lead. A barrage of stones and mud hit my dress, my knees, my face. I turned to run, but I fell, and they circled me. The mudslinging stopped, and Randall glared down at me. A large rock, bigger than any he had before, was in his hand. I met his ruthless gaze with my own. Randall gave a cruel smile.

"Why?" I asked.

"My mother always said it is best to beat the devil out of someone." His boot drew back and kicked me in the stomach.

I gasped as the impact knocked the air from me. I struggled to breathe. Stars flickered across my vision.

"She's so weird looking," Randall said. "Look at how black her hair is."

"All of them sisters are. But she's the creepiest. Do you see the way she stares at you?" the tall boy said. "Look, she's trying to get up." He reached out his long leg and knocked me back down, face first in the mud. "She needs to be taught another lesson."

"No!" I cried out. Forgetting the promise I made to my mother to not reveal my true nature to anyone, I shrank. My body burned as the muscles stretched, my dress disappearing to be replaced by long feathers; my vision narrowed, and I shot into the air. Flapping my wings in Randall's face, he cried out in surprise, calling me the devil once again.

Doing a quick circle in the sky, I took in the lay of the road before turning to barrel down on my targets. An angry cry rent the air. My claws flexed as I prepared to rake my talons across their faces.

"Maeve!" Rosalie's stern warning sent ice down my spine. I peeled away from my attack at the last second. The boys ran in terror, screaming abhorrent things in their wake.

Slowing the beat of my wings, shifting midair in an attempt to show off, I landed next to my older sister. I knew I was in trouble. I had shifted in public, created more discomfort and speculation against my family, and the fact that I had almost attacked them was the greatest sin of all. I would have too, if Rosalie hadn't stopped me.

Then the guilt and rejection hit me. Their cruel words ripping away at my fragile heart.

"Why Rose?" I sniffed, wiping my snot nose on the sleeve of my ruined dress. "I just wanted to play with them. Why do they hate us so much?"

"It's not hate. It's fear disguised as hate," Rosalie said. Pulling out a handkerchief, she wiped at the blood and mud on my face. "People hate us because they do not understand us. And that is why we live far away from others. Protected. Where *they* can't harm us and *we* won't harm them. For every time you harm others, you do more harm to yourself—here." She tapped her finger on my heart in a gentle rebuke. "So put a shield around your heart. Bury it beneath a wall of ice so their words do not harm you."

Under the pressure of her finger, my heart beat wildly, my soul burned with anger toward the boys. I didn't want to forgive them for what they did. I wanted revenge, and that very night, under the cover of darkness, I flew out of the tower in my raven form and scratched at their windows while they slept. Haunting them, leaving dead things on their windowsill, internally cackling as they screamed in fright and cowered under their covers.

When Mother Eville found out about my midnight escapades she lectured me, "What have you done, Maeve?"

"I exacted revenge. That's what you've been training us for, isn't it?"

She sighed and rubbed the crease in her forehead. "Revenge and justice are different. It is best when there is a lesson to be learned. What do you think the boys have learned by your antics?" Her eyes were hard, her posture straight as she sat in her high-back chair. My sisters all gathered in our sitting room, listening to the speech. Honor shook her head. Sweet Aura cried in empathy for me as Rhea patted her back. Rosalie sat in the chair nearest mother, her posture a perfect mirror of our mothers. Eden looked nervous as she practiced glamouring stones into coins by the fire, and Meri, with her red hair, looked just as disturbed as I was as she reclined on the sofa.

In submission, I kept my eyes cast downward and replied. "They have learned to *fear me.*"

"They already fear us, and that is why they attacked you. Fear is never the best ferry for delivering lessons."

"I'm not sorry," I said stubbornly.

Mother's eyes narrowed as she studied me. "No, I suppose you're not. For that is the nature of who you are. There is a time for vengeance, and that time has not yet come. Remember that, Maeve. You have great power, and if you can't control it, you will leave chaos in your wake."

The wagon dipped as the wheel hit a pothole, sending my body reeling against the bars of my cage, crushing my injured wing. I let out a cry of displeasure as it snapped me out of my childhood reverie. Velora, the girl with lavender-colored hair, reached out a steadying hand to keep the cage from rattling as Allemar drove the wagon further into the woods and off the main road down a hidden path.

We traveled under the cover of night, away from the destruction I had caused on the palace in Rya. I still remembered how the sky looked as the palace walls glowed a sickly green; a reflection from the mage fire I had released to save my sister, Aura. My untamed magic in the shape of a fiery dragon had caused the roof to collapse and had killed many innocents. It was that raw power that had caught the attention of Allemar, the sorcerer who kidnapped me while I was in my avian form. Injured and unable to shift back into my human self, he had placed a band on my clawed foot, trapping me as a raven.

The mountainous terrain made the travel slower, and by my calculations, if we went any farther south of the palace, we could encroach on the territory of Candor . . . and I doubted that was Allemar's plan.

The moon seemed to shun us, for she hid behind the clouds. Our way lit by mage light that floated inches above the horses' heads. Velora shuddered and pulled her hood over her hair, giving me a solemn glance. One of pity.

I hated her for her pity.

I cocked my head and gazed at the young man, Aspen, who rode on the large roan next to me. He was much more pleasing to look at. In his early twenties, with dark blond hair and intense eyes, his intricate blood magic tattoos ran up his arms and disappeared beneath the sleeves of his red apprentice robe. Inwardly, I scoffed at his need to use them to amplify his powers—unlike me. Sensing my gaze, Aspen turned and glared back at me.

"Stupid bird," he muttered under his breath.

My feathers ruffled at his comment. I was no more stupid than I was a bird. I couldn't wait for my chance to be free of the band to show my true power and put this half-brained young man to shame. After all, I knew more about him than he did about me. He was Rosalie's brother, the heir of Florin, except he gave up the throne when he became Allemar's apprentice. Allemar had killed King Basil and tried to take his place under guise of a strong glamour. Aspen had bartered royal power for magic power, and from the stories I heard, he was no match for his elder sister. But that was almost years ago, and the blood tattoos on his arm looked fresh. He may very well be stronger than I realized.

"She's not stupid, Aspen," Velora said, coming to my defense.

I hated her all the more for it.

"No, she is." He lowered his voice to a whisper. "Because of *her*, Allemar changed his plans. He wants to *train* her as his apprentice."

"Why not? I think it's a good plan. I would like to be trained too."

"Then you are both fools."

The surliness in his voice was one that I had heard often enough repeated from my mouth when I was displeased with my stepmother's pace of training, or lack thereof. Mother always criticized my training, saying I was often reckless or skipped steps.

I had an intense desire to be better than my sisters. Stronger and more powerful than my adoptive mother, Lorelai Eville, one of the most feared sorcerers in the seven kingdoms. But she refused to teach me the dark magic, going so far as to lock those books away from me. Now I'm bound by someone more powerful than me. And I hated them all for showing how weak I was.

The longer they imprisoned me, the deeper the resentment toward my sisters grew. Especially Aura.

How could she not come for me? How in the world with all of her mind-reading gifts and ability to read emotions could she not hear my cry for help? Could she not feel my terror, my pain? I came to only one conclusion. She did not *want* to help me, or she *couldn't.*

The wagon slowed down as we came across a picturesque two-story cottage. The home backed into a hill with a thatched roof covered in moss. The green shutters still had a faded pattern of painted flowers along the edges, with carefully tended flower boxes. Behind the cottage was a path that led down to a grove of willow trees, and beyond their swaying branches, I saw the reflection of a lake.

Smoke trailed from the chimney, and next to the cottage was a small barn.

"This will do," Allemar said, stepping down from the wagon.

Aspen slid from his horse. "I will prepare the cottage for your arrival."

Allemar waved off Aspen. "No, I'm in the mood to greet our hosts myself." He approached the front door and didn't knock, but raised his hand and blasted it inward with magic. The door swung open, hinges broken.

Within the second-floor windows, lanterns lit as the occupants realized they had an intruder below. A trail of light swept from one room to another as the owner's candle moved from upstairs down to the main level.

"What are you doing in our ho—" a male voice yelled. A flash of green light blasted outward. The man's voice instantly cut off. A feminine scream echoed into the night, then silence followed.

Velora's fingers gripped the sideboard of the wagon, her knuckles white, her breathing shallow. Aspen looked irritated to be cast aside once more. I knew then that he was his own worst enemy. His pride would be his downfall. If I was patient, I could use it against him.

A few moments later, Allemar beckoned for us to enter. Velora picked up my cage and carried me into the dark cottage. She paused, being careful to step around two blackened cinder marks on the floor in the main living area. All traces of the previous inhabitants were gone, other than the two piles of ash. I wanted to take in my surroundings more, but he did not give me the opportunity. Allemar took the cage from Velora and lifted a trapdoor in the floor, carrying me down the cellar steps.

I flapped my wing as the air cooled and I could smell the mustiness. It was small, not much more than a hole in the ground used to store food. There was a wall of jarred food and a small table with barely enough room to turn around.

Allemar placed me on a table in the cellar and turned to leave.

Kra! Kra! Kra! I cried, while mentally screaming, *No!* I

flapped my wings in protest, ignoring the pain of my injury. *Not in the dark. Please don't leave me down here.*

But Allemar was not a mind reader. He was a sorcerer, and I was his prisoner. His boots thudded loudly as he headed back up the stairs. The hinge creaked as the door slammed shut, imprisoning me in the blackness deep beneath the earth.

My heart thudded against my ribs and I screamed in mental anguish, crying out until my voice hurt and it died down like my dreams of escape.

CHAPTER TWO

I hated him with every fiber of my being. Every breath within my lungs was used to curse his very existence. My soul burned with revenge because I could feel the smallest seed of fear growing within me. The fear slowly consuming my mind as I desperately clung to my last shred of humanity.

Even now I could hear Mother's warning. "Maeve, you mustn't spend so much time as a bird. If you do, you can slowly lose yourself, and one day you may not be able to change back." I had rebelled by spending the night living outside in the tree as a raven. It wasn't until my hunger overwhelmed me and I had accidentally eaten two grubs did I come flying back home. I'd spent the next candle mark washing my mouth out and had primly changed into a clean dress and attended breakfast. Eating slower than usual that morning, the food had tasted bland, and my gaze kept straying to the moth trapped in a spider's web in the corner of our window.

My heart had thudded in fear and I had always returned to my human form, never staying in one form or another longer than necessary.

My sharp eyes picked up a flicker of movement; a

shadow under the trapdoor. I ruffled my feathers, burrowing my head down into my chest. Waiting. The cellar door opened, and I glared upon the intruder who entered, the lantern held high in his hand.

Allemar stared back at me. Long waves of black hair showed a hint of green when the lantern light touched upon it. A sneer marred his handsome features.

"Maeve, how are you enjoying your time?" He reached out and brushed his fingers across the edges of my silver cage, an astute reminder that he was my captor.

Carefully, on my perch, I flicked my tail and turned to give him my back. It was the same response I had given him every time he came to visit.

"Come now, is that the way to greet me? After all, I've come bearing gifts." His hand moved into a black leather bag at his waist, removing food.

I couldn't control the shudder of desire that began at my head and ran through my tail feathers. Carefully, I eyed the bloody rat carcass in his hand. The human part of me was disgusted, but the raven, a natural scavenger, was ecstatic. The small rations Velora had been giving me over the last week were getting scarcer. They were slowly starving me, hoping to control me by controlling my food.

My head snapped toward the door, and Allemar voiced the answer to my unspoken question. "She will no longer be bringing you bread or scraps."

Kraaa! I flapped my wings in anger, feeling the tightness in my muscle and the weakness in my still healing wing, but I was stronger. I could feel my body lift off the ground for a few seconds. It wouldn't be long before I could fly again. He couldn't control me or tempt me with that disgusting, but delectable, piece of rotting . . . juicy —*oh stars help me*—flesh.

"Is that your answer?" He quickly put the rat back in his satchel, and I inwardly groaned and cheered at my resolve. It was easier to resist once it was out of sight. The smell of blood was only slightly muffled by the leather, but I could still feel the raven within me fighting for a taste.

"We will see how long you can resist. After all, you will eat from my hand, or not at all." He grinned, revealing his pointed canines, the character trait of those from the Undersea. It served as another reminder that the body the sorcerer resided in was not his own, but that of a Vasili, once a guard of the Undersea. "Soon you will call me master."

Allemar left, and if I were still in my beautiful human form, I would have tossed the room, starting with the cage and table it sat upon. I would have called down lighting, summoned a poisonous fog, and destroyed him. Instead, I felt the flutter of disappointment and the slow grumble of my empty stomach. I'd hold out as long as I could. I must keep every shred of dignity I had left. This was a power struggle, and I had to win.

Each evening he returned with the carcass and tempted me, holding it out within a few inches of the cage. I resisted the urge. But with every passing night, I could feel my humanity slip away as the hunger grew stronger, and with it, so did the scavenger within me. Even the flies and maggots didn't seem to repulse me, but for the raven they were a mere treat. By the seventh evening, I barely had the strength to let out an angry cry as the sorcerer presented another offering.

How could I possibly hope to defeat him if I wasn't

strong enough to escape? But that promise had me hopping toward the door and pecking at the latch.

Allemar held out the maggoty flesh, and I snatched it away, accidentally drawing a speck of blood from his finger in my eagerness. Tipping my head back, I ate it in quick bites, refusing to contemplate on what was actually sliding down my throat. Soon it was gone, and I waited for him to hand me another morsel.

Allemar studied his bloody finger, letting the blood pool upon his skin. "Blood is so precious. It brings life . . . and the lack thereof brings death, but to those prone to the secrets of dark magic—it brings power. If you learn to obey me, I will teach you these secrets." His eyes darkened as he regarded me in the cage. "But that is not this day—for you dared to strike out against me." He tucked the bit of meat into his leather pouch and his voice lowered with a warning. "You will call me master. I will break you, and if you die, I will bring you back from the dead a thousand times until you are mine."

A rattle of challenge left my throat, and quick as lightning, he reached through the bars and grabbed me. My cry was silenced as I felt Allemar's power slice through my body and feathers like a knife through butter. A dark green mist rose from under his touch. My bones snapped and creaked as he forced a shift on me, despite the band on my foot binding my abilities.

Searing pain exploded in my body as his magic fought my own. Shrinking, forcing me to shift against my will.

No! Even starved and exhausted, I tried to keep from shifting, but it was too painful, and I was weak. I gave in and collapsed; my beak was shorter, body still covered in black feathers. A crow. He forced me from a raven into its much smaller cousin, the crow. He released me from his grip and stepped back.

"See, it's useless to fight me. Your magic is no use against mine. I can see that you can change into other forms. How many?"

My ragged breathing was his only answer.

"No matter. All in due time." Allemar turned to leave, but paused and gave me a curious stare. "Do you know what they call a group of crows?"

I trembled beneath his gaze.

"A murder. Ironic, isn't it? That is what you will do for me. You will become my right hand; striking vengeance and death, gathering power for me, and only by doing so will you earn your freedom."

My resolve was slowly breaking down.

"I will come again tomorrow, and I expect utter compliance from you, or this will be the last meal you ever eat."

The door slammed behind him, shutting me in darkness while I wished crows could shed tears.

Against my will, I anxiously awaited the sorcerer's return the next evening. I shuffled back and forth on my perch and stilled when heavy footsteps drew near, and the cellar door opened. Once again, Allemar offered me a treat, and I took the food, being very careful to not peck his skin. It wasn't much more food than the night before, but I sat and waited patiently. I even allowed him to brush a finger across my feathered breast. I swallowed the repulsion, the desire to stab him and bring about blood, but it was my own life I was playing with. Allemar wanted obedience, submission—and I was a rebel. Born to defy, create havoc and mischief, to test boundaries, and if someone told me no, I almost always went against it.

This was a game of patience, and the winner would receive power. And I craved power as much as I loved rebelling. A plan had formed as I lay imprisoned in darkness. I would play the charade of the perfect student and learn the magic my adoptive mother refused to teach me, and with it I would exact revenge when the time was right. Because it was obvious by the fourth week of living in the cellar, eating rotting flesh from Allemar's hands, no one was coming to save me.

It was time. I couldn't hold back my exuberance and felt giddy like a little child, but I knew outwardly showing my emotions would only annoy Allemar. Instead, I remained calm as he brought my cage out of the cellar and into the daylight.

Instantly, I was drawn toward the closed window and looked out upon the sunlight with desire, but quickly put it from my mind. I had to focus. In the main room, Aspen reclined in an overstuffed chair, reading a book. It was one of two chairs that sat opposite a blazing fire. On the far side of the room was the kitchen with another smaller fireplace and a wood-burning stove. Velora was fluttering around, making more of a mess than actually cooking anything. She tried to pull something from the stove and grimaced while the handle was hot. Using her skirt to pull the pan from the fire, she cried out at her burnt meal. She rushed to the closest window and opened it, using her apron to air out the room.

"So you think you've tamed the bird?" Aspen asked casually, turning a page in his book. My attention flickered back to Aspen, and I wondered if he was really reading, for it seemed quite the domestic scene if I hadn't known that I was in a room full of evil sorcerers.

"I have," Allemar grinned.

"I don't think it's a good idea to keep this one. We should throw it back."

"You need her, especially if you ever hope of becoming stronger than your sister."

Aspen seemed to have grown bolder over the last few weeks. He held up his tattoo sleeve. "I already am."

"Then you can practice against her."

He cast those dark eyes my way. "Very well. I will out of curiosity, then. To truly see who is more powerful."

Velora quit moving about the kitchen and stilled as Allemar used the key he wore around his neck to open the cage, holding his hand out before it. We had done this dance before. He had practiced this in the cellar when there was no escape. He would whistle and I would step out onto his hand. But down there, there was nowhere to go. Here, freedom was across the room with the window that Velora had carelessly left opened.

My heart thudded, and Allemar's eyes narrowed. He knew I saw the window. His left hand clenched into a fist, and I knew this was the last test. I could try, and there was a slim chance I could make it, but I would have a band on my clawed foot that wouldn't allow me to shift.

Plus, where would I go?

Home? Not likely. Mother would only blame me for disobeying and getting captured in the first place. I would not be allowed to study transfiguration, and that was only if she could remove the spelled band. It was better to stay. Only then could I learn his secrets and destroy him.

Ignoring the window, I hopped onto Allemar's outstretched hand and tucked my wings close to my side.

"Wise choice, my dear," Allemar said. "Your final test. To remain a crow forever or align yourself with me." He held me near the cage, and I shuddered. I couldn't bear to be locked away again. I desired freedom, even if that freedom meant a longer tether.

I refused to budge.

"Very good." Allemar whispered a word in an old language and a burning sensation appeared on my foot. I felt the weight of the band fall away and knew I could run. I was free. I should flee.

I stayed.

"She's already smarter than the others."

Others? Before I could ponder on his meaning. Allemar touched me again, his power coursing through my body, fire shooting through my veins.

"Shift," he commanded.

It was easier to not fight it; to give in. I raised my wings and felt my neck lengthen, the feathers shrank and turned into jet black hair, my rough claws turned into feet. What once was easy and filled with joy was now agony as my body fought the change, choosing to stay a bird. But I knew each day I stayed in the avian form, the more of myself I lost. I had to shift; it was too dangerous not too. In a flash of light, the shift was over. Dark feathers coated the wood floor, and I stood naked in the room. Nothing but my long ebony hair covering my body, and the loose feathers falling off me. A dangerous telltale sign of how close I was to not shifting back to my human self. I could always retain my clothes before. The feathers didn't want to release their hold on me.

A thud clattered along the floor. Aspen's mouth dropped open in awe at my unexpected beauty. The book he had been reading splayed on the floor, having fallen from his hands. I narrowed my eyes, knowing that in that moment, I held the power in the room. The power he could never possess. The power of being a woman. I walked over to Aspen, giving him a sly smile, completely unashamed. My hair covering my body like a dress.

He looked away, shifted in his chair, and I knew I had won. I reached out my hand toward him. He swallowed, and I pulled the red cloak from the wall hook behind his chair, slipping it over my body. Feeling the touch of the wool against my bare skin felt electric as I was unused to the million hairs that ran along my body once more. I shivered as I clasped the robe and returned to the spun rug in the middle of the room, being very careful to not make sudden moves. Once there, I clenched the robe to keep it from opening, and I kneeled in front of Allemar. Keeping my eyes lowered, I waited for instructions.

"Why did you choose to stay?" Allemar asked.

"I desire power," I said, my voice weak from disuse. "To learn without barriers or boundaries."

"Even if it goes against your own teaching?"

"Especially if it goes against my mother's," I said, my voice filled with heat.

From beneath his robe, Allemar pulled a long dagger with a black stone in the hilt. The stone once alive with magic, now burned out and dead. He sliced his hand with the dagger and put three drops in a cup he had already prepared. He handed me the cup and offered it for me to drink.

I knew the basics; had read about it in Lorelai's forbidden book—one that I had stolen and read numerous times. He was offering a blood contract, an unbreakable one at that. Inwardly, I panicked. This was not part of my plan. I didn't want to be bound to him but knew there wasn't a way out. He wouldn't let me out of the cage without putting another measure of control on me. It was drink or die.

Outwardly, without showing hesitation, I took the cup and drank. My mouth filling with the taste of mulled wine and the iron taste of his blood. I tried not to gag.

He reached out and placed his hand around my wrist. Gritting my teeth, I waited as he spun his spell on me. Feeling the curse course through my veins, I kept silent. One by one, he removed his fingers, and I saw the dark mark he had placed on my skin under my wrist. A triangle. The symbol of loyalty; the first of my blood tattoos. I was now one of his acolytes, his apprentice. He helped me stand and gave me a kiss on my forehead. I kept my revulsion under control.

"Velora, show her to her room and get her some clothes."

"But dinner," she said and pouted, pointing to the smoke-filled pan.

"Can wait," Allemar corrected.

"Hopefully, the new girl can cook," Aspen called out, having regained his composure again.

I bowed my head and waited as Velora took me upstairs to a small storage room that had been converted into a bedroom. A cot with a green, moth-eaten blanket had been shoved into the corner. Velora opened a trunk and pointed to the array of clothes inside. It was the only bit of help she wanted to give me. Now that I was no longer a pet, it seemed like she'd lost her interest. She closed the door, leaving me alone. The clothes were neither the right size or fit and were very out of style. The dress hung on me like a sheet, and I used a belt to help cinch the waist. The boots I found didn't fit either, but they would do to protect my feet. There was a shift and another baggy brown dress and cloak. Once dressed, I turned to survey my surroundings.

I knew why they gave me this room. It backed against the stony hill, revealing no windows. I could use the mirror to call for help—to speak to Rhea and mother—but it was the wildness of my reflection that stopped me.

The spelled wine dribbled down my chin like blood. My green eyes appeared even more vibrant as my anger rolled through my body. I saw that my transformation left me with a few feathers stuck in my scalp. I winced in pain as I plucked them out and laid them out on the cot one by one. Seven feathers in all. Seven sisters, seven kingdoms, and seven prayers I would say for forgiveness as I vowed to learn dark magic so I could have my revenge against my captor and escape.

Looking once more at the mirror and my reflection, I frowned and ripped it from the wall, slamming it into the floor. Over and over I repeated the brutal action until nothing remained but shards of glass that sprinkled over the wood like glitter. Gone was the temptation to call my sisters and mother, and with it I felt a release. Like I had taken a step away from my past and could now look forward to my future, whether or not it would be bleak.

Then a small voice in the back of my head muttered, "Break a mirror, seven years' bad luck."

No sooner had I swept all the mirror shards into a corner when my door was thrust open, and Aspen strolled inside, the book he'd been reading earlier tucked under his arm. His dark eyes took in my saggy black dress, but the way he looked at me in disgust made me feel like I was naked all over again. The tables had turned, and I felt his power radiate as he crossed the few steps to me. I refused to back down as he towered over me, and I was increasingly aware of how tall he was as I looked up at his angular face.

"Why didn't you run?" he asked, his breath warm on my cheek.

"Because he would have killed me."

"He will kill you, anyway," he warned. "It may not be today, or tomorrow, but bit by bit, he will twist your soul until you wish you were dead."

"Why tell me this now?"

"Maybe because I want to see your face as the hopelessness of your situation hits you." His lip turned into a smirk.

"At least I'm alive."

"No, you're already dead." Aspen backed away, turning to grab the door. His eyes held a look of pity as he sent me his parting remark. "You just haven't realized it yet. None of us are free. The mark on your skin is the first stage. He can drain your magic for his own, and with it, your life."

"Then why are you still here?" I hissed. "Why warn me," I grabbed his wrist and pulled on his sleeve, revealing the dark tattoos, "when you seem to benefit from his tutelage."

Aspen's eyes darkened as he ripped his hand away. "You know *nothing* of my past or what I've gone through."

"Do not take me for a fool. I know you gain your power from forbidden black magic. I know that each of those tattooed marks are because you murdered someone." I relished revealing my knowledge and waited for him to deny it. He didn't.

Aspen studied me through narrowed eyes, making his own observations. "You do not have what it takes to survive his training."

"I have to. So I can find out what happened to Aura and find out why she abandoned me."

He shook his head. "No, there's no need. She's in a spiral of her own self-destruction. She imprisoned everyone within the palace and placed them under a sleeping spell, surrounded by a forest thorns. No one can get in or out."

"You lie. That doesn't sound like the Aura I know."

"But it's the truth. You may not know her as well as you think you do. It is not the King of Rya that people fear now, but your sister."

I turned away, scared to let him see my doubt. It was our greatest fear; one that we knew was coming because of her magic. But then it proved my earlier thought. With Aura's gifts, she could have found me. Saved me, but chose not to. She'd gone mad, and I could feel myself following on the same path as her.

He closed the door, and the key turned in the lock. A moment of panic ran up my spine, then anger of being imprisoned again took over. I picked up the book he had left and tossed it at the back of the door. It fell to the floor with a thud, and I sighed.

My body physically weak and my mind mentally exhausted, my nerves having run the gauntlet of endless emotions over the last few weeks, I collapsed on the cot, letting a single sob of regret escape my lips before pressing my fingers over my mouth. No! I would not give in to emotion, to weakness, or to self-pity. I would never allow them to make me cry. Pulling the green blanket over my head, I curled into a ball, flexing my fingers and toes one by one, counting them repeatedly. Relieved each time I counted ten fingers instead of eight, somehow wondering if it had all been a dream. But my exhaustion won, and I fell into a deep sleep and wished briefly to never wake up.

CHAPTER THREE

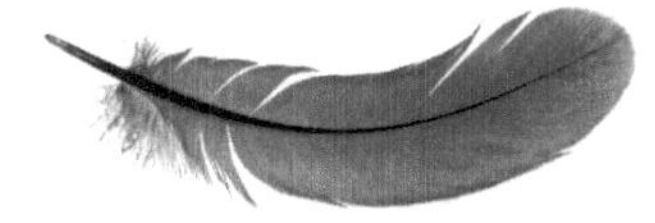

F ly! Fly! Faster; you must fly faster, I told myself, but no matter how hard I pumped my wings, how fast I tried to soar, I could never escape the darkness. A malevolent shadow would spring up from the ground and rise to where I perched on a branch. Taking flight, I tried to lose the thing in the sky, but the shadow's reach was endless. It consumed the trees and spread across the skyline, sucking the white clouds into its dark maw, devouring it and anything the darkness touched.

Farther! Farther! Faster! I flew, but then mid-flight my wings failed me. They stretched, and the feathers fell away, revealing my soft flesh underneath. Then I was no longer a bird, but a girl falling out of the sky.

My scream silent. The rock-covered ground loomed before me, growing larger as I raced toward the earth to meet my death. But I never crashed. Right as I should have been ripped apart by the rocks, a hole opened up in the earth, and I fell into the black abyss that I had been trying to escape. The pressure of the air changed, and it became thick like molasses and I was swimming in the black water. My lungs burned for air, and now death did not come for me in the shape of falling but drowning.

Just when I could handle it no more, I opened my mouth to scream. The inky, dark presence rushed between my lips eagerly, searching for my life and bringing me to death's door, whispering that salvation lie in another form. My skin flaked, turning to scales; my fingers elongated into claws covered in blood. Smoke escaped between my lips with each exhaled breath as I sat upon a pile of human bones. No!

Gasping, I sat up in bed. My body trembled from the echo of the night terror. All around my bed were more feathers, and I wondered how much of my dream was real. Was I shifting in my sleep? Was this a side effect of being trapped as a bird for such an extended amount of time?

No matter. I would need to dispose of the evidence. I gathered the feathers and hid them in a chest at the foot of the bed. Streams of light peeked through the wood slat in the roof where the moss had thinned and I must have slept through most of the day and through the night, for the morning sun danced across my wall. If it was midday, the rays would be on the floor. Running my fingers through my hair, I did my best to plait it and tie it with a string, refusing to grumble about having broken the mirror. When I was presentable, I tested the door, and the knob turned easily in my hand. Someone, either last night or early this morning had unlocked the door. Carefully, I pulled it open and was surprised to see an empty hall and not a guard or Aspen's furious glare. I was not expecting this amount of trust from my mother's greatest enemy.

Expecting a trap at every turn, I treaded softly. I stepped on a wood stair and heard a creak. I froze, waiting for something—anything—to jump out and destroy me. Nothing appeared. When I reached the main floor, I glanced around the empty room and felt confusion flood over me. Where was everyone?

"Shoddy starfish," Velora muttered angrily to my left.

I stepped around the pillar into the kitchen and took stock of the mess that Velora had created. Dishes had been piled high, nothing having been cleaned or washed in days. It seemed the daughter of the sea witch didn't know how to cook or clean. Food had been left out to rot, and I saw a cockroach scuttle behind a cupboard. My eyes snapped hungrily toward the roach and my stomach growled.

I turned, clutching my hand over my mouth, holding back the dry heaves that began to churn in my stomach and up my throat.

"You're hurt," Velora said, pointing to my hand and the piece of mirror that still clung to my skin in dried blood. She sat at the table staring forlornly into her burned stew. We were the only ones in the house. From outside came a repetitive thwack of wood being chopped, and with the frenzy with which it was being cut, I assumed it was Aspen.

"It's nothing," I said, wiping at my hand. Turning toward the kitchen mess, I shook my head and grumbled under my breath, "Useless." Of course, I didn't want to clean. I was the one who frequently skirted chores by flying out the window, swooping in when the chores were done, and dinner was about to be served. It didn't mean I didn't know *how* to cook, it was just that I didn't *want* to. Those days were over. Unless I wanted to go back to eating rotting meat, I would have to do what I hated doing. Menial labor. At least at home we had a brownie and a hob that would help us with chores. The couple that lived here before may have had fae that helped, but after their murder, I'm sure they left.

I went to the sink and lifted the arm of the water pump giving it a few steady pumps and waited for the water to spurt out. Nothing. Gritting my teeth, I grabbed a bucket and headed for the door.

"No, don't," Velora tried to warn me, but I ignored her, not in the mood to listen or take orders from her.

As soon as my foot passed the threshold, I felt an agonizing pain rip through my skull.

"Holy stars." I fell forward and collapsed to my knees.

"Go back!" Aspen yelled from across the yard. He dropped his axe and came running across the yard, waving his arm. "Get back inside."

I would have if the world didn't go black . . .

The pounding wouldn't go away. When I blinked and came to, I was laying inside the frame of the door on the floor. Velora was hovering over me wringing her hands.

"What happened?" I asked.

"You left," she whispered.

"Yeah, I know." I groaned in pain. "I went outside to get water."

Velora shook her head. "You can't go outside. Look." She pointed to the doorframe and the wards that had been magically placed within the framework. Wards to kill me if I stepped over them. I didn't need to guess that they were already over every window as well.

"You could have told me," I snapped.

"I did." She panicked and looked away as a shadow filled the doorway blocking the light.

"You wouldn't have listened," Aspen said. "Too stubborn. You should have died for your disobedience." He stepped around me and headed into the kitchen where he placed a stack of wood by the stove. With deft hands, he made a fire and took more logs to the living room fireplace.

"Then why didn't I?" I asked.

"Aspen," Velora whispered, her eyes going wide as if sharing a secret. "He dragged you back inside before it was too late."

I winced as I sat up, a weird crick in my back told me he hadn't done it gracefully. And more likely had done it out of fear for his own life. Something wet fell down my face. Brushing my hand under my nose, it came away bloody. It really was a close call. Where was the sorcerer? I cast a worried look around the room, and Aspen was the one who answered.

"He's not here. He doesn't know you tried to escape . . . yet." He let the threat hang in the air.

"I didn't try to escape. I went to fetch water." I pointed to the bucket that was laying in the flower bed in the yard.

"Excuses. He won't see it that way. When he returns, he will punish you."

"And when might that be?" I asked as I tried to get to my feet, wiping the blood away and instead smearing it across my face, calculating how long I may still have to live.

"Who knows? Days, weeks, months." Aspen sighed, rubbing his forehead as if being saddled with me and Velora was now giving him a migraine. "He comes and goes whenever he feels like it. He has important business within the kingdoms."

"What kind of business?"

"As if I'm going to tell you."

"But what about my training?" I asked, feeling a bit perturbed by the sudden disappearance of Allemar.

"It has fallen to me."

"No," I snorted. "I can't learn from you."

"Can't or won't? I *can* teach, but if you *won't* learn, not my problem."

"I'll learn!" Velora raised her hand and both of us rolled our eyes at the same time.

"Not now," we snapped in unison, glaring at each other. Neither willing to back down, both of us burning holes in each other with hate. But I came to realize, if I didn't play nice, I may inadvertently run into another one of Allemar's traps.

"Fine." The word seared across my lips, hating that I was agreeing to be an apprentice to someone that was only a few winters older than me.

"Fine." Aspen nodded and headed back outside.

"I still need the water!" I yelled at his retreating back. His shoulders stiffened, and I shook my head in frustration as I gazed upon the mess. Without the water, I doubt I could make any headway cleaning the kitchen.

My fingers dug into my palms as I wrestled with the anger inside of me. Did I feel this way because I was being cast aside and forgotten? Unloaded upon the ignorant Aspen to train instead of with the all-powerful sorcerer himself? Was I not worth his full attention? An all too familiar feeling of rejection washed over me, and I replaced it with a renewed sense of vengeance. I would just work hard and prove everyone wrong. Aspen, Allemar, and my mother.

A loud clatter interrupted my thoughts as a bucket of water clattered inside the doorway. Half of the water sloshed over the wood floor and I groaned at the waste. Picking up the handle, I stared at Aspen's back as he headed back to the wood pile, gripping the axe with ease. It was an odd sight to get out of my head, and I had to remind myself that everyone worked, cleaned, and did chores. Even us, the feared daughters of Eville, mopped and swept when needed.

Hauling the bucket to the stove, I filled the kettle and prepared to boil water for the dishes. Finding a somewhat clean rag, I began to clean.

Velora tried to help, but only mimicked my movements by following along and redoing everything I had done. More than once, she bumped into me, or made a mess dragging a dirty rag over the area I had already cleaned, but I bit my tongue.

"Can you get me more water?" I pointed to the bucket, using any excuse to send her out of the room.

She picked up the bucket and headed outside. I watched her through the window and groaned when she stared at the pump in confusion. Rapping my knuckles on the glass, I made a wild motion with my hands and yelled, "Lift the handle."

Velora lifted the handle and gave it a few tentative pumps. When the cold water sloshed onto the ground, her face lit up with excitement.

"The bucket!" I yelled. "It needs to go in the bucket."

She nodded her head and filled the pail before bringing it back into the kitchen. Her fair cheeks filled with color. "That was wonderful. Did you see it?"

"Yes," I drawled out, waving my hands in the air. "You made water."

Velora's newfound delight of drawing water from the pump had her frequently running back and forth, filling up my bucket. When that was done, she started on filling every tub, jar, and vase within the kitchen. I was now forced to move jars of water onto the window ledges and shelves and along the floor.

I took a quick inventory of food in the sparse cabinets and the cellar. There wasn't much, but I could make something palatable. I hoped. Now I wished I had helped around the kitchen more. I'd just made a roux in the pot when Velora, mimicking my cooking, grabbed a handful of salt thinking it was flour, and flung it into the roux. I couldn't take it anymore.

I snapped at her. "What is wrong with you?"

She backed away, her head hanging low. "I'm trying to learn."

"No, you're not. You're wrecking everything."

Her eyes welled up with unshed tears. "I'm not trying to . . . I just don't know . . . how to be a human girl."

That's when I remembered *who* and *what* she was. A mermaid who had only recently gotten her legs because of a curse they placed on my sister, Meri. A curse that almost killed her.

"Then maybe you should have stayed a mermaid." The wooden spoon I used to stir the roux slashed through the air like a knife. "Your selfishness almost killed my sister."

Velora's lips trembled, her voice barely a whisper. "Love makes you do reckless things. I thought Prince Brennon loved me too, but I was wrong, and I can't go back to the sea. I won't." She said *won't* with a strength and determination she hadn't yet shown.

She was a sea witch's daughter and had plotted to steal a kingdom by marrying the prince. Good for her. I applauded that tenacity because it's something I would have done. But her plans had harmed my sister, and that I wouldn't condone. I stirred the roux and slowly added water from an overly full flower vase, contemplating what her life had been like growing up in the ocean. Fire would be a foreign concept, cooking food another, as a mermaid's diet consisted mostly of raw fish, oysters, and kelp. No wonder she was desperate to learn.

I couldn't help but think of my sisters if they were in my position. If Aura were here, she would know what to say. She'd feel Velora's pain as her own and know the right words to comfort her. Rhea would teach her to read and write. Eden would use glamour to make her feel more at home. Rosalie would be the one to teach her herbology and cooking; Meri, the finer arts of life, like music. Honor, well . . . Honor would never find herself captured or imprisoned. She'd be the one doing the capturing. My fingers gripped the wooden spoon and the wood bent under my anger. It was easy to see each of my sisters' strengths and their abilities and how they would make the best of this situation. But my sisters weren't here, and it wasn't my responsibility to coddle her. It would only teach her codependence. I was the one who had the sarcastic mouth, and anger was the instrument with which I was most in tune.

Empathy was not in my wheelhouse, but I knew how to correct, challenge, and excel. Maybe if I pretended she was a project that I needed to fix . . .

"Fine," I said, mostly to myself.

"I don't understand?" Velora said, not having been privy to my own internal dialogue.

"I will teach you."

"You will?" She visibly brightened and wiped at her eyes.

I wasn't sure if I could stomach the girl. "Yes, but I will not coddle, or sing fake praises when you screw up because that only gives you a false sense of security and lets you think it's okay to make mistakes. But I'm sure you've witnessed by your own accounts that this is not a place you want to have errors."

Her head shook.

"Okay, then let's start with the basics because I don't want to starve. A roux begins with fat, which is butter, oil, lard, or bacon grease. Then we add flour slowly, mixing it together until it has a thick paste consistency." I spent the next candle mark walking through the simple steps in making a roux and thickening it, adding in chopped vegetables and letting it simmer.

An hour later, the kitchen was filled with the most pleasant of aromas. I couldn't help but feel pleased when Aspen stepped into the house, closed his eyes and took a deep breath, savoring the scent. He made his way toward the closer of two pots simmering on the stove and leaned over the smaller one.

"So she *can* cook. Wonder if it tastes as good as it smells." A wry smile appeared on his face.

The pleasant feeling dissipated as fast as a candle being blown out by a brisk breeze. Aspen's hair was dripping wet, the collar of his shirt damp, and it seemed that he had cleaned up at the pump before coming inside. He claimed an empty chair at the table in front of a wooden bowl and looked at me expectantly, waiting to be served. "Maybe you were worth capturing, after all, if I get a servant out of the deal. Serve me, apprentice," he mocked.

My temper flared up. I brought the smaller pot to the

table. Using a ladle, I scooped the hot soup, purposefully missing the bowl and dumping it in his lap.

"Youch!" *Thud!* Aspen tried to stand up and banged his knees on the table.

"Oops," I said unapologetically. Leaning close, I gave my own warning. "I'm no one's servant. Remember that, prince."

Velora gasped, her hands covering her mouth.

I glared at Aspen in challenge, waiting for him to lash out at me. His face red, he raised his hand as if he were going to strike me. My eyes brushed across the tattoos on his arms, and he saw my gaze and where they lingered. The hand lowered, his head dropped toward his chest and he let out a dejected sigh. He set right his bowl and served himself another portion of soup, ignoring the mess I made.

With eyes that accepted my challenge, he put his spoon into the broth and brought it to his lips. He gave it a cursory sniff before putting it in his mouth. Seconds later, it came back out, spewing across the table to join the earlier mess.

"It's salty."

"I know," I said sweetly. "What can I say? The mermaid likes her salt." I gestured to the second pot. "There's your dinner, Your Highness. If you want it, get it yourself." Unwrapping the apron from around my waist, I tossed it onto the table and headed upstairs to my room, making sure to slam the door loudly. I waited as the heavy steps on the stairs alerted me to Aspen's impending arrival. He paused outside the door. I tried not to imagine what my repercussion would be for the outburst. Ten lashes? Imprisoned in the dark, cold cellar? Would I be burned or marred? Then I heard the key turn in the lock, and the footsteps receded.

What? That was it. A night without supper. What kind of evil sorcerer was he?

A pathetic one, that's what.

CHAPTER FOUR

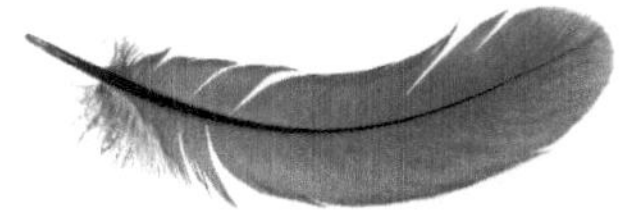

After another night filled with hellish nightmares, I awoke to my room having been unlocked during the early morning. This time before I came downstairs, I walked the other direction down the hall and explored the rooms on the upper floor. Part of it was curiosity, where I wanted to know the lay of the land and where my enemies slept. The closest bedroom to mine was void of personal belongings. The photos that had once graced the walls had all been removed, their absence marked only by the faded outline on the wallpaper. On the table next to the bed was a candle and a stack of books, tucked near the wall.

The next room tore at my heart as I entered a nursery.

A cradle, a single bed, and shelves of toys filled the room. Had there been a child here? Did Allemar murder the children? After closer inspection, there was evidence that the cradle hadn't been used in years. The toys on the shelves had a coating of dust, and the clothing in the trunks had yellowed with age.

Velora had claimed this room, using the single bed as her own. The windowsill was lined with various seashells, a bell, a rattle, and a small porcelain doll.

The last room on the end belonged to the previous owners. My hand grasped the door handle, and my imagination began to run away. If I opened the interior, I would see their private area and getting a closer look at their life. Their deaths would move from being a passing nightmare to reality. But then maybe the sorcerer had left something personal behind, and I could use it in a spell against him.

Pragmatism won out, and I pushed the door open, expecting to enter a full room of memories. Instead, the bed was turned on its side and had been pushed out of the way, the rug rolled up, and in the middle of the room was a spell circle.

I approached hesitantly and tried to read the ancient language, quietly swearing under my breath that I hadn't studied harder. Making a quick note of the markings, I noticed the hash marks spread around the circle like a compass. A transportation spell.

Quickly, before I was discovered, I backed out of the room. As the door clicked shut, I felt a hand on my back.

"What are you doing?"

I spun and stared into Aspen's accusing eyes. His mouth was pressed in a firm line, his hair wet as if he had just washed it. A drip of water trailed down his cheek.

The lie came easy. "Looking for an extra blanket. I was cold last night."

Aspen's eyes narrowed. He stormed into the first room I'd investigated, pulling the folded blanket from his bed and handing it to me.

The blanket was warm in my arms, as if I was touching him. I thrust it into his chest and walked away. "I don't need it anymore."

"Then why lie?" he called after me.

"I didn't lie," I huffed.

"You did."

"Does it matter?" I tossed over my shoulder and spun.

He titled his head in thought. "I guess not, since there's nothing you can do to harm me."

"Then I think you clearly underestimate an irritated woman. I can still kill you without magic."

"I thought that's what you tried to attempt with last night's dinner?"

"Knock off," I snapped and brushed past him, stomping loudly as I headed down the stairs and into the kitchen. I was surprised to see that the remains of last night's meal had been cleaned up and a fire was already roaring in the living room. I knew it wasn't Velora's work, so that meant Aspen had cleaned. But why now when he hadn't done so before? I was confused.

Velora rushed through the front door waving her full bucket of water, her face alight with joy as she set it on the table. "Are we making a roux today?"

I sighed. This isn't what I expected to use my free time for; cooking and cleaning when I wanted to be learning. The front door opened and slammed shut. I looked out the nearest window and watched Aspen stroll across the yard as he headed toward the barn, the sleeves on his shirt rolled up to the elbows, exposing his tattoos. He picked up a pitchfork leaning against the side of the fence and headed inside the structure.

"What's in the barn?" I asked.

Velora's face scrunched up as she tried to think of the word. "An ugly black and white not-horse thing."

"Cow?"

She nodded. "Yes, cow and horses."

If a dethroned prince had become a stable hand, then who was I to complain about a sorceress cleaning a kitchen?

"Come, Velora. Today I will teach you how to make bread."

We spent the morning making dough and letting it rise. Aspen only came in to bring a pail of fresh milk, which I then put into a small butter churn and set Velora on churning duty.

"My arms hurt," she whined. "Can't I do something else, or can't you use your magic?"

The flashback came quickly, and I was sitting in the kitchen with Rosalie when I was eight or nine winters. Ever the ungrateful one, I whined about churning the butter while my eldest sister kneaded bread. "What's the point of having powers if we can't use it to make life easier?" I had pouted.

Rosalie's long hair was pinned out of her face, and her cunning eyes regarded me. "Because magic doesn't teach us about life's lessons. We learn patience from work, and joy from a job well done."

I smirked and let my hands drop from the spelled plunger and it continued to move up and down without my help. She gave me a disapproving look as my charade was revealed.

Rosalie kneeled in front of me. She was the only one of my sisters who saw through my tough demeanor. With a finger covered in flour, she patted me on the nose, leaving a white print in its wake. "Using magic is a shortcut, and there are some things you should never cut corners on."

Her eyes strayed to the churn. She lifted the lid, revealing the separated butter and buttermilk. "Taste it."

Dipping my finger into the buttermilk, I brought it to my mouth and took a taste. My eyebrows had furrowed, and I shook my head. "It tastes wrong."

"Exactly, because your magic spoiled it."

"You mean my magic is bad?"

"No, just that all magic has a taint, a distinct smell, or taste. A trail, per se, that is left behind and alters the taste of the food you cook. You will have to do it all again." She picked up the wooden barrel and headed outside where she dumped out an hour's worth of my work. Coming back inside, she'd set it before me and handed me a milking pail.

This time it was Velora sitting in front of the butter churn, a pretty pout on her face.

"No, we can't use magic. You will want fresh butter to go along with our bread. Believe me, it will be worth it. Plus, I'm teaching you."

Midday came and went, and yet, Aspen never came inside. I wondered if he was avoiding me so he wouldn't have to train me, or did he really despise me that much? He kept busy with menial tasks. After he milked the cow, he mended a fence, continued to chop wood, and even repaired one of the loose shutters on the cottage. With each new task I was surprised, and at the same time secretly bitter at my circumstances.

When the sun set, he finally came inside. This time, as he sat at the table, his mouth dropped when he saw the fresh baked bread and butter. He reached for the loaf, but quickly pulled back his hand as if afraid it would bite him. "May I please have some bread?"

I nodded my head. Aspen picked up the knife, leaned

over the loaf and gently sliced it. Velora was so excited, she was practically bouncing in her chair. I'd taught her how to use her shells as a mold for the butter, and she thrust a plate of her creations his way.

"I made the butt."

I snorted and covered my mouth. Aspen let out a loud laugh.

She frowned. "What's wrong? That's not right, is it?"

"Er," I corrected. "Butt-er."

"Yes. That," she preened.

"I'm sure it will taste wonderful." He gave her a smile and then turned to me. The smile fell from his lips. He reached for the ladle and served himself a bowl, and then his spoon hung within the dish longer than expected.

"It's not poisoned," I said irritably.

"I know. For it would be foolish to poison me. You would be forever trapped in the house until the master returns. Then *he* will kill you."

The threat hung in the air between us, and I pinched my lips together.

He raised the spoonful of soup, and after a suspended moment, took the first taste. I waited for his reaction. Yesterday, I knew it was too salty, for I didn't have any potatoes to help soak up the briny flavor. Today, it was mediocre at best.

He swallowed and grimaced.

"Really, it's not that bad. I'm just short on ingredients and trying to make do with what is left in the cellar," I said in frustration.

"I think you are mistaken. It tastes fine. It's just hot."

The knot in my shoulders released, but not for long.

"Fine? Just fine?" My voice rose in pitch.

Aspen backpedaled. "No, it's good."

I took one of the eight water cups that Velora had filled and flung it in his face, lashing out and letting my temper get the best of me. Water dripped from Aspen's face, and his expression turned dark.

His fist slammed into the table, making the spoons rattle in the bowl.

"What is wrong with you, woman?" he roared.

"Everything's wrong!" I yelled back. "I'm not a cook. I'm a sorceress."

"And I'm a prince."

"A prince without a throne," I hissed, digging into his pride. I was angry. Angry at the world, angry at my predicament, just downright angry and I wanted a fight. I felt more trapped in the house than I did in the spelled cage.

Aspen's fist turned red, the tattoos on his arms glowed with power, and I smelled smoke as his anger burned through the table.

"Do not test me. As I said before, I do not need or desire an apprentice. I would rather end your life now than be saddled with your hissy fits for years to come."

"Hissy fit?" I laughed. "Who said I want to learn from you?" Eagerly, I reached for the power, the ley lines deep in the earth, and I felt it answer. The magic racing up my body, sending currents to my fingertips as lightning crackled across my palms. Velora gasped and ran out of the room. Aspen pushed the chair back, the legs scraping across the floor. I strutted toward him, the lightning dancing across my fingers. "Maybe it is you who should learn from me?"

Aspen's smug face only made my anger rage further.

His arms engulfed with fire, he reached out, grasping my wrist. I tried to shock him but gasped as my magic was quickly smothered. Not smothered . . . *drained*, and the more I fought, the quicker it was depleted. Then I released my hold on the ley line, the connection between the earth and me was cut, but not the pull—for Aspen wasn't done. I could feel him reach into my body, to my very essence, and drain me.

"Stop!" I gasped, my breathing shallow. I felt faint. "I concede."

But Aspen's eyes were wild with hunger. I could see his thirst for power far outweighed my own, and that hunger was not satiated by taking my magic. It wanted my life as well. He released my wrist and backed away in disgust.

My knees buckled, and I fell to the hardwood floor, clutching my chest as I fought for every breath.

"What . . . what was that? What did you do?" I struggled to form the words.

Aspen kneeled in front of me. His lip curled up, and he shook his head. "The mark on your arm. It connects you to not only Allemar, but me. Your power is mine. I can draw on it—and your life—at any time. Consider this lesson one. For the next time you try to challenge me— don't." Aspen stood and stormed off.

My vision blurred as tears filled my eyes. In all of my years training under mother, I had never had a lesson that had me fearing for my life. I couldn't help but wonder if Aspen had been right. I would never survive the training.

∽

We didn't speak again. Days went by and each night my room was locked, and every morning Aspen unlocked it. I spent the time teaching Velora to cook and clean the house. Warily, I watched the windows like a hawk. Whenever I saw him head toward the house, I would make myself scarce, leaving food covered under a towel for him at lunch, or a stew simmering for dinner. But with each meal, the stew was becoming more and more bland as our supply of root vegetables began to dwindle. I never saw his reaction to how the food tasted again because I was always in my room hiding before he was in the kitchen, leaving Aspen and Velora to have a lovely dinner together.

The barn door closed, and my head snapped up to look out the window. There were only a few minutes left because he followed the same routine. He would stop to wash up at the pump, and then head inside for dinner.

"Good night, Velora," I said quickly, making my escape.

"Will you not stay for dinner?" she asked. "Please."

I cast a wary glance at the table, noting the burn mark in the shape of Aspen's fist, then shook my head. "I'm not one who can control my temper easily, and by staying, I run the chance of mouthing off and putting both myself and you in danger."

"At least you're wise to your own shortcomings," Aspen said from the doorway. Dirt coated his shirt, and he hit his pants, a billowing of dust falling to the floor. Why would he skip cleaning up and come in trailing a pile of dirt? Did he do it on purpose?

I bit my tongue and turned to head up the stairs.

"Running away again?" Aspen drawled.

Stopping on the first step, my fists buried in my skirt, I

turned. "I'm leaving you to eat in peace, for you made it quite clear that my presence is not wanted."

"Not wanted, yes, but what if I commanded you?" He ran a finger along his arm and touched one of his tattoos. I felt a pull on my chest and a burning sensation began to build up inside. Was it hatred or his magic?

Spinning on my heel, I came back down and curtseyed. Keeping my eyes to the floor, I bit out between my teeth. "Is that your desire?"

The tension in the air was thick, and only the ticking of the clock on the mantle pierced the air.

"No. There's nothing about you I desire." His words and tone of voice sliced through, cutting me as a woman.

The dismissal was obvious. Retreating up the stairs, I headed back to my room. Hearing his heavy footfalls right behind me, I quickened my pace, and he did too. Rushing into my room, I slammed the door, and then heard a deep chuckle from the other side.

"Oh, Maeve. We really do make the best of enemies," he whispered through the barrier between us. I shivered.

Pressing my hand to the door, I sent a little shock his way.

"Whoa, what was that? A new trick, I see. This is interesting. Very interesting. But you do have to learn to come out and play nice, Maeve. After all, I love toying with you."

"Knock off," I snapped.

"There you are. There's the fighter." The key inserted into the lock but didn't turn. Instead, he pulled it back out and left. Waiting until the footsteps retreated, I checked to see if it was locked. It wasn't.

Had he made a mistake? Or was it a test, and he was hoping I would leave the room so he could punish me? It was a trick. It had to be. Or was he trying to regain my trust?

None of the options gave me comfort, but instead invaded my dreams. This time when I fell from the air to my death, I heard his voice echo from the darkness.

"We make the best of enemies."

CHAPTER FIVE

Allemar returned without notice. When I came down the following morning, he was in a deep discussion with Aspen. I paused on the bottom step and both men turned my way, stopping mid-sentence, a sure signal that I was their main topic of discussion. Allemar leaned back in his chair, a sly smile across his lips. Aspen was tense, his fingers digging into the arm of the chair, like an animal cornered.

"What say you? Feeling up for the task?" Allemar asked, but the tone of his voice was a command.

"As you wish." Aspen bowed his head, hiding his frown. "I will gather the information you require."

"Excellent. Now, both of you, come." Allemar stood, beckoned a finger my way, and headed out the front door with Aspen on his heels. I followed, halting at the doorframe. The sorcerer watched my wariness with interest. "So you've experienced the wards. Tell me, did it hurt?"

"Yes," I answered.

"Good. Aspen said you haven't given him trouble since then. You've been a good student. Is that true?"

My eyes flickered to Aspen. He stared at the wall, feigning disinterest.

"I've taken his lessons to heart."

"Very good. Come," he beckoned again.

I searched the doorframe for the wards. My hesitation displeased Allemar. With a flick of his wrist, his magic grabbed me around the throat and pulled me through the doorway. Expecting another attack, I stumbled to the dirt path and waited.

Nothing happened.

"You shouldn't act surprised. I deactivated the wards. Come, child." Allemar, in his dark green robes, walked the path toward the willow trees. His long black hair pulled back into a bun made him seem less scary and more youthful. A fitting disguise.

It was odd hearing the word *child* drop from the youthful face, but I knew that the soul behind the mask was much, much older. He never looked back to see if I followed but continued down the path and slowed when he reached the lake. Aspen hung back, his eyes watching me carefully, his posture tense.

Cattails flocked the edge of the lake creating a curtain of green and brown. Peeking out among the reeds was a white head on a long neck that glanced at me curiously. The curious beast left the protection of the reeds and paddled out into the middle of the lake. A black swan.

He gave me a curious gaze. "Beautiful," Allemar said. "What I wouldn't do to create an army of them."

My focus was still on the bird in the lake. "An army of swans?" I could never imagine them being intimidating.

"No, shifters . . . like you." He frowned. "Over the years I've used transfiguration magic on my apprentices, but not everyone's minds can handle the shift back and forth. My apprentices eventually go mad and kill themselves, unless they were bitten by a were animal, but those are rare. But natural born shifters—that is where true power lies."

He turned to me, brushing a finger down my face. I flinched.

"What I wouldn't give to learn your secret. Tell me about your parents."

My hands balled as I was flooded with the unwanted memory of my parents and their look of terror when I accidentally shifted into a bird in front of them.

"It's okay," he coaxed, reading my anger. "Let it all out."

"The first time I shifted, I was four. My parents were horrified. They chained me up and took me to the elders of their village, who tried to drive the evil from me. Starvation, beatings, everything short of killing me. When nothing worked, they brought me to Lady Eville, and she knew right away what I was. My parents abandoned me when they found out. But I don't see how any of this is important."

Allemar laughed. "You think it doesn't matter? Of course, it matters. Bloodlines are essential with true shifters. Those people were not your parents. Couldn't be. It's surprising that you never questioned Lorelai Eville, or sought out more of your kind."

"I did. She said that there weren't any more shifters. That they had died out long ago."

"Do you really believe everything she says? There are others. They're in hiding."

My mouth went dry as I suddenly knew he was right. "Where?"

"Patience, Maeve. All in due time. Be a good apprentice, and I will take you to them."

And with that promise, he held power over me once again.

"Can you imagine, Maeve, how powerful you can truly be under my tutelage? Not only are you a natural born shapeshifter, but a trained sorceress."

"You mean how powerful *you* will be when you use my abilities for your gain?"

He wagged his finger at me. "You are definitely the smartest of them. Can't pull one over on you. Yes, everything you do is for my gain, my glory, my success."

My lips stiffened in displeasure as I tried to keep my face neutral despite the anger rising up from within me.

Allemar read my face. "I see you dislike that idea. But you haven't proven yourself and I want to keep a close eye on you. And my apprentice is extremely loyal to me. Let's just say..." Allemar's eyes flashed, "that his life depends on the extent of that loyalty, and so does yours . . . do you understand?"

The mark on my skin burned, and I gasped, holding up my wrist and watching the red blister form before my eyes. He hadn't even waved his hands, spoke a word, or drew a sigil. It was as if his very thought seared into my flesh. A scream escaped my lips.

My anger rose in defense. I was not used to being harmed for no reason, and my instinct was to fight back.

Aspen tensed, his body ready to fight or defend, I wasn't sure. Ever so slightly, he shook his head, but I ignored his warning, drawing on the power of the ley lines deep in the earth.

"You dare to fight me?" Allemar breathed out, closing

his eyes, as if bathing in the sweet sense of my power. The choking pressure came again, and I gasped as I felt the mage begin to siphon my magic, and as quickly as I called it, I let go. The magic released back into the earth, but the siphon didn't stop as Allemar continued to drain my life energy. He could kill me with a simple thought, and I began to understand Aspen's earlier warning.

I should have run.

Allemar's head rolled side to side, and he grinned with pleasure. The mark on my skin throbbed as he continued to leech from me. Aspen stood still as a statue, never flinching, even when I cried out. The self-assured sneer on his face was gone, and instead he was void of emotion.

The world swam, my body weakened, and I was unable to stay upright. I fell to my knees, pitching forward headfirst to the cold ground. I passed out.

When I awoke, I was besieged by darkness. The muscles in my body ached. The damp smell was familiar. My eyes adjusted to the minimal light, and dirt covered my body. The shelves and table were all too familiar. I was back in the cellar. The dull ache in my stomach was my only concession for the passage of time. I must have been down here awhile. At least I wasn't in a cage or trapped in my raven form. Footsteps fell across the ceiling and slowed when they came to the cellar door, then it opened.

Light beamed down the steps, illuminating my pathetic body. The tall lithe shadow could only belong to Aspen. As he descended, I groaned in regret. He was the last person I wanted to see.

His boots came to rest inches from my face, and I waited for him to lift his foot and kick me.

"I knew you were a fool," he taunted. "I didn't think

you would value your life so little as to straight-up challenge him."

"I wasn't challenging him. I was defending myself."

"Same thing. He could have killed you." Aspen paced and muttered to himself. "Maybe I should kill you and save you from yourself." He rolled up the sleeves of his white shirt and held out a hand.

"Touch me and die," I hissed, ignoring the proffered hand, slowly pulling myself to my feet, and squaring off with him.

"You forget already. He doesn't need to touch you to make that happen."

When he didn't make a move to hurt me, I regained a little of my confidence back. "Coward," I shot out.

Aspen stalked forward, his face unreadable. I retreated until my back hit the shelf. I closed my eyes and waited. He gave me a cursory sniff before backing off with a disdain. "You smell." He turned on his heel.

I blinked in surprise and tried to take a covert sniff without him seeing. He was right.

"How long have I been down here?"

"Two days."

"What?" I breathed out. Trying to wrap my mind around the fact that I had lain unconscious on the dirty floor for that long. "Where's—" I began.

"Gone. It's best to assume he's never far. It's time to go. It seems you've recovered."

"You call letting me lay in a cellar recovering?"

Aspen didn't miss a beat. "You didn't die. I would say you've recovered well enough." He talked as he took the cellar steps.

Much slower, I followed behind, and when I reached

the main level, I almost fainted with exhaustion. Stars flashed before me and I gripped the frame to steady myself. The house was stripped bare, anything of value had been removed. A pungent odor hit my nose, but I ignored it as I was distracted by the wagon outside. Velora was sitting in the back among the trunks and supplies. Two other horses were tethered behind the wagon.

As I followed Aspen into the night, a third person stepped out of the darkness carrying a torch in hand. He looked like a mercenary. Long scars lined his muscular arms; his hair, a ruddy brown that brushed his shoulders, his blue eyes hollow, as if filled with years of grief. He was not unattractive at all, but his silent nature bothered me. He wore a brown vest, and strapped to his back were many axes of varying sized.

"Who's that?" I snapped, pointing at the strange man, my anger fueled by my circumstances. I hated feeling helpless.

"Marco," Aspen answered. "An old friend, and our guide."

The question, *what for?* died on my tongue as Aspen took the torch from Marco and brushed it across the cottage's moss-covered roof. Within seconds it blazed, and the fire hungrily chased a trail across the roof and down the frame. The scent in the house earlier . . . he had poured lamp oil. Aspen tossed the torch into the open door, catching a puddle of the accelerant. The fire trailed the fuel through the house and up the stairs. He closed the door, and with mixed feelings running through me, I watched as the cottage burned.

It was unexpected. I knew that it wasn't home. Knew that we couldn't possibly stay there. Someone would eventually come and find out that the previous owners were missing. Questions would be asked, soldiers would come. Our trail had to be covered. It made sense.

Velora sat stiff-lipped in the wagon. It seemed this wasn't the first time she had seen a house destroyed in her wake. In her arms was a cloth-wrapped bundle. When I approached, she opened it, revealing a loaf of bread and the pressed butter.

"Look, I saved the butt." Her smile was wide and proud.

"Yes." I sighed and climbed into the back of the wagon. Smoke billowed out of the open windows of the cottage, creating dark, fingerlike spirals reaching for the sky. "Yes, you did."

CHAPTER SIX

"This is dumb," I spouted angrily, crossing my arms over my chest, glaring at the paper in front of me like it had sprouted horns.

"What did you expect?" Aspen sighed. He tapped the scroll and pointed out an error. "If you are to learn magic, then you need to take notes."

"I already know all of this. When are you going to teach me something I don't know?"

"Really? Then how come you are making so many mistakes in your diagrams? I would have expected more from someone like you. Even Velora is getting the hang of it."

Scowling, I looked over at Velora as she painstakingly copied out the sigils for a spell circle, and I felt the jealousy rise. This wasn't fair. I wasn't great at studying, nor good at tests. I excelled at practical magic; using my gut and instincts rather than tried-and-true spells. This was my undoing with summoning the mage fire dragon and why I couldn't control it. In the end, it had become my greatest regret. I only wanted to learn the strongest spells, skimming over the lesser ones because they weren't as showy. I preferred the quick route.

We had stopped for the night and Aspen was using the free time to teach Velora and me. Well, mostly Velora because I had stormed away from the lesson and moved to stand by the stack of wood Marco had gathered and placed in the pit.

Kneeling before the wood, he pulled out flint and steel, but I didn't even wait. Angry and needing an outlet, I raised my finger toward the dry wood.

"Fiergo."

Flames engulfed the wood pile and almost took Marco with it.

"Dagnabbit!" Marco cried out as his sleeve caught fire. He jumped away from the fire and began to furiously pat at the burning arm. "Are you trying to kill me?"

With another wave of my hand, I whispered, *"Difinite."*

The flame on Marco's arm instantly went out.

"Whoa," Velora whispered. "I want to learn that."

I gave her a triumphant grin. "Of course you would."

Aspen glowered. "So reckless."

Curling my lips in displeasure, I spat out, "You're one to talk. I've heard you practically went on suicide missions to prove yourself stronger than my sisters."

Aspen's shoulders stiffened. He casually rubbed the blood tattoo marks along his arms and wouldn't look me in the eye. "You don't understand. You can't understand the lengths I have gone to just to survive. One day I won't have the strength anymore, and when that day comes, it will be you who pays the price—not me," he warned.

Aspen picked up the axe Marco had discarded on the edge of camp and began to hack at a log, splintering it into smaller pieces. The amount of aggression he was putting into each swing, he was probably picturing my head beneath the blade.

"Coward," I shot after him.

His shoulders tensed and I knew I struck a nerve. I felt like I won an internal battle. But it wasn't fun if I was the only one fighting. This time, just to test Aspen, I sent a flicker of power his way, causing his boot to sink into the earth, and the axe fell.

He spun on me, and I looked at him wide-eyed, as innocent as I could pull off, but secretly grinning in challenge. This is what I missed; antagonizing my sisters, getting into friendly arguments that turned into magical duels. Once Rosalie became so frustrated with me, she made it rain over my head indoors for a whole day. Mother had insisted I be banished outside so as not to ruin her rugs with the incessant puddles that formed wherever I went. I could never beat Rosalie. Meri would give me a run for my money, but with both of them gone, I never had the heart to challenge Aura, and Rhea wouldn't take the bait. She knew better than to fall for my tricks. It may be stupid, goading Aspen into a fight, but I needed to know. I needed the reassurance that I was better than him.

He flung his cloak off and the tattoos on his arms glowed, his fingers twisted and bent, and he created intricate patterns midair. *Conjuring.* Seconds later, a fireball launched my way, and I took joy in twisting out of its path as it scorched the earth.

Velora backed up, Marco had retreated to the other side of camp, grabbing the horses and keeping them at a safe distance.

Laughing, I raised my arms and felt energy trickle along the hairs. Flicking my wrist, I conducted the magic and lightning struck, sending Aspen rolling along the ground. The earth rumbled as the lightning raced skyward, missing him by inches.

"Aw, I missed," I taunted.

Aspen's eyes narrowed, and his fingers danced midair as he conjured his next spell.

The earth rumbled, and the ground shifted under my feet as a chasm opened beneath me. Just as the earth gave way, I lifted my arms and shifted into a raven, taking off for the sky, pushing my wings. Cutting through the air like an arrow, I flew straight over his head and shot into the tree line.

I remembered the feel of the wind under my wings. I had spent so much time imprisoned in a cage that I forgot the freedom that came with flying. Now that I was in the air, there wasn't anything holding me back. I flew fast, hard, and immediately discerned north. A few days of flying south and I'd be home.

Ack!

A piercing shot rang through my heart. I faltered midair, lost my rhythm, and fell. Furiously I beat my wings and remained airborne, but I felt the magical pull and another tug.

Looking down at the camp, Aspen conjured and pulled at the air and jerked his hands back. I felt the tug on my heart again and it fluttered in distress. I fought against the dark magic and tried to fly farther away. Aspen's magic reeled me in like a fish on an invisible string, except that it wasn't string, but a line of dark magic connected to my heart. Just like my dream and I couldn't escape it. *Would I die if I didn't obey?* They way my heart was racing, I was sure it would give out if I didn't comply. Another tug and I was falling, acknowledging that my dreams were a warning of the future of being consumed by darkness if I continued to fight.

I concede.

He felt me give in and the tension on the magic line lessened, giving me room to maneuver and land. As soon as I came near the ground, I had a moment of hesitation. This couldn't be it. I had to fight harder for freedom. He must have sensed my change of heart because he pulled so hard, I fell the last couple of feet to the ground. I shifted just before I made impact, letting my good arm brace for the fall. It wasn't graceful by far, and I landed in a clump.

Breathing became my only focus. If I could breathe, that meant I was still alive. Sitting up, I cupped my arm and felt a tenderness there, knowing that if I had hit the ground as a raven, I might have re-injured my wing.

Boots scuffed along the ground and Aspen stood before me, his face filled with fury. "Foolish girl. I told you that you are bound to me. It is not so easy to escape. Don't *make me* do that again."

It wasn't the warning I expected. He could have said, *don't do that again.* But he laid the blame on me for forcing him to be cruel. He could have let me go. Instead, he kept me bound.

My lips curled in loathing and I glared up at him. "I hate you."

"Good. Consider lesson two over. Hate me. It will give you a reason to survive."

Again, not the response I expected.

Aspen turned and told Velora that lessons were over for tonight. He moved across the fire to sit under an oak tree. He was done with me. I could tell that I irritated him.

But this was a lesson that I hadn't been taught in any of the books. And despite my earlier remark about hating him, I was curious. After a candle mark, I moved from my position in the dirt and cautiously approached Aspen.

His head was leaned against the trunk, and he watched me with narrowed eyes.

"What do you want?" He sounded tired.

"What . . .what was that?" I clutched at my heart and motioned to him, gripping the magical line. "It's what Allemar did too."

"You are connected. Just as I am to Allemar. A tie of the souls, if you will." He gave me a wry smile. "When a master calls, the servant must answer, or die a horrible, painful death."

My heart raced against my ribcage. Sweat trickled down my back. So that's what it felt like. Not only could Allemar do this to Aspen, but Aspen to me as well? It was terrifying to hold someone's life in the palm of your hands like that. And exciting. I wanted to know more.

"Teach me."

The smile fell from his face. His eyes darkened. "No."

"Why not?" I asked.

"Because you only want to know the spell so you can break it."

"Is there a way?"

"No." He leaned his head back and closed his eyes again dismissively.

"Then you're a lousy teacher," I said.

"And you're a horrible student," he countered.

My mouth dropped open, and I wanted to call him a thousand names under the sun, but that would only encourage his view of me. If I wanted to learn, I would need to become a proper student, and I had a feeling that it would be easier to learn from Aspen than the less forgiving Allemar. I was about to concede that I had burned my bridges.

Aspen gasped, his head fell forward, his hand going to his heart. He looked to be in pain.

"Are you okay?" I asked.

After a few moments of silence, he released a slow breath and rubbed his arms. A few of the tattoo marks on his arm had faded and disappeared.

His face fell to one of despair. "Tomorrow I will show you the cost of what it means to be an acolyte. But let me warn you, you will not like this lesson." He paused in thought. "On second thought, maybe you'll surprise me." I felt a moment of pride. He thought I might be good. The moment quickly passed as he added, "But who am I fooling? You'll just mess it up."

"What are we doing," I muttered, sitting at a table in the middle of a crowded pub. My arms folded over my chest, my knees crossed and my right leg swinging in irritation as I glared at every person in the River Run bar.

"You need to keep a lower profile," Aspen growled out. "You're drawing too much attention."

"I'm a woman. I will always draw attention." I smirked and decided to change tactics. Instead of glaring, I smiled at the nearest attractive patron. The man was in his late twenties with auburn hair. He smiled back and stumbled over his low stool as he tried to get up from his seat and move to me.

Aspen sighed. "I should have brought the mermaid. She would have at least listened." He adjusted the sleeves to cover up the tattoos along his arms, but I noticed more had faded and didn't appear as stark. My attention drifted, and I was caught by surprise when the handsome man I smiled at made it through the busy crowd and was by my side.

"How much?" the man whispered, shifting on his feet uncomfortably.

Aspen swore under his breath and rubbed his temples as if I gave him a headache. "Useless."

"For what?" I asked, my brows drawing together in confusion. I was taken aback by the stranger's question. *Could he not see the posted menu board? Did he think I worked here?* "The ale is three coppers, the bread is stale and not worth—" My answers were interrupted by the choking sound coming from Aspen. I looked up at him in surprise. Was he laughing? I had never heard him laugh like that. He clapped his hands over his mouth and was trying to stifle the odd staccato noise coming from him.

The handsome stranger's face turned as red as a high-lock flower. "I mean for your time?" he asked.

Now I was getting irritated. "Did you not hear the bells? It's after ten."

The glasses jostled as Aspen's leg shot out and he kicked the table. I was seriously wondering if he was having a seizure because he couldn't control the spasming of his body as he doubled over. He was shaking with laughter.

"Is this a joke?" The stranger reached out to grasp my upper arm clamping it painfully. It felt like a vice. "You dare to tease me, then pretend ignorance?"

Aspen's laughter stopped as soon as the man touched my arm. The stranger was about to lose that hand, but I didn't get a chance to react because Aspen was on his feet, a glint of a knife flashed, and he pulled him roughly away from me.

"I wouldn't touch her if I were you." Aspen pressed the knife into the man's side, and he jumped in response. His gaze flickered between the two of us, picking up that we were together. For a second, my heart warmed a touch at seeing Aspen defend me, but then it froze like ice and cracked when Aspen added, "She's not worth the money."

The knife disappeared between the folds and the stranger slithered off into the crowd.

"Do you see what I mean about keeping a low profile?" He rubbed his hand through his blond hair.

Feeling chastised, I hunched over the table, mimicking Aspen's earlier posture and pulled the hood over my long locks. Adjusting my position so my knees were demurely tucked under the table and causing fewer glances my way.

"Better?" I asked.

"Better," Aspen grunted as he gazed into his half empty glass. "Did you really not know what he was asking of you?"

I ran my fingers along the edge of my own cup and thought for a second before my cheeks flushed in embarrassment. *A lady of the night. A streetwalker. A bedwarmer.* There were many names for them, but I had always imagined them to be impossibly beautiful. "Why would he think . . .? I mean, why would anyone . . ." I fumbled with my words as my thoughts spun in an impossible cycle. "No man's *ever* shown any interest in me."

The glass Aspen had been holding hit the table hard. "I find that hard to believe."

Did he think I was lying? "It's true. No one can hold a candle to my sisters' beauty. They're all especially pleasing to the eye. I'm the one men are terrified of. Once a young man sent me a love letter and asked to meet me in the woods near the pond. I should have known better."

"What happened?" Aspen leaned forward, his weight on his elbows.

My voice hardened as I recalled the time when Randall and his friends tried to get back at me. Seven years had passed since the attack with the mud. We were no longer children, and I thought maybe his feelings had changed toward me. "It was a trick to lure me from my house. He set a trap with his friends and they tried to drown me in the pond."

Aspen winced, and his hand moved across the table to touch mine, but he pulled back thinking better of it. I felt his rejection . . . hard. It was just like the other men in my town.

"What happened to them?"

He didn't ask what happened to me? Did he only care for their welfare and not mine? "They won't be bothering me anymore."

He nodded his head. "Good. Cause now I don't have to kill them."

I never said I had killed them. In fact, I had erased their memories and sent them back to town like bumbling idiots.

"When it comes to men, their fear *of* me outweighs their desire *for* me," I said simply.

"Not all men." When his eyes met mine, it was the

briefest flicker before he turned away, but it was just long enough for me to notice his eyes were actually a warm hazel and not the dark brown I had always assumed.

Aspen cleared his throat, and his gaze went to the board on the wall, scanning the map of the seven kingdoms. It magically synced with sister boards in other waystations, keeping a current update on all blocked or impassible routes. As I watched, one of the green roads turned red and an X appeared. Swords appeared along other routes.

"What do the swords mean?" I asked, my focus on the ever-changing map. I was reminded once again of how sheltered I had been growing up in the small town that didn't even have an enchanted mirror.

"Bandit sightings. A transport driver updated the board near Packers Creek, which means it will magically update across all the maps."

Before my eyes, the map folded up and disappeared to be replaced by wanted posters of criminals. Aspen tensed, his gaze on the pictures, and I turned to study them as well.

Most of them were petty crimes of poaching on forbidden lands. A few minor scuffles, but then a familiar face appeared on another poster. It was my sister, Meri. A spitting image of her long wavy red hair, her intense green eyes drawn with a memory charm in dark charcoal. Above her pictures were the words: Wanted for Murder. Although it was for accidentally killing a man in defense of Aura, it didn't matter. There was a bounty on her head, and if I had heard correctly, Aspen and his crew had tried to apprehend her multiple times, but she had eluded him. They'd even gone so far as to chase her across the sea. Now it wouldn't matter. She was the queen, and the sea was her domain. Her power was immense; the poster hardly a threat.

Aspen muttered under his breath when he saw her, his hand gripping the glass so hard it shattered. He cursed as he quickly tried to clean up the mess.

"Careful," I drawled. "You'll draw unnecessary attention to yourself."

"Shut it," he snapped. "This is all her fault. If only I had succeeded. I wouldn't need to—" He lifted his hand and blood pooled from a cut on his palm. He wrapped a bandage around it and turned to study the posters. He shook his head in frustration, obviously not finding what he was searching for. "I'm running out of time."

I tapped my finger across the table and stared up at the info board and the wanted signs. It was then I caught a faded article about a notorious serial killer hunting in these parts. Leaving the table, I moved to the wall and plucked the paper from the board, reading the small faded script. The warning, scribbled by a hand that trembled, described a monster who murdered his victims in a cruel and horrible way. Not only did he stab them, but he removed their hearts, as if part of a ceremony. I took the paper and sat back down reading the page.

"Who would do something like this?" I asked showing the poster to Aspen.

In the dim light, he seemed more on edge. Over the last few hours of travel to get to River Run, he had begun to look sickly. His face became more gaunt. His behavior was becoming erratic, and his speech was regressing to odd patterns and repetitiveness, almost manic in nature. In short, Aspen was becoming desperate, and he wouldn't explain why. He read the poster, and he looked unwell.

"Lesson three." He took a deep breath. "Allemar, and those that use dark magic, gain their power through the death of others." He tapped the poster. "And now, so do we."

"Murder," I whispered. Remembering Allemar's warning to me that *I would become his right hand, striking vengeance and death where he wishes, gathering power.*

The door to the inn opened, and immediately a cold chill ran over my back. I stiffened as a dark and foreboding presence entered. I wasn't the only one who noticed because Aspen froze, his head dropping forward, the hood covering his face while he surveyed the room.

I wanted to turn, to look at the thing coming through the door. But I kept still, feeling the floor vibrate with loud steps as he passed into view. There he was, a barrel-chested man towering at almost seven feet tall. His hands the size of a blacksmith's hammer, and probably as deadly. His nose crooked, as if it had been broken on multiple occasions and never set right. My stomach roiled when he passed by, and I could feel the darkness within him. My breath hitched, and I subconsciously put my hand over my mouth to still my expression.

"Barboa!" a drunkard called out toward the man. Barboa ignored him and headed toward the counter.

"Don't move," Aspen whispered. He reached across the table and grabbed my hand squeezing. A faint flicker of magic passed over my skin and I knew he was conjuring . . . something.

"Why?" I whispered.

"I've found my mark."

A beautiful serving woman strolled past our table.

Aspen's eyes followed her, a smile played on his lips. I frowned.

Aspen whispered, "Stay here." He reached for my untouched drink and lifted it high in the air, making a show of polishing it off, swiping his sleeve across his face and stumbling directly in front of the barmaid.

"S'cuse me," Aspen slurred, dropping his money pouch. He made a grab to pick it up, but missed twice, swiping at the wood floor next to the bag. On the third try, he grabbed the pouch and tried to make his way toward the back door stumbling like a drunkard the whole way.

The young barmaid appeared next to Aspen. Her face had an appealing allure. Her sultry aura, a blinding beacon in the dark bar. She pursed her lips, gave him a coy smile and headed into the night. Aspen drunkenly followed after her.

Stay here, Aspen had said. My stomach twisted at the command. Sighing in frustration, I stared back at the poster, picking up the faded page. There were no eyewitness accounts, no picture attached, for no one had ever lived to tell the tale, or they couldn't remember the details in particular.

. . . gain power through the death of others . . .

Aspen's words echoed in my ears, and my heart raced as I replayed the scene in my mind of the barmaid and Aspen following her out into the night. I glanced back at the faceless wanted poster. *It's Aspen.* The barmaid! She's in danger. Dramatically leaping from my chair, I stepped out in front Barboa, almost bowling him over in my need to save the woman.

"Sorry," I muttered in my haste to leave.

A wicked smile fell across Barboa's lips as he mumbled, "Pretty."

The door to the bar slammed behind me as I rushed outside. The cobbled streets were empty, dimly lit by the enchanted lanterns. Across the way, a lone transport was travelling down the road.

Where did they go? I couldn't do a tracking spell, I didn't have an item of the barmaid's nor Aspen's. I would have to remember to always keep something of his on me in the future. Passing between two buildings, I felt a draft and glanced down the alley. I saw it turned a corner, and a shadow moved across the wall. Someone definitely went down there. Adrenaline overcame my fear, and I rushed down the dark path and turned the corner into a dead end. A lone lantern swung gently on a roof hook and a cat jumped onto a wheelbarrow.

Feeling frustrated, I turned to make my way back to the street, and I saw the brick too late.

CHAPTER SEVEN

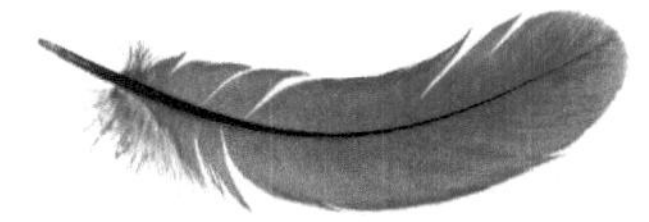

My head throbbed painfully, my ears rang, and I couldn't open one eye. Warm blood ran down my cheek and a copper tang filled my mouth. A cat hissed. A crash followed as the lantern was destroyed and the alley was plunged into darkness.

A blurry shape leaned over me, and a dark shadow filled my vision of my one good eye. It was Barboa. His lips pulled back revealing misshapen teeth too large for a normal human's mouth. He must be a half-breed. Part man, part giant. His breath smelled of death and rot. Bile filled my mouth.

I was wrong about who the killer was. It wasn't Aspen.

Barboa's hand reached for my head, his palm easily covering my face and smothering me. I struggled to breathe, my lips crushed against his skin. A whimper escaped my mouth as I desperately reached for my magic. Lashing out at him with fire, it raced up his hand, and he roared, pulling back to swat out the flames that engulfed his sleeve. It was a gamble, for I could have easily set fire to myself. It was the same for most of my magic. It did me little good in close combat situations.

I gasped for air, but I couldn't inhale. It felt like my

lungs were crushed. That's when I noticed his knee was on my chest, and in the giant's free hand was a knife that he was about to plunge into me.

"You monster!" I wheezed. He ignored the flames, his hand raised toward the sky, and I knew I would have to call down lightning. If it killed us both—so be it.

My head fell back, I arched my back, and prepared to feel the pain of death. Barboa let out a roar, reaching his hand behind him, clawing at the knife sticking out of his back. He fell backward and Aspen rolled out of the way at the last second. Before the monster could get to his feet, Aspen came around with a second dagger and stabbed him in the chest.

I closed my eyes and looked away.

"You idiot!" Aspen yelled. "Get back, or it will all be for nothing." He pointed to the glowing circle and runes on the ground around the half-breed's body.

Scrambling backwards, I exited the magic circle just as Barboa was engulfed by a dark purple mist. He screamed, and the mist thickened as it surrounded his body, hiding him from view. Then the screaming stopped. The mist dissipated, and Barboa's mouth was slack, his eyes lifeless as he collapsed to the ground.

When the circle stopped its ethereal hum, Aspen stepped inside, picked up the knife, and I saw the blood tattoos on his arms grow darker as if freshly applied with a wet brush.

It was forbidden magic. Blood magic.

I wiped at my forehead, and it came away coated with blood. I knew now how close I'd come to death. If I had been inside the trap circle, bleeding when it activated, I'd be dead as well.

"You killed him," I said numbly.

"I have to kill them," he said without emotion. Aspen pulled the sleeves down over his arms as if he was ashamed. "It's the only way. Allemar's power comes from blood magic. A sacrifice."

"It's murder."

His eyes glinted dangerously as he kneeled in front of me. He took in my battered and beaten face. He ran a finger down my cheek, and it came back wet with blood. "Is it murder or justice?" he asked. "I ended a serial killer's life. A slayer of innocent women."

"The barmaid," I groaned and stood to my feet, wobbling. "Is she hurt?"

Aspen's hand reached out to grip my elbow to help me up. "She's gone."

"What?" I yanked my arm out of his grasp. "How could you let her die? Was she just another sacrifice so you could gain more magic?" I couldn't control myself, and my pitch rose in anger.

Aspen snorted. "You really couldn't tell?"

"That you're a coward?" I spat out.

Aspen moved over his spell circle and with a wave of his hand it disappeared. The cobblestone showed no evidence of blood. "I'm not a coward," he seethed. "No one was hurt," his eyes went to my face, and he frowned, "except for you, and that was because you rushed in and tried to save an illusion."

"What do you mean?"

"She was an illusion. I created her in the perfect image of the killer's past victims. I needed a head start to lay out the spelled trap. The illusion would have led him right to me. But you didn't stay put. Instead, he followed you. I barely had time to recreate an entrapment spell."

It was a trap, and the girl was an illusion? I couldn't believe I didn't see it. Of course Aspen would be good with glamour and illusion. Hadn't they changed Velora into a fae queen for an entire banquet? I had seen firsthand how effective and strong his magic was. "I'm sorry . . . I should have known. But you should have explained to me what you were doing."

"Should I? Excuse me, I didn't really have time. He was about to pick his next victim in the bar. I had to act fast. I told you we gain power—"

"—through murder," I finished for him, my hands on my hips, my head held high as I challenged him.

Aspen flinched. "I'm pretty sure you would have tried to stop me had you known."

"Because it's wrong. There are other ways to gain power."

He shook his head. "Not for me, and soon—not for you." I blinked, taken aback. "You're an acolyte now. The earth's magic will slowly rebuke you. You'll be blind to its power, and the only magic you can access is the forbidden magic—that which you gain through blood."

"You lie," I said angrily, refusing to believe that I would lose my gifts. Magic was a part of my life. It was always there. What he said couldn't be true.

"It's true. First it will be just a small loss. Like the color blue. It may still be there, but not as vibrant. Then the other colors will follow until everything you see is only in shades of gray. The magic will still be there, but you can no longer see it or access it. The world will eventually become black and white. Lose its life, color, flavor . . . and you will just be existing."

I swallowed because what he described sounded like Hell. Fear raced up my spine.

"I can exist," I stated boldly. I lied.

"Can you?" Aspen shrugged, his hazel eyes filled with sadness. "I couldn't. It was dark and cold. I found that I would do anything to feel again."

"With the forbidden magic."

"Allemar says blood magic is gained through sacrifice. He never cared how. When I was younger, he would tie up servants in his workshop and torture them. I watched them go mad. Plead for him to end their suffering. Eventually he did, but not after leaving them broken. I swore to never take a life the way he does. I follow my own moral compass."

"Your compass is broken," I sneered.

He snorted. "I only murder those that have murdered others, or those that I deem truly evil." He gave me a side glance and his mouth pinched. I could almost hear his unspoken thoughts. He gathered the body of Barboa, dragging it onto a wooden wheelbarrow, and carted it down the road, stopping outside of the city guards' tower. He knocked on the door, and lights from within came on. A moment later, two guards answered. I stayed back and out of sight.

The guards were hesitant at first. Half asleep, but they seemed to recognize Aspen when he presented another certificate.

"Bounty hunter." The first one guard nodded taking the certificate. "Who do you have?"

Aspen spoke in low tones and gestured to the body in

the wagon, then he pulled out a separate warrant detailing the serial killer known as Barboa Black.

"It wasn't very descriptive. How do we know it's him?"

"It's him," Aspen assured them.

"Wait." An older guard came from the back of the room, still dressed in his nightshirt. "Show me his arm."

Aspen obliged, lifting the sleeve on the arm on Barboa, revealing twelve slash marks on his wrist. One for each of his kills, a few still fresh and healing. A characteristic left off on the warrant, but clearly known by the guards.

"It really is him." The old guard sighed in relief.

More guards came, and after a longer discussion, they took the poster and the body and gave Aspen a full bag of gold. When he turned to leave, the older guard grabbed Aspen's shoulder.

He leaned forward and spoke softly. "You really are one of the best hunters we've seen. Time and time again, you do what we cannot. I need your help. There's a crew of bandits on the southern pass. Everyone I've sent to dispose of them hasn't returned. Do you think you could—?"

"I'll take care of it," Aspen interrupted. "What do you want for proof?"

"The leader is called Pavel. He has a jeweled eye patch. Send me that, and I will pay you handsomely on your next visit through town."

Aspen nodded and left as silent as he came.

I had a thought and spoke it aloud. "Is this why you watch the wanted posters so carefully? You're a bounty hunter?"

"I rid the world of evil, and at the same time gain power."

"By creating more evil," I said.

"I dole out justice."

I didn't like the words coming from Aspen's mouth. It sounded too much . . . like me.

"Come, let's return to camp. I'm tired, and could use a good night's sleep," Aspen said.

Mother Eville's warning came back to me. Justice verses revenge. Is murder justifiable? *No.* I shook my head. But then I saw myself back in the palace of Rya as the magic thorns tried to attack. I used my magic to fight back, and in the end, it caused hundreds of senseless deaths. Deaths that could have been prevented had I used my magic more wisely.

My eye was almost completely swollen shut as I followed blindly after Aspen. Unbidden tears made seeing out of my good eye impossible. I tried to wipe it away but couldn't stop the flow. I had seen the evil being that Barboa was and had chastised Aspen for ridding the world of a killer. Yet, I was the one with more blood on my hands. I was the greater evil in this world.

We took the back alleys and side streets, avoiding the bar we had just left, and headed to the outskirts of town. Aspen explained it was imperative that we never stayed in the same place we hunted. That if you wanted a good night's sleep you can stay in a waystation or an inn, but if you wanted to hunt, you slept on the road. You could have one, not both. He explained that it was to cover our tracks so we didn't get caught.

It made sense, except when I was battered and beaten and I didn't trust my legs to carry me out of town. My steps slowed, much to Aspen's frustration.

Aspen ran his hands through his dark blond hair. "Can't you heal yourself?"

I shook my head. "No, only others."

He released a long, drawn out breath of frustration. "You really are hopeless." He brushed aside my hair, his fingers trailing along my cheek as he drew a sigil for healing. Warmth cascaded from his touch, and the wound on my forehead closed up. The swelling around my eye went down, but it wasn't fully healed.

"I'm just healing you so you can keep up and stop whining. That's all."

Grinding my teeth kept me from verbally attacking him outright, but he healed me, and for that alone, I kept my silence. When we came to the small fire in the clearing, I was emotionally exhausted and collapsed on my bedroll, rolling to face away from the group. I thought I was hiding my feelings well, but the shaking of my shoulders gave me away.

Velora tiptoed over to me with a cloth and gently wiped the dried blood from my face, making a soft cooing noise that sounded more like the blowing of bubbles. I'm sure it was a natural instinct for a mermaid, but to the human ear, it sounded odd. But her oddness was slowly growing on me. I let her clean up my face, and didn't insult her while she did it, proving that I too could grow and be a nice person.

Maybe.

CHAPTER EIGHT

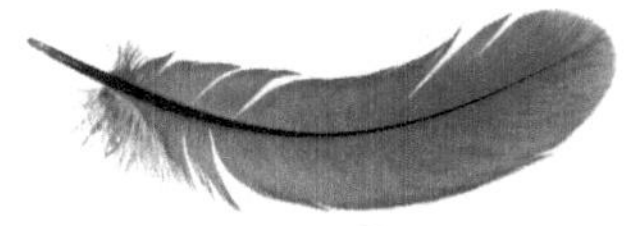

A foot nudged me roughly in the back. Opening my good eye, I recognized Marco's boot covered in mud. He said nothing, but once I was awake, he moved across camp and began to pack up the sparse belongings. Velora was already up and spending time with the horses, petting them, rubbing their snouts. Aspen was noticeably absent.

"Where's Aspen?" I asked.

Velora shrugged, ignoring me to focus on her horse. That's when I also noticed that the wagon and the workhorses were gone as well. After I packed up my bedroll, I moved to speak with Velora.

"Why are you here?" I whispered. "Do you know what Aspen did last night? He murdered someone."

Velora's eyes hardened, and she glared at me. Her nostrils flared, her voice becoming punctuated with her anger. "You don't know us. Don't judge."

"You could leave. Escape right now. Run away. You're not bound like I am." I held up my wrist, showing my mark. "There's nothing keeping you here." *Unlike me*, I thought angrily.

My futile effort at persuading her was interrupted as

Aspen returned with two more horses but without the wagon.

"Where's the wagon?" I said, letting my frustration ride out in my voice.

"I sold it," he said simply, dismounting with ease. "We need to get moving and we'll travel faster without it. Need to get to the southern pass as soon as possible to track those bandits."

The news made me uncomfortable. I wasn't the best at riding horseback. I preferred sitting in the wagon, where it was safe, or traveling in the air where I depended on my own wings—not on the whim of an animal that could throw me at any moment. These beasts were not like our gentle donkey, Bug, or Jasper, our slow and steady workhorse. They were built for speed, and they terrified me.

"Is this your plan, then? To travel the roads murdering bandits to gain power?" I said.

Aspen's lips pinched together in a smile as he adjusted the saddle on one of the newer horses. "And money. We mustn't forget that."

When camp was packed and we were loaded, I watched as Aspen gave Velora a hand up onto her horse and adjusted the stirrups for her legs. She blushed when his hand brushed her thigh, and I knew then the reason she didn't leave them. Velora was smitten with Aspen. Did he return her feelings?

All of a sudden, my stomach dropped and I felt sick. Was this jealousy I felt? No. Impossible. I couldn't care for him. He was a murdering fool. A psychopath that had tried to kill my sisters on multiple occasions.

When Aspen brought over the chestnut-colored horse

and held out the reins, I refused to take them. I was embarrassed to show how bad of a rider I was.

"I'd rather fly," I stated, and shifted into a raven. I flew to the nearest tree and glared at Aspen, who shaded his eyes as he tried to find me within the greenery.

"You can't go far from me," he yelled. "I will always find you."

Kraa!

"And don't do anything stupid," he added.

My feathers ruffled, showing my anger. *He was the stupid one.*

Aspen tied my horse to his own saddle, and they took off down a barely discernible path until they came up to a junction. Aspen headed south, toward the roads that held the most danger. I took to the air and flew from tree to tree, keeping near Aspen, scared that if I flew out of sight, he would pull that magical thread and stop my heart. By midday, I felt confident enough that I took to the sky for longer periods and flew in circles, scouting the road ahead and then dropping back to cover our trail, always staying in sight.

We stopped for a break and I flew down and joined them.

Aspen cut up an apple into slices and handed half to Velora. Her cheeks flushed again. I felt ire rise up in my belly and I wrote it off as hunger.

"Catch." He tossed me a full, uncut apple. Seconds later, a sheathed knife came flying into my lap.

"Hey!" I snapped. He didn't even offer to cut it for me. Just expected me to do it myself. I picked up the knife, slid it out of the sheath, pressed the edge to my apple and very carefully pared the skin from the apple in one curly slice.

"Nice," Velora said, as I took a bite of the pure white crispness, the juices flowing down my lips.

I grinned in response and wiped at the juice with my sleeve. Aspen's eyes dropped to my lips, his face a stony mask, and my smile fell. *What was that look for? Did I do something wrong?* Frustrated, I quickly ate. As soon as I could, I took to the sky, keeping as much distance between him and me as possible.

When the sun began to set, I felt a single tug on my magic, and I circled back to Aspen. I was irritated with him. He could see me just fine. I wasn't trying to escape. How dare he threaten me like that. I shot to earth like an arrow, and my anger roiled through my wings. I wanted to take off his head.

He made a motion with his finger ahead and he called out, "What do you see ahead? Is there a good place to camp?"

My anger dissipated. It wasn't a threat or a disciplinary action, but a signal. I had been so lost in my thoughts that I had forgotten they were below me. I continued to search the surrounding area until I found what we needed. I flew back to warn the rest, letting out a call and flying in a circle.

Aspen nodded. "Very well. We will make camp there. Show us the way."

Keeping low, I flew along the ground as he led the group to the spot I had found. I sat in the lowest branch of an evergreen tree.

"Very good, Maeve," Aspen said, when he dismounted. "This will do well." His praise made me unintentionally preen. "What about danger? Is there anything near us?"

I blinked at him slowly, showing my irritation. *Did he*

think I would purposely lead them into danger? Wait. That was a good idea. I probably could have led him straight into a bear den and then I would be free of him.

But that didn't leave me free of Allemar. He was the more dangerous of the two, and I never knew when he would return. I flew to the ground. My transformation in midair was seamless, and I knew I was showing off a bit. Aspen seemed impressed by my ability.

"*We* are the most dangerous things for miles." I didn't turn around, but got to work preparing dinner as best as I could, wanting to show off some of my skills, knowing that Marco and Aspen preferred my cooking over Velora's.

Cooking over an open flame on the road was different from cooking in our kitchen on our stove. For one, the elements played a huge part in how fast or slow the water boiled. Feeling frustrated, I reached my finger into the water and whispered a simple heating spell. The water boiled, and I began food prep.

Velora sat by me and stared into the flickering flame.

"Tell me about your sisters," I coaxed.

She flinched as if I physically hit her. "Why?" she asked suspiciously.

"I come from a large family. I have six sisters, and I wondered about yours. Rosalie's the oldest, Meri has the best voice, Eden is the funniest, Aura the sweetest, Rhea's the smartest, Honor's the wittiest, and I'm the . . ." I trailed off, not sure exactly how to describe how I fit into our family dynamic. I excelled at causing trouble, had the shortest fuse, and was not the perfect role model. "Well, I'm the most adventurous," I finished, figuring that described my late night exploits the best. I decided to open up a bit more to her. "But we're not actually related. We were all adopted," I said.

Velora tucked a strand of her lavender hair behind her ear. "The sea is home; full of life and color, and my sisters and I explored every edge of it. But the same sea was also our prison. Because of our curse, we were not born with the ability to shed our tails like other mermaids." Her eyes hardened, her knuckles clenched. "A curse placed upon us . . . by *your* mother."

I had forgotten the long rivalry between Lorelai Eville and Sirena. It was Sirena who caused Lorelai's father's ship to sink and lose all of their fortune, losing the engagement to a prince, thus starting the whole vengeance cycle we were currently embarking upon.

"But no longer," I said. "Meri broke the curse. *You* almost killed her doing it."

Velora crossed her arms over her knees and rested her head upon her hands. "Yes, we are longer bound. But I fear her repercussions. I do not feel safe in the sea any longer. None of my sisters do."

Meri had taken her rightful place as the song of the sea, the ruler of the ocean, with Prince Brennan at her side. A prince that Velora was in love with. She had tried to kill Meri to protect that love. I understood why she was scared to return home to the water. Could she trust the ocean to protect her when Meri's reach was far? She was running from her past and took up with the only person she thought could protect her. Too bad it was the enemy.

"How many?" Aspen asked, his eyes scanning the narrow road before us.

I was out of breath, my heart racing with adrenaline as I quickly recounted what I saw waiting ahead of us.

"Eight bandits. Three on each side of the road. Two with crossbows hiding in the tree line."

Aspen's lips pinched together in worry. "That's the largest group I've taken on without more fighters. I may not be able to take them down without spending too much magic."

"We could have avoided this route altogether," I said. "Forget about your promise to the old man."

His eyes hardened. "Bandits shouldn't be left unchecked." His hand reached for his sword.

"And who's keeping you in check?" I added harshly.

"If you're not helping, you're hindering. When the fighting starts, keep out of the way. Marco and I will handle the bandits."

"I'm not useless," I argued. "I can fight."

He gave me a seething look. "You yourself said you didn't want to do this. So either you're with us or not. I can't have a dull blade guarding my back, or one that has qualms when it comes to life-or-death situations. So choose a side."

He left no room for argument. Aspen marched over to Marco, and the two of them made a plan of attack.

"I hate this," I muttered as I walked along the side of Velora's horse. Aspen took the lead with Marco bringing up the rear as we entered the narrow trail. There was a cliff on our left and a heavily dense population of trees on the other. The attack would come from there, and we would be pinned against the rock wall. Above the cliff, hiding in the rocks, were three more men.

Aspen gripped his horse with his thighs, his hands tucked under his robe, and his hood pulled low over his head. Velora kept facing forward, trying to not give anything away, her fear evident in the tenseness of her shoulders. Marco's eyes scanned the tree line, his hand resting on his axe.

A poorly imitated whistling birdcall pierced the air. Men burst out of the cover of the tree line on our right. Screaming, they charged, swords drawn.

Aspen reacted. Conjuring a spell, he blasted the two closest backwards into a tree. He was quickly set upon by the two who swung out from the cliff and dropped down on him from above, knocking him from his horse. Aspen hit the ground, rolled and was up, his sword in hand as he dodged, then blocked a downward strike. Marco yelled. Launching from his horse, he swung his axe at a man's head. The bandit ducked to avoid being decapitated and fell backwards. The first man that hit the tree was back up and into the fray. There was so much going on. It was chaos, but I couldn't lose sight of the real danger. My eyes focused on the trees, and I was ready for what I knew was coming.

Velora struggled to stay on her horse as a bandit with a scarred chin grabbed the reins and tried to separate her from our group.

"No!" Velora kicked him in the shoulder, but he easily dodged.

"*Fulguri,*" I yelled. A lightning blast hit him, and he fell backwards. My sudden attack startled Velora's horse, and he reared, sending her to the ground. Her head hit the ground with a thud, and she didn't move.

Marco and Aspen were struggling. Every time Aspen tried to push them back to weave a trap circle, they attacked him again. The leader put his fingers to his mouth and whistled. The twang of the crossbows released, and Aspen tried to put up a magic shield, but I knew it would be too late.

"Incendium!" I pointed, and the bolts incinerated into ash midair.

We couldn't fight an opponent we couldn't see. There wasn't a way for Aspen to lay a trap circle while he and Marco fought off six attackers, while two more hid within the trees. I needed to even the playing field. Standing over Velora, I raised my hands and struck out with lightning bolts where I remembered the men hiding. A scream came from the woods as my magic hit close to home. One of the men jumped out of the cover of the boughs and rolled to the ground. After another wave of blistering attacks, the second man came running out of the woods toward us.

A searing pain hit as an arrow grazed my shoulder, and I cried out. A blinding fury came over me and I lashed out with magic, aiming at the cliff. Strike after strike, attacking the boulders and the men that had avoided my earlier detection.

"Maeve, behind you!" Aspen cried out. One of the bandits had snuck behind, and a flash of steel came from above me. I blinked as my attacker froze midair. The sword falling from his grip, he collapsed to his knees. Behind him, a furious Velora pulled a dagger from his back. Her pupils had shifted into dark slits, her teeth morphed, small and needlelike, and her skin reflected the sun like clear fish scales. Velora had taken on aspects of her deadlier counterpart, a killer in the sea, the mermaid.

"Thanks," I said.

The gentle Velora I knew was gone, and she turned, dagger in hand, to launch at the next closest bandit.

Marco rushed to Velora's aid, but he wasn't needed. She was extremely strong, easily disarming the man and tossing him over her shoulder.

Aspen was in a duel to the death with Pavel, the leader of the bandits. But his fighting was distracted as he kept trying to protect Velora and me. When one would break off to try and attack Velora or come my way, Aspen would use magic to pull them back toward himself.

"Where are you going?" Aspen laughed. "I'm not done with you yet." He cocked his head and a churlish laugh spilled forth. The tattoos on his arms glowed, and I knew he was using up too much magic. There was a madness that was building as he used his power. Insanity was following. The more injured he became, the more desperately he used his magic. I could hear it in his voice, and I didn't like it.

"End it already," I ordered Aspen. "Or I will."

With a cry, he sent out a wave of air that knocked everyone within a five-foot radius back a good ten feet. His lips moved, and he began to weave a spell. Knowing I was bleeding, I turned and ran, grabbing Velora by the arm and pulling her out of the way.

She snapped at me and swung the knife, nicking my hand.

"Velora, it's me. We need to move back."

With a quick glance around, she saw the trap circle begin to flare up, and she retreated with me. Marco was still fighting and bleeding from various cuts. I knew if he was too close, he would be pulled into the spell.

With a flick of my power, I pushed him to a safe distance. His yelp of surprise made me laugh. But Aspen wasn't done casting the circle. His eyes were focused on his hands and the glowing marks in the ground. The bandits rushed him, not fearful of the magic emblem, or maybe they were blind to what he was doing.

I had to decide to let him die, or aid in their death.

"Come on, finish it," I murmured under my breath. The circle was thrumming and slowly growing larger to cover a greater area. Then I understood his concern. Trapping one person was a quick spell, trapping such a large number required a greater area and more concentration.

"Die!" Pavel had made it within the inner circle and rushed Aspen.

Aspen's eyes were still closed, oblivious to the oncoming attack.

Pavel raised his dagger.

Velora cried out in fear.

I reacted on instinct. *"Glacias."* An ice spear shot from my hand.

Pavel's mouth gaped open as he stood over Aspen. The hidden dagger in Aspen's grip buried deep in his lower stomach while the ice shard I sent flying embedded in his chest. We had simultaneously attacked, and both struck our target. Pavel fell to his knees. Aspen took his jeweled eye patch and retreated out of the trap circle as it activated around not eight but ten bandits.

I closed my eyes and dropped to my knees, covering my ears. Not wanting to hear or see the killing mist as it encircled them. Cries filled the air, followed by a whistling wind, and then it was silent.

It was over.

Aspen stood over me, the marks on his arms glowing with a renewed power. His gaze met mine, and he said solemnly, "I guess you picked a side."

CHAPTER NINE

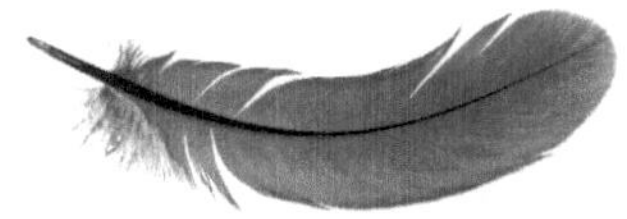

We spent the next week travelling south, hitting the more dangerous trails, and we had a surprise run-in with a rogue ogre who had a taste for human flesh. After seeing its home, a cave full of human skulls—some of very small sizes—I felt no remorse for his death, only a small bit of pride that a monster like that was gone from this world.

I guess you picked a side. Aspen's words sat uneasily with me.

Each night, the lessons continued by the fire, and they were strained as I barely said a word. Velora had long given up since her attention span was that of a gnat. I could easily conjure a trap spell that fed the marks, use a snare, and conjure many other dark spells that my mother had avoided teaching us.

In my mind, I had begun to call Aspen the dark prince, because when no one was looking, he often stared off into the distance. His eyes filled with a deep sadness that never lifted. When I didn't purposely irritate him, I found him to be quiet in his praise, and he rarely rebuked me when I did mess up.

This night in particular, I wasn't tired, but more contemplative. Marco was whittling Velora a wooden mermaid. She was leaning close to him and supervising his work; giving him little corrections like, "the tail's too long", or "a thinner fin", and "Oh, that looks like my sister now."

Aspen was rereading a letter that he kept tucked in his book. It seemed to be the source of his sadness.

"Okay, spill. What is it that has you turning so melancholy" I asked, turning on my side, propping my head on my hand.

"A letter from a friend."

"Is it good news?"

"Depends on how you take it."

"Did someone die?"

He shook his head. "No."

"Oh, I see. Then it's a girl, writing to let you know that you have a secret love child and you must come home right away or she'll forced to marry a baron?"

That got a wry smile from him. "No."

"Really, I could have sworn you were the type," I teased.

His eyebrows rose up in surprise. "What type?"

"The kind of man to woo a woman in every town."

His eyes twinkled with mischief as he looked at me. "I don't need another woman in my life. You two are exhausting enough as it is."

I wrinkled my nose and made a face at him.

Aspen laughed, and the cloud that was hanging over him seemed to lift.

"Then I don't see what the problem is. If no one died, and you don't have a secret lover or child, then why the long face?" I asked, pulling on my chin, mimicking a sad face.

"You really have a flair for the dramatic, don't you?" The corner of his mouth rose in a smile.

My heart fluttered. Did he realize how handsome he was? The firelight caught his hair, making it look like it was spun of amber.

"Eight women in one house. You have no idea the drama that unfolds. It can be as dirty as last week's laundry. Especially since Aura has a knack for *accidentally* reading our thoughts. In our house, there's no such things as secrets."

"She can't be trusted?"

I shrugged. "She talks in her sleep. Imagine having a fancy for a boy and not telling anyone, but then your sister spills the beans between snores."

Aspen chuckled. "Did you fancy anyone?"

My smile fell as I remembered Randall. Trying not to allow my past to cloud the conversation, I shrugged it off. "Once, but my affections were not returned. It was usually Rosalie or Aura that caught the attention of the town boys."

"I can't imagine living in a house full of women. I grew up an only child, well, that was until I met Rosalie." He sighed and slid the letter between the pages of his book, then placed it in his saddle bag.

Aspen laid down on his bedroll, his arms tucked behind his head, and he stared through the trees up at the sky. With my innocent questions, it seemed to give him permission to ask me a few. "What's it like to fly?"

"Freeing. The higher I go, the further away my problems become. It's easy because a bird doesn't worry about where it will sleep at night or what it will eat. It only focuses on the air currents."

"It must be great since you always want to fly and never ride with us." He turned on his side and looked at me, the glow of the fire turning his eyes molten. "I have to ask, and please be truthful. Have you refused to ride with us," Aspen lowered his voice so only I could hear, "because you're avoiding me?"

I glanced away, my mouth suddenly going dry.

"Am I really that terrible for company?"

"I thought you hated me. Resented teaching me. I thought it best to keep my distance and give you space, less I accidentally annoy you further." I blushed. "You have to admit, I can be very blunt."

"True. Is that also why you've been so quiet during lessons? I feel like the fiery woman I met the day she shifted and appeared with no clothes has become a timid mouse. I watch you bite your tongue with me and you keep your thoughts hidden. You're becoming more like Velora."

"Ugh, kill me now." I sighed, plopping back onto my back on the bedroll. "I hate that you have so much power over me. Being with you during the day, riding on a beast that is shackled to the ground, reminds me I'm not free. Whereas up there," I pointed to the sky, "I have no fear. Except bigger birds."

"I see." He sounded so accepting of my answer, and I felt a bit irritated that he didn't push me further.

"That and . . ." I dragged out my answer, and he perked up. "I'm not that great at riding."

"I knew it," he said smugly.

"Did not," I snapped. In my anger, I tossed the small satchel I used as a pillow at his face.

He caught it with one hand. "Thanks." He promptly tucked it under his head.

"Give it back," I demanded.

"Not until you promise to ride with us tomorrow."

"No." I rolled over and laid back on the ground, immediately regretting my decision. The hardpack soil was prodding into my head. I missed the small comfort the bag allowed me. "Fine. I change my mind. I'll ride with y—"

My words were cut off as the bag smacked me in the face.

"I hate you," I muttered, but it was hidden by Aspen's loud laughter.

The next morning, I contemplated my choices as I stood next to the horse Aspen had bought for me. A strong and fast Florinian steed, solid black with a white nose, and easily sixteen hands tall. Velora's horse was only fourteen and a half. Aspen held the reins out to me, and I took them, my heart racing at the sheer size of the massive beast. When the horse shifted, I flinched.

"Come on." Aspen patted the saddle, taunting me. "Do you need a hand up?"

"Don't touch me," I said. Turning my back to him, I put my foot in the stirrup and jumped, using the horn to pull myself onto the horse's back. It wasn't enough momentum, and I felt myself sliding backwards. Strong hands caught me around the middle, pressing me into his stomach. Being so close, I was caught by Aspen's scent; earthy like the tree he was named after, and a faint spice. There wasn't time to identify anything specific because he tossed me back up in the air, almost over the saddle. I caught myself and readjusted the hem of my dress to no success. The dress was one of two I found at the cottage, and the previous owner was much shorter than me. Now on a horse, the hem rode up to my calf, exposing more of my legs than was considered proper. Aspen noticed my conundrum, and he tried to adjust my skirt by tugging on it, but it wouldn't go anywhere.

He cleared his throat in embarrassment. "I think we need to get you some new dresses."

"How about a smaller horse?" The ground looked very far away, and I hated how my life was in the hands of the great beast.

He looked offended. "This was the best of the herd."

Had Aspen really picked out the best mount for me? I quickly shut my mouth and decided to accept his gift graciously. "What's his name?"

"Drake."

Reaching out, I patted Drake along the neck and gave him an encouraging word as we started moving. "Just don't throw me, okay, or I'll turn you into a pig." The horse shook his head, and I swore he understood me.

The terrain slowly changed from heavily wooded to lush hills. The farther south we traveled, the more anxious Aspen became. Surely we had to have entered Candor. Before long, I smelled the sea and knew we had traveled farther east than I had thought. Then I saw it on the horizon. A tall and foreboding castle overlooking a valley. It was a castle I easily recognized from my mother's scrying mirror. The sandstone walls, the three towers over the gate. The red banners flying in the wind.

Florin.

Aspen's home. The last time he was here, his father was murdered, he fought Rosalie in a battle, and accidentally sent Allemar to the daemon realm.

I watched Aspen out of the corner of my eye, waiting

to see what possible reasons he had for returning. I didn't think any of them were good.

"We're in Florin," I stated.

Aspen was looking at the letter in his hand. It had been folded and unfolded so many times it was falling apart. "Yes. We are."

"Why . . . I mean what . . ." I was unsure how to ask, so I just spat it out. "What reason could you have for coming home?" Immediately, I regretted my choice of words. From what I had learned from Aspen, he did not have fond memories of growing up here.

He swallowed, and I saw the muscle tic in his clenched jaw. "Are you scared I'm here to take revenge on your sister?"

"Yes."

He shook his head. "I've other more pressing matters."

I didn't believe him, but was quickly distracted as Aspen gave instructions to Marco, mentioning an inn.

"Inn?" I spoke up, letting the words sink in. "Do you mean it? We can sleep in a real bed?" I felt myself getting excited. I glanced at Velora who was grinning ear to ear.

Aspen couldn't hold back his smile. "Yes, you can sleep in a real bed."

"Then what are we standing around for, let's go!"

The capital city of Silverton was packed full of people in the midst of preparation. Two centaurs worked on raising colorful banners across the main square. Vendors, human and fae alike, lined the streets, bringing in the best of their harvest and goods. A wooden platform was being constructed for musicians, and barrels of mead and wine were being rolled out in preparation.

"What is this?" Velora asked excitedly.

"It must be Saint Autumnus Day," I answered softly. "It's a day celebrated throughout all seven kingdoms as the official start of the harvest season." Had I really been gone so long from Nihill that it was already autumn? I must have been locked in the cellar longer than I'd realized.

"It's a full week of drinking, dancing, and contests," Aspen said.

I put on a fake smile that didn't match how I was feeling. Of course, I had snuck out multiple times on Saint Autumnus Day and flown to the small town of Haversfield. I'd stolen my fair share of fruit pies, candies, and colorful ribbons, and watched all the activities. I'd always return home with my stolen goods to share with my sisters. It was our greatest secret. This trip felt different. Like a bribe.

"Most of the inns will surely be booked for the celebration," I said.

Aspen looked back over his shoulder. "There'll be room." He led us with ease across the square to an inn far grander than any we had passed by. The Singing Siren was three stories with mosaic glass windows and music notes embedded within the pane. The wooden placard outside said no vacancies, but it didn't deter Aspen. Dismounting, he handed the reins to a waiting stable hand.

"Sir, there aren't any rooms available," the stable hand said.

Aspen ignored him and headed inside.

"You don't think he would . . .?" I trailed off and looked to Velora in question.

She shrugged her shoulders.

A little fearful that he would kill someone to make room, I slid from the horse, half falling, half sliding down to the ground. I ran after him, praying that Drake wouldn't wander off or that the stable hand would grab him.

Bursting through the front doors, I was greeted with the warm sight of polished oak tables, benches covered in padded blue velvet, and colored lanterns that decorated every table.

Aspen was speaking in low tones to an elderly man with white hair and a trimmed mustache.

I bumped into a stool in my haste to save the innkeeper from a grisly fate. The stool fell to the floor with a thud. Both men looked up at me in surprise. I gave a little wave and Aspen raised a curious brow before shaking his head. They ignored me and went about their business.

"I received the letter. Thank you for the warning. Have I come in time?" In his hand was a soft black velvet cloth, and displayed in his palm was a gold signet ring with a flower.

The old man nodded. "Yes. The events haven't started yet. But I hear many of *their* kind plan on entering. They've grown increasingly restless over the years. I fear for what may happen if too many gain power. The queen doesn't know the history of our lands like you do." The innkeeper glanced my way and grew quiet.

Aspen nodded, covering up the ring and tucking it away in his pocket.

The owner bowed his head. "I will get what you requested.

"Thank you, Ibol." Aspen clasped the man's shoulder in gratitude. When the innkeeper left and we were alone, he turned to me.

"Eavesdropping?" He leaned past me and looked at the stool that I had knocked over. "You'd make a terrible spy."

"I just wanted to make sure that everyone was . . . still alive after you left the room." I accused him outright.

He frowned. "You thought I was going to kill him, didn't you?"

"You did it before," I whispered angrily. "You killed a couple just to take their house."

Aspen roughly pushed me aside, stopping to lean down to my ear. "I didn't kill them. Allemar did."

"You might as well have done it," I accused. "I blame you as much as I blame him."

"Why?"

"Because you didn't stop it."

"Can one stop a hurricane or a tornado by stepping in its path? No, but you can help others take cover."

"Are you saying you wouldn't have killed them?"

He took a deep breath. "Honestly, I don't know. I would have tried to warn them, or reason with them, but if they wouldn't leave, I would have made their passing as quick as possible, unlike Allemar."

I shook my head. "You're a monster."

"So you keep saying," Aspen said. "But this monster has just secured you lodgings for the week."

"How did you accomplish that—"

"—without spilling blood? I do have something of worth still, even if *you* think I'm worthless." He didn't wait for a response but headed out, giving instructions to the stable hand, Velora, and Marco.

A servant came up to me and took me to a room that overlooked the next building and had a view of the square. It was spacious; much larger than my tower. There were two beds with real down stuffed mattresses and thick embroidered quilts. When Velora came into the room, she immediately claimed the bed near the other window and proceeded to place her few treasures on the windowsill, along with the wooden figurines Marco had made for her. A large pole in the middle of the square caught her eye. "What's that, Maeve?"

"It's an autumn pole. They're attaching ribbons, and girls will dance, winding and unwinding them in an intricate pattern. There are also numerous favor dances during the festival."

"What's that?" Velora asked.

"The men purchase flowers, ribbons, or tokens to match the color of the dress of the girl they favor. They present it to her in exchange for a dance, and sometimes for a kiss." Velora at least had a dark purple dress that accented her unique hair. With a flower or ribbon, it could easily be made festive.

"We must go," Velora begged me. "We will dance with *all* the men."

I glanced at my gown and grimaced. "I don't exactly have anything to wear."

"It's not the dress that will chase men away, but your foul temper," Aspen teased. I'd been unaware that he was silently leaning against the doorframe, listening to me wistfully talk about the dance.

"I guess we didn't all have the etiquette training you did, Your Highness."

Now it was Aspen who winced. "Don't call me that."

"Why? It's who you are. Or are you denying that you flashed the innkeeper the royal ring of Florin to get us these rooms?"

"I don't deserve that title. I never did." He couldn't

hide the pain in his voice. The epic sadness, loss and rejection. It mirrored my own.

"Yeah, you couldn't handle the throne, instead leaving your sister to rule two."

I didn't know why I was so angry, other than I was unsatisfied with my own circumstances.

In a fit, I shifted into a crow and flew out the open window, waiting for the tug, the angry yank of the string tied to my soul. But he let me go. Maybe he knew I needed the freedom to escape, but there was no escaping what I had done. Neither one of us could run from our past mistakes.

CHAPTER TEN

I spent the next candle mark flying from rooftop to rooftop, scouting out the various passersby. Selecting my mark, an overweight gentleman, I hopped along the ground pretending to scavenge while keeping an eye on his coin purse. It was heavy, filled with more coin than he could spend in a week. Flying onto the overhang of the stall, I waited for my chance as he debated over which meat pie to buy. The smells of roasted lamb filled the air and it made me impatient, stepping side to side, drawing scrutiny from an old lady who made a cross symbol over her heart. Did she really think my presence was a bad omen?

The target finally pointed to the pie he wanted and opened his money pouch, setting the weighted bag on the counter.

Finally! I pecked and pulled at the leather strap on the corner post of the stall, releasing the pots and pans that had been tied up to showcase the wares. They fell to the cobblestone, creating a ruckus. I flapped my wings right in the man's face, cawing loudly, then hopped onto the table and snatched three coins from his bag before taking off, my claws filled with gold.

Normally, I thrived on my wits and trickery skills, but today there was a heaviness in my heart. Was it my conscience finally catching up to me? Where had it been my whole life when I made rash, selfish, and spoiled decisions without any repercussions? I didn't count the extra spell work mother gave me as punishment. It seems that my imprisonment had changed me. Maybe I had grown up and lost some of my self-centeredness. Or maybe it was the gravity of being responsible for the loss of so many innocent lives.

Landing in an alley, I shifted back. The coins clutched in my hands felt heavy. I had stolen them with the intent to buy a dress so I could go to the dance, but that seemed so trivial. So self-absorbed.

Looking at my reflection in the nearest window, I barely recognized myself. Before, I never balked at stealing; taking what I wanted when I wanted because I was angry. Angry at the world for my circumstances. Angry at my parents for having gotten rid of me. *Was I not good enough? Why didn't they want me?* Acting out had a purpose. Now, it felt petty. There was no joy in what I did.

Unfolding my fingers one at a time, I looked at the flower minted on the coin, the same on the signet ring. No wonder the innkeeper was helping Aspen. He was still a crown prince without a throne. Rosalie was the queen, and she spent half the year at Baist with Xander and half the year in Florin.

Picking up my pace, I headed back toward the town square, looking for the children I had seen earlier when I was scouting. I hoped they would still be there. As luck would have it, the three kids were playing in a puddle, trying to get a paper boat to float in the murky water.

Their clothes were a little small and on the thin side. Their faces gaunt as if they missed a few too many meals. The two older boys looked close in age, and they were very protective of the younger girl with freckles. Obviously, their sister.

"It's going to sink just like all the others," the oldest boy warned.

The young girl jutted out her chin. "Nuh uh, I said a spell over this one."

"Magic's not real. Just like wishes aren't real," the middle boy said.

Their skepticism broke my heart, and I found myself approaching the girl.

"Don't listen to them," I said, holding my hand out for the paper boat.

She gave me her sailing creation, and I made a gesture with my chin. She followed me to one of the lit candles on a table set out for the musicians. Picking up the candle, I carefully poured wax, coating the bottom of the boat, then returned to the puddle.

"Magic is real."

"Is not." The oldest boy crossed his arms over his chest. "It's going to sink."

I smiled knowingly, and gently placed the paper boat into the water, the wax having dried and successfully sealed the bottom—a trick Lorn had taught me when I was younger. Trailing my fingers through the water, I created a current. The boat set sail on her maiden voyage and didn't sink.

"Well, I'll be. How'd you do that?" the younger boy asked.

"My sister Rhea calls it science. Another form of

magic." Resting my hand on the boy's shoulder I asked. "What is it that you hope for?"

"Food and money for shoes, and tools for my dad. He's out of work. No magic can bring all of that." He looked down at the ground, his hands going to the refuge of his empty pockets.

Kneeling down so I was at the same eye level as the three of them, I gave them a smile. "Magic is real. It exists where there is hope, some even call it miracles. Let me prove it." I reached into my pocket and pulled out three gold florins and gave one to each child.

Immediately, the oldest boy broke down in tears, and the youngest one clutched the coin to his chest and shook his head. The girl threw herself at me, wrapping her thin arms around my neck.

"Thank you," she whispered, her small shoulders trembled as she began to cry. I gave her a soft pat on the head. I was not the motherly type but tried my best to mimic Rosalie.

"What are your names?"

"I'm Tate," the oldest boy thumbed his chest, "that's Francis, and my sister, Toryn."

"Well, go home quickly before the magic fades. Get the food and items you need," I said gently.

Toryn pulled back, her hazel eyes glistening with tears. "Are you an angel?" she asked.

Unable to hold back, I snorted. "If you asked my sisters, they'd say far from it, but I think I'm on a path of redemption." With a final hug, they were off, dashing out of the square heading home.

As I stood up, the skin on the back of my neck began to tingle and I turned, scanning the crowd finding nothing. I had an ominous feeling of being watched but could find nothing out of the ordinary. The sun had almost set, and the musicians were tuning their instruments. Defeated in my attempt to attain a better dress for myself, I returned to the inn in a very sour mood, despite having helped the children. My worn boots thudded loudly on each step. They felt heavy with my awareness of how old and ill-fitted they were. Pushing open the door, I headed into the room and let myself flop onto my bed, burying my face in the pillow.

The silence in the room had me sitting up and searching for Velora. She was always prattling around like a bird in her stilted English. My gaze settled on a table filled with brown wrapped packages. If I had any self-control, I would ignore them, but like the raven, I was very curious and drawn to pretty things. My name was written on them in black ink.

I opened the first package and couldn't hold back the smile when I saw the hunter green dress with a modest neckline and full sleeves. The second contained black boots and a gray wool cloak with a floral clasp. Opening the third, I was pleased to find another dress in a shade of dark blue. The final parcel was wrapped differently. Unlike the others, this one was wrapped in white silk with a gold ribbon.

Pulling on the ribbon, the silk fell away, revealing a deep red dress trimmed in gold. Holding it in the air, the many folds of fabric fell to the floor, and I was perplexed by its sheer elegance. The trim waist, the full sleeves, the intricate gold lattice lace across the bodice.

I gasped as the dress shimmered in the candlelight.

"What do you think?" Aspen said as he entered the room, grinning like a fool.

I could play his game. I smiled slyly. "Never have I seen anything so extravagantly . . . stupid."

The smile fell from his face, and I hid my own behind a stony expression and raised an eyebrow. Mother Eville would have been proud.

"And here I came bearing gifts." Aspen gestured to all the unwrapped packages on the table next to him. It was then I noticed his hair was glistening as if he had recently bathed, and the clothes he wore were new, finely tailored to accentuate his strong arms.

"I do not take kindly to bribery."

"It's not a bribe. It's a gift."

"The only gift I want is my freedom," I said, dropping the dress on the table.

"You know I can't do that," Aspen said firmly.

"Then leave me alone."

"So you can wallow in misery?"

"Misery gets a bad rapport. It's actually not so bad once you get used to the crazy looks from talking to oneself. Speaking of crazy—" I glanced around the room searching for Velora.

"Where's the fish?" I said snarkily, letting my childish anger get the better of me.

Aspen's eyes darkened at my name calling. "Velora has accepted my gifts and gone out to enjoy the celebration."

"Alone? You let her go out there by herself?"

Aspen's brows furrowed. "Why not?"

"She doesn't understand all of our customs. It's not safe for her out there alone." My heart thudded in my chest. "There are dangerous men out there, and they are only after one thing." I flung a finger toward the window, hearing the music that was coming from the streets, my mind replaying malicious attacks on my sister Aura.

Aspen laughed, his shoulders shaking as he came to stand uncomfortably close. Refusing to take a step back, I stood my ground, and he leaned in, his voice dropping to a husky whisper. "Oh, Maeve, there are dangerous men in here." The candlelight caught the specks of green in his hazel eyes. He leaned forward, his breath warm across my face. My heart raced as he reached out, tracing a finger across my cheek, setting my skin on fire. "And I'm only after one thing," he whispered, and plucked a stray raven's feather from my hair.

A warning or a promise? He took the feather with him as he turned to leave, looking over his shoulder in challenge. "If you're so worried for her, why aren't you looking for her? Or you can trust that she is fine, enjoy the hot bath I've ordered to be drawn for you, and then take advantage of the gifts I've brought. It's not right for you to be stuck wearing clothes that were made for someone else."

The promise of a hot bath changed my mind. I raised my chin. "This doesn't make us even."

"I wouldn't expect it too."

"Nor friends."

He smirked. "Definitely not. You forget that you're nothing more than my apprentice." He backed out the door, his hand on the handle. "And as your master, I order you to take a bath." He closed the door.

I turned to follow out the door after him, but paused and stared back at the gorgeous red dress and compared it to my faded black one. It wouldn't take me long to bathe and change. Servants came and took me to a private bathing room where I spent a few candle marks washing and scrubbing my skin raw with soap and scented oils. Feeling refreshed and renewed, I took my time getting dressed, running a comb through my hair until it shone and it hung down the middle of my back. I plaited the sides and made an intricate design in a figure eight. I knew it was the right decision to change as soon as my feet slid into the newer boots. They weren't perfect, and pinched a little from being new, but they fit. I didn't understand how he could pick out shoes or a dress for a woman and get the right size.

Witchcraft. I smiled to myself. He's a sorcerer. He probably has his tricks.

I felt like a completely different person as I headed out of the inn. The dress gave me a feeling of confidence, and I couldn't help but hold my head up high. A few unwanted, creepy looks came my way, but a dark glance in response had them shifting their gaze. I may have been beautiful, but I was still powerful and in no way scared of them.

As I passed down the rows of vendors selling spiced meat sticks, sausage rolls, fruit pies, and cinnamon pastries, I caught a glint of Velora's lavender hair. Weeding between the bodies, I'd almost reached her when I saw her head fall back, and she laughed aloud at something Marco had said.

Marco stood close to her, the silent guard dog. He slipped into the shadows and gave her freedom to move about. When she pointed to a particular trinket, he was by her side, his money pouch open, freely pouring coins into her hands with a smitten look on his face.

My lips pinched together holding back my smile. Of course she wasn't alone. Marco looked dashing in his new green shirt and leather vest, which also appeared to give him newfound confidence. Realizing that she was safe and happy, I didn't feel the need to interrupt her. I slipped back into the crowd, but not before a hand gripped my elbow.

"May I buy the lady a drink?" a slurred voice asked.

Pulling away, I glared at the stout man with puffy cheeks and glassy eyes. His mug of ale sloshed precariously over the rim.

"No, thank you. I'm fine."

"Then a sweet for my sweet." He hiccupped and swayed a little.

Reaching out a finger, I pressed it to his forehead, and whispered, "*Somnus.*"

The man collapsed backward against a wall and slid down, his drink still in his cup. Soft snores replaced his drunken words.

"A sleeping spell? I'm impressed," Aspen said over my shoulder. Reaching down, he relieved the drunk man of his cup and took a tentative sniff. He wrinkled his nose at the offending smell and poured the ale on the man's pants, making it look like he'd wet himself. "Not impressed with his choice of mead. This is the bottom of the barrel stuff."

I pursed my lips to keep my laughter in, for I would have probably done the same thing.

"I wouldn't know because I've never had anything more expensive."

Aspen placed the cup next to its drunken owner and looked up at me. "Come, then. The night is young. Let's drink to our heart's content."

"As long as you're paying and I'm eating . . . deal."

He chuckled and held out his arm to me. I hesitated. It was a courteous gesture, and not one I expected from him. His lips pressed into a firm line as he dropped his arm and began walking, thinking it a rejection. Taking a few quick steps to catch up, I wrapped my arm through his and kept a stiff pace beside him.

Aspen adjusted his steps to be more accommodating, but I never relaxed my posture. "You walk like I'm leading you to an execution instead of to dinner. Relax. I'm not going to harm you."

My eyes flashed and my temper followed. "I'm not scared of you."

He gave my arm a little squeeze. "I don't doubt that, my little dragon. You're not scared of anything."

Heat rose to my cheeks as he referenced my fire dragon magic. As long as he knew I could in turn scorch him if he harmed me . . .

We stopped at a vendor, and I inhaled, slowing my steps.

"What is that?" I asked, pointing to the wicker baskets stacked on top of each other.

"Steamed buns," Aspen answered, pulling out a copper florin and paying the young women for two. He carefully handed me a warm, white pillowy cloud with a flower designed into the top. After taking a bite, the meat-filling and sweetness of the bun filled my mouth.

"Do you like it?" he asked.

"Yes, I do, very much," I said, staring at the next table which had rice wrapped in rolls, and were decorated with edible flowers. It seemed that every vendor and all the food items available all carried the country's royal motif. A red rose.

We continued to walk, and I watched Aspen out of the side of my eye as he interacted with the people. He was aloof, direct, and to the point. He wasn't one to waste smiles on everyone just because they smiled his way, but he wasn't necessarily downright rude. He just wasn't one for small talk. But there was a distinct air of power about him, even in the way he walked. There was no denying that he was royalty. It made me wonder.

"Why did we come here?" I asked after licking the last of the sticky bun off my finger.

"Because you were hungry, and because you thought some crazy man was going to murder or take advantage of Velora. As if I would let anyone harm the two of you."

"No, back to Florin. Aren't you nervous that you'll be recognized?"

Aspen picked at the steam bun in his hand. He let out a long sigh. "No, I won't be recognized. King Basil, my father, never let me leave the castle."

"Why? You were the crown prince."

"It's been almost three years since I left the kingdom. Before that, my father was paranoid; saw enemies everywhere. He believed the shifters would try to take his throne. He was ashamed of me for not living up to his expectations. I never left the castle and was beaten almost daily for every error. It wasn't until Allemar came that the beatings stopped." His knuckles turned white, and the bun was destroyed in his grasp. He flicked it to the ground and kept walking, leaving me behind.

I let the weight of his words sink in. To a young boy, his father was the greater monster, and Allemar, although just as evil, probably seemed like a savior.

"And now my sister rules." He turned to stare up at the castle. "Look around you. At the people's faces. There is hope, prosperity, and even fae." A giant tree that had grown between two of the houses moved slightly, as if shifting to a better position, and a groan followed. A scattering of fairies flitted about, disturbed by the giant tree's movements, but then they resettled among the branches. "There were very few fae welcome in our lands. They are coming out of hiding now, and I fear what will come out as well."

"What does that mean?"

"Long ago, the shifters were the bodyguards for the royal family. Each royal had one or two shifters assigned to their personal honor guard. For generations, they lived in harmony. The shifters trained from birth in hopes of one day getting chosen to protect the king, queen, or their offspring. Until the day King Alder found his queen dead. Killed at the hands of her own guard. The shifter denied it, but the dagger was found in his hand. It was later discovered that the shifter had fallen in love with the queen, and when she rebuked his advances, he killed her in a fit of rage. Because of that, the shifter wars began. The king revoked the honor guard and destroyed seven of the strongest shifter families, then drove the rest into hiding. But a shifter can hide among humans easily. Since then, the kings of Florin have lived in fear of the shifters' retribution, and they have tried to keep them from gaining power."

"Rosalie doesn't know this, does she?"

"No, she wasn't raised in Florin. She doesn't know our history, and our record books are concealed deep within the castle in a hidden room. She would not know the danger the shifters place on the kingdom. Now that King Basil is gone, I fear *they* may return and try again."

"I can't help but wonder, what does Allemar have to say about this?"

"You heard him. He wants to control the shifters. And if they want to take the throne by force, he will help, just so he can turn around and control them."

"I thought he wants the throne?"

"He wants power, and he knows to keep the throne, he will need the help of the shifters," he said, his voice low and full of frustration.

As he spoke, Aspen was illuminated by the lamplight, and I saw a young man desperate to prove himself; a man with an unparalleled pride toward a land that was no longer his own. What would have happened if he had continued to live under his father's heavy-handed rule? Would he have turned into an even crueler king? Instead, he turned into an evil sorcerer. The only difference was he was no longer the one taking the beatings. He was on the other end of the stick. He had all the power.

Aspen's confession left me in a whirlpool of emotions, full of anger, pity, and understanding. I didn't speak up because it wasn't my place to. As we walked, he pointed out a certain statue of a tall man, covered in a fur cloak.

"That is my grandfather, King Alder. He was the one who defeated the shifter king and brought our kingdom peace."

I had more questions, but Aspen turned into the main square, and I saw Velora and Marco.

Velora's eyes darkened when she saw my arm wrapped around Aspen's. When we were talking, and he was reminiscing about his horrible childhood, I had instinctively wanted to comfort him and had threaded my arm through his again.

I didn't move away as she pounced over to us.

Grasping Aspen's hands, she pulled him toward the dance floor. "Dance with me," she said.

He dug his feet in. "Can't. It's only for eligible ladies." He motioned with his head to the pole and the ribbons and all the young maidens dancing with the colorful strings.

"That's right!" Velora turned back to me, her jealousy forgotten. "Show me!"

Flouncing around in circles, weaving between people did not sound fun to me. It seemed childish and girly, but I did it for Velora. The pole was already threaded, and a young girl handed Velora a long green ribbon and me a blue. This would be easier since we were unthreading.

"What do I do?" Velora squealed in delight, holding the ribbon up in the air over her head. Soon all the spots were taken.

A snobby girl with a petulant smile and wearing a yellow dress tried to forcefully take the ribbon from Velora's hand.

Anger roiled through me and I flicked my wrist, letting a burst of power hit the strange girl in the back. It caused her to stumble into the dancers in front of her, causing a colorful pileup up in the dirt and leaving Velora on the outskirts holding onto her original ribbon.

"Avis, are you all right?" A concerned girl reached out to help the bully in the yellow dress.

Now this was entertaining. I couldn't hold back my laughter as the mischievous side of me began to find ways to make the event more interesting. I spun on my heel and waved at Aspen, who was shaking his head at me.

"No more," he mouthed.

"Did you say more?" I yelled back.

He didn't have time to respond because the music

started, and the girls danced. Velora froze, and I gave her a gentle push in the back. "Look up! Follow the string and unwind," I tried to coach.

Avis had successfully confiscated some other poor girl's ribbon, and every time she passed under Velora's ribbon, I could see the hate rolling off of her. I knew she was planning something in retaliation, probably thinking it was Velora who pushed her down.

Avis became my target, and I almost ended up in a tangled mess as I was focused on her and not the dance. She was coming around the pole again, her grin widened, and I saw her foot shoot out to trip Velora.

She was an arm span away, and I twisted, putting my body between her and Velora. I bent, reached out, and touched the edge of her dress. "*Fiergo.*"

It was the smallest flicker of flame, and then I moved past. Velora was oblivious and still dancing and staring at her string in awe. Avis glared at me now, and I just smiled and shrugged my shoulders while watching the flicker of fire. The more we danced, the quicker it grew, until another girl pointed it out.

Avis screamed, dropped her ribbon, and began to frantically pat down her dress to stop the flame.

"Roll on the ground!" I yelled in encouragement, pretending to care.

Quickly, she dropped to the dirt and rolled back and forth until the flame went out, turning her yellow dress to a shade of umber. Knowing the dance was over, I lifted my skirts and headed to the outside of the dance square.

Aspen raised a brow at me. "You set her on fire."

I pinched my fingers together. "Just a little one." I grinned. "And besides, she had it coming."

I waited for the chastisement, but he nodded his head. "She did. If you hadn't done something, I would have." He gave me the smallest smile.

"I hate entitled people," I added.

"You're the most entitled person I know," he chuckled.

"Okay, maybe I hate competition." We watched Velora off in her own little world, spinning in a circle, holding the ribbon and dancing by herself. So innocent and child-like, but I knew the truth and had seen it with my own eyes. Mermaids were dangerous in the water and could frequently drown their victims and feed on their bones. Yet on land, she was different.

"She really is something else," Aspen whispered, watching Velora dance.

"Yeah," I said bitterly, feeling a sting of jealousy stab in my heart. It was utterly obvious that he cared for her.

"Thank you," he turned those hazel eyes on me, "for protecting her."

"No problem," I said uncomfortably, shifting from foot to foot.

"You shouldn't have used magic in public."

There it was. The Aspen I knew was back. The condescending tool who loved to boss me around. "Yes, Your Majesty," I snapped.

He blinked, taken aback. His brows furrowed, and his eyes darkened as I accidentally brought up the sensitive topic.

Not in the mood for a lecture, I stepped back into the crowd, disappearing among the many dresses and skirts as the men cleared the floor and prepare for the favor dance.

A hush fell over the crowd and the stage was emptied. Soldiers dressed in red began to fill the square. A red banner with a gold rose was lifted onto the stage, and the crowd quieted.

A tall handsome man with dark hair stepped onto the dais holding a toddler with dark colored hair. He held out his hand for the woman at his side to join him.

Immediately, I recognized her. Long hair, demurely covering half of her face, hiding a scar. Her one visible bright eye, so light it looked silver, glanced out among the people, and I felt my knees go weak.

Rosalie.

CHAPTER ELEVEN

"We welcome you to the St. Autumnus feast. This last year has brought both the kingdoms of Baist and Florin prosperity." Loud applause filled the square as King Xander began his royal address.

Did Aspen know they were coming here? Did he purposely put me within reach of my sister, or was he here to harm them? My heart thudded loudly in my chest, and I knew something was wrong.

"We've seen the return of the fae and hope that many more cross the borders and come out of hiding." A murmur came from the crowd; some speculation, others, a bit of discord. A few pointed to the statue in the square—to the king who'd protected them from the shifters. King Xander continued on, but his voice became a dull noise as I couldn't drag my eyes away from my sister.

Had it been three years? She looked even more beautiful, her face shining with love when she looked at her husband. Their young daughter, Violet, left the shelter of her father's arms and walked over to her mother. Rosalie knelt down and scooped up the young princess.

I felt like someone lost in the desert, and my sister was a spring of water. I wanted to drink in every detail and memory of her and my young niece. Tears silently fell from my eyes, and I brushed them away as I felt propelled by an unseen force, moving through the bodies toward the stage.

"Rosalie," I whispered, my hand raising up to wave at her.

She stopped and looked out among the crowd as if she heard my cry.

I was about to yell louder when I felt an agonizing pain in my chest. With each step I took, the pain became unbearable, and the tears only fell harder. My anger boiled on the verge of erupting. How dare Aspen keep me from her . . .

Another step and I would clear the biggest obstacle, the monument statue of King Alder, and I would be in view. But my heart was beating erratically, the pain was distracting, and I stumbled, having to stop and gasp for breath.

Rosalie, I cried internally. I was so close. The crowd erupted as they said their final farewells.

"No!" I took another step and felt a jabbing tug, my vision swam, and I fell to my knees. The royal couple and their daughter turned to leave the stage. Their forms became blurry as my vision faded and my tears fell.

The instrumentalists played their departing fanfare, and the royal family were surrounded by their troops and escorted into a coach that was waiting behind the stage. And then they were gone.

Sitting in the dirt on my knees, I refused to budge as the villagers around me began to pick partners for a Dredilly dance. I clung to the base of the statue and tried to pick myself up.

Aspen appeared out of nowhere, offering me his assistance. His hand grasped my arm, and he pulled me up.

"How could you!" I cried, hitting him in the chest. "How could you keep me from her?" Anger and pain collided as one strong emotion. I was hurting, and I wanted to hurt him, to make him feel the same pain I felt.

Instead, he pulled me into an embrace, burying my face in his chest, hiding my distress from everyone. He let me cry. And I did. All the pain I had hid from the world chose that moment to release in an undignified sob.

"I'm sorry," Aspen whispered into my hair, one hand gently stroking my back. "I'm sorry I couldn't let you go to her. It would have ruined everything. You would have revealed my presence, and I would have had to fight her. There's no guaranteeing that she would come out uninjured this time."

"You don't know that."

"I do. I'm not the young foolish apprentice she bested years ago."

"I hate you," I said. My voice was muffled, lost in the fabric of his vest.

"I know," he whispered.

Pulling away, I looked up at his strong profile. The muscle in his jaw tensed, and he swallowed. It was then I saw his own eyes were glassy and filled with emotion. What did he feel when he saw his half-sister? Anger, resentment, or remorse?

"You hurt me," I whined, rubbing my chest.

"I won't apologize for that," Aspen said. "You are my apprentice, and you need to listen to me."

"Yeah, don't count on it. I don't even listen to my mother, and she is way scarier than you."

A smile tugged at the corner of Aspen's mouth, and the tension between us lessened. It wasn't gone, but was at least more amiable. I still wanted to hurt him, drag him through the mud and make him pay. But maybe not kill him.

What I had failed to hear was the announcement marking the beginning of a Favor Dance. All the ladies moved in a line to stand along the front of the stage, and then the elder women, those married and with children, walked among the men holding baskets of colored ribbons, flowers, decorative combs, clips, and jewelry to sell.

It became a mad dash as the men looked among the ladies, purchasing favors that matched their dresses. The first young lad approached a girl in a daffodil-colored dress. He bowed and presented her with a yellow pin. The girl blushed and nodded her head in acceptance. They were the first to enter the dance floor. One by one, young maidens were presented with gifts of love and swept up in a dance.

"Excuse me." Aspen left my side and moved to Velora, who was looking excited and flustered. She had been swept into the mass of ladies, but being an outsider from this town, she was a stranger. I watched as Aspen approached her, pulling out a comb from his pocket. With the most noblest of bows, he presented the token to Velora. He must have purchased it earlier in the day because it matched her new pastel blue dress perfectly.

My heart flipped-flopped at seeing her face alight. She jumped into his arms and he caught her. She refused to unclasp her hands from around his neck, and he had to very carefully escort her onto the floor. Either she was a fluid dancer, or Aspen was a pro at leading because the two of them looked like the perfect dance pair. Her soft lavender hair was braided over her shoulder, and it looked almost silver in the moonlight.

Her face beamed with love, and I felt anxious. I didn't want to be left on the sidelines and forgotten, but I didn't really want to stand at the front of the stage and not have any suitors. Even now, there were still girls with wistful faces, waiting for a partner.

This is stupid, I thought angrily to myself. These girls were putting their heart on the line, and what if no one asked them to dance? What if no one asked *me* to dance?

"Excuse me," a voice said from behind me. "May I have the pleasure of this dance?"

The stranger had already bowed when I turned around, and I could only see the back of his dark head, a red rose held in his hand.

"This dance, yes. But whether it's a pleasure remains to be seen," I said wryly. "I already feel sorry for your feet."

"Then I will accept any consequences that befall my feet." He lifted his head, and his golden eyes met mine. I gasped. Never before had I seen eyes that color. They were certainly his most distinctive feature, followed closely by his angled jaw. He was medium build, and I could tell by the way he moved that he was fluid and muscular.

"I'm Silva." He held his palm out.

"Maeve," I answered, my mouth suddenly dry. I placed my fingers on his, immediately feeling the power radiating from his skin, and the tingling rushed through my body. My eyes widened, and I wondered if he felt the shock. If he did, he was silent.

With sure steps, he led me into the square, and his hand went around my waist. The music changed. It was much slower and more intimate than the first song, and it made room for conversation.

"You're not from around here," Silva said. The weight of his hand on the small of my back was electric. His eyes searched mine, and I felt like I was drowning, unable to take a deep breath.

"No," I whispered, wishing I didn't sound like a scared child. "I'm not."

"Where are you from?" he pressed.

"Nowhere," I answered playfully, referring to my town called nothing.

I heard the deep rumble of his laugh. "Playing hard to get, are we?"

I returned his laugh. "Not necessarily playing hard to get, but playing. I do love games."

"Then I am up for the challenge."

"Where are *you* from?" I asked.

"From a land far away." His eyes twinkled mischievously. "I didn't plan on dancing, but you caught my eye earlier in the day. As soon as I saw you, I knew you were something special."

Like all the girls, I felt the thrill of excitement at being noticed. I wasn't immune to charm and flattery.

He rubbed his thumb on the side of my palm. The electricity that passed between our contact was heady. It made me dizzy, like I had drunk too much wine.

"Do you see the effect we have on one another? My touch calls to you."

My breath caught in my throat, and through the sea of faces, I caught Aspen's. He was dancing with Velora again, but he wasn't focused on her. Instead, his gaze was dark and deadly, and the apparent anger was focused on one target. My dance partner.

"Why is that?" I asked.

He leaned close, his warm breath brushing against my ear. "Because we are the same, you and I," he whispered.

My heart raced. "How so?" I said, playing coy.

He reached into his vest and pulled out a black feather. Fear raced through me.

I pulled away, somewhat fearful that he knew my secret, had seen me shift, and had taken one of my lost feathers.

"Don't," Silva whispered. "It's not yours, but mine."

I blinked. "Yours?"

He smiled and handed it to me. On closer inspection, I noticed the vane was longer; the barbs fuller than a raven's. It still didn't give me a clue as to what type of bird.

"You feel it, don't you?" he asked. "When we touched. We're compatible."

"I don't understand?"

"Our magic calls to each other. We are meant to be."

"Okay, now that's enough." I stepped back. "I don't know what's going on, but I don't like it."

"You don't? Please forgive me." Silva quickly bowed. "I thought you understood the customs. When you said you're not from around here, I thought you were jesting, but if you truly don't, then I'm the one at fault."

My cheeks were burning in embarrassment. I stepped close to him and tapped his shoulder. He stopped his bowing. I grabbed his hands and continued to dance so people would stop staring at the handsome stranger. "It's true," I whispered. "I've never met another of my kind before."

"Really," Silva said. "I'm your first?"

I couldn't contain my smile. "Yes, and I have so many questions for you. How many are there? What kind of shifter are you?"

Silva looked behind me and he frowned. I turned, seeing a tall man with brown hair. He nodded his head at Silva, which made him uncomfortable.

"What's wrong?" I asked, immediately sensing trouble.

"Nothing, I need to go."

"Wait, where are you going? I just met you, and now you're leaving me?"

"Don't worry. We will meet again, Maeve."

The music came to a halt, he stepped back, and brought my hand up to his mouth. He placed the softest of kisses upon my knuckles, and as he did it, I felt them subtly brush against my own lips.

His golden eyes rose to meet mine, and I felt a pull in my soul all the way down to the tips of my toes. He was right. There was something magnetic about him. I could easily be lost in his embrace, his touch, and I even yearned for a kiss from a man that I had never met before.

He released my hand, and at our parting, a cold rushed over me like ice. Where moments ago I was bathed in warmth, I now felt cold and alone. His cloak billowed out behind him, and he disappeared into the shadows. I tried to follow him, but I blinked, and he was gone. I was left holding his black feather and feeling lost.

"Maeve!" Aspen's voice cut through the air like a knife.

I turned and looked at him in surprise.

"I've been saying your name over and over."

"Sorry. Distracted."

I turned from the shadows and my thoughts of Silva. Aspen bowed and presented me with a gold pin inset with a ruby, the jewel a matching shade of red to my dress. I stared numbly at the expensive token and wondered at the meaning. It seemed far more extravagant than any of the favors, and more than the one he gave to Velora.

I frowned. Aspen read my hesitation.

"It's just a pin, Maeve."

"Yeah, but what does it mean?" I asked suspiciously. "It can imply many things, a bribe—"

"I already know you don't take to bribes." His mouth held back a smile.

"You could have spelled it to ensnare me."

"You're already trapped by me."

"True, but I vow to break that bond one day. Even if it kills you," I said.

"You say it without any remorse," Aspen said casually.

"You could have cursed it to give me the hives, or pox."

"I take it you've done that to others?"

"Many times."

His deep laugh filled the air, and a warm feeling spread through my body.

"Well, I expect you to struggle under my authority, and try to kill me to escape our bond, but I assure you, there is no other hidden agenda behind this token other than I would like a dance."

"I'm not sure that's a good idea." My heart was confused after having a very pleasant and exhilarating dance with Silva. I wasn't sure if I could compare those feelings to the complicated emotions Aspen created within me. I tried to find a way to put some distance between us until I could sort them out.

"Why do you refuse? I won't hurt you."

"You already have." I gasped, not meaning to have said it out loud, my hand clutching my chest. I looked up, and his eyes softened as he glanced where my hand protected.

Stepping closer, Aspen whispered, "Does it really hurt you there?" His gaze flickered to my heart.

I took a deep breath. Maybe he didn't understand what he was doing when he pulled on our bond. "My heart feels like it's being ripped in two."

Aspen's eyes dropped in remorse. "I don't want my presence to cause you more pain."

He lifted my palm up and placed the gold and red pin in my hand. "Keep it," he said. "I don't deserve to wield the power I do over you. And I don't deserve a dance." With his head held high, he turned to leave.

Without thinking, I grabbed his cloak. Pulling him, keeping him from leaving me. There was something about the vulnerability he showed. Every once in a while, the armor would drop and I'd see the true Aspen. I wasn't sure if it was another deception, but I wanted to trust my gut.

He stopped, the wool cloak feeling heavy in my hands.

"No, wait. I'll dance with you," I said softly.

His shoulders stiffened. "I don't want your pity."

With a jerk, the cloak was ripped from my grasp and he disappeared in the crowd. I was left holding the golden pin, easily worth more money I had seen in my lifetime. The light from the lanterns flickered along the cut of the gemstone, and it sparkled. The stone reminded me of the color of blood. I wondered if he purchased it with the money he made bounty hunting.

CHAPTER TWELVE

The next morning, Velora couldn't stop talking about the festival. She lay sprawled out on the bed, the comb she had received from Aspen held up in the air.

"It's perfect!" she crowed. Flipping over to her stomach, her legs swinging in the air over her back. "And then I got all of these." She made a gesture to the table where it was piled high with ribbons, flowers, and other tokens she'd received from admirers. "How many did you get?" she asked innocently.

The pillow I was attempting to smother myself with did nothing to drown out her chipper voice. I punched the pillow a few times and folded it back over my ears.

"Go away," I muttered.

Her feet padded on the floor, and she came over to my bedside table, picking up the rose pin and the feather.

"These are nice," she said.

Like a snake striking, my hand blindly shot out from under my pillow and swatted her arm.

"Don't touch. Sleep," I muttered.

"Can't. Too excited for today's events."

"Curse on you," I grumbled, rolling over to try to get into a more comfortable position. Facing the day meant facing the feelings that I had. Whereas if I continued to sleep, I could just dream about Silva, the mysterious dance partner who made my blood sing at his touch.

"I heard that today at the training field they are beginning the contests."

"So what? People swinging pointing sticks at each other. Big deal."

"Aspen will be competing."

"What?" I sat straight up in bed, the pillow falling from my face. Is he crazy? What does he hope to accomplish by entering? He is a fool. He will be found out." Tossing the blanket off of me, I stormed out of my room, down the hall, and pounded loudly on his door.

There wasn't an immediate answer, and I worried he had already left for the tourney field.

"*Locherra*," I whispered. The lock clicked open, and I let myself in the darkened room.

Unlike our room that faced the rising sun, Aspen's window faced west, and his room was cast in shadow and darkness from the higher tower outside the inn. Nothing stirred, and I feared I was too late.

Moving toward the bed, I discovered it was empty.

The door slammed, rough hands grabbed me from behind, and I felt the cool steel of a blade against my throat.

"Who sent you? What do you want?" Aspen's voice growled against my ear.

Hearing his voice and knowing he was here, I relaxed, letting my body lean against his chest, inhaling the scent of his skin. I could tell he wasn't wearing a shirt.

His arm accidentally brushed my chest, and I gasped.

"Velora?" Aspen rasped out, the knife dropping from my neck.

"No, it's me," I snapped, turning to push his bare chest. My hands connected with a wall of muscle. "Why would Velora be sneaking into your room?"

"Well, I never would have expected it to be you. You're the last person I expected to come here in your under-clothes."

I remembered then that I was still in my nightdress. My eyes having fully acclimated to near darkness, I could see him moving toward his bed, wearing only his pants. He tossed the dagger onto the mattress and reached for his shirt. As he turned away from me, I saw the crisscross of scars across his back. Old and silvery white, they told a tale of his childhood. I couldn't hide my gasp when confronted with the horror of his injuries.

He paused, the shirt caught above his shoulders, displaying the gruesome reminder of his father's reign of terror. The air in the room changed and became tense.

I brushed my fingers across the scars on his back, and he froze at my touch. There was nothing I could do to change those marks, and if I were Aura, I would have been able to heal the pain of his memories. But I couldn't do either. I only knew how to hide the pain and bury it under anger.

"Your father?" I asked.

"Yes," he said, turning to me, looking at me closely. He roughly pulled the shirt down, covering the scars.

I knew what he was waiting for. Pity. I was used to the same look, and I hated it. Well, he wouldn't find it in me.

"Good thing he's dead. Otherwise I'd have to kill him,"

I said angrily, mimicking Aspen's own threat against my attackers.

Aspen seemed surprised at my response. He took a step closer, his breath warm against my cheek. "You would murder a bad man so easily, and yet, you chastise me. You are a hypocrite."

I inhaled at the insult. "He's not a man, but a monster."

He nodded his head. "Many, including you, say the same for me." He continued to dress, ignoring me as I stood silently in his room. It wasn't until he sat on his bed to put his boots on that he pointed to me. He leaned back on his forearms, his long legs stretching out before him.

"I'm sure there is a reason for you to have come into my room half-naked."

"I'm clothed," I argued.

"Half-clothed. And a lesser man would have already taught you a lesson for barging in wearing next to nothing."

"I don't need a lesson. I came because I think you're stupid."

Aspen laughed. "By the stars, woman, the things that come out of your mouth. I'm glad you got that out of the way, or I would have thought you came in here for something else. But since you've only come to insult me, then have at it." He waved his hand my way and reached for his boot. "Why am I stupid? Please, expound upon my many non-virtues."

"Velora said you are going to enter the tournament today."

Aspen pulled his right boot on, his hand resting on the second one before continuing. "Yes. The prize for winning is one I cannot pass up."

"Why? You must know that you will be seen by

hundreds of people. You're considered a traitor to the crown. If you're discovered, you'll be thrown into prison."

"I don't plan on being discovered." Aspen stood and reached for his dagger, then moved toward the door, which I was now blocking. When I didn't move, he raised an eyebrow at me. "Don't tell me you care about my wellbeing? I thought you would want me to get thrown in prison. Then you'd be rid of me."

"I—uh." I faltered. He was right. Wasn't that the answer to my problem? If Aspen was caught by the troops and tried for treason, I could then be free to go to Rosalie for help and she could break this bond between us. Or what if there wasn't a way? What if they killed him? And in doing so, killed me.

"I don't care about you. I just care about myself more."

Aspen shook his head, seeing through my facade. He stood, reached out his hands, each one grasping me on my shoulders, and he pulled me close. My head fell back. Was he going to kiss me? I held my breath as he leaned down and whispered into my ear. "Maeve, not every man has as strong as a resolve as I do. Don't come into my room again, or else I can't guarantee the outcome . . . or your safety."

He opened the door and left me standing alone in his room, reeling from our contact.

A smile graced my lips as I took his warning as a challenge. My safety. I think it's his safety he would need to worry about.

Heading back to my room, it took me longer than a candle mark to be ready for the day. Granted, I could have easily been ready. Velora was already dressed and downstairs by the time I entered my room. I took my time because I knew it would irritate Aspen. I wasn't sure of the feelings I was experiencing, and had trouble comprehending them. But every time I was near Aspen, I was both irritated and exhilarated.

I spent more than enough time in front of the mirror, braiding my hair into multiple layers and weaving them together into an intricate knot at the base of my neck. Pulling my black hair back made my green eyes starker. Wishing for rouge or makeup, I did the best I could with pinching my cheeks and lips.

As I pressed my hands down on the green dress, I spun in front of the mirror. I couldn't help but feel beautiful, exotic, and powerful.

The mirror flickered, and I felt a thrum of magic. I froze. Staring at my reflection, I heard my name echo softly back.

"Maeve," the cry came. I recognized Rhea's voice. "Maeve, are you out there? Please, I won't believe you're dead. Answer me."

Tears filled my eyes as I heard my older sister's voice cry out for me. She was using a mirror—a spell used to call out to me and only me—and it would ring out against any reflective surface.

My breath hitched, and I reached, brushing my hands over the air above the glass, inches away, not activating the spell to answer. Feeling the need to be close, I pressed my face to the wall and listened as I heard her cry out. I could feel her pain.

"You can't be gone," Rhea said, her voice filling with emotion. "I refuse to believe it. I would know in my heart if you were gone. So please, answer me."

A tear fell unbidden, and I whispered to her. "I can't. Not yet. I don't want you to see what I've become."

"If something or someone is keeping you from us, I will find a way to bring you back."

I shook my head, hoping she wouldn't. Not yet. I was tied to Allemar, and I couldn't endanger my sisters. I had to break the bond first. And Silva . . . I needed to find out more about him, about others like me. I desperately wanted her to continue talking just so I could hear her voice.

"I have to go away soon. I don't want to leave, but I have to. Something has happened." I felt a rush of panic as the anguish in her voice grew, and I was about to touch the mirror to answer her call when the glass flickered out and she closed the spell.

"No!" I screamed. "No." I hit the wall, the force causing the mirror to shake, but not fall. I needed more answers. What was happening to my sister? Where was she going? I could tell she was scared. Rhea, with her golden-brown hair, spent more time in the alchemy shop forging magic charms and items than she did brewing spells. She had a mind for advancement and was the brightest of us. Somehow, I'd always pictured her growing old in the tower, never leaving. But that is not our destiny. Ever since we were little, Mother told us we would leave, that we had a job to fulfill. Like the old fae tales, the kingdoms were no longer ruled by peaceful kings and queens. Their hearts had been turned to greed and evil, and the scales needed to be balanced again. Only through war, assassination, and by taking revenge on the kingdoms could the rightful rulers take their place. In the fae tales, it was usually a witch or a crone who came and tested the princes, and if they were found wanting, a new prince was chosen in their stead.

It was when Aura had left with Liam to go and fight

the blight did Mother Eville reveal the final piece of the puzzle to us. We were the test. We were the ones who would choose the next king or queen and put them on the throne, even if that meant doing it ourselves.

Of course, we didn't know that. If she had told us, we would have become greedy, knowing that we were meant to one day rule. Instead, she taught us magic. Rosalie, the long-lost princess of Florin, was engaged to the prince of Baist. Eden snuck into the ball and fell in love with a half-blood prince. Meri was the heir of the Undersea and married the Prince of Isla. Aura was . . . I don't know what happened to Aura. And that bothered me.

"What's taking you so long?" Aspen stormed into the room and halted abruptly when he found me crumpled against the wall in a heap, tears streaming down my face. I quickly wiped them away, hating that he saw me weak and vulnerable.

His face hardened, and I waited for the rebuke and lashing to come at being late. Instead, his voice was controlled and even. "When you are ready, I will escort you." He moved to sit on the chair and waited. He didn't ask questions, didn't rail against me for crying, or for being weak. He kept his face neutral.

I hated it. I was not one to show my emotions easily. I was not Aura or Eden. Getting to my feet, I wiped away the last shreds of my tears and raised my chin. "I'm ready to watch you stupidly enter a contest."

"Good, because I intend to win the prize."

"Prize? What prize?" Now my interest was piqued.

"Were you not listening last night, or were you too distracted at seeing your sister? The winners of the different events will be invited to the palace. Then the real tests begin."

My mouth dropped open. "The palace. You want to win so you can get into the palace." My eyes narrowed. "What are you after?"

"Respect," Aspen said, standing up, the chair scratching against the wood floor.

I snorted. "Respect is overrated. It is better to be feared."

Aspen ran his hands through his dark blond hair. "I've been hated and feared for the last three years trying to be the perfect apprentice, and I can never do that. But I can maybe regain a title."

"No," I said stiffly. "Not if it means harming my sister. I will fight you tooth and claw."

"You really should pay better attention. I'm not going to explain it to you. It's time to go."

Aspen headed out the door. I waited a few moments for the redness of my cheeks to fade away before heading downstairs.

Marco was already outside with Velora. They didn't have any horses, so I knew we were walking. Aspen was pacing back and forth anxious to be on our way. As soon as I appeared, he was off, walking with a purpose, and Velora and I struggled to keep up.

We soon came to the outside of town and the buildings became more spread out, then more stables and forges appeared. The Shoe Horn, The Goblin's Hammer, Gilded Arms. All blacksmiths' shops, and all packed with people wanting to get their weapons sharpened or buy new ones for the tournaments.

Rhea would have loved to see the magical forges alit

with blue and gold flame. The sound of hammer hitting steel filled the air with a rhythmic clang. A few even sang songs in tune with their hammer strikes, weaving charms and magic into them. It was easy to see the crowd gathering around the largest blacksmith, and I walked behind Aspen as he perused the wares. The swords were beautiful and deadly looking, and many had gold inlay and gemstones embedded in the handles.

My eyes widened in shock at the price when I heard one call out for a particularly embellished sword. "Four hundred florin."

Aspen shook his head and continued past the blacksmith.

"Amateurs," Aspen said. He slowed and stepped into the next shop while I walked along to a smaller establishment. There were many fine swords standing up, braced against a wooden display, but no one was flocking to his wares. That's when I noticed the large blacksmith move out of the enclosure into the sun. The centaur stood taller than Drake. His coat matched his gold hair braided over his shoulder. He took a sword from the stand and began to grind it, sharpening the blade.

I now understood why he had no customers. Even though a decree had gone out years ago, the racism was still apparent in Florin. Stopping to admire his wares, I lifted the sword and felt the balance in my hand. It lacked the decoration the other blacksmiths added to their pieces, but I could see the acid etch along the blade, showing the many layers of steel inside.

There were no defects, cracks, or delamination like I had seen on the other swords.

"You have an eye for steel. Do you forge?"

I shook my head. "No, that is my sister's expertise, but I've sat in her shop on many occasions and listened as she talked nonstop about metallurgy and magic."

His blue eyes twinkled. "Then you have come to the right place. Here you will find no finer blades in all of Florin."

Aspen strode past, and I grabbed his shoulder. "This blacksmith shop." I pointed to the centaur's wares.

"You sure?" he asked.

"Trust me," I said.

"I thought you didn't want to help me?"

"I don't want to help you, but I don't want you to die . . . yet."

I handed him the sword I had been holding, and as soon as his hand fit around the guard, he stepped back in surprise. "It's so light." He took a few practice swings, and I was mesmerized by the motion. His back straight, his shoulders relaxed, his body showed signs of being a trained fighter.

"I'm Corvallis Swiftfoot, and I can see you've had training. What kind of fighter are you? Do you prefer to take out your opponent fast? Are you strong, light on your feet?"

"I prefer to end the match as quick and painlessly as possible." Aspen looked among the blades, searching for the one that spoke to him.

The centaur didn't say anything, but I could see him looking at me. I reached deep into the earth and felt the magic come. Both magic and metal were of the earth, so maybe I could use my power to find the right sword.

I moved my fingers along the pommels of each blade,

brushing the tips and feeling the cold steel, waiting. When I brushed my fingers along a saber, my fingers tingled.

"This one." I grasped the sword and passed it to Aspen, feeling ashamed as soon as I did so. It was the least finished of the blades. The metal rough, and not polished like the others, the handle had no decoration, no insignia, and looked very mediocre. My stomach dropped as soon as I opened my eyes to see it. He would be laughed out of the arena.

Aspen took a few practice swings and nodded. "It is old magic."

"That one was made from steel mined in Kiln," Corvallis answered. "It is said there is ancient magic deep within the land. If you can be in tune with it, it will serve you well."

"I'll take it," Aspen said. "My apprentice believes that this is the one for me. Although, she has also sworn to kill me on many occasions."

Corvallis laughed, his head falling back, and I heard the deepest rumble in his chest, part neigh, part chuckle. "Don't all women threaten to kill us? My wife does so daily. I believe the more she threatens to kill me actually means the more she cares about me." The centaur gave me a wink, and I paled.

Aspen laughed good naturedly, slapping me on the back. "Unfortunately, I don't think the same can be said about this one. She always says what she means."

I quietly began to mutter curses under my breath as Marco joined us. The silent giant scratched his beard and pointed to a large axe.

"Ah, the Axe of Velhein. This one can cut through a

tree easily." Corvallis began a history lesson on the axe while Aspen pulled out his coin to pay.

"You don't have to buy it," I rushed out.

"Why not? It's a good blade."

"It's ugly."

"You should know never to judge a weapon based on its appearance. Just like people. This weapon will do well. Besides, if I lose, I can blame it on you."

"Then you better not lose," I warned.

"Women," Aspen muttered to himself. Velora moved over to speak with Aspen, using her feminine charms to ask a million questions. I didn't feel like my patience could tolerate her. For some reason, when it came to Velora, Aspen had the patience of a saint. That was not the impression I had received from my sisters when they'd encountered him. He had seemed on edge, hysterical, and mad even. But maybe that wasn't the true Aspen, but an Aspen driven by Allemar and desperation.

I moved to the edge of the glade and sat down under the trees on a stump and watched Aspen and Velora. What was different about him? Why did I not see the same person my sisters had? Was it because Allemar was nowhere near us?

He was puzzling, to say the least.

Marco came away with more weapons than he could possibly carry, but he easily strapped them together with leather and created a harness in which to carry the two axes on his back. Adding the sword on his side, and the multiple daggers along his bandolier, it made him look like a walking one-person arsenal.

A clatter of noise from the woods behind me had me looking over my shoulder. The sun blinded me, and I could only see a few meters into the forest, but I detected movement. A dark shape slunk through the hedges. My skin prickled, and I detected a subtle scent of magic.

"What are you looking at?" Aspen asked, silently coming up beside me. He peered into the woods trying to see what caught my eye.

"Nothing," I said, thinking it must have been a trick of the light. My eyes had been adjusting, and I had seen something that wasn't there. I sniffed lightly, no longer sensing what I had thought to be the scent of magic. The wind changed, and with it came an aroma of baked bread and roasted meats. Trumpets blared at the tourney field, and it was time to head to the arena.

"Here." Aspen handed me a small dagger. "For protection." The blade was small and its sheath thin, easily able to fit in my hidden pocket in the folds of my skirt.

"What do I need protection from?" I asked.

"Men. Any man. Me." He blushed. "I got it from the centaur. You seemed to like him, and he was reasonably priced." He pointed back to Marco and Velora. It seemed the four of us creating a crowd around the centaur's stand worked, and it brought him more customers. "Also, he had the best weapons, hands down."

I felt a moment of pride, but quenched it down quickly. We followed the men as they lined up to register for the tourney. Velora and I moved to the notice board and schedule. There was archery, hand-to-hand combat, swordsmanship, and even a joust. Between the events, there was a hawk show, two-headed dog combat, a foot race, and wrestling.

"There's nothing for the ladies?" Velora said.

"Yeah, apparently they don't think we can fight," I said,

snickering. If Honor were here, she could easily best most of these opponents. "If I remember right, there are events geared toward ladies that usually have smaller prizes."

"What kind of events?" Velora asked, seeming eager to win a prize.

"Baking."

"That's male dumb, female unfair. What's the word? Gah, never mind. I can't even enter because I can't cook."

"Maybe you'd win if they had a boiling water competition?"

Velora's head snapped up, and she looked hopeful. "You think so?"

"No. They won't have one."

"Maybe we should ask." And like a fish darting through water, Velora parted the waves of people and disappeared.

"How does she do that?" I groaned and took off after her. It was my fault. I shouldn't have teased her about the competition. I needed to find her before the next trumpets sounded so we could get seats to watch the first round of events. As I passed a notice board, I saw there was another feast scheduled for tonight . . . with more dancing.

"Oh yay," I said dryly. But then my heart picked up a beat. What if I saw Silva again?

A few minutes later, I found Velora speaking to the gamemaster on the stage. Her hands were flapping about in the air wildly as she tried to convince him of the need to add a new contest. Even from across the road, I could see the poor man try to keep from laughing.

He didn't make it.

A loud guffaw filled the air. "Are you mad? Who

would ever in their right mind try to enter that competition? It's ridiculous."

As soon as he said the words, her shoulders dropped in rejection and my anger rose.

My finger flicked through the air, and the gamemaster in his formal vest and hat, fell backwards on his bum as if knocked by an unseen force.

"Ooops," I said to no one.

I linked arms with the dejected Velora and headed her back toward the fields, trusting her to not run off or get lost again. A few times, I had to squeeze my arm as she saw something new and shiny and wanted to dart away. When we passed a stand selling cooked mussels, she about tore my arm off in an attempt to buy a plate.

"Not now. I promise you I will buy you some after."

Velora wrinkled her nose after she smelled the mussels. "It's okay, they ruined them, anyway."

"They cooked them in butter and garlic," I said.

"Ruined. They're better raw."

"I'll take your word for it."

When we made our way back to the fields, I stopped when I saw the men warming up, breaking into sparring partners. My heart fluttered when I noticed a familiar dark shape. Silva. Tall, lithe, dressed in dark colors with a white cravat on his neck. He moved with an unspeakable grace, and he put his partner through the paces. Without missing a beat, he easily disoriented his partner, spun around, and disarmed him.

The sword went flying into the dirt to land near the edge of the fence, near me. Silva turned and our eyes met. He raised his hand and bowed his head in greeting. Velora waved back, and I tucked her hands into my side.

"Why did he wave at me?" she asked.

"He didn't."

"Yes, he did."

"Whatever," I grumbled.

I found Aspen near the edge of the field with Marco. He made a motion for me to follow him into the woods. We easily caught up, and when we were far enough away, I asked him what he was doing.

"I'm going to need a glamour," he said, looking at me.

"Nope, you kidnapped the wrong sister," I said dryly. "Eden's the one you want."

"You think so little of my abilities." He pulled back his sleeves and bent his fingers together in a steeple. His mouth moved, and he began to conjure. Sigils appeared midair, and I watched in fascination as he began to summon a different kind of magic. I had missed the glint of gold in his fingers before, but between his palms was the signet ring.

Aspen's hair turned a lighter blond, his nose widened slightly while his eyes became a dark green. They weren't significant changes, but enough. I still saw Aspen, but there were enough differences that he looked like he could be a distant cousin. Then I noticed why he seemed familiar. He had pulled the traits from his ancestors. He looked like a younger form of the statue in the square. King Alder.

CHAPTER THIRTEEN

"Winner!" The gamemaster called out, raising the hand of a muscle-bound fighter who paraded over his opponent lying motionless on the ground next to him.

"Is he dead?" Velora asked, a little too excited at the prospect.

I studied the body of the young man who barely looked out of his teens. He had broad shoulders, but he hadn't grown into them. The battle had been quick and brutal, with the fighter I nicknamed Rooster, because he liked to strut around the ring, taunting his opponents with his blade.

"There." I pointed. The young man's hand moved, and he tried to get up. "He's alive."

"Oh, too bad." She had already lost interest and was bouncing on the balls of her feet as the next round of competitors entered the field. "Look at that one!"

That one was a mountain of a man, not as formidable as Marco, and definitely on the shorter side. He carried his two-handed axe onto the field. His eyes were narrow and hidden under a large brow, his red beard long and braided.

"Dwarf," I said. "Probably from the mountains of

Kiln. I wonder why he came here?" They were obsessed with gold, precious gems, and much of their loot was cursed. A way to keep others from stealing their treasure.

"He's funny looking," Velora said, laying her chin in her hand as she leaned on the wooden barrier.

"Says the woman who has a tail."

"Nyah." Velora stuck out her tongue, one of the newest mannerisms she'd learned from a village child that morning. It was now her favorite response to everything. "Do you like the dress?" Tongue. How's the food? Tongue. When a guy tried to flirt with her? Tongue. It was actually quite funny how often that response worked in her favor. I shook my head and went back to observing the battle before us.

The dwarf didn't say anything, but marched out to the middle of the field, waiting for his assigned partner. We could have stood by the crowd and the notice board, following along with the list of contenders on the bracket, but it was too nerve-racking. I knew that Marco and Aspen entered, and I had mixed feelings about the reason behind it. Did I cheer for them to win or lose?

Speaking of Marco, the silent mercenary was the contender assigned to the dwarf. Marco was large, a giant of a man himself, especially in comparison.

"I see you favor the axe, my brother," the dwarf spoke, his voice filled with respect for the axes Marco carried.

Marco nodded. "I do so in remembrance of my master." His voice rumbled like rocks tumbling down a hill. It always surprised me when he spoke, because he so rarely did.

"Then I hope they will do your master proud." The

dwarf bowed and grabbed the axe from his back, shifting the weight of it between his hands.

Marco didn't pull his newest axe, but instead reached for the little one he carried on his hip.

"It looks like a toy," Velora said.

She was right. It wasn't a match for the weapon the dwarf had. "What is he doing?" I muttered and watched as Marco waited.

The dwarf attacked first, swinging his axe low. Marco stepped backward, avoiding the large blade, and using the quick one to aim for his opponent's back. I flinched as I expected it to make contact with skin. But the dwarf moved, almost disappearing into the muddy earth. Seconds later, he was behind Marco, the blade aiming for his ankles, but he missed as Marco sensed the attack and rolled forward on the ground.

"What just happened?" Velora blinked, standing up and leaning over the railing, rubbing her eyes in disbelief.

I smiled. "Earth magic. He used the earth to move him through the ground. Like a mermaid through water."

"He's nothing like me."

"I don't know, I think he'd make a cute mermaid. You know, with the red beard and all." I mimicked pulling a beard.

She puckered her lips. "So he's a mud mermaid."

I sputtered, holding back the laughter. "Yeah, a mud mermaid."

A second guffaw of laughter joined mine, and I glanced at the dwarf. His eyes twinkled with mirth as he glanced at us. He couldn't possibly have heard us . . . could he?

Marco realized that his opponent—though small and

extremely quick—tried to stay away from the wet sections of earth, keeping on the harder more packed ground. It wasn't that the moist earth stopped the earth magic, but it seemed harder for the dwarf to move through the damper areas.

Even with his feet firmly planted on the ground, Marco struggled to get the upper hand on the dwarf, but he managed to hold his ground, the small axe easily defending against the blows of the dwarf's double-handed blade. After almost a candle mark of fighting, both were getting tired, but it seemed that it was our mercenary that was on the losing end.

"Marco," I called out. He swept an arm across his sweaty forehead and looked at me. I could see the defeat in his eyes. "Get him off the ground." I motioned with my hands to lift him up. "Keep his feet from touching the ground."

A spark of recognition appeared on Marco's face.

I knew I was right in my assumption when the dwarf growled immediately following my announcement. Marco threw his axe to the ground and charged, catching the dwarf's handle on the downward strike. They both battled for control. Marco used his muscular left arm and braced it around the dwarf's waist and tried to lift him into the air.

But he was stuck. Having heard my plan, he had sunk his feet deep into the earth, and it had hardened around his ankles like stone. His grin was malicious. He knew he had won. As long as his connection to the ground was secure, there wouldn't be a way he could lose.

Grinding my teeth together, I glared at the dwarf as he raised an eyebrow at me. He smiled, full of triumph, as if asking what I planned on suggesting now?

"Marco," I pointed to the dwarf's axe that he now held, "chop his legs off," I growled out.

The dwarf's face paled. Marco grinned, raising his arm high in the air, preparing to bring it down, severing his opponent below the knee.

"Wait!" the dwarf yelled out. "I concede!"

The axe blade stopped inches from the knee cap. The crowd let out an exuberant roar of applause and approval. Marco released the blade and dropped before the dwarf, bowing low.

The earth magic pushed the dwarf up out of the ground, creating a pedestal of mud, and he hovered over Marco as if he were the victor and it wasn't the other way around.

"That was a good battle, my friend. May I ask, who was your master?"

Marco's face was obscured, and when he rocked back on his heels, there were tears in his eyes. "My master was Gridlock of the Goldiron clan."

"Then you are our brother in name and spirit. I have heard tales of you. The giant dwarf. I am Grimkeep."

I watched as the two exchanged words. The smaller of the two leaning over the larger man and knowing that even though the dwarf had lost, it didn't feel that way. Marco had won a greater prize, and that was the respect of the dwarf clan.

The gamemaster made an announcement of Marco winning, but the mercenary respectfully pulled out of the rest of the games. The crowds booed at Marco's withdrawal, but it seemed to not bother him.

The dwarf came over to the fence, immediately

seeking me out. I shivered when those cunning brown eyes found me.

"Oi, you," he pointed a stubby finger my way, "ye know things," he accused.

"Are you saying I cheated?" I pretended to be aghast at the accusation.

"Wouldn't hear of it." He planted his feet, and the earth helped him rise until he was eye level with me. He reached out a hand and touched my wrist. My magic stirred, and he closed his eyes like was settling in for a nap.

I waited a bit impatiently, and he muttered. "Just a sec, This mud mermaid wants to know."

I flushed red, but he released his hands and looked deep into my eyes, as though he was peering into my soul. "I felt something familiar come my way, and I had to know."

"Know what?"

"Lorelai Eville."

I stepped back, his hand reaching out to grasp mine. "She's from Kiln. We know her, worked closely with her family before her father passed. I sense her magic signature within you."

"Well, she trained me, raised me as her own daughter. How can you tell?"

He shook his head, and a spattering of dried dirt fell from his hair. "Earth magic is the oldest, for all magic is rooted *in* earth. But I sense Lorelai's magic and—" He quickly pulled away as if bitten by a snake. He turned my arm over and saw the faded triangle on my wrist.

"Bad," he muttered, turning as if rejecting me.

"Wait. Grimkeep." He turned along the fence, making his way to an opening to leave the field. I chased after him, leaving Velora behind me. He stopped, giving me a look like I had betrayed him.

"Lorelai would be devastated."

"Help me," I begged. "How do I free myself from this binding?"

"Bad magic. You've been tainted. It's like a poison. Slowly sucking away your magic to feed its own. Like a parasite."

"How do I stop it?"

"It's still early. The spell isn't absolute." He pointed to the triangle. "When it is complete, another mark will appear here trisecting it. Don't fulfill the final step."

"How do I know what that is?"

"I deal in earth magic. He shrugged, looking at my wrist. "*That* is the rejection of all that is good."

"Someone must know a way."

"Maybe. The one who casts always knows of a way to uncast. You just have to find it."

"Allemar could have hidden that secret anywhere in the seven kingdoms."

"Then you'd best start looking." Grimkeep turned, dismissing me as if I were three-day-old garbage.

A roar of applause and noise erupted as the next battle was about to start. I didn't feel like watching anymore, and instead followed the field around to a shady area by the woods.

What did he mean when he said he could feel Lorelai's magic in me? She trained me, so wouldn't it be my magic that he would be feeling? Perhaps, as my teacher, our magic signatures felt similar. That was what made the most sense. As far as not completing the final step in the spell. I wasn't sure what he meant by that. How could I stop something I didn't know anything about?

There was my answer. I needed to learn more about how Allemar used his blood magic and bound his apprentices to him. Secrets that Aspen had not been very forthcoming about. Looking up over the tree line, I saw the great castle of Florin in the distance. With its pointed parapets, it looked cold and unforgiving. A seagull flew overhead, and I remembered the ocean was about a day's ride from where we were. Allemar had spent years at Florin castle. Eden told me stories of discovering his underground lair.

"*His notes!*" My head popped up, and I looked at the forbidden castle with more determination. They were at the castle and that is probably why Aspen came back. He wanted to find Allemar's books. The castle was heavily warded, and the only way to get invited inside was to win one of the contests.

Eden had said that when King Basil was killed and Baist almost declared war on the kingdom, many of the servants and staff had fled. The kingdom was on the brink of ruin, and this must have been why King Xander was holding the event. He was trying to bring goodwill back to his wife's kingdom. Bring prosperity.

The mark on my skin was an ugly blemish. I promised myself I would do everything in my power to not give Allemar full control over me. I would find a way.

"Aloe Fields," the announcer called for the next fighter. I wanted to laugh. All the members of the royal family had been named after flora. King Alder, King Basil, Prince Aspen, Queen Hyacinth, Rosalie. I thought it interesting to hear the name Aloe, a plant I frequently used to treat burns.

Turning back, I saw Aspen's glamoured form enter the dirt ring. "Really, he couldn't have just picked a name like John? He *had* to keep a royal moniker."

Quickly, I assessed the two combatants.

His opponent was well muscled and seemed familiar with the sword. He wore no shirt, and his body was laced with battle scars. He flexed his muscles and brought his heavy two-handed sword to the ready. Aspen was tall, lean, and quick. With the sword he had, he would have to rely on speed, not brute strength. I'd seen him fight an ogre. I wasn't worried about this match.

The round started. Aspen dashed forward, swung his sword, and a glint of steel hit the ground. Speed won in a surprisingly short amount of time. In about three moves, he had disarmed the man. Aspen turned his back on his opponent and headed to the sidelines. The crowd wasn't happy with how fast the round ended. They booed at the obvious lack of respect shown.

"That was fast," I said smugly. "You could have at least drawn it out, making it look like the poor fool had a chance."

"I can't waste the energy," Aspen warned. "It will be too draining to keep the glamour in place and fight. I have to dispense each of them as quickly as possible."

It made sense, but I wasn't going to let it go. "It's okay to be the champion of the tournament. But there is also something called the people's champion. It was one thing to win, another to win *hearts*. Which one do you want to be?"

He looked startled, as if only just realizing the hidden meaning of my admonishment. Aspen swallowed. "I will try to do as you ask." His hand gripped the pommel of his sword, his knuckles baring white. By the second round, Aspen had taken more time.

His opponent was older—a farmer by the looks of him—his back tanned from working the fields, but his handling of a weapon was sloppy. Aspen put on a show, letting the farmer think he had a chance. I caught an elderly female that was cheering loudly, and she waved at her spouse. Aspen must have noticed the same thing because he even went to one knee and let it look like he was about to lose. But I knew differently.

Aspen wasn't straining; his face was a mask, and he was only pretending. When the farmer looked up at his wife in triumph, Aspen came alive and rebounded quickly, but not as fast as I knew he could have. I watched him and Marco spar every morning when we were on the road. Aspen was deadly with almost any weapons, having spent years working as a bounty hunter. And here he was, letting a lowly farmer with a dull blade have at him.

The farmer's wife jumped up and down in excitement, and I quickly became impatient.

"Oh, come on. Now that's too much," I called out.

Aspen heard and quickly changed his strategy. Within two moves, the farmer was defeated and on the ground, a look of shock across his face. Aspen looked toward me as I slapped my hand over my face and then mouthed, *Help him up.*

Aspen frowned but extended a hand to the farmer who gladly took it. His smile went from ear to ear, and even though he'd lost, his hand rose to the sky. The crowed hollered. The farmer ran to Aspen and gave him a pat on the back.

I chuckled as Aspen's face blanched from the intimate

contact. He looked horrified as the man grasped his palm, held it up in the air, and paraded him around the field.

He dragged Aspen over to his wife, and I watched as the surly prince's face flushed when the woman leaned over and gave him a friendly pat. Even though the farmer had lost, he had fun, and because Aspen made him look good and impressed his friends, he had become one of them.

Aspen kept craning his head, looking to me for help as he was mobbed by the people.

I shrugged my shoulders and laughed. He looked so uncomfortable being touched.

Then I remembered that for most of his young life, being touched meant pain.

After a young aggressive female planted a kiss on Aspen's lips, I had to intervene. I barged through the fence gap and grabbed him around the wrist pulling him from her grasp, but not before she covered his face with kisses, leaving almost no place untouched.

He was a bit starstruck by the sudden attention. He reached for the woman, and I slapped his hands away.

"All right, lover boy," I snapped, dragging him away from the crowd, and making him sit on a bench. "Focus."

"You were right," he sighed, looking a bit dazed.

"About what?" His face was as red as the lip stain the girl wore. Grabbing the edge of my sleeve, I tried to wipe away the color, but it smeared across his face more. I frowned . He looked like a painted jester.

"I think I get what you mean. I *like* being the people's champion."

"You didn't have to take it so far," I chastised.

The young prince ignored me, his head craning back

toward the petite brunette who kissed him. She posed with her hands behind her back, accentuating her slim waist and pert chest.

"I'd like to take it further." He was about to stand up, but I roughly pushed his shoulders, keeping him in place.

"Down boy. Save your energy for the rest of the fights."

"There's only one more, and then the rest pick up tomorrow." He spoke, but his eyes never met mine. They were constantly searching for the woman, but I could see his glamour start to waver.

I grabbed his cheeks, holding them between my palms, and forced his eyes to meet mine.

"I—uh . . ." I lost track of my thoughts as we stood only inches apart. The blue eyes faded to hazel, his lips thinned, and my breath caught as I saw him. Truly saw him, not the glamour. "You're losing focus, which means you're losing control of your glamour."

His eyes hardened, he nodded slightly, and the glamour strengthened. He was handsome, and I felt a rumble of magic pass between us. A tug on my heart string that was a bit painful.

Then something deep within me cried out.

Mine.

As soon as I heard it, I dropped his face and backed away, putting a proper distance between us. I forgot to breathe. For a second, Aspen wouldn't meet my gaze, and I felt guilty. Did he hear *my* thoughts? Was he connected to me enough to have actually heard me?

He stood, using his sleeve he wiped the rest of the rogue. I searched for clues, but his face was a mask.

"I think I will take a break before my next fight. You don't need to be here for it." He reached into his vest and pulled out a few gold florins. "Take this and find a way to occupy your time until tonight."

The gold florins dropped into my hand; the weight of it felt like guilt. "But don't you need me?"

"I don't," Aspen said coldly. "Nor do I want you here."

Anger flooded me at his rejection. "Fine then, I'll—"

I felt the tug on my heart, cutting off my words. "And don't think of running." His voice was hard.

"Noted," I said sourly. "What about Velora? Do you want me to take her?" I turned to point at the mermaid who was surrounded by a group of fighters. They looked like giant peacocks preening before a maiden. Marco stood near her, his brooding face doing little to deter the suitors.

"She's fine where she is."

I felt like I was the only one being punished by being sent away. "Well, then I think I'm going to go shopping and buy a lace kerchief."

"Fine," he said, turning to take a drink out of his flask.

"And silk gloves, and a riding habit."

"Whatever you want," he said nonchalantly, still ignoring me.

"And a revealing dress to attract all the men in the village." He finally turned to give me a scorching look. I smiled and spun on my heel, heading down the stone path back to the town, tucking the gold florins in my pocket.

I didn't really want to buy lace trimmings or silk gloves. They were too frivolous and not me. I walked silently, knowing I said it all because I wanted to get a reaction out of Aspen. What was I thinking?

CHAPTER FOURTEEN

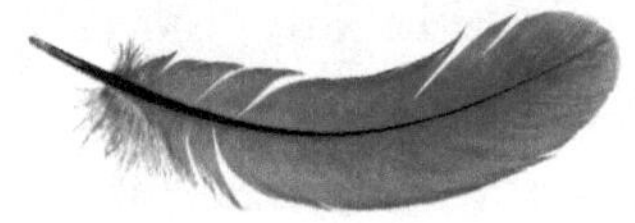

Feeling vindictive, I broke into Aspen's room and stole all of his books, taking care to spell the door closed again behind me. I spent the afternoon researching, but finding nothing in his books on how to break the binding spell.

"Waste of time." I tossed the last book onto my bed.

When the sun began to set, I headed out into the streets in hopes of seeing Silva again. Tonight's festivities included a menagerie of entertainers, acrobats, fire-breathers, tightrope walkers, and sword swallowers. When I snuck away as a child and flew to watch these events, I always felt like an outsider looking in. Even now, as I threaded through the streets, shoulder to shoulder with strangers, eating delicious and foreign food, watching the exhilarating shows—I felt like I didn't belong.

Somehow in my wandering, I ended up in a section of town that became less populated the further I went. I wasn't sure, but it seemed like most avoided the area all together, for I found very few walking in its direction. Narrow roads and uncharmed lamps made it feel derelict. A cat hissed at me from a dark alley. The hairs on the back of my neck prickled, and I could feel an ominous foreboding. Most would have turned and walked the opposite way. Not me. My curiosity always got me into trouble. As I walked, the roads narrowed even further, and there were a fair number of birds that hung on the rooftops ahead and animals that lay in the middle of the street. I was about to cross a marked stone when a dark shadow passed over me and a flutter of feathers sounded from behind.

"Don't!" Silva grabbed my arm. His face was deathly white as he dragged me away from markings along the cobblestone.

"What's going on?" I asked, disturbed by his behavior.

He glanced right and left, checking the markings along the doors, pulling me back until we were standing near some houses. "It's not safe for you to go into the narrows."

"Why not?"

Silva pointed to the designs along the walls. "Those are warnings." He shook his head. "Those that do, don't ever come out."

A young woman, her head covered with a kerchief, entered the narrows pushing a small cart. The animals scattered at her sudden arrival. They hid in the shadows and behind crates as she began to unload the contents of her trolley. I stuck out my thumb toward her and gave him a disbelieving look.

"She's not a *shifter*." Silva pointed to the scratched markings on the stones and walls. What I had thought were childish scribbles were actually wards in an old language. "It's to keep the shifters inside. The first are warnings, but if you would have passed the last ward, you would have been trapped inside permanently . . . as a raven."

"Do you mean to tell me those are all shifters back there?"

He nodded.

"Who did that, I mean? How? Why?"

"It's been this way for a few years. The wards suddenly appeared one day. Once a shifter passed the wards, they instantly turned into their animal and couldn't shift back. More powerful shifters have crossed over the years and tried to free them, but they too have been trapped inside."

"Years. That's a long time to be trapped in that form. I bet most have . . ."

"Gone mad," Silva nodded. "The townspeople are too scared to even go into this section of town anymore, except for a few of the younger maidens that live nearby." He pointed to the young woman who had been scattering food along the ground. A mix of dried food and corn. She went back to her cart, pulled fish out of a wooden barrel, and tossed them along the gutters. When she had emptied her cart, she pushed it farther into the narrows to spread more food. "The shifters won't harm them because they pose no threat."

As he spoke, a large, lumbering bear came out of the nearest house and picked up a fish before heading back inside. Even as I watched, shadows moved toward the food. One shadow in particular looked as big as a horse.

"Has anyone told the king and queen?" I asked.

Silva shook his head. "Why would they care? Years ago, the shifters revolted against King Alder's rule. They were defeated, and the strongest killed. The shifters went into hiding, staying out of sight, blending in with the humans. Then the wards suddenly appeared. Most believe it's a fit and just punishment for the shifters, placed there by the king himself."

"No, he wouldn't do that because the king's a wer—I mean, the queen's a sorc—" I struggled to explain how they could help. "They just wouldn't do that, that's all. We need to do something," I snapped angrily.

"Maeve, come away. There's nothing you can do. Only an incredibly strong sorcerer can break this spell."

"Exactly," I muttered, making a decision that I would probably, most definitely regret.

I walked back to the final ward, slapped my hand on the stone before it, and reached deep into the earth. The same way the dwarf touched my hand and could recognize my mother's magic, I was doing the same. Searching.

First it was a tickle as I traced it, then I began to unwind it, following the path further back until I doubled over in pain. I sucked in my breath between clenched teeth and tried to not throw up. I found it. The castor was . . . Allemar.

This was his doing. These were the poor souls he was experimenting on to create his so-called shifter army. A spell he had put into place years ago when he was the under the guise as Earlsgaarde, the ambassador for Florin. Did Aspen know about this? My mouth went dry as I traced the magic, feeling along the edges, testing the wards. It was very similar to the one he had placed over the door of the cottage. Except that one was meant to kill *me* if I crossed it. This one would only trap shifters.

I paced back and forth, chewing on the corner of my lip. Frantically thinking of a way to save them. The shifters noticed my pacing, and a fox moved to the edge of the ward and whined at me, as if warning me to back away, or perhaps it was a plea to save him.

I kneeled in front of the gold chalk line, closed my eyes, and reached deep into the earth, searching for the ley line of magic, beckoning it to come. Coaxing it like a child with a treat. It was just as Aspen warned. It was slow to respond, not a willing participant, and I could feel sweat beading across my forehead. My magic was starting to rebuke me, and when it answered, I grabbed ahold of it and forced it into the ward. The wards were like a lock that needed a special key, but over time, they drained and weakened and needed to be replenished. These wards hadn't been recharged in a few years, so they were weaker than the one at the cottage. I could overload it with magic and break it. I hoped.

"Maeve, what are you doing?" Silva kneeled by me.

"I'm going to overload the wards with magic to release them."

"I wouldn't do that if I were you," he warned. "You could get injured. Most of them have been trapped too long. They're no longer human. If you release them, they could do more damage than good."

"I will free them." I pointed angrily to the fox that was making his way over to me. He carefully dipped his nose, touching the same stone ward I touched. A current ripped through my body and because I was touching a ley line of magic, I was granted a glimpse into the past.

My heart fluttered as a vision swam over me. Fire burned around me, screams of the innocent echoed in my ears. The ground was soaked with blood. Everywhere I looked, I saw swarms of animals running for their life.

I could hear their internal thoughts, feel their terror.

My heart bursting with fear as if I were there when it happened.

"Stop!" I said, covering my ears as I tried to keep the screams at bay. "No more!"

The human fear of the shifters consumed me, and even though I closed my eyes and tried to keep the vision at bay, I saw him.

King Alder as he stood over me.

As I lay frozen in the body of a fox, unable to shift back to my human form, the great sword rose in the air. It came down, the blade slicing into my spine.

I screamed, my pain mirroring that of the shifter whose vision I was trapped in. In an attempt to fight back, I unconsciously released a blast of magic into the wards and into the air.

Under my touch, the buildings around me exploded in a ball of fire. Stone debris flew across and blasted upward; fire and ash fell. My body flung across the road like a rag doll, smashing into a wall. I looked up as the sky burned with fire.

Not again, I thought, before I passed out.

CHAPTER FIFTEEN

"Maeve!" Silva called.

The voice called to me from the darkness. Locked away in my mind, hiding from the terrors, I retreated. I was being carried, and the movement was too much. Feeling nauseous, I pushed at the chest that pressed against me. The strong arms tightened, but I wiggled, and he put me down.

My feet touched the ground, and I immediately collapsed, throwing up the contents of my stomach. With each heave, I could feel my head spinning, and I feared I was going to black out again.

"Easy." Silva's hands brushed at my face, and they pulled my long hair out of the way.

I felt myself tip forward, and he caught me, laying me back on the ground. "You shouldn't have done that. The repercussions will be terrible."

"Don't lecture me," I mumbled.

"Maeve! Where are you?" Aspen's voice called out in panic.

"I have to go," Silva whispered, pressing his forehead to mine. "You'll be safe now."

My eyes fluttered close, and I passed out.

"Maeve." Aspen's voice cut through the murkiness. "Are you all right? Answer me."

I withdrew, finding safety in the nether where I could sleep.

"Don't make me do it," Aspen said.

It was easier to let the blackness consume me. There, it was quieter.

"I warned you."

He pulled on our link. Pain ripped through my chest, and I awoke with a gasp.

Aspen held me in his lap, my head pressed against his shoulder. "You're alive."

"That hurt," I muttered, rubbing my chest.

"I had to. I couldn't wake you."

"Hate you," I muttered into his shoulder.

"I know. Keep arguing with me. It shows me that your mind is still functioning."

I shook my head and immediately wanted to vomit again.

"Take it easy. Your head is bleeding." As he held me, I could see the sky was bright like daylight.

No, not daylight. It was on fire.

"What h-happened?" I said. Then I heard them . . . the screams. I pulled away and saw the sky—a bright, burning orange—and I was immediately confronted with what I had done. The narrows were on fire. Tears of regret filled my eyes. My cheek was pressed against a soft linen, and the scent of the woods on a rainy morning drifted across my senses.

"Nooo," I groaned and tried to stand up. Aspen helped me to my feet. But it wasn't on my own as he held me pressed against his chest while I saw the devastation that I had caused . . . *again*. A man came running out of a house closest to the narrows, his arm on fire. Townspeople came to his rescue and tried to put him out. I could hear the screams of those inside and tried to enter the nearby houses with blankets covered in water. But I knew the flames were too high. They wouldn't be able to get far. I destroyed the wards *and* obliterated a section of the narrows and nearby houses.

Tears ran freely down my cheeks. "Not again," I cried out angrily. I covered my ears as the screams of the dying mimicked the screams in the vision. So much death. "Help them!" I cried out, pointing at the burning section of the city. I knew if I tried to put out the fire, I would black out, and I didn't trust myself not to cause further damage.

"You can't save them. It's too late."

"You can!" I hissed. "Do something!"

"We let nature take its course," he said. "Let their sacrifice be for you." He began to conjure a trap circle.

"It wasn't a sacrifice. I did this!" I cried out, my guilt all-consuming. "It's my fault. I can't let it happen again. I can't let them die because of me."

Aspen took a deep breath, and I felt his hesitation.

"They're your people," I said. "What kind of prince lets their people die?"

Aspen's jaw clenched. His hand dug painfully into my shoulder as he debated my words. "They're not my people. They're shifters."

"You knew?"

"No, not until I saw three of them transform and run out of the narrows. I put two and two together. Most have made it out. The others . . ." He looked sadly at the fire that was rolling through the narrow alleys and further into town.

"You said yourself you wanted to be the people's champion. Be the champion," I said softly.

Aspen looked at the blaze and I felt his hesitation for a moment; then it was gone, replaced by stone determination. "I will do what I can." He marched toward the wall of fire and drew the entrapment circle on the earth.

"No," I whispered, recognizing what he was doing. He was going to use the entire narrows as a trap and feed his magic that way. He wasn't going to help them survive, just die faster.

He spread his hands wide, and I stood, rolling up my sleeves. Preparing to fight him, take him down. This wasn't right.

I took two steps and collapsed on the ground. The screaming stopped.

The smell of salt hit my nose, and I awoke inside an unfamiliar tent. The red and blue stripes made me dizzy, and I rolled over just in time to dry heave over a ceramic bowl. Nothing came out, thankfully. I collapsed back on the cot and stared up at the fluttering canvas roof. When the world stopped spinning, I turned my head and saw that I was lying next to others on cots. It seemed the acrobats' tent had been turned into a recovery center.

A woman in a light blue dress was moving from victim to victim. Her long black hair fell down her back. Though she was facing away from me, I recognized her. Rosalie.

She was leaning down and using magic to heal each of

those injured in the fire. Three bodies covered in white linen were on the floor next to me. I did this. I had killed them. Guilt flooded my system, and I knew I needed to leave before she saw me.

"There. You will be better in no time," Rosalie encouraged an elderly man.

"I couldn't find her. My daughter. She went into the narrows and didn't come out again." He began to sob. "I tried to find her."

"We still have people searching. She may still be alive," Rosalie said.

"What happened?" he asked, his hands reaching out to grab her arms, clutching her like a lifeline.

"An explosion of some kind. By the time the king and I arrived, it had died down and was under control."

"How?"

She grew somber. "I don't know."

As the man sobbed, the flap on the tent opened and Aspen rushed in holding an injured girl. She was the one who had gone into the narrows to care for the shifters. His face was covered in soot, his clothes and hair singed. From my angle, I could see a blistering and painful burn on his side and along his hands.

"Help me," he called out frantically. "She's not breathing."

Rosalie spun around and they both froze when they saw each other.

Aspen clutched girl to him protectively and Rosalie looked like she was ready to bring the world down around him.

"You do not belong here," she hissed. Brother and sister stood toe to toe, neither moving to help the girl.

"Forget about me for once," Aspen pleaded. "Help her." He carried the girl to an open cot.

The man on the cot sobbed. "Faye! It's my daughter, Faye."

His cry spurred Rosalie into action. She pressed her hands into the girl's chest, and I knew she was searching for what was blocking her breathing. A few seconds later, the girl started to cough, and she rolled over, Rosalie helping her as she spat out black bile. Within seconds, she began to breathe and cry out loud.

The man had rolled out of his cot and made his way over to the girl. He wrapped his injured arm around her, and they embraced, crying loudly.

Rosalie confronted her brother, and he didn't try to run.

"What are you doing here?" she said, her anger evident. "Did *you* cause this?"

Aspen shook his head. "It wasn't me. I swear."

"Then who would be so reckless? They killed over a dozen people. I personally want to see them held responsible. It was Allemar, wasn't it? I'll kill him, then I will see *you* thrown in prison."

His posture stiffened. "I wasn't the one who lost control this time." He glanced to me. "She's the one who broke the wards and decided to rescue a whole clan of imprisoned shifters."

Rosalie followed his gaze, and she turned, her face paling when she saw me. "Maeve," she whispered, but then her voice rose to a scream. "Maeve!"

I winced at the sound of her voice as she wrapped her arms around me in a tight hug.

I immediately started sobbing, my shoulders shaking as she held me.

"Shh, it's okay. Everything's okay," she soothed.

"No, it's not." I whispered. "He's right. I did do this. It was an accident, but I killed those people."

"You saved them too, didn't you?" She cupped my face and looked at my bandaged head. "Someone used a lot of magic to quench the flames. I felt it, the echo of the magic used."

I tried to shake my head, but it was trapped in her palms. "It wasn't me. It was Aspen." I tried to look toward the young prince, but he'd disappeared. The tent door flapped in his wake at his sudden departure.

Having remembered her brother, Rosalie called the guards. Soldiers wearing the livery of Florin rushed in. She gave them a description and sent the guards after him. I could have told her it wasn't worth it. He would use glamour and hide in plain sight.

With her attention back on me, the questions came pouring out of her one after another. "How are you alive? I was told you died in Rya. What are you doing here? Does Mother know? How do you know Aspen? Maeve, tell me what's going on, now!" The last command set my teeth on edge.

I pushed her hands away and crossed my arms over my chest, glaring at her. "Slow down."

"I'm so sorry. I must tell Mother right away."

"No," I said, louder than necessary.

She sat back, brushing the hair behind her ear, highlighting the faded white scar that went down her face. Her icy eyes narrowed. "What do you mean *no*? Maeve, what's going on?"

I released a long breath. "They saved me."

She grew quiet. The air in the tent filled with tension. Her eyes blazed with anger and distrust. "I don't believe you."

"They did. And whether you believe it or not, I'm the one who lost control, just like I did at Rya. And it was your brother, Aspen, who saved the people in the narrows."

"I don't trust him," Rosalie said.

"I'm not asking you to. I'm asking you to trust me."

Rosalie's voice softened. "Maeve, what happened to you over the last few months?"

"I don't want to talk about it."

"That's fine, but why can't we tell Mother?"

Raising my chin, I met her glare with my own. "I'm not sure I'm ready to come back from the dead." My fingers buried in the light sheet covering my legs. "I've never been the good one. You know that. You've covered up for me enough times in the past. I'm too wild and unpredictable."

Rosalie stilled, head dropping forward, the hair covering her scarred face again. "I see. Then I promise not to tell her right away." She would have said more, but the flap opened, and King Xander came in. He stopped when he saw me.

"That looks like . . ."

"It is," Rosalie smiled. "She's alive."

Xander nodded his head. "Welcome, sister of my heart."

Rosalie blushed. "Stop it with cute nicknames."

"It's true, my love. You hold my heart."

I wanted to roll my eyes and barf at the nuances between the two of them. Gone was the cold sister I once knew, replaced by a maternal woman who blushes.

"Aspen is here." Rosalie's voice changed as she gave Xander the warning. His face darkened.

"Then we will double the guards around you."

"I hardly need protection from my brother, but my daughter—"

"He won't hurt Violet," I said suddenly.

Rosalie turned to give me a look. "How do you know? Do you know what he and Allemar did while they were here? All the servants that were murdered, sacrificed to feed his addiction to power."

I quieted. How could I explain to her that it was Allemar that slew the innocents? That Aspen only murdered criminals, and if I did manage to explain it, how would I explain how I came by that information? If she knew I was bound to Aspen, then she would definitely tell our mother. They would find out.

"I just know," I said.

"I hope you're right, for his sake" Rosalie said. She stood, becoming the ice queen I once knew her as. "Because if he so much as touches a hair on my daughter's head, there will be no place he can hide where I will not find him and destroy him."

The air chilled with her fury. I knew it was a subconscious trick of hers to alter the temperature of the air around her when she was angry.

Then Rosalie swayed, her body exhausted from healing so many people. Xander swept in, his arms wrapping around his wife, holding her close.

"You've done enough, Rose. It's time to go back to the palace." Her head drooped against his shoulder and she nodded weakly. He addressed me over Rosalie's head. "My men will continue with the rest of the rescue attempts and clean up. The festival will resume on the morrow. You will come with us."

"I don't think this is a good idea." I began fidgeting with the sleeve of my dress that covered the mark on my arm.

He gave me a royal stare. "That wasn't a request."

CHAPTER SIXTEEN

I never thought I would love a castle so much. The room I was given was larger than the whole main floor of our tower. The four-poster bed was big enough for multiple people to sleep on, and the fireplace could hold Drake standing up. Two stuffed chairs faced the fireplace, and a red crested chaise lounge was in front of the double doors that led onto a private verandah. Rosalie was nice enough to give me a room with easy access to the outdoors.

Flinging the doors open, I gazed out onto the valley below, the gardens to the left, and a great glass dome of the flower conservatory. The many panes sparkled in the light, and I knew that was where the magical imperial roses were kept. To my right, I could see the town of Silverton at the bottom of the valley. Even now, dark smoke trails could be seen from the still smoldering buildings. Guilt weighed on me heavily as I tried to remember what had happened when I lost control. It started with that vision.

Was that vision I had real? Was I tapping into long-lost shifter memories? Did King Alder really kill shifters in cold blood with a silver embedded sword? I gnawed on the inside of my cheek and debated what my next course of action would be.

Allemar had promised he would tell me where the shifters were, and Aspen brought me right to them. This must have been his plan. What would he do to me when he found out I broke the wards and released them? Nothing good.

Maybe now that I was in the castle, I could search for Allemar's study and find his spell books. Find a way to break the bond he held over me. As I paced the room, I heard a disturbing noise coming from my wardrobe.

I had assumed it to be empty since the suite was clearly for guests. Walking close to the furniture piece, I put my ear near it and listened. There was a rattling noise, followed by a loud thump.

I jumped back as the door unlatched and slowly swung open. A long green arm snaked out and pulled the door close again.

"What in the stars is that?" I muttered. Preparing for an attack by a beast, I flung the door open wide and looked into the shocked face of a green-skinned goblin. His long ears were drooping, and his nose round and red, but what surprised me the most was he was wearing a pair of earrings and had wrapped a silk scarf around his body in the form of a skirt.

"Grabberr dath," the goblin sputtered.

"Get out of my closet," I shouted at him.

The creature stuck his tongue out at me and preceded to ignore me as he focused on a pair of satin slippers embedded with blue beads and lace. One came flying at my face. I ducked, and it hit my shoulder.

"Ouch!"

He grasped the edge of the wardrobe, flipped me an obscene gesture, and then slammed the door.

"Rude!" I yelled back.

The door to my room opened, and a worried Rosalie stepped in and scanned the room.

"Have you seen Gobbersnot?"

I placed my left hand on my hip and motioned with my right. "Is he about yay high, green, rude, and has an affinity for women's clothes?"

Rosalie visibly relaxed. "You've seen him?"

I pointed to my wardrobe. "In there."

She was about to open it, then turned her back and changed her mind. "Do you mind if he stays in there for now?"

"What? No!" I said.

"He's been really jealous lately, and feels put out."

"He belongs with the rest of the red caps. The murdering little rascals."

"As you can see, he is . . . um, different."

"You can say that again."

She smiled wanly. "I think he's just trying to find where he belongs in our family." Her hand rested on her stomach.

"Are you pregnant again?"

She blushed. "Yes, and that's what's got him on edge. He is like a very loyal pet, and the perfect guardian for Violet. But ever since we found out about the newest addition, he's been a little off."

"You mean crazy."

She moved farther into the room and sat on the edge of the stuffed chair. "Sorry we didn't get to talk more earlier. I've been exhausted."

"You shouldn't have been down there," I snapped.

"You shouldn't have healed those people if you're pregnant. You could have injured the baby, or worse."

"I'll be fine. I know my limits."

"You almost passed out. I saw you."

"Well, okay, I may have done a little too much. But the people are my responsibility."

"It's two kingdoms. The strain is too much for you and Xander both."

"We know. We are trying to solve the problem, one of many, and then I heard about the narrows. How did I not know about their situation? No one told us." Her hands trembled.

"Fear disguised as hate," I said firmly. "Just like you once said to me: people hate shifters because they don't understand us. Not all of us are evil."

Rosalie nodded and wiped at her eyes. "Yes, we need to change the way they see you. We may have a solution, but I need to ask you something, and you have to tell me the truth. What is Aspen doing here?"

"I don't know," I lied.

"Then I will have to assume he is here as a threat to the crown."

"No, I don't think so," I added quickly.

Her lips thinned, and I knew she didn't believe me. "Then why, if Allemar and Aspen saved you, have you returned here to his place of birth, if not to try to take the throne by force?"

I chewed on the inside of my lips and breathed out. "I think he's after something that Allemar left behind."

Rosalie stared into the fire, her hands clasped on her dainty lap. "I've locked the tower and forbidden anyone to go near it."

"What about Aspen?" I asked.

"What about him?" She turned slightly to face me.

"He's your brother."

Her eyes hardened, and she shook her head. "No, he is nothing to me. A stranger of my blood. You are more family to me, and we share no blood at all. I cannot trust him. For one, he was raised by our twisted father, and then warped even further by Allemar himself. There's no telling what kind of hold Allemar has over him. I can't allow him near my daughter, ever."

My mouth went dry, and I covered my wrist with my hand. There was so much hate and distrust directed toward her brother. Would she reserve some of that malice for me when she found out that I was bound to them in a way that would terrify her? That Allemar had control over me . . .

"Are you okay?" Rosalie noticed my sudden shift in mood.

"I'm just tired," I said, brushing my hand across my bandaged forehead. "I have a lot to think about."

"You said that you were the one who caused the fire. What happened?"

"I broke the wards on the narrows."

Her eyebrows shot up toward the sky. "By yourself?"

I patted my chest, and the pain in my heart grew heavy. "I lost control and the closest wards exploded. I didn't mean for the nearby houses to catch fire as well."

She reached across the two chairs and grabbed my hand in between hers. "Well, it will be okay. You're safe here. Get some rest. Stay as long as you like."

"What about the people in the town? The shifters and the innocent victims?"

"Xander is taking care of it. There will be a public funeral and mourning period. He will search out the shifters and speak to them. We're prepared to help them rebuild their homes, find lost families, and help them heal after that ordeal. After all, he is a werewolf. He's close to their kind. But I heard many have taken to the woods and have not regained their former selves."

"It's not fair," I said angrily, picking at a string on my dress, fighting back the hate I had for Allemar. "That should never have happened."

"No, it shouldn't. And my husband knows this. He has a course of action that may help them build trust with us. Tomorrow, we will resume the festival."

"Don't you think it's a little too soon to be celebrating?" I ground out between clenched teeth, partly from my own guilt.

"The last forty years have been hard on them. The people need a reason to celebrate and have hope. Xander will make sure the families are compensated for their loss."

"Hush money," I said angrily. "Coin will not replace a family member."

"It doesn't. But it gives them time to close shop, grieve properly, and not worry about feeding their family while they do so. It is all we can do. We cannot bring back their dead, but we can help them bury them."

"You should punish the responsible party," I said, turning toward her. "If I were you, I would want revenge."

Rosalie shook her head. "I just got you back. I can't lose you again."

This was *not* the sister I knew. So easily she put her convictions aside and became a ruler of the people. She should punish the culprit. Me. But instead, she was going to hide me away and pay off the people to forget.

She wished me a good night and left me. Exhausted, I moved over to the bed and fell upon the mattress, sinking heavily into the blankets. She may not wish me harm, but I soon began to see that I caused more harm than good. Another epic disaster caused by my anger and lack of control.

It wasn't Aspen she should fear, but me.

CHAPTER SEVENTEEN

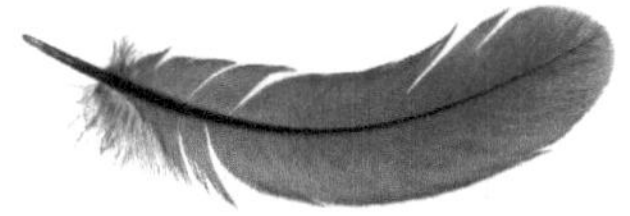

Pain exploded out of my chest. I couldn't breathe. Reaching toward the sky, I fell out of bed, landing on the cold, hard stone. Aspen pulled at my heart string, and it was becoming desperate. Stumbling, I went out onto the balcony on my bare feet. The cold stone made me shiver, and I tried to pinpoint which direction the pain was coming from.

Another pull. I sucked in a breath through my teeth.

"By the stars, I'm coming," I raged, unsure I could even fly straight. But maybe I didn't have to fly so much as fall . . .

Climbing to the top of the stone bannister, I let my toes hang over the edge, then let myself slip forward. Shifting into a raven, I flew off the balcony and headed deep into the woods, following the ebb and flow of pain. They were in a clearing just outside of the village, and I felt Aspen's final tug as I came into land, half shifting, half collapsing as I almost blacked out.

"You shouldn't have done that!" Velora chastised, her voice full of worry. "Can't you see, she's not well?"

"I had to." Now it was Aspen's voice that was

distressed. "I had to see if she would come. That something hadn't happened to her."

I could hear them discuss me like I wasn't there. Whenever I opened my eyes, my vision swam, and I felt dizzy again. I'd clearly hit my head harder than I thought during the explosion.

"H-hate you," I muttered painfully, without opening my eyes.

Aspen laughed. "I know." He kneeled by me and waited for me to recover. "Are you okay? That landing was a little rough."

I frowned and wanted to close my eyes again. "What do you expect? I'm recovering from a concussion. I shouldn't even be shifting right now. There was no guarantee I could even fly."

"Then why did you?"

I glared at him. "That wasn't flying. That was falling recklessly."

"Where were you? Are you safe?"

"I'm safe for now, but they have the whole kingdom looking for you. My sister has me staying in the palace."

He nodded. "It will be safer for you there."

My brows knit together in confusion. "Safer from who?"

Aspen didn't say. He looked away, refusing to meet my eyes.

"You were the one who stopped the fire, right?" I asked.

Aspen seemed annoyed. "Yes, I did, but I used up most of my reserves ." He pulled up his sleeve, revealing the fading blood tattoos. "I hesitated at first, and doing so, more died. I smothered the fire, but it took time. It wasn't fast, and that is how the young girl was injured. But I wasn't the only one in there. There were others roaming among the smoke and haze. I believe they were shifters. They helped evacuate the invalid or elderly, and others put out the fire.

I sighed. "I did it. They're safe."

Aspen frowned. "You did, and Allemar won't be pleased."

"I never told you about the narrows and the trapped shifters. You already knew about them."

"I knew. Allemar wanted you to come—"

"Look over this way," a voice echoed in the woods. "I think I hear voices."

Aspen put a finger to his mouth, silencing us. He made a motion to Marco and Velora and they stepped out into the open. He grabbed me around the waist and pulled me against a tree. He took his cloak and covered us both with it, pressing my back into the bark.

"Can you—" he asked.

And without even finishing his sentence, I held up my hand and wove an invisibility spell over the cloak. "Don't move," I whispered.

It quickly became warm, and I was consciously aware of how close Aspen was to me. They may be looking for him, but he also didn't want me to be found with him. Crashing noises drew close, and I heard guards enter the clearing.

"You there, identify yourselves," one of the guards began to interrogate Velora and Marco.

A rough knob of bark bit into my back painfully, and I moved to adjust myself so it wasn't jabbing into me. Aspen groaned in pain ever so softly, and that was when I remembered he was injured.

Feeling my fingers along his side, I found the frayed edges of his shirt. I could feel the heat radiating off of his skin from the burn. Very gently, I cupped my hand around the area and sent magic into the wound. Cooling the burn, softening the skin. He wavered and fell forward, his head dropping onto my shoulder. The full weight of his body pressed against mine, and I felt his lips move ever so softly against my neck in the lightest of kisses. Or it could have been the lightest of curses.

I tried to focus on healing the burn on his hands.

"Is this all of your party?" a guard asked. A branch snapped only a few feet from us as they beat the bushes.

Aspen lifted his head, his fingers moving across my lips to keep me from calling out. I wouldn't give him away after all I had done to heal him. Even though we were hidden by an invisibility spell, he pressed even closer to me, as if trying to cover my small frame with his own, hiding me beneath him.

Light still trickled through the cloak, and his hazel eyes met mine. I saw a burning question within them. I pushed my face against his hand, wanting him to remove it, and as soon as he did, it was replaced by his lips.

Aspen's kiss wasn't gentle. It was demanding and possessive, and it awoke something within me. A need so strong that could only be satisfied by the desire to taste him. I parted my lips, and he moaned. His hand wrapped around my waist, my arms reached around his shoulders, pulling him deeper into the kiss. My breathing came in gasps, and he pulled away, immediately silencing me again with his hand. His eyes were wild with fear as he looked around us, suddenly remembering where we were, or perhaps, *who* we were.

I wasn't satisfied at the abrupt ending to our kiss, and I glared at him angrily. Aspen's own breathing was ragged and didn't lesson once the guards moved away. We waited agonizing moments and heard nothing, but he refused to pull away from me.

Look at me! I mentally cried. When he did, I saw his eyes full of regret.

He slowly removed his fingers from my mouth, brushing them across my lips gently. "This should never have happened. I'm sorry."

Rejection felt like a slap in the face. I stood there as he pulled away, removing the cloak from both of us, and stepping out to be greeted by Velora and Marco. Fuming, I stormed away and sat on a downed log.

"They were looking for you. We shouldn't stay. We will draw too much attention. We should hunt elsewhere," Marco spoke up.

Aspen's hands cupped into fists. "I told you we are not hunting here."

"Does your master know about . . .what she did?" Marco asked the weighted question.

A long silence followed. "He knows enough." Aspen spared a glance over at me and quickly looked away. "But we will just be more careful. I will have to keep my disguise on permanently, and now we have someone on the inside that can help me."

I was paralyzed as I knew what he was referring to. They were going to use me to get what they wanted. If what Aspen wanted was the same as my own goal, then maybe it wouldn't be so bad. That was the only thing that gave me comfort.

"You will keep my presence a mystery," he said, giving

me an order. "You will feed me any information you find out about the upcoming trials." His voice had grown cold, commanding, and I bristled at the change in him.

Standing up, I bowed mockingly low. "My only *desire* is to obey you," I said with as much disgust as I could, putting emphasis on the word desire and watching his face like a hawk.

I saw the twitch at the corner of his mouth, but that was the only break in his mask.

"What about the competition?" Velora asked.

"It will resume as scheduled," I said.

"Yes, I will continue to win, and the winners are allowed to enter the palace for the final trials."

"But what if you don't win?" I said.

He gave me a cool look. "I will."

"But what if you don't?" I challenged again.

He turned his back on me, and I felt the wall between us grow even higher. I sighed. What did I expect? I shouldn't have feelings for my captor. It was a stupid.

Sitting on the outside of the circle, I listened to them plot and plan. I felt left out, and it bothered me to be excluded. What had happened? Was it because I spent weeks traveling with them? Did I let Velora and her insipid questions slip under my defenses? Had Marco, with his quiet demeanor, somehow become the big brother I never had? And Aspen . . .? My cheeks grew warm thinking of Aspen. Had I somehow developed a desire and feelings for the second most vile person in the seven kingdoms?

I dropped my head into my hands. I was an emotional mess. I didn't trust myself. It was just a kiss. A kiss to keep me quiet. That was it.

". . . can you do that?" A shadow had fallen over me,

and I looked up in surprise. I had been so lost in my own thoughts, I didn't hear his question. Instead of asking him to repeat it, I opted for rebellion.

"Why should I?" I snapped, irritated at the knot of feelings that sat in my stomach and how I couldn't get them under control.

Aspen gripped my elbow and pulled me away from the group, further into the woods. "Don't be a fool. Don't be sullen. Just forget about what happened between us. Do as I say, and I'll do what I can to protect you."

Protect me? I didn't need his protection. "Only if you stop trying to rip my heart out," I said. He paused as he tried to decipher exactly which way I meant it. It hurts when you summon me. And what if I can't leave, or come to you? Are you going to destroy me in a fit of rage?"

Aspen's jaw clenched angrily. "You will come to me when called. And if you don't, I will find you and punish you. There's nowhere you can run where I can't find you."

"I wish I had never met you," I ground out angrily, ripping my elbow from his grasp.

"I know." Aspen sighed. I could tell my words affected him.

In a fit of feathers and mist, I shifted and flew up into the sky, desperately trying to escape the trembling of my frantically beating heart.

CHAPTER EIGHTEEN

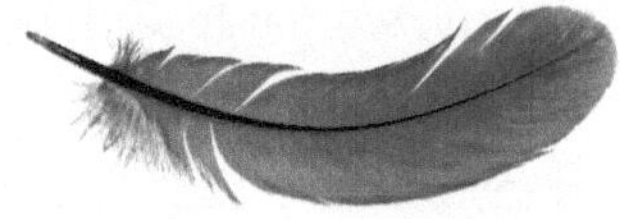

I flew to the narrows to survey the destruction I had caused. The southern half was nothing but a burned husk. Only the framework of the buildings remained like blackened skeletons whose mouths were gaping open to the sky. Smoke still trailed from hotspots that kept popping up, and the breeze carried the acrid smell of ash.

A stray dog sniffed in one of the burned buildings, and I wasn't sure if this was a lost shifter or a real dog. The burned shell of buildings and the neighboring streets were still cordoned off, but signs and barricades never deterred me. I simply flew over them and landed in a section that hadn't been destroyed by fire. When I found a safe place to land that was out of view, I shifted back to a human. The change made me dizzy, and I had to grasp the nearest open doorframe for support.

A sudden movement within the dark interior of the house caught my attention .

"Hello?" I called out warily.

A snuffing sound followed by soft footfalls met my ears. Not in the least scared, I entered and was surprised to see a fox scratching around in the corner by the fireplace.

His nose was burned, and part of his backside was missing fur.

Carefully, I approached the shifter, my hands held up in the air. "My name is Maeve. I'm like you."

The black nose rose in the air and sniffed, catching my scent. The beady eyes were wary, and he slinked and hid behind a wooden chair that had a thin, partially burnt quilt over the back.

"It's okay. You can come out," I coaxed.

His distrust was evident. His lips pulled back in a snarl, showing his teeth. I kneeled on the ground and waited patiently, but I didn't think I was gaining any headway. Closing my eyes, I shifted back into a raven and flew to the table, flapping my wings to show that I was just like him.

Kraa! I called, flicking my tail. A reddish blur flew through the air, knocking me down. The fox pinned me. He snarled, and I pecked his foot. He yelped but didn't let up. Before he could attack, a thick golden paw smacked the fox in the snout, causing him to jump back and retreat behind a blackened chair.

I lay on the wood table, my blood thrumming in my ears. My body was still frozen in terror from almost being eaten alive. Solemn amber eyes peered down at me, a red-gold mane surrounding his face. The sweltering heat of the lion's breath hit me as he snuffed and nudged me to make sure I was alive. I flapped my wings and righted myself, and the lion shifted into his counterpart.

He looked around in distress when he had no clothes and yanked a tattered curtain down to surround his hips. "Sorry. It's been a few years. I forgot clothes don't always return." The man was in his fifties, and had faded cross scars on his chest. The red-gold of his mane remained, but he was white at his temples and goatee. When he was covered, the lion turned toward the cowering fox.

"Brekken, you mangy dog. You shouldn't eat the person who saved you." The lion shifter's voice was calm and deep, like the ocean.

The fox yipped but didn't seem too pleased to obey the lion. "Careful now, watch your language. That's no way to address a lady."

Brekken didn't like that at all. In a flurry of red mist, he shifted into a thin man with a wiry face and reddish hair. He was about to open his mouth and yell an expletive when he realized he had no clothes. His mouth fell open, and he grabbed the blanket from the chair and tied it around his waist.

"It's been a long time, friend." The lion went over and gave a pat on Brekken's back.

"Yes-ss, it hasss." Brekken shivered, struggling with speaking after so long as a fox.

"I'm Cross." The man extended his hand toward me. Still in my bird form, I had slowly worked my way to the door. "It's okay. No one will lay a finger on you if I'm here. We may be crotchety old shifters, but we still have manners." He rolled his eyes at Brekken. "Or at least some of us do."

Feeling at ease, I shifted back into my body. "I'm Maeve."

"You were the one that broke the ward spell?"

Heat rose to my cheeks in shame. "Yes, I did, and I'm sorry for the chaos afterwards . . ." my voice dropped to a whisper, "I didn't mean for anyone to get hurt.".

Cross pinched his lips and placed a hand on my shoulder. "You did what no one else could do. It was a battle for our freedom, and like any battle or war, there are bound to be casualties. We shifters understand that."

"You shouldn't try to make me feel—"

Cross's voice rose with authority. "Don't carry their deaths on your shoulder. It was not your fault, but the one who imprisoned us."

It was no use debating with a lion. I could tell that he was adamant about his beliefs.

"Why didn't you leave?" I asked. "Why did you stay once the wards were broken?"

Cross moved to a window and looked out into the dirty street. "I stay to protect those that can't protect themselves. Not all have moved on and left the narrows. There are some that are truly lost and can't return to their human self. Others have nowhere to go. This is their home. But their home isn't safe. For there is someone who walks among us, whispering lies and dissension."

"Is his name Allemar?" I asked.

Cross cleared his throat. "We do not know his name. He comes at night calling himself the shifter king. He promises power and freedom if we follow him. The shifters that went with him were somehow able to leave the narrows despite the wards."

"How long has this been going on?"

"A few months now."

"Well, isn't that a good thing?" I asked. "That someone was helping the shifters leave the narrows?"

Brekken shivered. "Not when they wind up dead."

Cross nodded. "It's true. In here, we protect each other. Out there . . . we're not safe from the humans and other things that hunt us. The world is bigger than we remember."

I thought about it. Whoever had been crossing into the narrows called themself the shifter king. But yet, a shifter couldn't cross the wards without getting trapped inside. It had to be someone else. A human . . . Allemar.

Cross's eyebrows drew together as he searched the sky for something or someone. When he couldn't find them, he put his fingers to his lips and whistled. A hawk came, sat on the lamp post and gave Cross a side-eye.

"Where's Joanna and Pak?"

The hawk shook his head and bobbed up and down.

"What do you mean gone?" Cross groaned.

"What's going on?" I asked.

"Two of our oldest predators, Old Joanna—a puma—and Pak the coyote, have disappeared since the wards were dispelled."

"Do you think they escaped the fire?" I asked hopefully.

Brekken kicked a pebble on the wood floor. "Probably left the narrows and the human's killed them, or the shifter king got them. Either way . . . still dead."

Cross glared at Brekken.

A white snake slithered into the kitchen, and I almost smacked it with my slipper—then it shifted. The snake elongated, and I focused on his red eyes as one of the most handsome man I've ever seen stood before me. His white-blonde hair pulled back with a leather cord, his pale skin shimmered, and it looked like the sun never touched his perfect body. Thankfully, he was dressed in fine black pants and a white long-sleeved shirt. His silver vest only accentuated his skin and hair color.

"Warden, what's wrong?" Cross addressed the scout.

"We've got company. A retinue of armed soldiers have entered the narrows. Never before have they cared about us. Why now?"

Hooves rattled along the cobblestone and Brekken yelped, ducking under the table, his much larger form struggling to get his whole body under it. Only Cross and I headed toward the doorway.

Florin soldiers dressed in red uniforms rode single file down the road. Shifters ran, hiding in the shadows, under wagons, or in alleys. I stepped into the middle of the street to confront the oncoming army.

The commanding officer, a harsh man with cunning eyes, abruptly pulled up to a stop. He sneered at me. "Out of the way."

"Not until I know why you've come bearing arms into the narrows."

"That's none of your business, woman." The commander pulled the reins on his horse, making his mount dance around me. I was fearful of being trampled, but kept my footing, refusing to budge an inch.

"It does if it involves the shifters," I said proudly. Standing with my legs apart, I raised my chin in defiance, my hands glowing with power.

"Are you threatening the royal army?" The commander's eyes alit with challenge. "I would love to take you on." His hand reached for the blade at his side.

"Hold, Commander Harn," a voice called out.

The soldiers parted way, and King Xander rode up to me. He shook his head and chuckled. "I should have known it was you causing trouble."

"I'm not causing trouble. I'm here to protect them."

"And so am I," King Xander answered. He coughed into his hand. "Or do you forget I may be a bit partial to their specific needs as well?"

My cheeks flushed red at my werewolf brother-in-law's reminder. "No, Your Majesty."

"I'm very glad that you've shown initiative in helping the shifters recover from this ordeal, but I'm also here to offer them aid." He sat up straight on his horse. "Know this. I, King Xander, am hereby declaring peace between the shifter nation and the kingdom of Florin. We will help all of you in your search to regain a life of peace and prosperity here."

Leaning back along the wall, his bare chest exposed, Cross had taken in all of the ceremony from the doorway. "Pretty words from a pretty king. How do we know that you'll stand by us?"

"How does becoming a lord sound to you?" Xander grinned. "With lands and vassals of your own."

Brekken stepped forward and raised his hand to volunteer, accidentally dropping his waist cloth in his hurry to claim what the king was offering.

Cross elbowed him roughly. "Idiot. It's the king. You're not decent."

A loud bellow of laughter followed as Xander couldn't hold back his amusement. "I've been in similar situations . . . you know what I mean?" He winked.

It took Cross a moment before his eyes widened with understanding. "Yes, Your Majesty. What you offer sounds too good to be true. I can't help but wonder if there is a catch to all of this."

Xander swept his hand to encompass the narrows. "I may not be the king you chose, but I'm the one you have. I will do my best to right the wrongs done to you in the past. We've decided to allot titles and lands to those we deem worthy. We will invite the bravest and smartest to our palace where they will compete in a few trials to prove their mettle. Win, and I will give you all that I promised."

"What about if we lose?" Cross asked.

King Xander smiled. "There are no losers. I still intend to help the shifters rebuild and thrive. I hope this is a way to bring our kind together."

"What do you need me to do?" Cross asked suspiciously.

"Choose seven of the smartest and bravest among you. You, along with those that have already won the various challenges during our St. Autumnus festival, come to the palace.

"They want the smartest? Well, that rules you out Brekken," Warden said and stepped into the street, laughing at the fox.

Brekken peeked his head out of the house before he was spooked and went back inside.

"We didn't win any of the events. The humans will think that we cheated before we even begin. They will hate us," Cross pointed out.

Xander shrugged. "They hate you already. I've been hated and feared my whole life. I just had to find a way to prove them wrong. I thought that you would be up for the challenge. Am I mistaken?"

Cross's eyes burned with fire. "You're not."

"Good, then. Seven shifters. Come to me tomorrow and I will present you to the town."

With a crack of his reins, King Xander spurred on his horse. A few soldiers at the end of his retinue stopped and unhitched wagons full of provisions. Clothes, food, and household items in the first wagons; in the second, building supplies and tools to start the rebuilding process.

As Cross, Warden, Brekken, and I watched, men, women, and children came out of the houses and approached the soldiers with fear and trepidation.

"Come on." I waved Brekken and Cross over. "We need to get you some clothes."

"I don't know. I kind of like the freedom this brings." Brekken wiggled his hips, showing off his blanket skirt. "Clothes are too itchy." He scratched his hairy chest to prove a point.

"You're wearing clothes, Brekken," Warden snapped. "I refuse to see your pale backside strutting through the narrows."

"Pale?" Brekken barked. "Look who's talking, snake boy. You need a tan. And I don't strut." He pouted and strutted across the street.

"Enough!" Cross scolded them. He pulled pants from the wagon and a soldier handed him a white shirt and belt. "Has anyone seen Hela, or Torren?"

Warden shook his head. "Not lately."

"Torren is probably sleeping. Warden, go wake him, and get Everett. Brekken, find Roman and Hela. We need to see who is still around." Cross took his clothes and went down an alley to change.

I climbed into the wagon and began to sort through the clothes and help hand them out. Most of them still had a wild look about them. Their mannerisms were very abrupt, and they often grunted instead of speaking. A young woman walked barefoot toward me, and I wrapped a cloak around her thin shoulders. Her eyes were wide as saucers, and she blinked against the sun, shading her face from the light. A few stray spotted feathers were still stuck in her hair. I plucked one out and handed it to her.

Her cheeks flushed pink. "I'm so embarrassed, thank you."

"Don't be. The feathers are the worst. Owl?" I asked.

She bobbed her head. "Yes, is it obvious?"

"A bit."

"I'm Nora. A snow owl."

"Maeve, raven and crow."

Those owl-like eyes blinked in disbelief. "Two forms? I've never heard of that."

Cross came from behind the wagon. "Did you say raven and crow?"

"Hmm, yes," I answered. "My mother said I can shift between them because they're similar in nature. Can't you?"

Cross shook his head, and he eyed me suspiciously. "No, we only have the single form. There's only one kind of shifter that can—"

"Dead!" Brekken came running down the street, his hair as wild as his face. "Roman's been stabbed through the heart."

CHAPTER NINETEEN

Brekken dove into the cart of clothes, digging under them and hiding like a frightened dog. Cross gave a worried glance at Nora who dropped the clothes she was holding. Her lip trembled, and she looked ready to faint.

"I got her, go!" I told Cross.

With feet that barely touched the ground, Cross took off running down the street toward Roman's home.

The pile of clothes moved, and I placed my hand on the mound. "Brekken, it's okay. You're safe."

A pair of long johns moved, and only the top of Brekken's eyes were visible. "Nope, not coming out. It's not safe out there. It's too bright. Too noisy. I don't like it." The long johns flipped back over his face.

Nora giggled, and then her eyes went wide. "Wait, that's my laugh? That's what I sound like? It's been so long, I couldn't remember the sound." Tears filled her eyes, and she collapsed to her knees and began to cry.

I stood next to her awkwardly as I tried to figure out how to comfort her. Reaching toward the wagon of clothes, I found a pretty silk scarf and handed it to her. "Here. Wipe your eyes."

Except I didn't hand her a scarf. Nora unfolded the silk to reveal a scantily clad nightshift.

The long johns moved again, and Brekken let out a wolfish whistle.

"You really are a mangy mutt!" I gave a slight punch to the pile, and I heard Brekken's snotty voice.

"You missed." The clothes moved, and he laughed.

Using more oomph, I measured exactly where I thought his head was and gave him a hard whack.

"Oomf!" A thin arm holding white breeches waved at me from under the mound. "Ya got me. I surrender."

Nora had stopped crying and was now in a fit of giggles. When we had picked out outfits for her and her mother, we walked to the second wagon. One of the soldiers stopped and stared when he handed her a crate filled with food. She blushed, and he smiled, instantly smitten. She stayed to talk with him before heading home.

The next few candle marks, I worked hard, unloading the wagons, parceling out the food, and speaking to every shifter. Each one I met, I committed their name to my memory and learned their story.

With each shifter I talked to, I asked what their form was, secretly hoping to find a connection to my family. Most were smaller creatures, like cats, coyotes, and birds. I even met a turkey vulture. But I never found another raven.

When Cross finally returned, his face was grim. Behind him Warden came with a giant of a man who I assumed to be Torren. Thick in the shoulders and body, he was pure muscle, and his eyes were a piercing blue which disappeared behind an enormous yawn. He looked at me sleepily.

"Is this her? The one who broke the wards? She looks small, like a child." Torren yawned again, scratching his chest.

Cross nodded. "Hela, Torren, this is Maeve. She's helping us.

Hela's piercing gaze was predatory in nature. She ran her caramel-colored eyes over me and raised one brow as if surprised by my stature. She obviously wasn't intimidated by me. Her golden hair was pulled back in a twist. She wore a green pantsuit with long billowy sleeves that covered her arms.

"Hello," she purred.

Torren's greeting was lost in a yawn.

"Is it true?" Hela turned to Cross, "Roman is dead?"

Cross growled and looked toward me.

"Not just Roman. I found two more dead in their homes."

"It's like it's become open hunting season on shifters," Warden murmured. "We should fight back. Kill a few of them so they'll leave us alone."

My breath caught in my throat. "No. We do not know that the humans did this."

"Are you saying a shifter did?" Hela scoffed. "We've been safe inside the wards, and as soon as they come down, all of a sudden we're getting picked off. Who else could it be other than the humans?"

"We don't know anything about how they died. We need proof before you do anything reckless."

Hela laughed. "Reckless? Honey, you're the one who brought the wards down. Maybe you didn't realize that some of us had it pretty good on the inside. We were safe, fed, and left well enough alone by the humans. They forgot about us. Now, we are an eyesore to them. A reminder that we still exist." She flashed her teeth in her anger, and I heard the slight feline growl.

"I seem to remember someone," Torren yawned, "coming into my cellar and disturbing my slumber. They spoke in an odd language, but I chased them out. They haven't come back."

"When was this?" Cross asked.

Torren shrugged. "Could be days, or weeks ago. I don't remember. It all runs together."

Cross rubbed his chin and sighed. "Maybe we should take the king up on his offer. I would feel better if a few of us were given lands. We could move the shifters there and we'd be safe."

"Or they'd just hunt us there." Hela sniffed.

"No, I will speak with the king. We will find out who did this, I promise."

"Big words from such a little girl." Warden patted me on the back. "I like it."

"Do what you can." Cross said. "I will bring the seven tomorrow night." The man squinted his eyes and glanced up and down the street. "Where's Brekken?"

I smirked and lifted a blanket on the wagon. Brekken was curled up asleep in his fox form. When he wasn't looking, I'd healed his burns, and already the missing patches of fur started to show new growth. He was so terrified that I had to spell him to sleep to do it.

"Sleeping like a baby," Warden chuckled.

"Move over," Torren growled. The giant man shifted, the heavy fur cloak he wore disappeared, and a great black bear pawed along the cobblestone and crawled up onto the wagon, the wheels creaking beneath his weight. Torren was careful to not crush the tiny fox. He plopped his head down near Brekken's and closed his eyes.

Brekken shivered and nudged closer, releasing a sigh of content. He felt safe. Who wouldn't nestled in the arms of a giant bear?

"Want to join them?" Cross teased Hela.

"Not on your life." Hela looked affronted at the prospect. "Brekken bites in his sleep."

"Oh come on, you never complain when Everett bites." Warden wiggled his eyebrows at Hela, and she hit him in the shoulder.

She rolled her eyes at Warden before addressing Cross. "I'll take the first watch. I don't feel comfortable unless some of us are patrolling the streets."

"Good idea. Warden, get some of the birds. We'll make a rotation until this is settled." Cross turned to me. "I sure hope you're right and we find the murderer soon."

"Me too."

The next morning, I awoke as the door of my room creaked opened. A young toddler about two summers old walked in wearing a pink dress, her eyes filled with delight and wonder. Her dark curls and violet eyes were the spitting image of Rosalie. I was having the mother of all fits by burying my head in my pillows, and I peeked out from under the downy softness to glance at my niece.

Violet wasn't alone, for right on her tail was Gobber-snot dressed in a matching outfit. The young girl was in her own little world and babbling in her own language, or I thought it was until the goblin answered her back.

Totally enraptured by the conversation between the

two, I remembered what mother had said about young children. Children are a gift and are born already knowing the language of the fae. As they grow older, they forget as they make room for the much headier English language.

"You can take her out," I muttered to Gobbersnot. "I'm not in the mood to babysit."

He ignored me as Violet came over to my bed and tried to pull herself up onto the mattress. Her fists balled into the covers; her face scrunched up in a mass of wrinkles as she sputtered out the command. "Boov!"

Gobbersnot jumped forward and gave the uncoordinated girl a boost onto my bed. What is it with young children and their incessant need to climb on things? I sat up, crossing my knees and covering them with my dress. Resting my chin in my hand, I watched as my niece held out her doll to me. I awkwardly accepted it and released a loud sigh.

This was not in my nature to be motherly. Aura's—yes, Meri—absolutely. . . me, not a chance. I thought children were cute at a distance. Not so much up close. They smelled.

Except for Violet. She smelled of roses and soap.

"What do you want me to do with this?" I waved it back and forth like it was dancing. She didn't look amused. Even Gobbersnot gave me a bored look. "Hey, I'm not great with kids. Starting fires, blowing things up . . . yes. Playing . . ." I immediately recalled Randall and the game of stones, the memory a reminder as to why I hated games.

Violet didn't move but looked at me expectantly.

"Okay." I slid from the bed. "Do you want to see a trick?" I closed my eyes, shifted into a raven, and flew around the room.

"Birdy!" Violet hopped up and down on my bed. "Birdy. I wanna touch it."

I landed on the coverlet. Violet had the biggest smile reaching from ear to ear. Gobbersnot, on the other hand, was licking his lips eagerly. I ruffled my feathers at him angrily and hopped over to my niece, inwardly preparing myself for the hard pat I knew was going to come down on my head or spine.

Instead, she held out the back of her finger and gently brushed across my chest. I was momentarily taken aback by the flood of feelings coursing through me. I wasn't used to being touched in this form but being caressed by one so young and gentle was very peaceful. Her love and awe poured out through each stroke. Her eyes glistened, and she leaned down to give me the softest kiss on my beak.

"Love you, Birdy." And just like that, she shattered my walls and broke into my heart.

Love you too, kid.

She leaned back and shifted into a wolf pup, and I fluttered back in response. Violet hopped off the bed and wagged her tail at me. Her fur was a silver gray, but her eyes remained violet. She yipped at me and rolled onto her back, exposing her belly, wanting to play.

Gobbersnot jumped off the bed and began to berate her. She ignored him.

Well, I'll be. She's a werewolf.

Apparently my little niece took after King Xander, after all. I flew into the air in circles, and she followed me around my room, barking and yipping, giving chase. For fun, I flew out the door, and Violet followed, her little paws scrambling on the cold stone tile, her tongue hanging out of her mouth with glee.

Down the halls I flew, giving her a good workout as I dashed into a library and hid among the top shelves. I saw her skid past the opened door, and then she backed into the library entrance, her nose sniffing the air as she tried to catch my scent.

Having fun, I flew to the ground and hopped along a row, brushing my feathers across the rug before flying onto another stack of books. Violet came in and paused on the rug, her nose sniffing where I had laid a scent, her snout now targeting the air.

She let out a little howl when she saw me.

Kraa! I cried out and flew down to greet her. We both shifted back to humans.

"Good job, little pup." I congratulated my niece who smiled widely. She held up her arms, and I picked her up, moving over to one of the overstuffed chairs, sitting down to face the fireplace. Violet didn't seem inclined to move. She yawned and leaned her dark head against my shoulder. Moments later, she dozed off, but not before I felt a tug on my skirt. Gobbersnot climbed into my lap and laid his head on her shoulder.

I looked at the ugly goblin wearing a dress, and my sleeping niece, and my heart felt full to overflowing. Not wanting to disturb them, I closed my eyes and fell asleep.

Two candle marks later, I heard someone calling for the princess and I opened my eyes.

"Violet!" Rosalie's anxious voice called out. She peeked her head into the library and I waved her over. When my sister came around the corner, she looked surprised to see a sleeping wolf pup and Gobbersnot both curled up on my lap. In her sleep, Violet had shifted back into a wolf.

"Oh, so now you know our secret." Rosalie sighed.

"That she's amazing," I said softly, counteracting whatever she was going to say. "No secret there."

"Some don't think so." Her eyes were filled with worry. "I try to protect her, but I can't help but feel uneasy whenever we are in Florin. The palace staff are used to King Xander and his unique needs. The place is even warded to protect him. But no children want to play with her for fear of her hurting them. You are right. There's so much negativity because of what happened after the shifter wars years ago."

"Anyone who doesn't love her is a fool," I said harshly, my hand reaching for Violet's back protectively, automatically feeling the need to protect her with my life.

"There's no one else like her. But Violet wasn't bitten like Xander. She was born a werewolf, and the staff here at Florin are wary of her. No one knows how to raise a were-child."

"You're wrong," I said simply. "I'm like her."

"I forget. Forgive me, sister."

"Did Xander find anything last night?" I asked, referring to the king's plan to hunt the killer in the narrows himself.

"No, and he couldn't sniff anything out with his wolf senses, either. There are too many shifters down there. The smells get mingled, and it's impossible to track anyone."

My shoulders dropped. "So, we still don't know who's hunting them."

"No, but we will find out, Maeve. I promise."

CHAPTER TWENTY

The palace halls were empty this morning, filled with silence and secrets. A constant reminder that this was the childhood home of Aspen and Rosalie, and I was but a stranger. The well-worn red floral carpeting, tapestries, and even curtains were the same now as they were two decades ago. If I closed my eyes, I could almost imagine them as children walking down this darkened hall.

"If walls could talk," I whispered. "What secrets would I learn?" If only there had been someone with Rosalie's death seeker gift the day the queen died. They could maybe find out if her shifter guard really killed her out of jealousy. Or was there more to the story? But we would never know, for the secret was locked in the past, and the shifters would forever pay the price. As I walked back to my room lost in my thoughts, a pain tore through my chest. Aspen summoned me. I slowed my pace and leaned against the palace walls, gritting my teeth until the throbbing went away. But every few minutes, it came again. A painful reminder that I wasn't free, but a sharpened weapon that belonged to others. He wasn't letting up.

Did he not heed my warning when I said that it hurt

and to not do it again? Another tug came, and I physically stumbled, gripping a table until the ebb and flow went away. Sweat beaded across my forehead, but I knew I wasn't going to fly to him. No matter how many times he summoned, I would not answer his call. Even if it killed me.

By the time I made it the wing of the palace where my room was located, I was shaking, shivering, and muttering curses under my breath. No doubt, I scared a few palace servants in the process who probably thought I was a raving lunatic. With each painful step, I swore vengeance on Aspen, describing verbally how I was going to rip his heart out, just so he knew what it felt like. The pain was so intense that tears were slipping down my face unbidden. My hands shook as I tried to turn the knob to my room. If I could only get inside, then I would be safe from the stares and whispers of the servants.

With a click, the latch unlocked, and I slipped into my room, collapsing against the door as it closed. The painful throbbing of the summons disappeared as soon as I crossed the threshold, and I sighed in relief. With wobbly knees, I got to my feet and made my way to the chairs that faced the fireplace.

Except someone was already in my spot, eating my bread and jam from the domed tray that held my breakfast.

Aspen sat in the chair; his hands clasped casually in his lap. His head was slightly leaned back, and his eyes were half closed as if waiting for me to serve him his breakfast. Aspen's top button was unbuttoned, the wind had tousled his hair, and I wanted to run my fingers through it. Opening his eyes, he leaned forward and reached for the bread and slathered it with jam. "I summoned you." He placed the knife down.

"I was busy," I said.

"Doing what?" He took a bite of my breakfast and I watched him close his eyes, enjoying my meal.

I wasn't about to mention his niece. "Taking a bath."

The corner of his lip twitched downward, easily catching my lie. "Nevertheless, when I summon, you must come."

"I told you, I'm not a dog."

"No, but you are mine." He reached for a slice of warm ham, folded it, and took a bite.

When he said *mine*, I felt a tug deep in my soul. It felt good. Possessive.

"And what if I'm indisposed," I challenged.

"Then I guess I will wait," he said nonchalantly.

"Then be prepared to permanently wait."

"How many baths do you take?" Aspen said in exasperation. He covered the platter with the dome and leaned back to give me his full attention.

"I will live in the tub and become a permanent prune if it means avoiding you."

"Why are you so irritating?" He sighed, pushing himself up from the comfortable chair, standing face-to-face with me.

"Maybe it's because you bring out the worst in me," I snapped, trying to not stare at his lips or think about kissing him.

He snorted. "I don't bring it out. It's already there, bubbling on the forefront of your emotions. Ready to lash out at anyone who displeases you."

"You're right," I said, feeling the truth of his words as

they ate at me. I moved away from him and sat on the edge of my bed, knowing that I was mentally exhausted and needed something solid underneath me. "I cause more destruction than good. I have a tendency to react first, then think. I guess I'm tired of hiding who I am."

"You don't have to hide with me."

He said the words, but at the same time, he still hid his true self behind a glamour.

"And yet, you are hiding."

"True, but not for long," Aspen turned and headed out toward the balcony. "Allemar's work here is almost done."

With renewed determination, I launched from the bed and stormed to the balcony. "He *is* here. I knew it."

"At this moment, no, he's not. But his reach is long." Aspen tensed when I drew closer to him. He turned away and stared at the darkened blemish of the narrows. Even from the palace, the fire's destruction was a heavy blight and an eyesore. He pointed it out. "You have a habit of repeating the same mistakes. This looks just like the mess you left back in Rya." A sadness came over me as I was cruelly reminded of what I had done. "You probably don't even care about what happened to them. If your sister is okay, if the people of Rya are okay . . .

My hands trembled as I bore the brunt of his rebuke. I dropped my head in shame.

Aspen noticed my sudden change of mood. He cleared his throat awkwardly. "Are you okay?"

"No, you're right," I whispered. "All those people I hurt. Who's taking care of them? I wish I had closure. I have so many unanswered questions."

Something was bothering Aspen. He paced and ran his

hands through his hair. Finally, he sighed. "I don't have the answers you seek, but I will take you back if you like."

I spun and looked at him suspiciously. "Back to Rya? You can do that? I didn't think it was possible."

Aspen seemed reserved. "It's possible with my magic, but there's always a risk."

I ignored him and began to think out loud. "I want to see Aura. I have to know why she gave up on me."

He shook his head. "She's no longer at the palace."

"How do you know?"

"Allemar keeps tabs on her. Just like he keeps tabs on *all* the daughters of Eville," he stressed. "So going back could be putting *us* in danger."

Why did he suggest taking me back, but then change his mind? "Either way, I'd like to see for myself."

He seemed hesitant and studied the tattoos on his arm, gauging how much power he had left. He took a deep breath, and his fingers began moving at an impossible speed. He whispered under his breath as he conjured a circle. I had seen one similar only once before. My mother had used one to send Aura back to Rya, and I had crashed through the spell at the last second. But I knew they came at a great cost to the caster. When he was finished, I could see the tension he held in his jaw. Aspen stood in the center of the circle as it began to thrum with magic, his arms glowing red as his magic fed the spell. He thrust out his hand, daring me to take it. "I don't think you'll like what you find."

I stared at the proffered hand. "What's wrong? I can tell that you're hiding something."

Aspen's lips pinched in anger and his hand dropped. "I

can't do this. Forget the consequences. I change my mind," he yelled out to the air.

He wasn't speaking to me, but to himself. He was about to step out of the circle, but I rushed in and grabbed his hand, activating the spell.

Darkness surrounded us; the wind screamed in my ear, and it felt like we were falling. Terrified, I clutched him tighter, burying my face into the crook of his neck, my arms locked around him. Seconds later, it stopped, and we stood in the middle of a town square.

Disoriented, I was reluctant to let go, not sure if I could trust the ground to not move beneath my feet.

"Where are we?" I stepped away from Aspen, taking in the nearest shop with a thatched roof. Peering into the store, a closed bookshop, I saw Aspen's pale reflection behind me. He took one step and collapsed to the ground.

"Aspen!" I rushed to his side to feel his skin. Cold. *What happened? Why would he collapse like this, suddenly and without warning?* I noticed the tattoos and that most of them were faded. Gone, even. Had he used up most of his magic reserve on a travelling spell to take me here? The fool.

A door opened, and I quickly covered up his tattoos. I looked up as a shopkeeper, an elderly faun in green pants and spectacles, came out of the bookstore.

"It seems your friend is in need of assistance," the faun said, his curled horns yellowed with age. His hooves clipped softly on the road.

"We traveled a great distance, and I think the strain finally got to him," I answered.

"Come, come. Inside we go. A good cup of tea will make him right as rain."

I put Aspen's arm over my shoulder and with the faun's help, we got him to his feet, partially dragging him as we maneuvered to inside the bookshop. Past the few shelves of merchandise in the front, we headed toward the back where there was a settee. I pushed Aspen, and he collapsed on the small couch. His sleeve fell back, revealing his tattoos. Even before my eyes, some of them farther up his arm began to fade from ash gray to nothing.

The faun's keen eyes picked up the faded marks. "Ah, that explains it."

"What is going on?"

The faun gripped my arm and pulled up my sleeve. The short fae only came up to my waist, and I was surprised at his strength.

"So you're bonded, but not yet bound," he muttered to himself. He scratched his chin and hobbled over to a book-shelf, pulling a small ladder behind him. With his goat feet, he easily ascended the steps and pulled out a thick leather book. He plopped it on the table near me and quickly began to thumb through the pages.

I tried to read over his shoulder.

The faun glanced my way, and I was struck by his slitted gray eyes. "What did he do?"

"A traveling spell."

"That's it?" The bookkeeper frowned and looked at Aspen's arm. "That wouldn't have drained him this much." He put his finger on a mark and it faded even further. He studied Aspen's symbols and tattoos, then tapped his cheek. "This is bad."

"What is?" I was getting frustrated by the lack of answers.

"A travelling spell would not do this, but it seems that

someone else is repeatedly drawing on his strength." He pointed to a tattoo that faded before our eyes. "When they're all gone, he will die." He dusted his hands and trotted over to the small stove in the corner. "Do you like sugar in your tea?"

"Wait, how can you be so calm? Isn't there anything else that can be done?"

"Not when you deal with dark magic like this." He pointed to the small triangle mark on my wrist. "You're safe because you are not fully bound, otherwise you would be affected alongside the prince."

"How do you know?"

"That he's the prince of Florin? Because of this." The faun waddled back to Aspen and pointed to the signet ring that now hung from a silver chain around his neck. When he had gone from hiding it to wearing it, I wasn't sure.

"It's not right," I said angrily. "He's the victim here."

"Is he now?" the faun said. "If you say so, then it must be right because I don't know him."

My heart thudded in my chest. What was I going to do? Did I let him die? I didn't want to . . . but how to save him? I reached out and grasped his hand. Using my magic, I reached deep into the earth searching for the ley lines. I coaxed it to my bidding and tried to pour it into Aspen, but it rolled right off of him, parting ways, never touching him. Even when I tried to grasp the magic and force it into him, it avoided my touch because of his current condition.

I quickly thought back to Velora, left alone in the woods with Marco. What would happen if we didn't return? What would Allemar do to her? Could I make the sacrifice to save them?

Leaping forward, I unstrapped Aspen's dagger and put it into the pocket of my dress and headed for the door.

"Will you watch him for me, Mr. Faun?"

"Eh, why not? He will be dead soon, anyway," he said nonchalantly and went back to making his tea.

"Not if I can help it. Where is the most dangerous part of the city?" I asked.

The faun turned and gave me a strange look. Before turning away. "If ye asked me a month ago, I'd say you'd be mad to wander into Somnielle, but ever since that magic forest appeared and the king disappeared, we've had some strange ones appearing on Farthing street. But I wouldn't go there if I were you. A maiden like you won't survive long in that area."

"I don't plan on being there long."

Rushing out the front door, I headed in the direction the faun pointed, wondering if I had really gone as mad as my sister. As I walked the street, I looked up at the palace on the hill, and the thick forest of thorns that once surrounded it had disappeared. What did the people think happened? Without a sovereign ruler, there wasn't anyone to hold the law. Who was protecting the innocents in the town, or had they fallen easy prey to the ruffians?

I turned onto Farthing and immediately could feel air become colder. Most of the shops were boarded up, *No Vacancy* signs hung on the doors of inns, and I could feel the fear of those hiding behind closed shutters. It was the same fear that accompanied me every time I ventured into the town of Nihill. The distrust, the fear, the hate.

My nails dug into my palms as I struggled under the turmoil. A curtain moved, a shadow followed, and the fabric quickly dropped back into place. I knew I was in the right neighborhood by the amount of trash that was left in the streets. People were too afraid to leave their houses and were dumping the garbage out the window. A smell rose up from the gutter, and I had to cover my nose with my sleeve. It was no use. I wouldn't be able to find what I needed in this form.

Ducking into a doorway, I shifted into a raven and took to the skies. My fine-tuned eyes picked out the slightest movement in a dead-end road, near a stable. A man in black had cornered a young kid, pinned him to the wall, holding a knife across his throat. Even from a distance, I could feel the boy's terror.

"Give me your money."

"I-I swear, I don't have any!" Tears filled his eyes.

"Then you make me money in a different way." The man motioned to the shadows and a second accomplice slithered out of a doorway. He put a sack over the boy's head and they began to tie his hands together.

"We can get coin for him at the slave market," the second man said.

I didn't hear the first man's response because my blood was ringing in my ears. They weren't people, but monsters.

I let out an angry cry, flew toward them, shifting midair. Black feathers littered the floor, and my scream of vengeance took over as I landed, one knee to the ground. I flung out my arm, and the first man went flying through the air, crashing through the window of a building. Still kneeling, I hastily scratched out the trap spell into the ground using the dagger. It was small and rushed, and I would have to lure them to step on it with one foot. It was like walking through mud, trying to control my rage because I needed to save the boy and Aspen.

The second man dropped the kid, pulled a knife, and rushed me.

I took to the air, shifting again, my claws raking across his cheek, the blade of the knife nicking my tail feathers as I only shifted for a few seconds, my body slipping into a mist in between shapes as I reappeared behind him.

He spun, the circle appeared under his feet, and a bright light appeared enveloping him in a dark haze. I heard the scream, then the ominous silence. The second man stumbled out of the door and fell across the circle. As soon as he crossed the line, his bleeding cuts activated the trap, and he was surrounded by the darkness. A loud gasp escaped his lips before he died.

I kneeled on the ground, gathering the crying boy in my arms, soothing him as I untied the cloth sack from around his face.

"You're safe. It's okay. Nothing will harm you. I'm here." I flung the sack across the alley and looked into the tear-filled eyes of a child no more than nine winters.

His lip quivered, and he flung his arms around me and sobbed.

"I'll protect you." As I rocked the child in my arms, my heart was full. Proud that I saved him, but even as I spoke, I saw the triangle mark on my wrist become darker, and another mark slowly transcended the tip of the triangle down the center. I had completed the initiation and was now a full-blooded acolyte. Two more marks appeared below the triangle toward my elbow. Two, for two lives taken.

Getting to my feet, I wiped the young boy's tears away.

"Where do you live?" He pointed down the road. "I'll walk you home." His small palm slid into my hand, and I felt an immense desire to protect him. I knew then that I would do anything to keep him from falling into the hands of those men. Would I do it again? Yes. Because I had wished when I was younger there was someone to protect me.

Mother was wrong about justice. There didn't need to be a lesson taught. They didn't deserve a second chance, especially if what they did was harm a child. I would never forgive men like those in the alley. On the short walk home, I learned that the boy's name was George, and he went out looking for work doing odd jobs to help provide for his family. He lived in a cellar below a workhouse.

When his mother asked what happened when I returned him, I quickly explained. Her face paled, and she gathered George into her arms and started crying as I gave her a few Florins. I became uncomfortable at her show of gratitude. I needed to return to the bookshop. I needed to check on Aspen.

"I need to go," I said earnestly. "Please be careful." I waved to George as I left. Taking to the skies, I flew as fast as I could to the bookstore. Not being careful of who saw me, I shifted in the street and barged through the door.

"Aspen!" I called out, rushing past the shelves to the back of the store only to find the couch was empty. I turned toward the faun who was sitting on a stool by his table, sipping a cup of tea. "Where is he?" I demanded.

"Isn't that sweet?" He swirled the tea in his cup and put it down, motioning to my arm and the blood tattoos. "Took a life, did you? Oh, make that two."

"I did what I had to do to save him."

"You went out all on your own, willingly conducted

the spell circle, and killed. I'd say she's fully initiated . . . right, Aspen?" The faun turned to a hallway and Aspen stepped into view. Something was wrong. Physically he seemed fine, but he wouldn't meet my gaze.

"Yes." He stared at the wood floor; both of his hands clenched into fists.

"Wonderful. I knew you could do it. Now there's no going back. She's one of us." The faun clapped his hands.

"Aspen, what's going on?"

He flinched at the anger in my voice.

"She hasn't realized it yet." The faun laughed. "That you betrayed her." He took off the glasses, and the glamour dissipated, revealing the much taller and more forbidding Allemar. His dark hair braided over one shoulder; his long legs crossed as he gave me a malicious grin.

I sucked in my breath, realizing that once again I was a fool. How could I not see the barest shimmer of glamour? That Allemar had stolen the glasses from the shopkeeper and used them to take his place. The real faun was probably already long gone.

"That's the real trick to becoming bound to me. The first sacrifice has to be done willingly. I can't force you to use blood magic, but I can trick you. Now, you truly belong to me." He cackled, and I felt sick. "Take her back," Allemar ordered. "I don't want to be bothered with her incessant questions. As long as you get her power, and she is obedient, then I will be satisfied.

Aspen bowed his head. "Yes, Master."

He stood up, reaching out for me, but I backed away.

"Don't touch me."

Aspen's eyes darkened, and he lunged for me. As soon

as his hand touched my arm, I screamed, and he pulled me into his strong embrace as we blinked out.

When I opened my eyes, we were back on the balcony of my room.

"What have you done?" I asked, looking at the marks on my arm. "I can feel the darkness. It's like a poison creeping toward my soul."

"Allemar was furious that I had yet to complete your initiation. I tried to give you as much time as I could, but he was adamant. He wants access to all your powers."

"You didn't have to do it," I yelled.

"He would have killed you. Or worse, *made me* kill you."

The dark marks felt like sins, visible for the entire world to see.

"I wish you would have," I whispered. Taking a step away I felt the toll of being linked. Even my physical energy felt drained. I almost fainted.

Aspen reached out to catch me. "Careful. I wasn't lying about my strength being depleted on the way there. I wasn't strong enough to get us back. I had to use your marks as well. You will feel tired. Sleep will only rejuvenate you so much. You're going to have to take another life soon."

"You tricked me," I said, pulling away from him. "You used the feelings I have for you against me."

"No, I didn't. I told you not to care about me."

Anger roiled through me. "I should have killed you. Then I would be free of you and Allemar!"

He looked me straight in the eye. "By doing so, you would have completed the final initiation on your own. And you would be in the same place you are now."

I started pacing back and forth, my shoes slapping against the stone, and I wanted to lash out at something—someone in particular—but I had been trying to turn over a new leaf. *New leaf? What's the point now?* I was an acolyte of Allemar, and would have to spend the rest of my life committing murder to feed his power. I had to find a way out, or a way to stop him.

"Is this why when you sent him into the other dimension, he didn't die?" I asked, stopping, and wrapping my mind around a thought.

Aspen nodded. "His body was destroyed, but he was linked to my mind and fed off me. It took me some time to understand that he could take control of me. I'd wake up covered in blood, miles from where I'd gone to sleep. Other times, I was mad with a desire for revenge and to prove myself. He took my fear and drove me to the point of madness."

"That isn't an excuse for your actions."

"I'm not saying it to gain forgiveness, for I never expect that from you or your family. But you must know that he will use your weaknesses and exploit them."

He reached out a hand to touch my shoulder, but I ducked.

"Maeve, with the connection newly established, these next few days will be hard on you. You are going to have to find a way to retain your marks. They will drain quickly in the beginning."

"I don't care," I said. "He won't control me. I'm not like you. I'm not a murderer. I won't murder again."

He shook his head. "I know you don't want to hear this . . . but with your magic alone, you've already murdered more people than I ever have."

Aspen's words cut me deep. I covered my face and let the silent tears fall as he spoke the truth. He was right. I was a murderer.

"Go away," I muttered.

"Maeve . . ." Aspen's voice turned pleading.

"I don't want to see you again."

"It doesn't matter. You are still my apprentice, and you are untrained. It is too dangerous to let you be alone right now."

"I said, *go away!*" The earth rumbled beneath my feet in answer to my chaotic emotions. Birds took to the sky, and thunder cracked in the distance.

He looked pained. "Okay, I will leave." He took a deep breath, his hazel eyes met mine, and they were filled with regret. "Maeve, I had hoped you would have let me die in the street. Then you would have been free . . .but thank you . . . for saving my life."

I blinked, and he was gone.

CHAPTER TWENTY-ONE

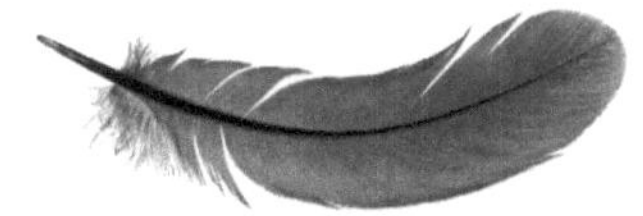

Sunlight came through my open window and tickled my eyelids. Aspen was right, I was exhausted. I could feel myself dragging, my energy fading, and even sleeping did little to restore me. By the way I was feeling, I would have to sleep for a century to regain enough energy to use magic. Rolling over, I buried my face into my pillow and decided I would live in my bed forever. Until I died. That sounded great. Or until someone broke the curse on me.

I held my arm up in the air, saw the dark marks, and groaned. I could almost hear Mother's voice in my head. "You let your anger rule your mind, and now you have to pay the consequences."

Yes, I would make a pact to never harm another person ever again. Even if it led to my eventual death.

The door opened, and I felt the mattress dip as a very small wolf jumped into my bed and begged for attention. Violet nipped and growled, trying to get me to play with her.

"Not today, pup," I said, ignoring her pleading. "I want to stay in bed." *Forever,* I mentally added.

A candle mark later, the door opened, and Rosalie

found us both curled up in my bed. I was careful to keep my arm hidden under the blanket.

"What?" I grumbled, looking at her out of one eye.

"You've been in bed all day."

"So?"

"Today we bring the shifters and the winners of the games to the palace."

I had forgotten about that. My days blurred together, and I didn't know how much time had passed. "Who had the idea for the contests?" I asked, sitting up, fully awake and wary.

She ran her finger down her hair and tucked a stray strand behind her ear. "I did. It was something that Lorn had said they did back in the old days. Ceremonies and contests to give out titles and knighthoods. But we didn't want just soldiers or the wealthy to win, so we opened it up to the people, and created events that we thought many could enter. Now come the real tests, and I hope you will help me choose those that are worthy to become the future leaders of our kingdom."

"How many people knew about this?" I thought back to the letter that the innkeeper sent Aspen.

"People talk. Word may have gotten out ahead of time," she admitted.

"Do you have to bring them here?" I asked. "Isn't it better to test them in town?"

"No, for with a title comes pressure, and we want to see how loyal they are to me and Xander. We can't have a wolf in sheep's clothing get in and murder the herd when we aren't looking."

My heart dropped, and I felt sick to my stomach. I opened my mouth to warn her, but I felt a coldness run through my veins. Sweat beaded across my forehead, and my neck felt clammy.

"Of course," I said. "When do we start?"

"They will soon arrive at the gates, and I would like you to greet them, give them a tour, and show them to their quarters. Here are their room assignments." Rosalie handed me the list and a map as she stood up, giving me a warm smile. "And try not to scare them off. We truly do want the best for our kingdom."

"I know nothing of being royal or how to act." I reminded her. "I'm a terrible example. I can't even curtsy right, and you know I run off at the mouth a lot. I'm guaranteed to make a bad impression."

"And that's why *you* are the person for the job. You are the queen's sister, and it shows that anyone can be in a position of authority, no matter their background."

I smiled wryly. "Does this position of authority come with a title as well?" I teased.

"Of course. Royal Pain in the Butt." Rosalie laughed.

Violet stretched her back and trotted off into the hall. Rosalie's gaze followed her daughter. "And Maeve, please keep an eye out for Violet. She's the final test. If they can accept her as their future, then we know they are the right person to be our nobles."

A surge of protectiveness overcame me. I could do this. I could run these mere men through tests of loyalties. All I had to do was make sure that Aspen failed and would never gain a title. But that would mean leaving the bed.

Decisions.

"I will."

"Thank you. I'm really glad you're here." She gave me a smile and left.

Stretching, I crossed the room and opened the wardrobe door. I wasn't even surprised anymore to see Gobbersnot sleeping among the silk dresses.

"Hey, you!" I nudged him with my foot. "I need to wear a dress to greet the future snobby nobles."

Gobbersnot opened one eye and reluctantly unwrapped himself from the clothing. He sorted through the dresses and withdrew a deep blue gown with white laced sleeves. Then hopped out of the wardrobe, opened a drawer, and retrieved matching blue slippers—the ones he had the first day I met him.

"Thank you," I said as I took the offerings and proceeded to get dressed. I had thought that was the end of his help, but as I sat at the small table in front of the mirror, he tossed up a silver comb with sapphires and even matching garters.

I held back a smile as I very carefully pulled back my hair, rolling it up and securing it with the combs. With my hair off my shoulders, it exposed my long neck, and I briefly wondered if Aspen would notice.

Stupid, I told myself. *He doesn't really care for me. I'm just a tool. A means to an end.*

A green hand slapped a set of pearl drop earrings on the dresser. Then I heard his mutterings as he went back to the wardrobe and shut himself inside it.

Such an odd little fae. But the drop earrings were stunning, and I couldn't help but see a strong, powerful woman staring back at me. With my confidence built, I knew it was time to greet the future nobles.

Waiting at the doors of the palace, a page named Ned introduced himself to me. He wore the red livery of Florin and a floofy feathered cap. He handed me a scroll and gestured to the steps.

"What's this?" I asked, holding the scroll out like it was a snake.

"You are supposed to read it," Ned said.

"Isn't that your job?" I pushed the scroll back at him. "I'm just supposed to show them around."

"I was told that you were to give the address." He pulled at his cravat.

"Why would she do this to me?" I whispered angrily, taking my frustration out on Ned. He looked to his right, and I saw the men waiting below. I was causing a scene. "Fine." I yanked the scroll out of his hands and stood on the top step. A red carpet had been rolled out for their arrival, but none had dared to step on it. Most of them looked shocked, a few smug. Even though he was glamoured, I easily spotted Aspen standing near the back of the crowd. But in front of him, I was pleased to see a few familiar faces. Cross was chastising and trying to coax Brekken into the open. The fox shifter kept pulling at his clothes as he wanted to rip them off. Torren looked like he was sleeping standing up. Warden was drawing the most attention, for he already dressed the part of a noble in his soft pale blue vest with matching pants and polished boots.

Hela stood next to a brown-haired man with icy blue eyes and an angular chin. His ears were a little too pointed, as if that was the one aspect that didn't fully convert back to human. I wondered if this was the shifter they'd called Everett. The seventh shifter was none other than Silva. He raised a hand and waved at me. He beamed with excitement that was contagious. I couldn't help but smile back at him.

There did seem to be a definite divide between the humans that won the contests and the newcomer shifters. Maybe it was the way they stood absolutely still that made them seem more than human—except for Brekken who never stopped shivering. Or it could have been that they were wary of their counterparts and expected to be attacked at any moment.

A long breath passed between my lips as I realized just how big of a job it was going to be to bring these two warring factions back together.

I unrolled the scroll and briefly read through it. It was so droll and filled with elaborate welcomes and formalities. Rosalie should know better than to entrust me to follow the rules.

I tossed the scroll over my shoulder, clapped my hands together, and took a deep breath. "Okay, so here's the deal. Congratulations on winning your event or receiving the personal invitation from King Xander, but the final prize has yet to be won. If you walk through these doors, you will be challenged with more tests to see how worthy you are. If you pass, you might get a title and lands bequeathed to you. If you don't, you will leave here in utter embarrassment. If you do anything to harm, insult, or so much as even think of doing something to the royal family, I will personally ensure that you leave here in a wooden coffin, nailed shut." I rocked back on my feet, my hands primly clasped behind my back, with a mad grin on my face. "Any questions?"

Silva's shoulders were shaking with barely controlled laughter. Everyone else seemed terrified of me. Brekken was trying to slip his pants off and ditch them in the flower bed. Warden whacked him on the back of the head until he pulled his pants back on.

A man that looked to be ex-military raised his hand. "Are you threatening to murder us if we so much as get out of line? I find that hard to believe coming from such a small one as you."

Oh, I liked him. I grinned evilly. "Oh I never said you'd be dead when I put you in the coffin."

Aspen rubbed his temples, his head shaking with exasperation.

"Follow me." I waved my finger in the air and spun on my heel, deciding that if I was going to be tasked with the boring job of the guide, then I would have fun with it. I kept a quick pace and was almost running as I headed down the main hall. Turning back around, I pointed to the double doors. "Throne room; don't go in there. Lots of people died in there. Keep up. Let's go." The rest of the tour followed along the dialogue of, "For those that can read, there's some books. Oh, look, the dining hall. You can get food here three times a day. Bathing chambers, visit them often. Don't want you to stink up the place." As the pathetic tour continued, Ned continually tried to interrupt me and point to the instructions on the scroll.

"Maybe I should take over, Miss?" he begged, his fingers reaching for the scroll. Aspen had calmed his features to an almost stoic stance, but his pressed lips and gleaming eyes told me he was amused by my antics.

I gave the page an evil glare, and he backed off until it came time to take the men to their assigned quarters.

"Here, I'm bored." I handed the scroll back to him and gave a dramatic wave. "Have fun." I sashayed out of the hall and ducked into an alcove. Quickly shifting into a raven, I flew up to the top of a statue of a maiden holding a basket of flowers. I believed it was supposed to be a representation of the very first Autumn Queen.

But the reason for my lack of manners was just. I decided to test the men to see how they would react to an independent and insubordinate woman.

Ned tried desperately to cover for me. "Well, you must excuse the queen's sister. She has only recently returned, and has quite the unusual, um . . ."

"What kind of greeting was that?" Adam asked. "I'm confused. That's the queen's sister?"

"The queen is originally from Florin, but she wasn't raised here. What can we expect from a family raised outside our kingdom?" another said.

I made note of the speaker indirectly, and the tone that came from his voice. He didn't seem pleased to have outsiders running the kingdom.

"Don't apologize for her," Aspen interrupted. "There's no excusing her bad manners." Aspen looked directly at me as he spoke. He must have seen me shift, or he knew I would be watching.

"I found it quite endearing," Silva added. "A little rough around the edges, but overall, quite a pleasing package. And you have to admit, it was a most entertaining tour."

Heads nodded, and the earlier confusion turned to a chuckle of appreciation. With only a few words, Silva very easily calmed the discord that I had created earlier.

Ned began the process of taking the men and lone woman to their assigned quarters, giving last minute instructions. "Dinner will be brought to your rooms. Afterward, you will meet in the ballroom for your first test."

Aspen held back, leaning against the statue he pretended to be adjusting the fit of his boot. "I'm not sure what you're trying to prove with your attitude, but you may want to rethink your strategy. You don't want to ruffle the wrong feathers, otherwise you may get your wings clipped."

What kind of warning was that? I wondered.

"By the way, you look nice. Blue suits you." He stood up and left.

My teeth ground together in anger, and I decided I was tired of being passive. I needed to find a way to beat Allemar.

Assuming that no one would miss me for a while, I headed into the library and began a coordinated search of the vast shelves of books, finding very little on spells or magic. If Allemar kept any of his books or notes here, they weren't in the palace library. But I did find the annex that held volumes of kings' reigns, and grabbed a book that dated back to the shifter war. I carried the large tome over to one of the long study tables. Pulling out a chair, I started at the beginning and read the history of the shifters. It seemed that there were many shifter families or clans that once lived in the kingdom of Florin. There were several smaller clans, but the largest and strongest were bear, lion, asp, jackal, and cougar. From those families, the royal honor guards were chosen. I found the history of the raven families. They were spies and assassins for the king. One named Atlas was assigned to King Adler's wife. I wondered if it was Atlas who killed the queen and started the war. If a raven was the one behind it, it was no wonder I couldn't find any of my kin.

I became lost in the pages, reading until late evening,

missing dinner entirely. My neck bent at an awkward angle, and even the addition of the light charms did little to ease my tired eyes. I soon fell asleep, hunched over the book.

The slamming of a door woke me. My candles had gone out, leaving me in the dark. Urgent voices filled the air, and by instinct, I ducked under the table as two people moved between the rows of books.

"I'm telling you, this is a trap. They brought them here to taunt us," a voice whined.

"Why would they do that? You heard them. They want to reward us with lands, a province, a title." The voices were hushed, and it was hard to tell who was speaking.

"I don't trust them. It's like the king is trying to start another war."

My mouth went dry.

"No, we stick with the plan. We will lie low, and when the time is right, we act—but not a moment sooner."

Rage, burning rage.

I jumped up to confront them at the same time the door closed, banging my head on the table. Sucking in my breath, I crawled out from under it and raced after them. I flung open the door to an empty hall. There was someone just there. I picked a direction and raced down the corridor, catching a maid by surprise.

"Did you see anyone come down here?" I panted.

The startled maid shook her head. "No one's been here, just me."

I cursed under my breath and took off running in the opposite direction. I had chosen the wrong direction at first, and my speed was hampered by my long skirt. By the time I passed the library a second time and rounded a corner, I ran straight into a crowd, almost bowling over one of the men.

"Sorry." I fumbled to stand up and tried to look at all of their faces. Two of them were guilty of treason. I had to find them. But no one looked at me with disdain or hate, just surprise. And one very amused Aspen, who had been the one I had nearly knocked over.

Panic and concern filled me. As I looked at Aspen, I made a quick decision. One I hoped I wouldn't regret.

"I need to speak with you," I whispered, tugging on his long sleeve.

The corner of his mouth rose in a smile. "Oh, so now you wish to summon me? When before you wanted nothing to do with me and told me to go away. That's not how it works."

"You deserved it. But please, it's important."

He sighed loudly. "This is important too."

"Please," I urged.

When no one was looking, Aspen grabbed my arm and pulled me down the hall, stopping in an alcove. "Now that you have my full, undivided attention, what is so urgent?"

"Someone is plotting something," I whispered.

He snorted. "Only one person? I'd expect more than that. If they were going to attempt to take a kingdom, they would at least need a small retinue of men, have paid off servants, and know all the secret ins and outs of the palace. Someone like myself."

"Who are you?" I said in shock. The Aspen before me was a different person.

"I am who I've always been," Aspen whispered. "I never lied about my intentions. You, on the other hand, are playing a dangerous game. You know what you will have to do to stay alive, and yet, you pretend that everything is all right."

I ground my teeth. "I will expose you and make sure that you never pass a trial."

Aspen gripped my arm, and I winced. "You think that because you are the queen's sister, you're untouchable. Let me tell you, a title doesn't protect you, or have you forgotten the scars I bear? Being a prince did little to protect me."

"What is Allemar after? Is my family safe?"

Aspen grew quiet, internally debating how much to tell me. "They're safe for now. He is not after the throne of Florin. He wants something else. But the real question is why haven't you told your sister about him? About me? I'll tell you the answer. *You can't*. Because if you did, you'd have to explain how you knew, what was done to you, and then you'd lose her trust. You'd become the enemy. She'd never be able to look at you the same way. I know. Because I've been in your shoes."

Aspen was right. I couldn't bear to share what was done to me. Not when I felt I could still beat this.

My breath became a whisper filled with worry. "You'll tell me if he is going to hurt my family?"

The air hung heavy with silence.

"I can't believe I thought you were someone who cared," I said.

"I *do* care. Just not about the same things that you do. I want different things."

My fingernails dug into the beds of my palms. "What do you want?"

Aspen reached out, cupped my face with his hand. He

leaned forward, his lips brushing across my cheekbone as he whispered into my ear, "I thought it was obvious." He pulled back, his gaze dropping to my lips.

A knot of confusion, frustration, and longing formed in my stomach. I wanted him to say it out loud.

"I thought you hated me."

His voice dropped to a rough whisper "There's a fine line between hate and desire."

"So which one is it?" I felt a needle jab through my stomach, not wanting an answer.

His hands fell away from my face. "I have to hate you. It's the only way to keep you safe."

Aspen spun away, his cloak billowing after him.

His words were a slap to the face that left me cold. In a flurry of anger and uncontrolled power, every sconce and candle in the hall flashed as they were lit. The flames burned six inches tall before settling down to a soft ember.

My heart fluttered, and I felt dizzy after the sudden use of magic, but I pressed on, regardless of the affect it had on me.

CHAPTER TWENTY-TWO

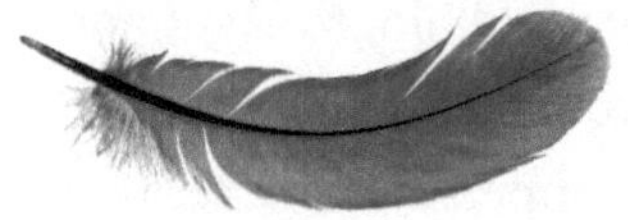

Aspen and I were the last to arrive outside the doors to the ballroom. There was a clear divide between the shifters and the humans. Brekken was hiding behind the curtains, only his feet were visible, and I silently prayed he was still clothed. Torren was rosy-cheeked from being deep into his drink. His cup was easily the size of a pitcher. Everett was running his hand through his hair while casting a bemused smirk to Hela who didn't notice. Cross nodded to me when I came in, and I cast him a small smile.

Silva's face lit up when he saw me. His black hair was slicked back as he cast his golden eyes my way. The corner of his mouth dipped for a second when he saw Aspen with me, but he swept across the room and leaned toward me.

"That was quite the tour you gave," Silva teased, his eyes glistening with mirth.

I grinned. "Glad you enjoyed it."

"I'm also glad that you're okay." His voice dropped to a whisper. "I was worried about you after the fire, and I didn't get to speak with you earlier today."

"You carried me to safety, so you're the one I need to thank. But why did you disappear so quickly?"

Silva cast his eyes to the ground. "I'm a shifter. I was scared for my life and the life of others once the ward was gone. Plus I saw your beau was on his way." He tossed a thumb toward Aspen.

I frowned. "We're not like that."

"Really? That's good. Then he won't mind if I steal you away for a while." He grinned, flashing me straight white teeth. "I wouldn't mind another private tour of the palace, if you have the time. I'm sure that there's much more to learn about the palace, the trials, and you."

Voices filled the air as the candidates became more excited. Aspen noticed Silva's hand on my arm. I could feel his disapproving glare, which only made me want to step closer to Silva.

Ned came and opened the ballroom doors, letting the candidates enter for the first test: diplomacy. The ballroom had been cleared out, and long tables filled the middle of the room. Scrolls sealed in wax were aligned every few feet, and quills and ink wells were provided. All the candidates were escorted in, and each took their assigned seat in front of the scroll with their name.

King Xander explained the first diplomacy test and how it was based on taxes, wages, religion, or policy. Each of them were given different scenarios based on the regions of the province. As landholders, they would have to collect taxes, be the governing factor for any disputes, oversee the resources of that province, and find a way to have the land produce goods and be prosperous. But each one had a different natural disaster or issue that they had to deal with: flooding, fire, drought, famine, bandits.

Reminding them that only one person had been assigned this scenario in their scroll, he cited an example.

"A drought had caused riverbeds to dry up. The only available waterway would have to be redirected to bring water downstream to three large villages and to the biggest farming community in the province. But in doing so, it would remove the only water source for a small town whose well had dried up, thus leaving them without water. What do you do?"

You sacrifice the small town to save the larger villages and the farming community, I thought to myself.

Immediately, many of the people in the room paled at the thought of the responsibility that came with the title. Hela opened her scroll and looked thrilled, her hand immediately reaching for the quill, her hand racing across the paper.

Aspen unrolled his scroll and stared at the script. He didn't move.

What was the matter? I thought. Surely, he would have been raised to understand what was needed to run a country? Of course, I didn't know exactly which scenario Aspen had been given since each were different. Silva's dark head was down, his eyes gleaming with intensity, a grin running across his face. Many of them had never had to think about the country as a whole. They'd only been concerned with their own farm or family, but now would have to make decisions that considered more people for the greater good.

A candle mark had passed, and Aspen still stared at the scroll, refusing to write anything. Most everyone had managed to have an opinion on some of the questions. Even the farmer had written a great deal. Those in attendance were not permitted to draw closer to the tables to see the questions or the answers, and they had until sundown to finish.

Chewing on my lip, I paced along the outskirts, wishing that I could see the moral dilemma he was given. Aspen finally reached for his quill, dipped the tip into the inkwell, and began to write.

Hela was the first done, her movements were fluid, and she walked in heeled boots without making a sound. She brought her scroll up to Xander. He quickly read over her answers, and he gave a nod. "I'm very impressed, but how would you go about financing the workers?"

"I would use those who owe back taxes to help dig more wells, or deeper wells. For it was because of the drought that they were unable to have a harvest and not bring in any money for their family or the taxes. It seems that they could work off the money owed that way instead of going to prison and letting their family starve the following year."

"And if there wasn't any water to be found if they dug deeper, then what?"

Hela raised her chin. "Then I would go to the naiads and beg them to come to my lands."

A murmur rolled through the crowd. A few were shocked by the answer. I only heard one or two mention blasphemy, but there were fewer naysayers that I would have expected. Those that were silent were nodding their head in affirmation.

"You would include the fae in your affairs?"

"I would, and I would promise them protection if they could help bring the water back to the province."

Xander smiled. "Very well spoken. I agree in your assessment."

Hela curtseyed and moved to the side the room. One by one, others brought up their tests. Xander challenged almost everyone on a question or decision. Not in that they were wrong; he wanted to test their conviction because the way things are done are not set in stone. There's room for new rules, changes, and a new government that can include the fae.

Torren, Cross, and Warden all presented equally challenging conclusions to their problems. Cross was praised, Warden preened when he was told he excelled, and Torren was still half asleep.

Xander had the hardest time keeping a straight face when reading Brekken's response. "Yes, this does solve the issue with linen shortage after the flax crop failed to yield, but I don't think also giving a tax break for those that go nude is quite the way to go."

The whole room erupted into laughter; hard, knee slapping, hooting laughter that took quite a while to settle down. Most thought Brekken was joking, but I could see by his earnest eyes he was serious. Even the stone-faced Cross couldn't hide how hard his shoulders were shaking. King Xander had to wipe the tears from his eyes.

Brekken was sweating and pulling at his vest. "They're just so itchy," he muttered.

"Pass," Xander chuckled.

Finally, Aspen brought up his test. My throat was dry, and I found it difficult to swallow. His glamour held strong as he faced another royal.

Xander frowned when he read his answers. "Aloe Fields, is it?"

"Yes, Your Majesty," Aspen struggled with saying his brother-in-law's title.

"It seems that most of your answers are right along

with the current system of policy. Are you a student of Florin law?" he asked.

"No, I've just read many history books."

"You gave the most diplomatic answers here."

"Is there something wrong with that?"

Xander shook his head. "These are textbook answers, as if written by our current monarchy. I'm not asking for you to uphold the status quo here. There's room for change. There's room for growth." He pointed to an answer we couldn't see. "You've upheld the justice system but also have shown little leniency for those that have broken the law. You've shown no mercy."

For a second, I saw Aspen's glamour flicker as his emotions began to get the better of him. He was struggling with what he had been taught versus what was right. His hand clutched the edge of his vest. "My father always said mercy was for the weak."

Xander sighed. "I was taught the same thing by my father." He looked across the room and met his queen's eyes. "But I learned our parents are not always right. Mercy bestowed upon the worthy is a seed planted that will one day produce much fruit. You must learn to be a farmer. Cultivate the trust of your people with mercy, then you will become a harvester of their loyalty and love."

Aspen's back stiffened. "Do-does this mean I failed?"

Xander shook his head and handed the test back to Aspen. "No, you passed." He looked out the window as the sun set behind the horizon. "Time is up." A flurry of quills and groans were heard by the rest of the group. One by one they came up, and Xander either let them stay or they were dismissed. When all was said and done, there were fourteen of the twenty hopefuls left.

"Get some rest. I will administer your next test in two days," Xander said.

Aspen did not look pleased when he stormed out of the ballroom.

After the test, there were light hors d'oeuvres served to the candidates in the library where they could mingle. Much of the discussion revolved around the tests and Brekken's nudist tax break. Those that had passed were sharing their answers and results. Not wanting to draw attention to myself, and because I was invested in the trial, I used a glamour on myself, shifting my dress into the plain dress of the servants. Glancing in the mirror, I took stock of my quick spell work. My hair was lightened to a soft honey brown, my vibrant green eyes were dulled to a muted green, and I overlaid a nondescript face over my own, widening my nose, bringing my eyes closer together and thinning out my lips. There was no way that anyone would recognize me. The only downside of my plan was it meant I was having to work and bring trays of food in and out of the kitchen, so I was missing much of the conversation.

Someone was disgruntled and could be plotting against the shifters or my family. I couldn't assume that they had failed the first test and had been dismissed.

Even now, the candidates were separated into two groups. Aspen stayed on the outskirts, sitting on a padded window bench, staring out into the kingdom. His eyes were closed, his head resting against the frame, and he seemed at peace. I could almost imagine him as a young boy doing the exact same thing.

"You did very well with your question on solving the unpaid taxes and digging the wells, Hela," Silva praised the woman. "Wherever did you get the idea to bring naiads into the kingdom?"

Hela smirked, tucking her hair behind her ear. "I've learned it's King Xander's and Queen Rosalie's desire to bring the fae back to their homelands. It is proven time and time again throughout history that when fae and humans live side by side, the land has always prospered."

"Except when it came to King Alder," Brekken said. "We've never fully recovered."

Everett looked up, his eyes hardening like glass. "What do you expect when a king declares genocide on a whole clan for the sin of one person? There was no justice, no mercy, just pain, imprisonment, and death."

"They got what they deserved, if you ask me," a man name Renold snarled, overhearing their conversation.

"Atlas was framed. He was her honor guard," Everett snapped.

"He was found with the knife in his hand." Another man pointed to his palm. "Guilty as charged."

"That's because," Everett seethed, "he was the one who found the queen slain. He removed the knife. He was her *protector*. He would give his life for her."

"And why would someone kill the queen and frame a shifter?" Renold asked. "To what purpose?"

Torren stood up, his voice low and steady. "Because some believed the shifters had grown too many in numbers. They believed we were a threat to the king. The purpose was to cause a divide between us. To breed fear and hate. It was an excuse to destroy a community. To exterminate a race."

"Enough," Aspen said, his voice filled with authority. The room listened. He rose from his position on the window ledge and moved across the room. "There's no room for past prejudices if you want to pave a way for the future. Didn't you hear what King Xander said? Or was I the only one listening?"

"What was *your* question?" Silva asked, his voice dripping with sarcasm. "It seemed you had the right answer for everything, and *yet,* you were wrong."

"Punishment for treason," Aspen said, looking directly at Silva, his voice cold like steel. "I deemed it necessary to execute not only the one responsible, but the entire bloodline."

A hush fell across the room. I had been reaching for a dirty cup that was left on a side table, but I froze midair. I let out a little gasp, and Aspen's hazel eyes narrowed and went right to me. I backed away into the shadows, but his gaze followed me wherever I went. There was no way he could see through my glamour. I wasn't as gifted as Eden, I could feel the tension, a faint throbbing in my temple as I strained to keep the glamour in place.

"I can see why you answered the way you did." Hela broke the ice, and the tension lifted. "I can also see where there is room for a different punishment." The conversation shifted, and I continued to work my way around the room, drawing close to each person, listening to the lilt of their voice, hoping to identify the speaker I'd overheard in the library earlier. I couldn't. But even when I stayed out of Aspen's view, he continued to follow me with narrowed eyes. He slowly walked onto the open balcony. He tapped his half empty glass and shot me a glare. I grabbed a flask of wine, and carefully made my way over to refill his glass.

As I reached for the cup, his hand snaked out and grabbed my wrist, pulling it down low. No one could see what he was doing, but his thumb rubbed over the invisible mark. I could feel his power testing me, and mine answered. He rolled his magic over me, and an electric spark ran through my body, making me jump. It was the same way that Silva's magic called to mine.

A chuckle followed, and he whispered, "I thought so." He released my wrist, and I quickly grasped the cup and refilled it before heading back inside and out of sight. He followed, and took up a reclining position in a chair, his eyes narrowed, and he looked to be asleep.

Not much time had passed when I started feeling unwell. My heart began to race, my body felt warm all over, and I felt faint. *Was it the glamour?* No, I was strong enough to hold it longer. But I felt drained.

Torren waved me over for a refill, and as I crossed the rug to him, I could feel my knees wobble. I accidentally slammed my hip into the heavy wooden chair. Wincing, I reached for the glass, but even it felt like an anvil. The glass slipped from my fingers and shattered onto the floor.

"S-sorry," I mumbled as the floor seemed to move beneath my feet.

Aspen launched from his chair, no longer feigning sleep. Grasping me around the waist, he led me out of the room.

"Look at him, rushing to the aid of a servant," someone sneered.

"That is someone who cares about those less fortunate than himself," Cross's voice shot out. "That is the kind of person I would serve under in a heartbeat."

"Drop the glamour, Maeve," Aspen ordered when we were away from prying eyes.

As easy as blinking, I felt the glamour fade away, and it was immediately easier to breathe.

"H-how did you . . ."

"You are a horrible servant. Too proud. Dead giveaway."

"I d-don't feel so good," I murmured, my head dropping forward against his chest.

"You need to stop using your magic. It's no longer coming from the ley lines, but from within you. And if you don't fill your marks, you will pay a higher price."

"What does that mean?"

"You'll go mad. Believe me, it's not a pretty sight. I've tried to withstand it on a few occasions, but I was driven further down that path. Your sisters have seen me at my worst. I don't recommend that route."

I struggled against his grip. "No. I can't do that. I *won't*."

Aspen didn't lead me to a room. Instead, he passed down a darkened hall meant for servants. A click followed, and a cold breeze brushed across my arms, and I knew he was using a hidden passageway.

The air became cooler as he led me down a dark stone path. Without light, he easily took the turns needed, climbing a flight of stairs, and then we entered a familiar room. Mine.

He laid me on the bed, being careful to not jostle me. Aspen's own glamour faded, and I was surprised at how much I liked seeing his face. "Hey, it's you," I muttered, feeling like my limbs were heavy and my mind drunk.

His mouth turned down. His hand reached for my

forehead, and he cursed. "You're running a fever." He held up my arm and studied the lack of blood tattoos. I could see his were fading as well. "Maeve, you need to replenish your marks."

"No." I shook my head. "I'd rather die." A shiver ran through my body.

"I can guarantee that you most certainly will, and that is if you don't go mad first. Can't you see Allemar is testing you? He felt you use magic earlier. He is purposefully draining you to test your will to survive."

"I'm not like you." My voice was raspy; I felt weak and small. "I don't want to kill."

"No one does. Sometimes you have to do what is best for the greater good."

"But I'm not good." The tears stung, and I could feel myself slipping into unconsciousness. "I'm evil. No one will care if I'm gone."

Aspen's head dropped as he clasped my hands between his. "You're wrong. I do." I could have been my feverish mind playing tricks, but I thought he laid the barest of kisses across my knuckles. "Rest. I will return the favor. I will do what needs to be done for both of us."

He may have said more, but I slipped into a dreamless sleep.

CHAPTER TWENTY-THREE

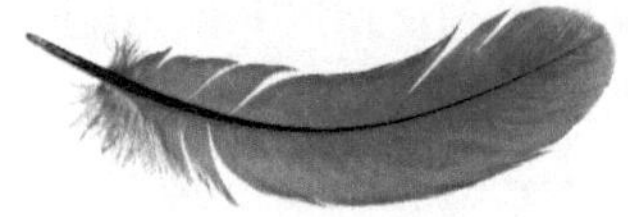

The next morning I awoke in my bed. The balcony doors were closed, and my door was locked from the inside. I felt better; stronger than I had felt in days. Stretching my arms above my head, I crossed the room and headed toward the wardrobe. That's when I noticed my arm. The marks had been replenished. They were thicker, and deeper in color. I pressed my finger into my skin and knew it was true.

A high-pitched scream resonated from down the hall, and I rushed out of my room wearing only my shift. Racing down the corridor, I turned as a servant was backing out of a room, her face pale, her hands covering her mouth and face.

"What is it?" I asked. She didn't speak but backed away in horror. Steeling my nerves, I stepped into the room and quickly turned away. Torren looked like he was sleeping. His eyes closed, his mouth slightly ajar as if mid-snore. Except he wasn't breathing, for a knife was sticking out of his chest.

Creeping closer to the bed, an aching pain filled my heart. It was just like the story of the murdered queen that started the shifter war. Was this someone taking revenge on Torren for speaking up last night?

"No," I shuddered, stepping back just as the room filled with guards. Commander Harn was at my back, his hand reached for the sword at his side. "What is this, and what are you doing here?" he accused.

"I heard a woman scream," I muttered, pointing behind me.

"What woman?" he turned toward the empty hall.

"There was a servant. She screamed. Didn't you hear it? How else did you know to come here?"

"I'm the one doing the interrogating, and I ask again, who are you?"

"I'm the queen's sister." I crossed my arms over my chest, feeling vulnerable. It looked really odd that I was in a strange man's room in my nightdress. Not just any man, but a murdered man.

"Then that means you're like her." His voice dripped with disdain.

I saw red. "What do you mean *like* her?"

"Commander Harn, what is the meaning of this?" King Xander declared.

"A candidate is dead, Your Majesty. Murdered. And this one," he gestured to me, "was discovered hovering over the body."

"I wasn't hovering," I gritted out angrily. "I was investigating."

"In your nightdress?" Commander Harn snapped.

"I heard a female scream." I flapped my arms in exasperation.

Xander glanced to Commander Harn who shook his head. "We found no servant, sire."

Xander studied the scene, his face void of emotion.

"Find the servant. Send for the queen and keep my daughter in the nursery."

It wasn't long before a sleepy-eyed Rosalie entered in a red silk robe, the belt knotted at her waist. She took in the grisly scene without any emotion. Commander Harn was ushered from the room, and Xander closed the door, leaving only the three of us.

Rosalie stared at the body and hesitated, her hand going to her belly.

"You shouldn't," I warned. "I don't think you should use your death seeker abilities while pregnant."

"I must." Rosalie moved to stand next to Torren. She reached out a hand and touched his wrist. A gasp followed, and Rosalie bent over as if in pain, her eyes clenched shut, her teeth biting into her lower lip.

Moments later, she stepped back and shook her head. Xander was there wrapping her in his arms. "What did you see?"

"Nothing. I felt only pain and darkness. He was heavily sedated before he was killed, which meant he didn't see anything. The vision was a jumble of dark shadows, and then a sharp pain."

"He was drinking heavily last night. It could have been the wine, or someone could have slipped him something. But why would someone go to the trouble of sedating him before killing him?" I asked.

"To make him easier to control," Xander answered. "Torren was a very large man, and a bear shifter. He wouldn't have gone down without a fight."

"Do you think it has something to do with the trials, or a hate crime because he's a shifter?"

Xander rubbed the back of his neck. "Maybe, or it could be—I don't know."

"I overheard disgruntled candidates yesterday in the library. They're upset that the shifters are here. I think this may be because of that. Or it could be someone else entirely," I added, thinking of Aspen and his promise to refill the marks. My stomach dropped, and I felt sick with remorse.

"I doubt it," Rosalie said. "What should we do? Do we cancel the tests?"

"No," he said. "Then the murderer gets free. At least now we have all of our suspects under one roof, and Maeve can help us find them."

Rosalie nodded. "Maeve is good at reconnaissance. There's only one other person that would be able to find the culprit faster, and that's Aura."

At the mention of Aura's name, I felt conflicted. I had so much to ask her. So much to say. But if she arrived, there was no way I could hide my secrets from her.

"How is she?" Xander asked.

"She's doing better. She's retreated to the fae court, and Liam is with her. She's healing and grieving, but I think she would heal faster if she knew you were alive, Maeve."

I shook my head. "Not yet." Rosalie's lips pressed together in disapproval. "Let me find your murderer. I will bring them to justice. I promise."

Xander and Rosalie gave each other solemn looks before agreeing. "We must move Violet to the northern wing and double her guards. Xander and I are able to take care of each other."

Of course they were. I pitied any man who thought they could attack a werewolf and a sorceress.

"Let's keep this as quiet as possible. The candidates must be notified, but beyond that, I don't want anyone outside of the palace to know." Xander gave the order and left, the door closing behind him.

Rosalie wasn't as swift to leave. "Maeve, I know a lot has happened in the last few years. We've grown apart, but I still hope that if you were in trouble, you'd tell me."

"I'm a big girl." I cocked my head. "I can solve my own problems."

"I know you can. But if Violet is in danger, you get her out of here, okay?"

"She's not. I'll kill anyone that lays a finger on her."

She grinned. "That's the Maeve I know."

I gave her a half smile as she left, and I followed behind her. I hesitated when I caught something in my periphery. The rug. It was disturbed, the corner of it slightly flipped up. I lifted the edge. My breath caught as it revealed a spell circle scratched into the floor.

"What did you do?" I hissed, assaulting Aspen as soon as he came out of his door. I'd been pacing the hallway waiting for him to make his appearance, unsure of which room he was in.

He pushed past me and headed toward breakfast. His shoulders straight, his eyes boring into mine. "I did what needed to be done."

"I will fight you. I won't let you get away with killing Torren."

Aspen stepped back, his eyebrows rose in surprise. "What? I didn't kill Torren."

My mouth dropped open. "Wait, then who did? There was a spell circle. I . . . I assumed it was you."

His surprise was quickly masked as he pushed passed me angrily. "I'm not the only one who uses magic."

Spinning on my heel, I picked up my pace and trotted after him. His long legs quickly outdistancing me as he headed down the main stairs.

"But how did you . . . I mean, me. I'm better." I tripped over my words as I struggled for the explanation. My marks were dark; his were darker.

He rolled his eyes "Maybe if you were a better student, you'd know what I did." His words were clipped. He was angry at me, and I didn't blame him.

We passed through a side hall, headed toward the servants' quarters, and then exited outside. With sure steps, Aspen headed across the yard. Troops were practicing and going through their paces on the other side of the training field and by the barracks.

"Where are you going?" I asked breathlessly as I tried to keep up with him.

He was silent in thought as we drew closer to the abandoned armory tower. When we came to the door, it was bound shut with a heavy chain.

Aspen's fingers wove a spell, and it unlocked. Looking around to see if anyone noticed us, he slipped the lock off, and we snuck inside.

The darkness within the tower was suffocating. There was a musty odor that covered up something darker and more sinister in nature. I followed Aspen down a long hall before he took a short set of stairs down into an old workroom. He lit the lantern, illuminating the interior space.

A sickness roiled through my stomach as I saw the

chains on the floor, and the dark stains marring the wood. Allemar's workroom for his sacrifices. I shuddered.

Aspen moved to the empty shelves, running his fingers along the back wall, searching for a hidden nook. "There has to be something here."

"Rosalie said she destroyed everything of his." I used the sleeve of my dress to cover my mouth, holding back the nausea that came over me.

"He wouldn't have left it out where anyone could find it."

"What are you looking for?"

Aspen slammed a leather-bound book closed and gave me a sly grin. "Wouldn't you like to know."

"Of course, that's why I asked the question," I said irritably.

He frowned. "No, that's not how it goes . . . never mind."

As Aspen continued his search, I was drawn to a trapdoor in the floor, my hand picking up the metal ring. With a groan, it opened, greeting me with its darkness and dank smell. My heart raced as it reminded me of the cellar in the cottage. I couldn't do down there.

"Those are his personal cells," Aspen said without emotion. "He kept his prisoners down there."

"Was Rosalie kept here?"

He nodded. "Among others." He took the stone steps two at a time and held the lantern high above his head.

Refusing to let fear and emotions paralyze me, I followed, my eyes searching the small room and the empty cells. A door had been blasted off the hinges and lay on the ground a few feet from the frame. I stepped into the cell and turned in a circle. One small window that let in air and very little light and the floor was cold and I stepped around puddles. This was where Rosalie was kept until Eden found and freed her. I thought I was hiding my feelings until I caught Aspen looking at me.

His eyes were downcast. "You must think me a monster for letting her rot down here."

"You said it, not me." My voice was cold.

"She was a stranger to me; a ghost returned. I believed her an imposter."

"Stop. I don't want to hear excuses."

His lips pressed together. He turned and headed into a back cell. For a moment, I imagined closing him in and walking away. My hand reached for the door as he brushed back the straw and dirt with his boot.

"There." He pointed to a stone with a strange symbol on it. "This cell was always kept empty."

I released my hand on the door and stepped in closer to look. Aspen was kneeling on the ground and digging out the loose stone with a sigil scratched in it. Under the stone was a book wrapped in wax cloth and twine.

Aspen didn't unwrap the book or show it to me but tucked it into his vest.

My lips puckered in anger. "Are you going to tell me what we've found?"

"Are you going to continue to call me a monster and murderer?"

"Yes," I said.

"Then, no."

Inwardly, I railed at his flippant attitude. None of my sisters acted like this. He acted like... me.

As quietly as we came, we left Allemar's workroom, closing the trapdoor. Lost in my thoughts, I said nothing as

I contemplated his actions. *What was in that book? Why did he want it? Where was Allemar?*

Aspen had just replaced the lock on the door to the armory tower when we were surprised by a visitor.

"What are you two doing out here?"

Silva stood behind me, a swoon-worthy perfect vision, his dark hair loose and brushing his collar. His tan pants clung to his long legs, and the white shirt he wore accentuated his tan skin.

"Taking a walk," Aspen answered, his hand unconsciously touching the book hidden in his vest.

Silva's eyes narrowed, catching the movement. "You've heard about Torren?" His gaze flickered between the two of us as if he was secretly judging our actions.

"We heard," Aspen said.

"What do *you* think happened?" Silva asked.

"Someone had a grudge." Aspen turned to push past him. "He spoke words of truth that must have offended someone."

"Then I would look closer to your kind," Silva said, turning to respond.

Aspen's eyes darkened, and he took a threatening step forward. "There's a reason the shifters are no longer guards to royals. They can't be trusted."

"And yet, you keep company with one." Silva nodded toward me.

"Believe me when I say this one is the worst kind of company."

I frowned at Aspen's disparaging remarks.

Silva jumped at the chance. He bowed his head. "Then I would find it a deep pleasure to have her accompany me this morning." He held out his hand to me.

"No. Let's go, Maeve," Aspen ordered.

I hesitated.

Aspen glowered. Silva smiled, knowing he had won. I stared at the two of them. One calm, cool, and collected, the other on the verge of exploding.

Feeling the urge to make Aspen uncomfortable, I placed my hand within Silva's and immediately felt that spark as our magic called to each other.

"I think it would be best if I spent some time with my own kind," I said.

Aspen turned cold. "Fine." He spun on his heel and headed toward the main palace.

When he was out of earshot, Silva spoke. "He treats you like you're more than a friend. What is he to you? Your lover?"

Heat rose to my cheeks. "No, more my prison guard."

"Well, we have some time till lunch. I wanted to check on you to make sure you're okay. This morning's events didn't have a lasting effect on you?"

My lips pursed as I had to think. Was it only this morning that I had found Torren murdered? It seemed like such a long time ago.

"I'm fine."

"Really?" he asked.

"Really."

I let Silva lead as we walked and headed around the palace to the back gardens toward the glass conservatory. As soon as I stepped through the door, the air immediately became warmer, almost hot, filled with a mix of pleasant aromas, but it was cooled by the moving stream that passed through the giant dome.

It was a utopia of fragrances, flowers, and colors;

winding paths and walkways led through a maze of hedges and tall bushes. Scattered throughout the gardens were stone statues of various beasts. I knew by looking at them, they were representative of the seven clans. These told more of a story. A beautiful and serene woman was kneeling over the stream like she was about to scoop water, an empty bowl in her hands as if she were frozen in time. At first glance, what I thought to be a kerchief tied around her neck was actually a snake. A playful fox batted at the hem of her dress; a raven perched on her shoulder. Behind her was a stone bear, his paw half in the moving stream, a lion lay sleeping in the grass and a cougar stood watch over him. Away from the others, with his back turned away from the intricate statues, was a lone stone figure. The size and point of his ears reminded me of a wolf, but I knew it was the elusive jackal. At the base, the imperial rose bush grew. The buds closed up, for they only bloomed when touched by the blood of a Florin royal.

Silva paused and sat on a bench near the middle of the garden, leaving a space for me.

"Do you know that I dreamed of coming to the palace? Now I'm here. My brothers would be jealous."

"You have brothers?"

"Six." Silva rubbed his hands along his knees. "They're far away in other kingdoms, but like those in the wards, they can't turn human anymore."

"I'm sorry."

"Don't be. I believe I can save them. I'm so close." His features filled with frustration.

"You believe what happened can be reversed. "

"Yes, I've been searching for a long time, and I think I'm close to the answer."

We fell silent for a few moments and watched a bird hop along the ground, pecking at the dirt before flying up into the sky to land on a tree.

"I remember rumors about a young prince that was in line for the throne before Queen Rosalie reappeared. But no one has seen him since King Basil's death."

I shrugged my shoulders. "Rumors."

"That's interesting. I would have thought he would be here to claim his birthright instead of letting it get parceled out to strangers. And by strangers, I mean shifters."

"To some, birthright is a burden."

"That's true." Silva nodded and reached for my hand. Threading his fingers through mine, he rubbed the back of my palm. "I know all too well the pressure birthright brings."

"Of being the oldest?"

"Of trying to redeem my people. To them, I'm the weakest of us all." He seemed hesitant.

"Silva, what kind of shifter are you?"

His eyes lowered, he held his breath, releasing it in a long drawn-out sigh. "I'd rather not say, if that's okay. I was teased mercilessly as a child. I will show you one day. I promise."

"Okay, I'll keep your secret."

Holding his hands felt comfortable. "Thank you, Maeve." He leaned forward and kissed me. It wasn't full of passion, but sweet and comforting. I pulled away first. Silva smiled, running a finger down the side of my face. "I still can't believe we've never met before. If you had grown up in Florin, then we'd be engaged, maybe even married by now.

"Are you kidding?"

His cheeks flushed red. "I presented you with my feathers. That's the first step in shifter courtship."

I was taken aback. My cheeks felt warm as I glanced up into Silva's confident golden eyes. "What's the second?" I teased.

His eyes filled with mischief. "A kiss."

"Oh great, does that mean we're engaged already? Are you sure you're not making this up? I've never heard of these customs."

He clutched his heart, pretending to be mortally wounded by my words. "Well, then I will have to woo you the old-fashioned way." He ran his finger over my palm, and again, I felt the jolt of electricity. "Unless there's something between you and Aloe?"

"No, no, not at all." My heart thrummed, guilt flooded me, and I answered too quickly. "I am sort of bound by a different contract. I'm looking for a way to break it."

"I see. So you're not free."

"Yes and no." I sighed. "Or I hope to be free of him soon." Silva's golden eyes made me melt as I gazed into them. "But forget Aloe. Tell me what it was like where you grew up."

Silva's face clouded over. "My childhood was not filled with whimsical stories or fantasies. We lived in fear of the humans, of being hunted and persecuted for the mistake of a single shifter guard. Many refused to shift, and they stayed human. For others, that was too much of a sacrifice, and a few—including my own grandfather—took their own life."

"I couldn't imagine not being able to shift anymore. It's a part of who I am," I said.

He nodded. "That's why it's so important for me to try

and gain back protection and land in Florin. My brothers will have a home, and maybe one day respect." His eyes glittered with hope and he flashed me a smile. "Maybe you could call it home?"

"I have one." My mind immediately flashed to the tower with my sisters, but it didn't feel like home anymore. Then a vision of Aspen chopping wood, and Velora trying to boil water while Marco sharpened his axes filled my mind, and I smiled but quickly shook my head. That wasn't really home either.

"We should get back," I said.

I headed out the conservatory doors, but Silva hung back and stared at the imperial rose bush. "I'll be right with you."

CHAPTER TWENTY-FOUR

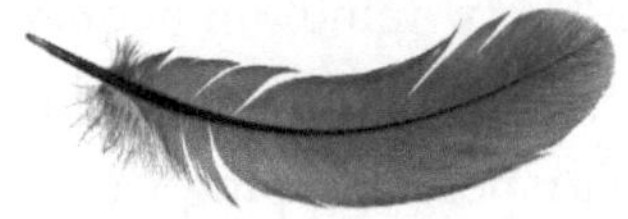

"This is an impossible task," a guard whispered. "But we are not allowed to interfere."

"It's crazy," another added.

"They're all going to fail before the test even starts."

"You would think that after all the competition events that there wouldn't be need for this."

The conversations continued from amazed to downright confused as the last thirteen were spread out among the ballroom and chasing down a dress-wearing goblin.

Since the king and queen were busy handling the morning's events, the trial was going to be administered by proxy. Right before the second trial started, Gobbersnot had burst through the doors to the room and had stolen the test. The butler had tried to regain the scroll from Gobbersnot, but he wasn't having any of it. He easily climbed up the closest column and perched on the top, waving the scroll.

"Pffftttt!" Gobbersnot's pink tongue flapped in his audience's direction before he made it to his feet and made a show of putting the paper in his mouth.

Three of the human candidates had tried to climb up the marble pole but quickly slide back down. The whole somber affair had quickly turned into a sideshow. I found it marvelous fun as Gobbersnot cussed in fae and then proceeded to flash everyone a rude gesture. For some, this was their very first encounter with one of the lesser fae.

"No!" Hela cried out. She stamped her foot and wagged her finger. "Bad goblin." She pointed to the ground. "Bring that here, now!"

Gobbersnot looked slightly amazed by the woman's commanding voice, and he slid down the column, but when he was still out of reach, he launched from the pole and over the heads of the onlookers, doing a somersault as he landed. He then proceeded to climb the tapestry.

Silva left shortly after Gobbersnot ran up the column and he returned with a tray full of food.

"Here you go, my friend." Silva held out the tray.

Gobbersnot looked interested. "Sangue?"

Silva lifted the lid to reveal cooked turkey legs, ham, and pheasant. The scent of the rosemary and thyme roasted meat filled the room, and even I began to salivate. But despite the grand show, Gobbersnot turned up his nose.

Cross brought a ladder and leaned it against the wall, quickly scaling it, but as soon as he was in reach, Gobbersnot jumped onto Cross's shoulder and then launched off, scrambling up another column.

"Can no one get that creature down? What if we don't finish the test before the time is up and we all lose our chance?" Warden said.

"Bring me my bow. I will shoot the thing," a man named Adam yelled, motioning to one of the servants.

A collective gasp came from those watching.

"Don't you dare," Cross growled. The low thrum of his lion voice came through and echoed through the room.

But the more they tried to coax Gobbersnot down, the more stubborn he became. Only Aspen seemed undisturbed by the commotion. He had settled into a wooden chair by the window to read a book. From a distance, it looked like it was the same book we had recovered from Allemar's tower.

Every once in a while, he would look outside at the setting sun and sigh.

"Are you going to do anything?" Warden challenged. "You heard the page. We need to complete the test by sundown, or we fail."

"There's still time." Aspen turned the page in his book, ignoring the commotion.

I stood at the front of the room near the butler who had given the instructions for the test, and I couldn't help but gaze at Aspen. He didn't seem bothered by the noise, voices, and commotion. He looked relaxed, at home. Then I remembered this was his home. When he would look out the window across the gardens, he would take a deep breath, and I could see the faintest of smiles. Was this who he truly had been before he was abused by his father and corrupted by Allemar? Was he a contemplative bookworm?

For the next candle mark, a few of the candidates had left, only to return with all sorts of items to use to barter or coax the goblin down.

Money, desserts, weapons. Warden had almost coaxed Gobbersnot down with silk slippers. But the wily goblin had slid across the floor, snatched the slippers out of his hands, and was back up the marble column.

Brekken spent most of his time hiding under the table. I'd occasionally see a hand reach up and take a pastry off of it before it slipped back under the tablecloth.

Gobbersnot used a long drapery to swing across the room to one of the chandeliers, and swung recklessly about.

As the sun sank lower into the sky, I began to worry. What would happen if Aspen didn't participate at all? Would he disqualify himself so easily?

Silva came up to me, his face full of sweat. "I don't know what else to do. Do you think you could fly up there and steal the test from him? I'm just not comfortable doing it myself."

Aspen's head snapped up as soon as he heard the question.

I nodded my head. "Of course."

"No." Aspen's voice echoed across the room. "Do not interfere. I'll do it."

"Do what?" Everett called. "We've tried everything. He doesn't want anything other than to make us fail."

Bently was impatient. "We should kill the creature now while we have the chance."

"That *creature*," Aspen said as he slid out a dagger, "is a red cap. You can't barter with him because you have nothing he wants. They only desire one thing." He sliced the palm of his hand, leaving a trail of red. He held his hand up in the air.

Gobbersnot froze, his nose searching for which direction the scent of blood came from. His eyes filled with desire, and he jumped from the chandelier to the curtains to slide down the drapes, leaving a trail of claw marks behind as he shredded them in his descent. In the blink of an eye, he stood in front of Aspen, his eyes wide with need. He held out the scroll in offering as he licked his lips and pointed to his bleeding hand.

"A red cap?" Hela said.

"Their kind deals in blood." Aspen nodded, took the scroll, and let the goblin lick the wound on his hand, much like a dog licking his bowl.

Just as the sun set, the doors to the ballroom opened, and King Xander and Queen Rosalie entered.

"Time is up," Xander announced. "What do you have to show for yourselves?"

Warden and a few other of the candidates groaned.

"I knew we should have shot it down," Bently grumbled.

The room grew silent, heavy with disappointment, but Aspen was still letting Gobbersnot lick his hand. He pulled his fist away, and placed his palm on Gobbersnot's head, leaving a smear of blood upon the faded patch of red on his scalp.

Gobbersnot took off and dove under the skirt of the queen, popping up with an outer layer of lace around his head like a veil. Rosalie didn't even react to her personal space being invaded by the goblin.

Aspen kneeled before King Xander and presented the scroll. Xander took the scroll and didn't even unroll it. He glanced around the room, his eyes alighting on each candidate. "All of you passed except for Adam, Bently and Renold."

"How's that fair?" Renold shouted. "How do they pass, and I'm eliminated? We didn't even take the next test yet because the stupid goblin stole it."

Xander unrolled the scroll to reveal a blank piece of

paper. "This was your test. To retrieve the scroll from Gobbersnot. Those that resorted to violence instead of bartering are eliminated."

"That's not fair," Adam huffed.

Xander's eyes turned cold. "Is it fair to kill my wife's familiar just because that is the fastest course of action?"

Bently paled. "That thing is the queen's familiar?

"Yes, and her companion. There are many fae in our lands, and you should never strike first. Warden studied the goblin and knew he had an affinity for clothes. That was an acceptable course. Silva was the first one who tried to bribe Gobbersnot with food, although he had the wrong kind of food. Gobbersnot likes his food raw."

After having presented the scroll, Aspen had gone back to his chair by the window and sat down, staring into the night sky.

"It was Aloe who first recognized the goblin as a red cap and successfully negotiated the trade for the scroll. You should thank him that he was here to help you," Xander added.

Aspen's mouth tensed as those that had not seen him as competition now did. No wonder he had tried to stay out of the way. This had painted a giant target on his back. I wondered why he did it when I could have easily stolen the scroll out of Gobbersnot's hands.

"Did you know?" Silva turned to me. "That the test was to retrieve the scroll?"

"Yes, I knew." I pursed my lips to hide my amusement. "We were told to not interfere unless someone asked us for our help, so I couldn't have offered my services."

Rosalie was speaking in hushed voices with her husband. They were discussing the candidates, and I saw her frown when she regarded Aloe reading by himself. Our eyes met, and she smiled seeing me and Silva together. I had revealed to her that he was a shifter like me.

Silva groaned and rubbed his hand across his face. "If only I had realized that sooner. I could have asked you, and this would have all been over. Instead, he gets the credit." Silva tossed his thumb toward Aspen, who was no longer reading, but watching our interaction with intense eyes.

"You could have flown up yourself."

He shook his head. "No, I have no desire to reveal myself as a shifter to anyone here. But you're the queen's sister. You have some level of immunity."

"You revealed yourself to me."

He grinned. "That's because we are the same, you and me." He threaded his hand through my mind and led me into the hall, away from the prying eyes of the room. "Come, you must tell me all about your family. I didn't know she had a red cap. What else don't I know?"

At that moment, I saw the barest gray shadow sneaking around the corner to duck behind a curtain in an alcove.

I unthreaded my hand through his and gave him my apology. "I'm sorry, there's something I must attend to."

The barest flash of annoyance crossed his face, but was gone, covered by a smile. "I understand." He bowed and left me alone, making his way down the opposite hall.

When I was sure I was alone, I moved to the curtain to reveal the wiggling blob that was hiding under it.

"Someone is sneaking about the palace unescorted again," I teased.

"Don't you mean you are," Aspen said from behind. "You shouldn't be sneaking off with that shifter. It's not proper."

Turning, I stepped in front of the curtain, blocking the wolf pup. My anger flared at being told what I could and couldn't do. "I'm a shifter too." I snapped. "And you and I are alone together all the time."

"That's different."

"How?"

Aspen struggled to respond while hiding his jealousy. He didn't get to answer because a low growl came from the curtain, and it surged forward to attack his leather boot. A furry snout poked through and began to angrily chew on his toe.

"I think the curtain has teeth and is attacking me." His brows rose in confusion, and he leaned down to pull the curtain away.

"Don't." I pushed him back and stepped between them as Violet batted the curtain and flopped around, growling and snarling.

"Don't what?"

"Stay back, or I'll hurt you," I warned.

Aspen grew angry. "Why are you threatening me?"

Panicking, I scooped up Violet in my arms quickly and put as much distance as I could between Aspen and us. My heart raced as I ran with my niece toward safety.

"Maeve!" Aspen called, his voice resonating down the hall, his anger and confusion evident.

Turning into the first open door, I attempted to hold it shut with my back, but his strong hands slammed it open, pushing me farther into the room. I retreated toward the far window.

We were in a private study. Whose it was, I didn't know, and I didn't care.

Aspen stalked after me, turning to close the door and

turning the key in the lock, trapping us inside. "Now that you have nowhere else to run, I want an answer to my question."

"Get back!" I placed Violet on a chair and stood in front of her. I held out my hands and reached for my magic and hesitated, remembering that to do so would have repercussions on my body.

"Maeve, stop it. Be reasonable." Aspen cocked his head to look at the young pup.

I couldn't control my fear. My heart and mind were at war with each other in my desire to protect her from the threat in the room. Violet didn't see the threat but was pawing at the air, wanting attention.

"Don't make me fight you." My voice was low as I searched for a form to shift into that strong enough to protect my niece, even if it meant dying in the process. Never had I tried something bigger than a crow or raven. Could I even do it? I would more than likely go mad.

Mist swirled around me, my neck cracked as I could feel my bones stretch as they tried to take on a new form. My eyes clouded over with anger, and before I could complete the transformation, Aspen was gone. He was no longer in front of me.

Instead, he had used magic and transported behind me and was kneeling before Violet. The wolf leapt up in playful banter to try to attack his hand. Aspen chuckled and rolled her on her back, exposing her belly. She tried to nip his fingers, her back legs kicking as she wrestled with his hand.

"She reminds me of my dogs I had before Father—" His voice was soft, wistful, and then became saddened. I could only imagine something bad happened to them.

My anger dissipated, but I was still worried. "Aspen, don't hurt her."

His eyes flashed. "Do you think me such a monster to hurt this little one?"

"I don't know what you would do if Allemar commanded you to. You said that you can't always control yourself."

"This is true." His smile widened as he stood up and backed away. The wolf pup lunged off the chair to attack. She sneezed midair, shifting back into a young girl with long dark hair.

"Whoa!" Aspen reflexively caught Violet and stumbled backwards, holding her in his arms protectively as he fell onto his back.

Violet laughed as Aspen sprawled on the floor and looked into the grinning face of chubby cheeked toddler.

"Who is this?" he asked sternly, sitting up and setting her a good distance away from him. Knowing that he was holding a shifter instantly changed his mind about her.

I took a protective step forward, ready to separate them if needed.

"Aspen, now be calm."

Violet had thought jumping into Aspen's arms was quite entertaining, so now she was climbing up into the chair and jumping into his arms as he sat on the floor. He caught her as if she was the most precious thing in the world. Setting her back down on the floor. Helping her up onto the chair when her human legs wouldn't reach.

"Don't tell me to be calm. Who is she?"

"She's a werewolf. But not just any werewolf. She's your niece."

"My . . . niece?"

"Catch!" Violet cried and flung herself out of the chair. Aspen almost missed her leap, but he swept her up and spun her around. Looking deeper into her face, his mouth tightened .

"What's your name?"

"Vi-yet."

"Hi, Violet." He swallowed, and his eyes turned glassy. "I'm your uncle." His eyes met mine. "She looks so much like her."

"Who?" I asked.

"My mother, Hyacinth, but with Rosalie's hair." Aspen patted Violet on the head and set her down on the chair before walking away, his shoulders stiff, his eyes hard as he marched toward the door.

"Where are you going?" I asked at his sudden departure.

"You were right about me. You shouldn't trust me with her. It's best if I leave now."

Violet didn't like being suddenly abandoned by Aspen. She ran after him, shifting into a wolf so she could run faster. He unlocked the door, closing it quickly behind him, cutting off her advance.

Violet, unable to stop on the wood floor, slid into the door. She scratched at the opening and whimpered. When he didn't return, she swept her head back and howled.

"I feel the same way." I picked up Violet and cradled her in my arms.

CHAPTER TWENTY-FIVE

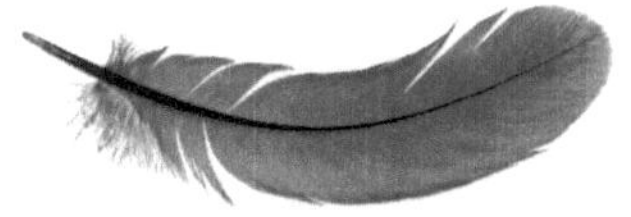

The following morning was the announcement of another test in two days. There were rumors among the staff and servants of someone coming from another kingdom to help administer the last trial. Rosalie had been very tightlipped about the news and had refused to share any information with me. The proclamation had put the remaining candidates on edge, and King Xander decided it was best to send the candidates into town to enjoy the last night of the St. Autumnus celebration.

Aspen had been especially annoying of late. Avoiding me. Refusing to speak to me as if blaming me for the unwanted family reunion with his niece. When we gathered outside to head into the town, he made sure to get in the carriage farthest away from me.

"Come with us." Hela looped her arm through mine and pulled me toward an empty stagecoach.

I smirked as Warden was trying to pull on Brekken's leg to keep him from climbing into a trunk strapped to the back of the carriage. Warden gave up as Brekken slinked inside, closing the lid on himself.

I took a seat between Cross and Hela, while Warden and Everett sat across from us.

"Are you really the queen's sister?" Warden asked. As always, he was dressed more impeccably than the rest of the candidates, wearing polished white leather boots and a white cravat that accentuated the dark red velvet coat.

"Not by blood," I said. "We're both adopted."

"I heard you were raised by the most powerful sorceress in the seven kingdoms." Hela leaned forward. Her voice had a soft purr to it when she said *heard*. "Is that why you were able to break the wards on the narrows?"

"Yes." I leaned back, crossing my arms over my chest. I was careful, not wanting to reveal too much, but at the same time studying them.

"Are you not competing as a candidate?" Everett asked. "You sure made quite an impression."

"No. I have no use for a title," I said, heat rising to my cheeks.

"She's right. A title does not guarantee power," Cross said, his voice a deep rumble.

I studied the four in the carriage and addressed the topic that had been hanging in the air. "I'm sorry about what happened to Torren."

"It is not your fault. We knew the risks coming out into the open again. We painted a big target." Cross's brows drew together, and he bowed his head. "He was the best of us."

Warden sighed, stretching out his long legs. "Many years ago when I was young, I remember Torren was caught in a snowstorm, and he shifted into a bear to stay warm. He found a cave and accidentally hibernated through winter. His wife was worried sick until he wondered in three months later, skinny as a bean pole, with no memory of what happened.

Cross chuckled at the memory and then sobered up. "Slow and steady, but the most kind-hearted guy around. It pains me that someone would take his life."

The coach became silent as we mourned his passing.

"Do you think it was the humans?" Warden asked, voicing the question no one wanted to ask.

"Had to be. Who else would try to kill a shifter?" Everett spoke up.

My knees bounced up and down as I debated sharing what I knew. What I had been thinking about for hours. That it was dark magic, the kind a sorcerer would use. The kind I would use. That he was killed in the same way a shifter killed the past queen. But I didn't dare tell them, or they would accuse me of his murder. But it left me with a question . . . if it wasn't Aspen, what purpose would they have for using a spell circle? Who else would use it?

"He was drugged." I decided to share with them information that wasn't released to the public. That way they could protect themselves. "Which means someone knew he was a bear shifter, and how to incapacitate him. But it also means it could be anybody, human or shifter."

Hela gritted her teeth together and growled. "I will tear anyone apart who tries to stab me through the heart."

"The kitty cat is showing her claws. Ooh, I'm scared," Warden teased.

Hela let forth a hiss and the hairs on my arms rose. The tension grew, and the carriage was filled with power and the familiar scent of shifters.

"Enough!" Cross growled out a warning, and immediately the two sat up straight and obeyed. "There's plenty of time to fight later, but for now, you two get along. We need to watch each other's backs."

Like petulant children, Hela and Warden continued to shoot nasty glares across the way. Finding a new topic to debate, the three shifters started a heated discussion. Cross closed his eyes and pretended to nap, feigning indifference to the fighting.

"Thank you for choosing Silva as one of your seven," I whispered to Cross. "I know how important it is for him to do this."

Cross didn't move, and he lowered his voice as the others were still arguing. "I didn't choose Silva. Aside from myself, I only found five shifters brave enough to step foot in the palace. You have to remember, the last time shifters were here, they were slaughtered during the shifter wars. But I'm glad your friend made it. You'll have to introduce me."

I didn't know that. It seemed that not all shifters knew each other. "Cross, I've been meaning to ask. The shifter that started the wars, the one who supposedly murdered the queen. It's not mentioned in any of the history books. What kind of shifter was he?"

"He was the shifter king," Cross answered, his eyes still closed.

"I don't understand what that means."

"He was an omni."

The carriage came to a halt before he could explain further, and we were in the middle of the town square. The candidates were escorted out and brought across the grand stage. Cheers rose up from the people and flowers littered the air. Aspen looked uncomfortable, and he hung back, pulling a green cloak over his head.

Hela and Warden seemed the most at ease, parading themselves across the platform. Cross came to the center of the stage and the crowd became silent, as if sensing the quiet power he exuded. As I stood by the steps leading up the platform, I gazed out among the crowd. I wondered how many of them were also shifters.

"Maeve!" Velora moved through the throng of people and wrapped her arms around me in a hug. "You're okay?"

I frowned. "Of course, I'm okay. I'm at the palace."

"I mean you survived the final initiation phase with . . . Allemar." She whispered his name, looking sideways in case someone overheard.

My stomach dropped that she knew what had been coming, and I didn't. I also wondered why she wasn't bound like I was. "Yes, I did. Because I was tricked by Aspen." I pulled away from her.

"You understand, right?" Velora pleaded.

"No."

"He had to. Allemar is back. He came to us shortly after you were taken to the palace. He threatened to kill you and me if Aspen didn't obey in getting you to take the final step." The color drained from Velora's face. "He had no choice."

"There's always a choice," I said. She recoiled as if I slapped her, but I quickly softened my voice. "Where is *he* now?" I asked.

Her voice dropped to a whisper. "I do not know, but he's not far. He's never far away."

Marco appeared out of the crowd and hovered over Velora's shoulder like a shadow. His eyes narrowed in on the remaining candidates. Velora looked up as well, and her mouth dropped open. "Oh, I've never seen so many . . ." she searched her limited vocabulary for the word, "pets."

Turning, I tried to see what she saw, but knew that with my magic cut off to the ley lines I was limited, and I couldn't see the faint aura of power that surrounded the shifters. "You can see them?" I asked.

"Mmm, like a mini shadow." Velora pointed to Brekken. "That's a dog."

"Fox," I answered.

Velora, one by one, pointed at the others on the stage. "Cat, worm thing, bigger cat."

I chuckled as she tried to point out cougar, asp, and lion. When she pointed to Silva, I awaited what her answer would be, wondering since he never told me.

"Dark thing."

"Come again?"

She wrinkled her nose and squinted her eyes. "I don't know what to call it. It's weird looking."

And as fast as it came, her attention span was gone, and she was bouncing on her heels like a puppy when she saw Aspen.

"You're here!" Velora raised her hands as he stepped off the stage and she jumped into his arms.

He caught her easily, without missing a beat. He didn't make a big fuss or seem to even mind the childlike adoration she had for him. But it was hard to read anything more. Did he like her attention? Did he return her affection?

"Glad to see that Marco's been taking care of you," Aspen said. He patted her head, but the motion was automatic, his posture was tense, and he scanned the crowd. He leaned forward, and it looked like he was giving her a kiss. "Any news?" he whispered

She leaned into him in return. "No, he hasn't made an appearance at the inn, or in town."

"That's troubling. He was the one who sent us here. I wonder what he's doing?" Aspen looked worried.

Velora grasped Aspen's elbow, and I saw the fear in her eyes. It seemed that Allemar was as much of a mystery to them as he was to the rest of the kingdom. His motives were similar to my mother's; revenge. But like my mother, he had his own secret agenda. Rosalie and Eden had been pawns used to advance her vengeance, but at the same time, her abrupt moves were actually to each kingdom's advancement.

"Why are you all back? What happened?" Velora asked.

"I think Xander and Rosalie wanted us out of the palace for a bit while they prepared the next test. It's being proctored by someone from another kingdom," I answered.

"Do you know who?" Aspen asked me.

"Why does everyone think I know what's going on in my sister's head? I'm not Aura . . . wait. I bet it's Aura. It would make sense. If I were looking to find out who killed Torren, and wanted to vet the best candidates. I would bring in Aura."

"She's the one who can read minds, right?" Velora asked.

"If that's the case, there will be no hiding anything. I might as well give up now," Aspen declared.

"I still don't understand why you are doing this. There's no way that Rosalie or Xander would give you control of lands when you tried to kill her."

"Why haven't *you* told them about me yet?" he accused. "I expected you to turn me in the minute you saw her. Even when I came to the palace, I waited for you to point to me and have the guards arrest me."

"I don't . . . know." I let his words sink in. Words that I had asked myself over and over. But each time I wanted to, something held me back.

"When do you go back?" Velora asked.

"Late tonight."

"Then let's celebrate," she squealed in excitement.

It was easy to be swept up in her exuberance. But coming back to the town square and seeing the first statue of King Alder made me think back to the shifter wars. The magic ward on the narrows, the person claiming to be the shifter king, the disappearing shifters, the spell circle in Torren's room. There was something nagging me that I couldn't quite put my finger on, but I wasn't sure if I straight out asked Aspen if he would tell me the truth.

"Hey, may I join you?" Silva jogged up to our group and brushed his dark hair out of his eyes.

"No," Aspen said.

"Sure!" Velora added at the same time, brightening up when she saw how good-looking he was.

Silva looked at me for assurance.

I nodded.

"Great! Who are your friends?" he asked.

"Marco, Velora." I pointed to each of them. Velora batted her eyes, and Marco grunted in greeting. "But friends is a loose term. I would say more acquaintances."

"Nice to meet you, Velora and Marco. What do you do for a living?"

"I make a great butt," Velora answered.

"—er!" I added. "She makes butter, and Marco is . . ." I trailed off, unsure how to answer his questions.

"What we do is of no concern to you," Aspen admonished. "Unless you are willing to tell me what you do for a living and the reason you're here?"

Silva was wary with his tone. "I'm here for the same reasons you are."

Both men stared at each other in an uncomfortable impasse.

"Who's hungry?" I piped up, feeling extremely nervous. "I'm hungry. Starving. Could eat a pig. Not a whole pig, but a roasted pig, or at least part of one. Can someone tell me where to get a pig?"

My babbling lessened the tension, and Silva laughed. Aspen turned his back to me giving me the silent treatment again. The next few candle marks were spent shopping and walking among the vendors. Silva was being very generous and buying me desserts and sweets. The whole time Aspen continued to refuse to talk to him or answer any of his direct questions.

The lower the sun sank in the sky, the livelier the town became. As lanterns were lit, the stage was once again filled with musicians. Silva paused by a flower stand and pulled out a very beautiful rose.

"Hey, Aloe," Silva called out. "I believe we should buy the ladies a flower." He pointed to a cart filled with various blossoms .

Aspen turned and frowned at the flowers. "No."

"Oh, please," Velora asked.

Aspen sighed and headed over to the vendor. The men stood close as they each picked out a flower.

Silva turned toward me, a beautiful red rose in his hand. "I think this one's for you." He held the rose out to me, but at the last second, turned and thrust it into Aspen's hand. The thorn pricked into the side of his hand, drawing blood.

The closed rose bud immediately began to bloom. "An imperial rose. That which only blooms when in the presence of a royal of Florin."

"Where did you get that?" Aspen growled. "That wasn't at the flower vendor."

"No, I plucked it from the royal gardens earlier when I was with Maeve. I know the story of the imperial rose. One taste of blood of the royal bloodline and they bloom. I was correct in my assumption."

"You're wrong."

"I'm not, Your Highness," Silva smirked.

CHAPTER TWENTY-SIX

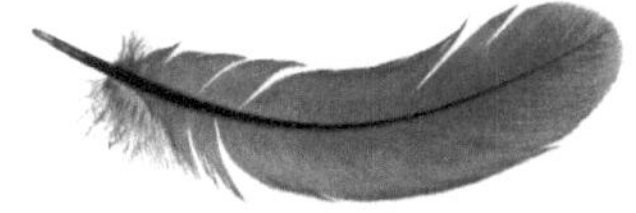

Aspen's fury was a raging storm. He grabbed Silva by the front of his jacket, pushing him backwards until his head thrust into the wall of a silversmith's store.

"What are you going to do about it?" Aspen seethed.

"You can drop the glamour. I'm going to do nothing. It just seems that you and I are the same." Silva held still, his voice soft and non-threatening.

"I don't trust your kind." Aspen's hands glowed, and Silva winced under the burning of Aspen's wrath and power.

"Yet, you travel with one. Is it because you are using her for pleasure?" His voice was cruel and taunting. "Are you going to cast her aside as soon as you're done with her? Just like your grandfather cast all the shifters aside because of one."

"Don't speak another word if you value your life." Aspen's voice had turned deadly. This was the side of him that my sisters had seen.

"What are you going to do, Your Highness? Murder me in cold blood? Hide my body in a cell beneath the armory tower, to grow your dark magic, like your master?"

Aspen's grip lessoned, and he pulled away. "That wasn't me."

"And you . . ." Silva moved to stand by me. "I wonder what the queen will say when she finds out you, her sister, are friends with a traitor to the crown." He cocked his head, and I shivered.

This wasn't good.

Silva moved away from the wall and rubbed his throat. "You, Prince Aspen, will help me save my brothers."

Velora hissed and attacked, her hands turning into sharp claws. She raked the air where Silva had been moments ago, but he easily sidestepped her.

"Don't even think of it, big guy," Silva preened, holding a finger up at Marco who moved forward to crush him in a giant bear hug. "I'm not alone." He held up his fingers and blew a sharp whistle.

In the darkness of the alley, shadows appeared all around us—from within the buildings, attic windows, and around the corners. As they moved and looked at us, golden eyes reflected back. We were surrounded by at least twenty shifters.

My anger and disgust were rolled into one big rush of attitude. I couldn't believe I'd thought he was nice. He was going to use me just like Allemar, just like Aspen, just like my mother. I hated being used. I was about to give Silva a very verbal not polite piece of my mind when Aspen did instead.

"Go ahead, you piece of garbage. Then see how far you get with the next test. Because we know who is administering it. It's Maeve's sister, and she is the strongest mind reader ever."

"What?" Silva said.

"You won't stand a chance with her inside of your mind. If you want to pass, then you need to make sure that Maeve is able to weave a shield over your mind."

Aspen was lying, and I wasn't sure to what end.

We weren't sure who was giving the test. It was only a guess. But then again, could Aura handle coming to this large of a crowd? I wasn't sure if her mind was fully intact or healed from the last battle. If she hadn't, she would've probably healed faster if I told her I was alive.

"Is this true? A mind reader?" Silva swallowed, his bravado gone.

"Yes," I nodded emphatically. "No secrets are safe from her."

Silva seemed uncomfortable. He whistled, and the crowd of shifters watching us faded into the background. "Okay, you help me, and I will keep your secrets safe. No one has to know. Deal?" He held out his hand, and I looked at it in disgust. There was no way I was touching his skin again.

"Deal. But stay far away from my family." Aspen shook his hand as he gave his warning.

"I won't touch the royal family as long as *you* help me pass, and you help me break the curse on my brothers." Silva shifted his gaze between me and Aspen.

"I don't mean the royals. I mean them." Aspen thumbed his finger at Velora, Marco and me.

When Aspen made a deal to protect me, a small ember began to ignite and grew anew in my heart. I never thought I would consider this ragtag team of villains to be my family.

"Fine, fine." Silva waved Aspen off. "Just remember your promise."

"Fine," Aspen spit out.

"See you tomorrow." Silva slipped away into the shadows.

"You don't know what kind of promise you just made. We don't know what kind of curse it is. Or what it entails."

"It doesn't matter. If it means I never have to see that snake again, it's worth it."

"Aspen, there's something else," I said.

"What?"

"I haven't told you everything. I didn't think I could trust you because it's obvious you hate the shifters."

"I do."

"Don't interrupt and just listen."

"I'm listening."

And he did. Aspen listened without judgment or interruption as I relayed everything I learned about the missing shifters in the narrows, the suspicious person calling themselves the shifter king, and the strange spell circle on the floor around Torren's body.

"Something was off about it, so I went back in the middle of the night and took another look at it. It's not the same as the one we use for our marks."

"Did you get a good look at it? Can you describe the spell circle?"

"I think so?"

"Show me," he demanded.

Velora and Marco kept watch as I kneeled down on the ground and drew out the shapes I remembered for the spell. "Except this one had been altered and replaced with a sigil like this." I traced out a swirling S.

He kneeled back and shook his head in disbelief. "It can't be. They would have to be crazy."

"What is it?"

Aspen looked uncomfortable. He stood up quickly and scanned the dark streets. "Where did Silva go?"

Velora shrugged her shoulders. Marco pointed toward a side street.

"Aspen, what are you doing? Do you think it's Silva?"

"I have my suspicions, but I won't know until I follow him."

"I can do it." I raised my hand.

He shook his head. "No, I need you to not distract me. Stay with Velora and Marco. If someone is killing shifters, then they could come after you. You, Maeve, are the most special one of them all."

"I don't understand."

Aspen came and gently grasped my shoulders. "Not here. Tonight. I'll come to you and tell you everything I know."

"Promise. No more secrets?" I asked.

He pressed his forehead to mine. "No more secrets." He squeezed my shoulders gently and disappeared into the shadows, hunting Silva.

The rest of the evening should have been spent dancing and celebrating, but instead, I was nervous. I couldn't focus on the music or the people. All I wanted to do was get back to the palace and wait for Aspen to come to me. Velora stopped at a candy vendor, and I sat staring into the window of the shop thinking of what was coming.

In my absentmindedness, I looked up and found myself alone. I had somehow become separated from my group. I tried to search over the heads of passing patrons, but couldn't find them anywhere. Walking past an alley-way, I thought I saw a girl with lavender hair, and I turned down the narrow passageway until it broke off onto another side street. With each turn, I quickly became more lost, and soon I was in a section of town I hadn't yet ventured into. A cloudy mist began to form, and a familiar tang filled the air. I recognized the scent as dark magic.

An ear-piercing scream rent the air. I ran toward the cries and turned a corner to see a cloaked figure attacking a man on the ground.

"Stop, Aspen! Don't," I cried out.

The hooded figure turned toward me, their face cast in shadow. A glint of silver flashed in the night as a knife flew through the air toward my face. I raised my hand to protect myself and turned, the blade slicing my arm.

I gasped and counterattacked. *"Fiergo."*

The fireball was slow to activate, and the figure easily dodged it and disappeared into the night.

A low moan came from the bleeding man. His body was covered with slashes as if a knife had been raked across his body multiple times. Under all the injuries, I recognized Everett. On the ground around him was a spell circle chalked in the stone.

"You're okay, now. I've got you."

Everett looked up at me, his face filled with terror, and he screamed. The loud wail echoed through the streets.

"Everett, settle down, you're safe now."

"Don't kill me. I promise I'll be good."

"Stop yelling, I don't know what you're talking about." He ignored me, and soon I could hear footsteps running toward us.

"Over here!" I called out as I saw the lanterns flicker along the brick walls.

The ground grew warm as the spell circle began to

activate. "No!" I tried to pull him from the circle, but he was too heavy. My arm was bleeding heavily from the knife wound. The mist rose out of the ground, and I cried out in anger. I would not be fast enough.

At the last second, I released his arm and fell back just as Everett was trapped within the spell. The purple mist swirled around him.

"No!" I pounded my fists into the pavement in anger at my uselessness. The mist departed, and Everett lay on the ground as if asleep. I crawled toward him, but he was already gone.

Guards in Florin uniform were the first to arrive. They rushed toward us, but pulled up short when they saw the jagged cuts on Everett and me hunched over his silent, prone body.

"It's you again. Why am I not surprised?" Commander Harn said, his cold eyes staring at me. "Arrest her. Now," he ordered.

"What?" I cried out, not even struggling because I didn't believe what has happening. Did they think I killed him?

"Commander Harn, it's like before. It's happening again."

"Yes, but this time we caught the culprit."

Cold shackles were placed on my wrists.

CHAPTER TWENTY-SEVEN

The air was dank, and the ground was moist from the runoff from the night rain. A chill ran through my body. My dress did little to insulate me, and I was scared to use my magic for fear of the repercussions. I could feel the lack of connection to the ley lines. Like the world was void of color, and I was scared of draining the little magic I had left. So creating a fire was out, breaking the door off was out. But shifting wasn't magic, it was a part of me, and I wasn't worried about escaping. That was never the issue. I could leave at any time. All I had to do was shift into my raven form, slip through the bars, and fly away.

As soon as I started to shift, agonizing pain coursed through my body. I screamed as my bones felt like they were being snapped. My skin burned. The torment was unbearable, and I collapsed to my knees. My mind went blank. Stars flashed across my vision, and I could feel myself begin to pass out from the pain. I laid on the ground, too terrified to move. *Was my body still in a human form? Was I mangled beyond all repair?* Time stood still as I refused to open my eyes to address my own nightmare. When I gathered the courage, I opened my eyes to see that

I was still human. There was no permanent damage, except what I suffered mentally.

What was that? What happened to me? Why hadn't Rosalie come?

Crawling to the bars of the cell, I noticed the scratch marks on the metal frame. Similar to the ones I had seen on the doors in the narrows. On closer inspection, they were another ward. Is this what was keeping me from shifting? I wasn't in the hidden cells in Allemar's old workshop. These were the main prison cells of Florin, and every single one was warded against shifters.

In that moment, I understood the shifters' fear. This is where King Alder sent the shifters to await their execution.

A sharp pain ripped through my chest, and I recognized it as Aspen pulling on our link. We were supposed to meet up. Another tug, this one much harder. It became almost frantic. My heart skipped a beat as it was shocked. I gasped aloud. It didn't let up. Every candle mark he continued to pull on the link, and I had to muffle the cries of pain.

"Stop, Aspen," I murmured to the emptiness surrounding me. "You're killing me." It eventually became more and more tolerable as my mind began to succumb to the numbness. Or I was going mad. Soon, I started to hear voices.

"Is it true?" A voice broke the darkness.

"Is what true?" I sat up and peered at the shape moving toward me.

"That you were at the scene of a candidate's murder?" Rosalie stepped out of the shadows, her face void of emotion. I detected no sympathy behind her eyes.

"Purely by accident," I said. "I had nothing to do with it."

"And it was purely by accident that you were the one who discovered Torren dead?"

"Are you accusing me of murder?" I asked.

"No, we are accusing you of being in league with Allemar." Rhea stepped into the light.

"Rheanon!" I cried out at seeing my sister, her golden hair pulled back away from her face. Her cunning eyes were inspecting me as if seeing me for the first time.

"When did you suspect?" Rhea addressed Rosalie.

"The day she showed up and didn't want to tell anyone she was still alive. She was very protective of Aspen, and if my brother is near, that means Allemar isn't far off. That's why I summoned you."

Rhea nodded coming forward to lean against the bars of my cell, studying me. "Show me your arm." I froze. "Show me," Rhea demanded. "I need to see."

Pulling my sleeve up, I revealed the mark, and the three tattoos.

She inhaled and stepped back, her face one of revulsion. "How could you?"

"Well, let's see," I said sarcastically. "I was almost burned alive, rescued by the enemy, locked in a bird cage in a dark cellar for I don't know how long, unable to shift, and starved until I almost went mad. I would have done anything to get out of there. I tried to wait. Tried to hold off . . . for someone . . . *any* of my sisters to rescue me." I glared at them. "But no one came."

Rhea's shoulders dropped as she heard my accusation, a single tear slid down her face and she kneeled in front of the cell.

"No one cared," I said. "So I did what *I* needed to do to survive."

Rhea's smile felt forced. "I never gave up on you. I never believed you died. But Mother's scrying mirror refused to show you to us."

"That mirror always hated me," I murmured. "Now what do we do? Knowing who and what I am, bound to Allemar."

My sisters gave each other a solemn look, and Rosalie nodded.

"We let you go," Rhea said. Her arm snaked through the cell, and she grabbed my wrist, slapping a familiar magical band on it. Instantly, I felt sick. Like someone hit me in the stomach and sucked all the air out of the room. "Until I can find a way to reverse the bond, I would prefer if you didn't run about the kingdom unchecked."

"What the—" I cried, pulling my wrist away. "What did you do?"

"I bound your powers. My alchemy magic is stronger than anyone else's. There isn't a simple counterspell for this." Rhea looked to Rosalie and gave her a signal. "You can release her. She's harmless. Can't even shift now."

Rosalie reached into a hidden pocket in the folds of her dress and removed a key, which she inserted into the cell's lock. She pushed the door open, freeing me.

Anger raged through me as I stared at the band on my wrist. Once again reminded of the horrible treatment I received at Allemar's hands. "How could you? I'm your *sister*."

"Are you?" Rosalie asked and raised an unbelieving eyebrow at me. "I don't know the sister who stands before me."

"It's me," I said, knowing how pathetic I sounded. "I'm still the same."

"No, the Maeve I knew wouldn't have kept secrets from me. She would have told me I let an enemy into my home."

"Aspen isn't your enemy."

Her head snapped up, eyes wide at my confession. I covered my mouth, realizing my mistake. "So he *is* in the palace? Is he using glamour?"

My silence was enough of an answer.

Her lip quivered. "I'm glad you're alive, Maeve, I really am. But you are too much of an enigma right now. We can't let you leave the palace for you are still under suspicion."

"I didn't kill them. Your death seeker gift should tell you that."

"My powers are unreliable at the moment. So until the baby is born, or until we find the real culprit, you will not leave the palace."

"What?"

"I'm the queen," Rosalie hissed. "You're lucky I'm not leaving you in this cell. You've always been the most dangerous of us. You have the least amount of control. So I will do what I deem necessary for the safety of my people and my family."

I stared at the band on my wrist and my stomach dropped. I wanted to rail about how the treatment was unfair. But it really wasn't. I would do the same if in their shoes.

"You're not a prisoner," Rhea said, trying to lessen the blow of what they had done to me.

"No, I'm just in a bigger cell with fancier food," I snapped. "But for you to bind my shifting abilities as well is just cruel. Now I know why the shifters revolted." My anger simmered just beneath the surface. I could imagine their fear as they cowered in the cells, their hate toward the royal line. It was easy to let it consume me as well.

"What do you want, Maeve? I'm trying to be as kind and forgiving as I can, but it's never enough for you. You always take more than you give."

"Rose," I whispered, instantly feeling the rebuke. Her words hurt. Burned into my heart.

Rosalie let out a long sigh and dropped her head. "Forgive me, I'm sorry. That is unkind of me. I'm under a lot of stress right now with the trials and we have now lost two prominent candidates."

"Shifters," I said, moving out of the cell, crossing my arms over my chest. Rosalie's head snapped up in surprise. "Everett and Torren were both shifters, not humans. I overheard disgruntled candidates talking in the library. They are not happy with the way things are going, or their arrival. It could be one of the human candidates.

"But we don't know for sure?"

I shook my head. "All we know is that they're also using dark magic."

"Which would point to an acolyte of Allemar," Rhea said, being very careful not to look at me when she said it.

"Or someone else," I quickly added.

"Maeve, what do you know? Are we in danger? Is Violet?" Rosalie was shaking.

When I saw her fear, I felt my anger lesson. It was unfair of me to unnecessarily increase the anxiety of losing her child when there was no call for it.

"I don't know. I don't know what Allemar's plan is. I'm not even sure Aspen knows. He's very good at hiding his true intentions, even from his acolytes. I just know that he is always watching us."

"You should have told me," she rebuked.

"I know."

"We could have helped."

"I know," I repeated, once again feeling like I let everyone down. "But so far, we don't know who it is behind the shifter attacks, but I promise I will find them and stop them."

"Will you do everything in your power to find the person responsible?" Rosalie questioned me.

"Yes, I promise."

Rosalie nodded her head. "Then do so, and I will unbind your powers. But one last thing . . ." Her eyes turned to ice. "*You will* stay away from my daughter."

Goosebumps ran up my arm, the air freezing, and my breath released in a white puff. My sister was showing her power; her warning adamant.

My heart dropped as I realized how much I loved Violet. This was almost worse than having my powers bound.

"I understand," I gritted out, my heart slowly breaking into a thousand pieces.

CHAPTER TWENTY-EIGHT

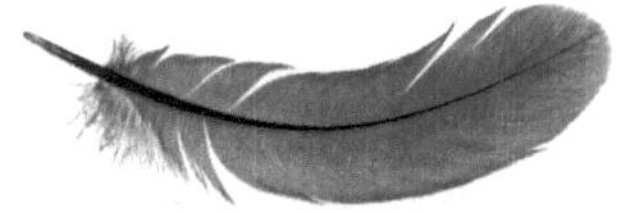

Ipushed the door to my room open and shuffled in. I had been in the cell through the day and well into the next night. In a few hours it would morning, and I had hardly slept from being cold and scared. I made my way across the carpet and collapsed on my bed. The feel of the coverlet was warm against my frozen skin. Once I was there, I inwardly raged against the injustice of it all. Then felt saddened at being cut off from the sweetest and most pure thing in my life. My niece, Violet.

"Where have you been?" an angry voice seethed from the corner of my room. Aspen stepped out of the shadows. "You didn't answer any of my summons."

"I was detained," I grumbled into my pillow.

He stomped across the room, and I stood up to face him, waiting for the angry words to flow. His eyes were a turbulent storm of emotions, and I prepared for the verbal battle that would ensue.

Aspen stopped a foot from me, his eyes searching me from head to toe, taking in my unwashed hair, the dirty dress that I had worn the last time I saw him. His hand lifted toward my face, and I closed my eyes, awaiting the expected slap, but what followed was a caress.

I released the breath I was holding. His hands squeezed my shoulders and his forehead dropped to touch mine. "You're okay. I heard there was another murder, and someone was arrested, but I was told nothing more. When you didn't show up at our appointed meeting, I feared you were dead."

"Why does everyone always think I'm dead?" I shot out. "I'm not dead. I was in a prison cell."

"What?" he said in surprise.

"It was Everett that died." I lifted my head to look at him in confusion. "I thought it was you who killed him. I could smell the magic circle, and I just assumed it was you."

"No. It's not me."

"But then how have you been keeping your powers?" I ran my hand down his arm, lifting the sleeve of his shirt, revealing the newly filled dark marks.

Aspen sighed. "I've been hunting."

I pulled away, but he gripped my shoulders tighter, forcing me to face him.

"No—Maeve, don't reject me." His head lowered. "I've been hunting deer in the woods. It's not as potent, or as powerful, but Allemar hasn't noticed. I bring the meat to the poorest sections of town and distribute it to those in need."

"Why?"

"Maybe because I want another chance to become the person I was meant to be." Aspen's voice became a whisper, his eyes met mine, and I could see the desire within them. "I ran away from everything when I was younger because everything here only reminded me of pain. I was led astray and believed that power would heal me, or at least help me forget. I was wrong. I've seen too much, and I've turned a blind eye to the wrongdoings for so long that I am just as culpable as Allemar."

"There's still time to seek help. My sister, Rhea, is here. She and Rosalie are going to find a way to break the blood bond between us. If anyone can figure it out, she can." I explained what had happened, and how Rhea bound my powers.

Aspen looked angry. He hands dropped, and he stepped away from me. "Rosalie knows I'm here? You told her?"

"I didn't mean to, but yes."

Aspen paced the room, worry on his face. The announcement seemed to disturb him greatly. He turned and faced me. "And is that what you truly want? To be free of me?"

The hurt in his voice was evident. I wanted to scream out, '*Of course not, I want you by my side forever.*' My head and heart were at war with each other, and I wasn't sure who would win if I answered aloud. So I nodded meekly.

"Very well. Then I will do what I can to grant you that one wish." Aspen sounded grim, as though he could see the future and I couldn't. "But I cannot promise you anything else."

He moved to the door, and I must have been insane because I rushed to him, grabbed his shirt, and kissed him. The shock of it had him pulling back in surprise, but then he leaned into it. His strong arms wrapping around me, sealing us closer together. My lips parted, and we deepened our kiss. Desire flooded through me.

Aspen pushed forward, kissing my neck, my chin, my nose, until the backs of my knees hit the bed and I fell backwards onto the mattress. He looked at me and he whispered, "I should go."

"No," I reached for his hand. "Stay near me. I don't want to be alone."

He swallowed and moved to the far side of the bed, keeping a respectable distance. "Just until you fall asleep," he said.

That was not what I had in mind. Somehow the thought of being abandoned while sleeping was worse than him leaving now. "No, you're right. Go."

He reached across the bed, grabbed my hand, and pulled me into his arms, tucking my body against his. "This is very dangerous." His breath was warm against the back of my neck.

"What is?" I asked, happy and content for the moment.

"My feelings for you. I've tried so hard to not have any . . . for so long. Anger has been the only emotion I've known, and then I met you and I don't know what I'm feeling anymore."

I brushed my fingers on his arm that was wrapped around my waist. I felt safe, secure, so I thought it would be the time to tell him how I felt as well.

"I hated you."

I felt his grin against my skin. "I know."

"But then somewhere along the way, my hate turned into something else . . . a fondness, perhaps." I wasn't going to admit to love.

His laughter was short staccato breaths on the back of my neck. "Thanks, I guess I don't despise you either."

I smiled. "Don't get me wrong. This doesn't change anything. I still hate you, but maybe not as much."

"I'll take it." I felt the softest of kisses on the back of my head. "I'm just glad you're not dead."

"Me too," I whispered, and snuggled against his warmth. Soon, my eyes felt heavy, and I fell asleep.

The chilly air woke me. I reached out behind me to feel the coverlet cold and the mattress empty. A torrent of emotions came but were silenced when I heard soft voices from the balcony. Laying perfectly still, I saw Aspen, and he wasn't alone. The wind carried whispered bits of their conversation my way, and what I heard terrified me.

"Don't delay . . . you must keep your promise . . . them killed . . . final trial . . . death . . . or else."

"I promise." Aspen's voice was clipped.

The curtain moved, and a shadow flickered across the stone floor, and the speaker was gone.

Keeping my eyes half closed, I feigned sleep as Aspen let himself out of the room, the door closing with a click. Sitting up, I rushed from my bed to the balcony, and it was empty.

Hurrying across the room, I threw open the door and chased after Aspen, except the halls were empty. Of course he'd gone through another secret passage.

Gritting my teeth, I glanced at the band on my wrist and cursed Rhea and her hand in binding my powers.

"Stars above," I muttered.

After three wrong turns, and waking many servants, I found my way to the right bedroom. I pounded on the door until my fists hurt. When it swung inward, I gazed at Rhea's sleepy face.

"Maeve, do you know what time it is?" she asked.

"Time to save a kingdom." I grabbed her sleeve and pushed her into the room.

CHAPTER TWENTY-NINE

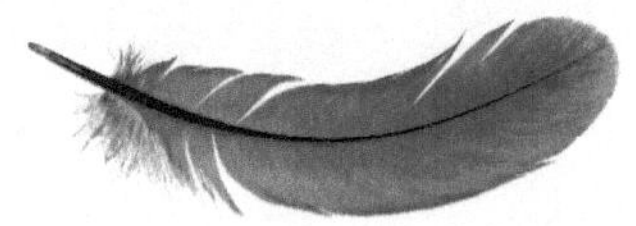

"Stop fidgeting, Rhea. Our plan will work if you don't give it away."

We stood on a balcony overlooking the garden where the final test was about to be underway. To the left of the garden was the entrance to the beautiful domed conservatory. Below us, guards stood off to the side while Commander Harn looked forbidding as ever, guarding King Xander. The last few candidates were meandering in the outdoor garden by the fountain, most clustered together in groups of two or three. Aspen, as always, stood apart from the rest. Thinking about it, it was probably because he was in glamour and didn't want anyone to suspect. When I glanced at him, I immediately thought of our kiss, and how he was scared to think I'd been hurt. Then those kind feelings turned toward anger knowing that he was on the verge of betraying us all.

"I can't take this. Are you sure this will work?" Rhea blurted out nervously.

"No, but that's the case with all plans. There's always a small chance of failure."

Hela and Silva made their way to each other, and she leaned in as he whispered in her ear. Hela's head fell back in a laugh, a blush rushing to her cheeks. Silva looked up at me and gave me a thumbs up, confident that he would pass the last test. I glanced away, angry that I had felt anything toward him.

Warden reclined on the stone bench, his eyes closed as if he was soaking up the sun. From a distance, I could almost see the sun sparkle on his skin. Cross sat in the shade of a sycamore tree.

Rhea looked queasy. "That is not the kind of reassurance I need. If only Aura were here."

"No," I said firmly. "There's too much death in this kingdom. She's still very fragile after what happened at Rya. You have to play her part."

Rhea nodded.

I softened my voice. "How is she, really? You said she's okay."

"She is, but she's different. Liam is helping her recover and heal. He turned down the kingship." Rhea's hands clasped together, and I saw the barest tremor. She always looked calm and in control whenever she was holding a beaker, book, or magic charm. But today, as she stood on the stage in a soft butter-yellow dress wearing a glamour to appear like my older sister, Aura, she seemed unsure. She patted her pocket where she had tucked Aura's spindle, the personal item she was using to keep her glamour. The wind tugged at her white-blonde hair, showing off her soft blue eyes. It was weird to see Rhea's mannerisms across Aura's face.

Rhea stifled a yawn.

"Stop that," I chastised.

"Sorry, but I was up most of the night working on the glamour charm you asked for. I'm beat. Wait—" She reached into her satchel and pulled out a small yellow stone. Giving it a squeeze, it glowed softly, reflecting a gold hue on her face. She sighed and gave me a big smile; one of Aura's smiles.

"What was that?"

"An energy charm." She grinned. "Here." She placed it in my palm and closed my fingers around it. Immediately, I felt alive, rejuvenated, like I could run for hours.

A trumpet pealed out as King Xander took to the stage, Rosalie and Violet nowhere in sight. I breathed a sigh of relief knowing that they were at least doing their part and staying out of the way.

Below us, the candidates stood facing the stage.

"Here we go. You can do it, Maeve." Rhea patted my shoulder.

She had all the confidence in me, but I was sorely lacking. I was about to find out if my stupid plan would work, or if I was wrong. We stepped inside the study and closed the doors. Rhea pulled out a lock of Everett's brown hair and wrapped it around a charmed string, tucking it into my skirt pocket.

I instantly felt the glamour settle over my body. My hands tingled, and when I held them out, they were larger and calloused. Looking in the mirror, Everett's angular chin was prominent, and his deep blue eyes stared back at me.

"My charm is as strong as any glamour spell you would weave. Just don't lose it and you'll be fine."

"Okay." It was weird to rely on a charm for a glamour rather than my own magic. I would have to trust her. "I just hope I'm right about all of this."

"You said the guards never released the information of *who* was killed, only that it was a shifter."

"Yes. Only the murderer would know his identity."

"Are you armed?" Rhea asked.

I nodded, patting the dagger Aspen gave me. "I'd be better armed if I had my magic."

Rhea grimaced and cast her gaze toward the flower conservatory. "Better not. It's going to be dangerous if you lose control in such a confined area. I'll be here monitoring everything through the mirror." She held up the handheld mirror and gave me a wink. With all the reflective surfaces inside the conservatory, she'd have eyes everywhere. "I'll step in and neutralize any threats, plus I gave you a few extra charms."

"Gee, thanks," I grumbled, tapping the truth charms in my pockets.

Heading down the stairs, I followed a short hall and stepped out into the garden behind Cross. Taking a deep breath, I stepped into view.

"Hey Everett, you're late!" Warden turned and gave me a nudge. "You sly jackal. Scouting out the gardens, were you?"

I nodded, too scared to talk.

Hela smirked when she saw me, placing a hand on my chest. "I was wondering where you went off to." Hela's voice dropped low into a seductive purr. "I missed you last night. It's not nice to keep a lady waiting." She made a show of adjusting the cravat on my neck, her fingernail trailing along under my chin. "I can't wait until we can be alone together again." Her lips made the slightest of pouts, and I felt extremely uncomfortable, having forgotten that they were a couple.

"Later, I promise," I said, trying to sound like Everett.

She made a huff and turned to saunter back toward Cross who watched our whole exchange with interest.

Silva was taking a sip of wine out of a glass and raised it in a toast toward Aspen who glowered in return, and I saw a slight nod. I turned my attention back to King Xander.

Rhea—in Aura's glamour—took a different set of stairs and came out by a side door near the stage. Commander Harn gave her his arm and escorted her up the steps, and she stood next to Xander. Her face calm; eyes calculating.

I groaned. Aura would never look that fierce. She'd be on the verge of tears. But since no one here had met Aura . . . *wait*. Aspen had met her.

Aspen was staring at Aura hard. His brows knitted together, causing him to look suspicious.

Oh, please, oh please, just let this work.

"I would like to introduce to you, Aura Eville. She will be the one doing the final exam, and as you may have heard, she has a very unique set of talents." King Xander smiled.

Hushed whispers followed as a few turned to each other and nodded. "Your test will take place within our flower conservatory." He pointed to the glass dome hothouse that looked like a mini-forest grew within. "Aura has hidden six stones. To win, all you have to do is find one."

"That's it?" Warden said. "Sounds easy enough."

"True, but by collecting it, the first person to touch one will be forced to reveal their deepest secret."

"That's a bit unorthodox," a man named Caven called out.

"I've got nothing to hide. Let's do it," Warden called out. The snake shifter seemed thrilled at the idea, and he shot Hela a smirk.

A few of the candidates seemed far more uneasy at the prospect, Aspen being one of them. He gave Silva a suspicious look. Cross and Hela didn't show any reactions. Brekken just looked as scared as always.

"Are there any rules as to how we go about collecting them?" Aspen asked.

Xander glanced to Aura. "Good question. However you choose to search will be up to you. Just know we can't see inside the dome. Only when all six are collected will the doors open, and then whoever is holding a stone is one of the chosen."

Lies. I knew we would be watched by Rhea, Xander, and Rosalie. He may have said the doors would open when the stones were collected, but he failed to explain we would be *locked* inside. All of us were to fend for ourselves.

My fingers trembled as I ran my hand over the band on my wrist. I would have to rely on my wit and my knife to unearth the culprit.

"With that out of the way, let's begin," Xander announced. The glass doors swung outward, and the final candidates headed into the dome. In the center of the flower conservatory was a great tree, its branches twisted upon itself. It was likely one of the oldest trees in the kingdom. The conservatory was close to a quarter mile in diameter. Large hedge rows, tall grasses, and trees made for many excellent prospective places to hide the stones. A natural stream filled with river rock passed through, and a bridge crossed the stream, signaling the beginning of the many forked paths. It would be very easy to get lost within.

As Aspen passed an imperial rose bush, I couldn't help but notice the vines reached out to him. He gave it a wide birth and moved to stand on the opposite side of the plant. Commander Harn was the last one in, and he closed the doors behind him. He crossed his hands over his chest to make sure that no one left before the stones were found.

"You may begin," Commander Harn yelled.

Everyone scattered, running down the small trails, weaving between the different flower beds. Cross pointed to Hela, and they took off running toward the great tree. It's exactly where I would have searched first as well.

Instead, I took off after Aspen. Keeping a safe distance, I trailed him as he took a path that looked like it led away from the rest of the group, but quickly circled back and brought him to an intricate collection of statues. The woman with the bowl, the same one I sat next to with Silva.

Aspen dug around the statues and kneeled, picking something up with a piece of cloth. He stood and tucked what he found in his pocket.

"You can stop following me." Aspen's voice cut through the heat of the dome. "I know you're there, Maeve."

I cussed under my breath and stood up. His eyes widened, and he snorted when he saw Everett standing before him. "Well, I have to say that's *not* an improvement. But you should know better than to hide from me."

"Why?" I accused him, not falling for his charm. "Why are you working with him?"

"Who?"

"Oh, you know exactly what I mean. I heard you last

night at the window. You are planning to kill people at the trial."

His lips parted, and I heard his intake of breath. "It's not what it sounds like."

"That's exactly what it sounds like."

"No, you have to trust me."

"I don't," I snapped. "That's the problem, and I realize I never should have trusted you."

Grass shifted by my feet, and I froze as a wolf pup ran out of the bushes and practically tried to climb up my leg in terror, her claws scratching at my legs. Violet was able to recognize my scent despite my glamour.

"What's the princess doing here?" Aspen's voice sounded panicked, but he made no move toward her.

"I don't know. I thought she was with Rosalie." Leaning down, I picked up a shaking Violet. "She's scared. I should take her—"

Aspen cocked his head and held up his hand silencing me. "Quick. Hide."

My choices were limited. I took Violet, and we ducked into the tall grass, squatting low, but I was still able to hear what was going on.

Aspen called out. "I'm here, just like you asked."

Silva stepped onto the path, his gold eyes beaming. "I can't get one over on the prince."

"What do you want?" Aspen sounded annoyed.

"You know what I want. I told you last night." Silva sighed dramatically. "I think I've waited long enough."

"I found a stone!" Caven called out excitedly from nearby, interrupting them both. His voice immediately turned to one of regret. "Wait, what, no. I didn't mean to betray you. Oh stars, no!"

The hair on my arms rose as I heard his remorse. I could only imagine the repercussions he was dealing with from Rhea's alchemy magic.

Seconds later, I heard a bloodcurdling scream.

That *was not* Rhea's magic.

Silva's face paled.

Aspen turned. Sweat was dripping down his back, his lips pressed into a thin line, and I saw him debate going to help or continuing on with his task. Both of them chose to race toward the scream. Still keeping my distance, I watched as Aspen almost tripped over the body.

Caven was dead in a spell circle, his chest slashed open, the faint purple mist still hung in the air. The stone was gone.

That was not what I was suspecting to happen. Not here. I knew that we were trying to lay a trap, but not at the cost of innocents.

"Did you do this?" Aspen sneered, pointing at the body.

"You know I didn't. I was with you when it happened," Silva answered.

"I mean *your kind.*"

Stepping out of the brushes, I confronted Aspen, Violet still in my arms. "What do you mean his kind? What did you find out?" I said.

Silva gave me a curious stare, unable to figure out what was wrong with my voice.

Aspen kneeled by the path, the spell still faint in the dirt. "It's as I feared. The last sigil in the spell. I know what it does. Someone is killing shifters to steal their abilities."

"But Allemar said it doesn't work. Humans can't become shifters. They go mad, like Gaven and his bracken-beast," I said, referring to the time Xander and Rosalie had battled, Gaven, Allemar, and Aspen.

Silva grew quiet.

"Right, it doesn't work. A *human* can't become a true shifter because their body and mind can't handle it. But a shifter trained in dark magic can steal the powers of another shifter," Aspen said. "Especially if Allemar trained them."

"You mean he has more than two acolytes?" I gasped in surprise.

"He has many," Silva said furtively, his face filled with guilt.

"You!" I hissed out. "Why would you do such a thing?"

Aspen grasped Silva's arm and rolled up the sleeve to reveal an arm empty of marks. "You're not a true acolyte."

Silva shook his head. "No, I don't know anything about dark magic. He trapped me and my six brothers long ago. He didn't have any use for us as shifters. He said we were too weak. But he placed a curse on them, and we've been forced to be his spies across the seven kingdoms."

"What about the wards on the narrows?" I asked.

"It was my job to lure the strongest shifters out of the safety of the wards under the guise of the shifter king." Silva looked saddened by his admission.

"But you said they couldn't leave. Why take them out?"

"Magic doesn't work within the wards." He showed us the silver band on his ankle. "It allowed me to enter the warded narrows to come and go as I pleased. If I touched them as we crossed the wards, they could leave the narrows. I lured them out while another person wove the trap spell."

"Who is it?" I ground out, my grip tightening on Violet who sensed my anger. She growled out as well.

"I don't know. I just know it's another shifter." He looked up, his eyes pleading with us to believe him.

"Why would they do that?" I asked.

"To become a stronger shifter," Silva answered, his face pale and filled with guilt. "Or to become the shifter king. I only did it because Allemar trapped my brothers. He holds their lives in his hands. Please believe me."

"So that means whoever killed Torren stole his ability to shift into a bear?" Aspen asked.

Silva counted off his fingers. "And Caven's hawk."

"Hawk?" I turned to look at the man on the ground.

"He pretended to be a human. Hated his own kind. He even tried to help the others sabotage the shifters in the trials. He won't be missed."

I pursed my lips as I put together that he was the one I had overheard in the library.

"Also Everett's jackal," I added.

"What?" Silva seemed surprised and gave me a curious look, but neither Aspen nor I explained what Everett was doing standing with them.

"Help me find the other acolyte, and I will break the curse on you and your brothers." Aspen turned and held out his hand to Silva.

Silva nodded his head. He gave a neat bow. "I take you at your oath, my prince."

"Maeve, get Violet out of here," Aspen commanded.

Silva's head turned in surprise. "That's Maeve—" He would have said more, but Aspen's hand gripped his arm and pulled him away.

They took off down the path, hunting another of Allemar's apprentices.

Violet gnawed on my thumb, and I winced. "Your mother is going to kill me when she finds out you snuck in. I have to get you out and get help." Tucking her under my arm, I raced for the unguarded double doors, wondering where Commander Harn had run off to. I grabbed the handle, and it didn't turn. I could see Rhea, Xander, and Rosalie in a frantic discussion.

Something was wrong. She was pointing to the mirror and shaking her head. It seemed that the magic spell wasn't working, and they were blind to what was happening within the conservatory.

Violet was getting heavy in my arms, and I pounded the glass with my free hand to get the attention of the guards outside the conservatory.

They turned toward me, and I held Violet up to the glass window.

Rosalie's face paled, her voice muffled even as she yelled, "What are you doing with my daughter? Open the door, get my daughter out of there!"

Rhea tried to shush Rosalie. "It's okay. That's Maeve in glamour." She reached for the door handle, and it didn't turn. She frowned. "It's locked."

"Unlock it!" Xander commanded.

Rhea panicked. "I did. It won't open."

"Break it down," Xander yelled.

Violet whimpered in my arms as guards used one of the heavy stone benches to try and break in the glass door. When the bench hit the wall, a spark of green light reflected back at them, and they were knocked unconscious.

Rhea frowned. "Someone placed a ward from within, sealing them inside. They're trapped until that person releases the spell." She did a test on the glass and shook her head.

Rosalie pressed her hands against the glass, her frantic breath causing it to steam up. She tapped the glass hard, pointing to me and her daughter. "Maeve. You protect her! Do you hear me?"

"I will. But I need help. The killer is a shapeshifter, and an acolyte of Allemar. I can't do this on my own."

Rhea nodded to Rosalie. "Go ahead, tell her."

Rosalie looked ashamed. "I lied. Your powers aren't bound. Rhea just placed a nausea charm on the band to make you feel sick if you used your powers. Like we did as kids."

"What?" I gasped, shifting Violet in my arms. She whined again, wanting to go to her mom.

Rosalie's hand covered her face in remorse. "We just did it so you wouldn't try anything stupid. But right now, we need you. *I* need you to protect my daughter. Do whatever you can. Use whatever power you have within you to protect her. You're the only one who can."

Rhea put her hand on the glass. "This isn't good, Maeve. You can't use magic without thinking. You are in a sealed dome. Using magic will be extremely dangerous. Be careful."

I nodded numbly and looked around at the conservatory, seeing it for the giant trap it was. If I lost control in here, we'd all die. Violet wiggled in my arms, and I put her down. "Stay close to me. You hear?"

She yipped in response.

Heading back into the maze of flowers, I felt more

confident knowing that my powers weren't truly bound. Except I didn't know who my enemy was . . . or did I?

I paused on the path and tried to think through all of the shifters. One of them was a killer. I never knew Caven was a shifter. Aspen didn't either. That was a surprise to both of us, so that left Brekken, Cross, Hela, and Warden. One of them was the murderer. I thought through conversations. Our carriage ride.

Stupid! I hit myself in the forehead. They gave it away. If only I would have caught it sooner. I picked up my pace, running and searching the conservatory.

Sweat trickled down my back, and I heard someone speaking up ahead of me. Walking into the path, I stumbled upon Hela with Cross. His head was in her lap, and she was rocking him softly as if he was asleep. I could smell the scent of magic in the air.

Hela slowly ran her hands through his long red hair, her hand reaching for the pocket in her skirt.

I tucked Violet into the bushes and motioned for her to lay low.

"Get away from him," I snapped, stepping into the open.

Hela froze, her face crumpled, and she released a loud sob. "He needs my help."

I glared at Hela. "He doesn't need a knife in his heart."

Her features changed. "I know you're not Everett," Hela snarled. "Who are you?"

I tugged the braided hair and the charm from my pocket, tossing it aside. The world shifted before settling into a stable view, and I knew my glamour was gone.

"You?" Hela's eyes glittered dangerously, and a smile spread across her lips. "You're smarter than you look."

"You gave yourself up. Allemar wouldn't be pleased."

"I did?" She frowned.

"In the carriage to town, you said you would kill anyone who tried to stab you through the heart. But the only person that knew the details of Torren's death were a select few, and the killer."

She smirked and clapped her hands. "Good for you, but you didn't catch all of it."

"It was you I saw backing out of the room in the guise of a servant. I just don't understand why you screamed. You could have left without anyone knowing any better."

"Oh, could I? But that wasn't his plan. It wasn't about me or the shifters, but you. We wanted to frame you for the murder of the shifters. Start another war."

Hela stood up, being careful to step over Cross's prone form. "Once I kill you and finish off Cross, I will have nine forms." She sounded a little mad, which reminded me of . . . me.

"Why are *you* doing this?" Reaching into my pocket, I pulled one of the charms out of the bag and tossed it at Hela. With catlike reflexes, she caught it and the truth immediately spilled out of her lips.

"Their sacrifice will aid me in my quest to become the strongest shifter, and when I do, I will be the new shifter king, and all will bow to me." She blinked, and her lovely face looked around in confusion. "What just happened?"

"Congratulations, you caught a truth stone," I said dryly.

Hela stared at the charm and shook her head. She pulled up the sleeves of her arms revealing the blood tattoos, and they glowed as she began to shift. Below me, I could see the spell circle already hidden in the stone.

I heard the slapping of boots as Aspen and Silva came over the path. They froze when they saw what moved out of the mist.

"Maeve!" Aspen cried

A great bear loomed over me. I froze as its gaping maw opened, and a roar echoed in the dome. The bear swung at me, and I shifted into a raven, flapping out of reach just as its mighty paw nicked my tail feathers. I flew straight up toward the ceiling, out of reach as the bear turned to attack Aspen. He rolled out of the way and quickly conjured a spell.

Kraa! I cried, but I couldn't warn him.

A fireball burst forth. Hela dropped to all fours, and the spell hit the warded glass wall of the dome, ricocheting upward toward the ceiling, bouncing off and hitting a tree. It exploded, and flames fell down around us while a dozen other little fires flickered to life.

Hela roared and charged Aspen. I dove straight for her left eye, scratching and flapping my wings, trying to distract her.

I didn't see the black paw until it was too late.

"Maeve!" Aspen called my name. I blinked but could barely see what was going on. "Are you okay?"

My body hurt, but I didn't think it was broken. Across the way, I could hear Hela roaring furiously. Smoke rose from the fires that were quickly spreading along the bushes. I shifted back into my human form, but I was unable to get off the ground. I laid gasping for breath, part of my body on the path, partly in a flower bed.

Hela snarled, spit dripping down her jaw. She roared in pain as a lion launched onto her back, clawing and biting at her neck.

The bear rose up and knocked the lion down, his head cracked against one of the statues and he didn't move. Aspen started to conjure another spell.

"Stop! You can't use magic. It's too dangerous," I said. I tried to think quickly, worried that Cross was going to be killed.

Silva appeared at Aspens' side. "If anything happens to me, promise you'll keep your word and free my brothers."

Aspen glanced down at me, then over his shoulder at the bear that was about to kill Cross. "If I survive this fight, I promise to find a way to free them."

"Thank you, my friend. I will be in your debt forever." Silva bowed before turning to face the bear. "And I'm no longer afraid." He tilted his head back and closed his eyes as I got to experience the pure joy across his face as he shifted into his true form.

"So beautiful," I gasped. Tears filled my eyes as I beheld a black swan, realizing I had seen him before, swimming in the lake by the cottage. Silva's glorious neck shook as he took off into the sky.

Honk!

Silva dove in front of the stirring lion, rising up, his black wings held wide, and he flapped in front of the bear, trying to be as distracting as possible.

"Silva! I cried, tears pouring from my eyes. I saw the bear lunge, biting the swan in the neck. I heard his strangled cry as Hela swung him to the side, flinging him away from her. The swan fell to the ground and didn't move.

"Silva!" Anger coursed through me, and I grabbed my dagger, ready to fight the bear head-on.

Cross slowly got up, saw Silva's prone body, and then bared his teeth. Digging his claws into the dirt, he attacked with a renewed vigor.

Aspen grasped my shoulders and gave them a hard squeeze. "Maeve, listen to me. I have to tell you what I know before it's too late."

I struggled to focus as I watched Cross attack Hela. The air was getting thick with smoke as it filled the conservatory. Cross pinned Hela, his teeth buried into the bear's throat. With a shift of magic, Hela turned into a jackal, surprising Cross and slipping from his mouth before she shifted back into a cougar. She used her powerful back legs to scratch at his stomach and kick him away.

Two powerful cats screamed in challenge at each other.

"You're an omni."

I blinked and stared into Aspen's hazel eyes. "How can that be?"

"It's why you have more than one form."

"No, that's not possible. It's because I'm a sorceress."

"No, like a hive that can only have one queen, there's only ever one omni in a generation. Maeve, that makes you the shifter king. You have access to all their forms."

"But Mother would have told me."

Aspen smirked. "Really? What would you have done if you knew you had that kind of shifting power? You would have been a nightmare growing up."

"You're right." A sly grin crossed my face. I was a force to be reckoned with just as a bird. What would have happened if I had shifted into dangerous predators whenever I was mad?

I had never tried to shift into another form that wasn't a bird. How could that help me now?

Commander Harn stepped from behind a burning tree. "What have we here?"

Using the sleeve of my dress, I tried to cover my mouth. "Commander Harn, we have to open the doors. Princess Violet is trapped inside." I coughed again.

"The princess is here?" Harn looked around, suddenly excited. "What a pleasant turn of events."

"That's not the Commander," Aspen coughed. "It's Allemar."

"You knew?" I turned to him.

His head dropped. "I knew he was involved but didn't know what mask he chose to hide behind."

"I'm disappointed in you, Aspen." Allemar dropped his glamour. "You didn't train her to be loyal. Get rid of her."

"No."

"No," Allemar choked out laughing. "You *dare* to defy me. I saved you. I took a frightened little boy and made you who you are. You are *nothing* without me."

"Yes, I didn't know any better. For years, I was lost and confused, looking for direction, but now," Aspen looked toward me and gave me a smile, "I think I've found my compass."

"How touching, and just when I thought we were finally getting somewhere. It seems you are no longer useful."

Allemar raised his hand and yanked on the bond between them.

Aspen gasped aloud, falling to his knees, clutching his chest. "Run, Maeve!"

"No!" I screamed. Aspen was dying before my eyes and my niece was trapped.

I gasped as Aspen's pain tore through to me, unable to breathe, my lungs struggling for air, my heart beating wildly. I could feel Allemar reaching through his apprentice to kill me too, but Aspen was blocking the link as much as possible. My blood pounded in my ears, and I fell face first to the ground. My hand splayed out, and I saw the mark fading, my vision going black.

Aspen tried to crawl to me, blood pouring from his mouth. "I'm sorry I failed you. I wasn't brave enough to break our bond." He stumbled and fell on the ground next to me. His breath was weak, but I could feel the warmth of it brushing across my cheek. "This is my fault."

"No," I whispered.

"I won't fail you now. It's the only way. Know that . . . I love you," Aspen gasped out, his eyes filling with tears. A flash of silver appeared in his hand, and he plunged the dagger into his chest.

The stabbing pain was mirrored in my body.

I screamed as I felt the bond sever between us. Like a reversed suction, all of the sound and color came flooding back to me as my connection to the ley lines was restored.

A sacrifice. A sacrifice to complete the bond . . . would mean a sacrifice to break it. Now I understood why Aspen couldn't release me. It meant one of us had to die.

The pain in my chest passed, but the numbness didn't abate. Tears of grief made seeing difficult. I pushed myself to my knees.

Allemar stood still, his face full of surprise. "Well, that was unexpected. Never thought he would ever care about anyone enough to do that."

"Then you really underestimated him . . . and me." I wiped Aspen's blood from my face and stumbled to feet. Trying not to look at his still form.

"No, I always knew he was weak. Unlike you. I know the rage that burns deep within you. The hatred that you can't quite control. I know you. Know your darkest fears. Don't be weak like him, Maeve. Join me. He was right. You are *the* omni. You can control all of them."

"Then why did you corrupt Hela? What was the point of teaching her the forbidden magic if you had me?"

He smirked. "You think I'd only settle for one? That you're enough for my plans? Of course, I want more omnis. I just had to find shifters who had no qualms about killing their own kind. I made a mistake trusting Aspen with your training. He failed me."

A cry of duress caught my attention, and I saw Violet backed into a corner, her small teeth bared as she tried to show her strength and intimidation against the much larger cougar. Cross was defeated, his body lay in a pool of blood, and Hela had turned toward the young princess.

With my connection to my magic fully restored, I reached through my powers and tried to find them—the shifters. I felt their heartbeats within my soul. I felt a connection, not just to the earth, but to every shifter in the kingdom. I knew that Silva was at the end of his life. Cross's heart rate was erratic and struggling. Reaching deep into the ground, I poured earth magic into Cross and Silva, healing their wounds, giving them my strength. But I had to do it without alerting Allemar.

"You should know by now, I always have plenty of apprentices willing to do my bidding." Allemar made the smallest of gestures, and I turned, seeing the cougar move to attack Violet.

An animal rushed out of the grass and blocked Hela's path to the cub. A low protective growl came from Brekken's throat as the much smaller fox dared to take on the larger, deadlier cougar.

"Brekken," I breathed out, knowing how hard it was for the small shifter to face his fears. Brekken bared his teeth, his body low to the ground. When the cougar tried to go around him, he snapped and lunged before dancing back and away from the cat. He lunged again, trying to draw the cougar away from Violet.

It almost worked. "Kill it already," Allemar yelled.

Hela turned her head, distracted for a moment.

Brekken attacked, but Hela was faster. She swatted him to the ground, and he cried out in pain.

Violet collapsed on the ground, her small chest barely moving as she struggled to breathe through the smoke.

I felt another shifter connect with mind; heard the question in my head, asking permission.

"Do it," I commanded.

A white asp sprung out of the grass and bit the cougar in the foot. Hela yelped and turned to snap at its neck, but the snake was too fast. Warden in his true form was brilliant, a pristine white, his hood flared as he attacked again and again, his poisonous strike true. Hela whimpered and backed away as she shifted into a hawk and took to the air.

Warden coiled into a ball, his head pulled back and ready to strike the hawk as she circled the glass ceiling preparing to come down on him.

"It seems that you have achieved what I could not," Allemar sneered. "You can control the shifters."

"I don't control them. I ask them. Now, release the ward on the doors," I said to Allemar. "And I may let you live."

He scoffed. "I don't answer to you."

My smile grew wider. "Just kidding. I really don't care if you live."

"I don't die easily girl."

"Neither do I."

I closed my eyes and reached back through the shifter lineage. Searching for the first one, the eldest one. Like when I touched the statue and felt the history of the shifters; when I touched their minds, I could find our ancestry.

There was one particular creature I was looking for,

one that I dreamed of, knew was in my blood—and then I found it. Grasped it. Called it to me.

The confident smile on Allemar's face fell as great wings sprouted from my back. My body and neck grew long, scales appeared across my body, and my belly burned with rage. I knew she was in here. The fire within me had to come from somewhere. My spells often took on her shape, calling to her when I didn't even know it.

My dragon.

My wings spread and I beat at the air.

Hela, as a hawk, dove for Warden and I intercepted her. With strong powerful claws, I grabbed her midair and felt her struggle to escape. Shifting into a bear, then a cougar, and a jackal. One form after another, none saving her from the strength of my grasp.

Her heart pounded frantically. I could feel the poison of Warden's bite take effect. While in my hand, the poison slowed her heart, paralyzed her lungs, and she died in my palm. I laid her on the ground and turned to confront Allemar.

"Release the ward," I breathed out, my jaws snapping within an inch of Allemar's body, causing him to fall backward.

"I will teach you to challenge me. You are no match for my strength." His face curled into an evil grin, and his robes billowed as he gathered power for a killing spell.

Cross was rushing back and forth, trying to drag Silva toward the stream to escape the heat. Warden took cover underground. Brekken tried to reach Violet, but a flaming branch fell, cutting off his path. The fox was trying to get through the flames, and he yelped frantically when he couldn't reach her. Cross gripped him by the neck and pulled him into the stream.

I needed to get to Violet. This had to end now.

My eyes flickered once to Aspen, his body surrounded by a pool of blood.

Rage built up within me and I wanted to reach for my power and destroy Allemar. Send a scorching mage fire at him, rip him to shreds, make him feel the pain he'd caused me. I shook my head and remembered the last time I summoned too much power and lost control.

Stay calm, I told myself. *You can do this. Outthink him.* My claws dug into the ground, and I gritted my teeth and watched him through narrowed eyes.

Something was wrong. Allemar staggered and grasped for his chest, his eyes wide with disbelief. His mouth turned down in an ugly snarl as he screamed into the air, "How dare you try to steal from me?"

His incoherent shouting confused me, and I moved in front of Aspen's body as an ice spear blasted from Allemar's hands, cutting through the air. I recoiled, my wings pulling up to protect my chest. The spear pierced my right wing and I roared. Despite the pain, I shook my wing causing the ice spear to crack and crumble. My confidence wavered as I was once again surrounded by fire, injured, and trapped.

"You're not much of a sorcerer," Allemar taunted. A black shadowy orb formed in his hands. If I could sweat, I would have as I saw the depths of the life-sucking spell he was creating.

"And you're not much of a man," I hissed.

I watched his eyes, looking for the tell of where he was aiming. His gaze betrayed him as they strayed toward

Aspen and my niece and I panicked. *Don't you dare harm her!*

He snarled and hurled the magic not my way, but toward Violet. Faster than I have ever moved before, I flung myself in its direct path, taking the full brunt of his deadly spell. The impact stung, and I grimaced. This was the end . . . and then it wasn't. His spell deflected off my dragon scales' magic, then ricocheted and hit the dome. Just as it had before, the warded glass sent it right back. I turned, raising my wings to take cover

Allemar's grinning face dropped to one of panic and fear. He raised his hands to stop it, but it was no use. The spell hit him in the chest and he gasped. His mouth gaped open and a low rasp escaped his lips as he fell to his knees.

"No," he wheezed out. "No more. It . . .hurts." Allemar raised his hand in supplication, reaching out toward me for help. "I can't . . . make it stop," he begged. I didn't know what kind of spell he had cast or what he was hallucinating, but I knew he'd intended on using it to kill me.

The color continued to drain from his skin, leaving him to resemble an ashen-like corpse. The last words he breathed out were to his acolyte. "Aspen . . . I always thought of you . . . like a son," Allemar groaned. He fell forward and collapsed into the stream. His body slowly disintegrated into ash, washing away as the water rushed over him.

The fire burned hotter and faster. The ward was down, but we needed air. Violet didn't appear to be breathing, and the shifters were passed out on the banks of the stream. I had to get rid of the smoke and get air to them. I didn't know a spell for that. I couldn't think. I panicked.

With a mighty cry, my wings pinned to my side, I

launched straight up into the air, crashing through the glass ceiling, and soaring into the sky . . . forgetting about the dangerous glass shards that would rain down on my unconscious niece.

No! I'd made a grave error. I dove back down but was too late. Clouds of smoke blocked my view, flames rose toward the dome ceiling. I couldn't fit through the hole I created without bringing more of the glass down around them. I roared in distress, trying to stand on the dome, but my weight broke off another piece in my claw, and more glass rained down on those inside.

Rosalie's magic coated the dome, smothering the fire until nothing but the smoke remained. It slowly cleared, and when it did, I saw the damage I had caused.

Glittering and beautiful, the glass had fallen like snow covering Aspen's body.

Rosalie and Xander rushed through the ash and glass, stopping beside Aspen.

Great sobs racked Rosalie, and I heard her heart-breaking cry as she pulled her daughter's limp body out from under Aspen's still form. Using my shifter senses, I tried to reach Violet.

But I couldn't hear her heartbeat.

NOOOO! I shot into the sky, letting my grief burn a way for me as I torched the sky.

CHAPTER THIRTY-ONE

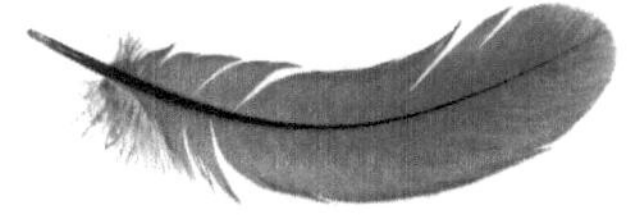

I was in the depths of despair, but yet found comfort in the hatred I had toward myself. I lost control. Once again acted without thinking, and others paid the price. My dragon body slept in a cave hidden within the mountains. My dreams were chaotic. My mind spun, full of fanciful wishes that always turned toward fire . . . and death. They always returned to death. Even in my dreams, I slept on a pile of bones and ashes.

Aspen.

Oh, my heart was breaking. What I wouldn't give to have him spitefully yank on our bond, tugging painfully at my heart.

Violet.

Guilt racked my body, and I fitfully sobbed at the innocent death of a child.

Silva, Torren, Everett all dead because of me. No, it was better if I stayed in this form and slept for a millennium. Maybe then the world will have righted itself again. My turbulent thoughts continued to ramble. My anger vented in a mist of steam that continued to surround the mountains, hiding me from all who hunted me.

"Get out of the cave," a familiar voice commanded. "I know you're in there, Maeve. I can hear your thoughts."

Then go away, I mentally shouted.

"Not going to happen. I tracked you all the way to this mountain range. I won't let you hide from your mistakes."

Hate you!

Aura sighed. "I know. I kind of hate myself. I've been where you are, Maeve. So wrapped up in my own guilt that I shut myself away. Hid from the pain of what I'd done. It was easier to be angry and feel nothing than to face my past. It was that mistake that kept me from searching for you. Maybe if I had, I would have found you sooner. Allemar would never have captured you, and we wouldn't be where we are today. So if anyone should feel guilty, it's me."

My anger dissipated as I imagined Aura, sweet Aura, carrying the burden of my death.

"Can you ever . . . ever find it in your heart to forgive me?" Aura yelled into the cave.

As much as I hated her for not searching for me, I finally understood. We were the same. I sent a soft thought of love toward her, then quickly retreated behind my walls.

"Good, now can you forgive yourself?" Aura called down.

NO! I released an angry breath, steam rose and shot out of the cave.

Aspen, Violet, dead. Their bodies lying there covered in glass and blood flashed across my mind.

Aura gasped as she caught my thoughts. "I see. Well, maybe you need to get your dragon butt out of the cave and tell me in person, you big coward."

When had Aura learned to get a backbone? I raised my dragon head and sniffed the air, contemplating sending a fireball toward the entrance. I could imagine her running for cover, but the thought quickly dissipated when I heard it. A soft whine. A wolf pup.

Violet?

"Don't know. You need to see for yourself." Aura said.

I was too big for the cave—barely had enough room to crawl in to begin with—and getting out wasn't possible unless I became human again. But then my heart would be vulnerable. With the dragon's mind, hatred numbed the pain. Could I do it?

I tried to shift but found it impossible. My heart raced as I tried again to become Maeve, the woman I once was. Reckless, and immature . . . GAH!

Nothing.

It was no use. I was trapped in this form forever. Cursed.

"No, not forever," Aura called down, hearing my thoughts. "Not until you forgive yourself, can you let your demons go. You are trapped in a curse of your own making."

It wasn't possible. There was no such thing, was there?

"Love yourself," Aura called out. "Forgive yourself. Let your past be the past."

It was a command filled with magic and I couldn't help but reflect on stolen moments of love with Aspen. Rhea begging in the mirror, refusing to believe that I had died. Laughing with my sisters in the tower as we tried to weave sleeping spells on each other. Racing Violet down the palace halls. Despite my mistakes, there was so much to live for, so much to love. In each memory, I saw their eyes filled with love, friendship, adoration. I was worth being loved. They proved it. If they loved me, all I had to do was love myself.

A sob ripped forth from my chest. A loud groan rocked the mountain, making it tremble beneath my power. Healing came from my tears and when the quaking stopped, I was human once more.

The darkness grew cold against my naked skin, and the rocks dug into my bare feet as I tried to find my way out of the shadows and into the light. The sun burned my eyes but cleansed my soul as I stepped out onto the misty mountain top.

Rosalie was quickly by my side, placing a robe around my naked shoulders. She pulled me into a hug, her very pregnant stomach bumping against my side. "We missed you."

"Violet," I murmured into her shoulder. "Is she?"

"She's fine. Look."

Blinking against the pain, I looked down at the wolf who shifted into my adorable rosy-cheeked darling niece. Being very careful, I lifted the small child. She felt so fragile in my arms.

"Birdy is back," Violet whispered. "Big birdy." I broke down and cried when her chubby arms wrapped around my neck.

"Yeah, pup," I kissed her nose. "I'm back. But how?" I asked Rosalie. "I thought she died?"

Rosalie took a deep breath. "It was Aspen."

"What? How is that possible?" I asked.

"He pulled himself to her. Protected her by shielding her body with his own as the glass ceiling collapsed."

My chest tightened and I fought against the tears. "He sacrificed himself to save me too."

Rosalie nodded. "Yes, he did. His sacrifices made this possible."

"I knew deep inside he was good-hearted."

Rosalie's head lowered in shame. "He was. I regret how I treated him. There's so much I need to apologize for . . . to both of you." She opened her mouth to say more, but I waved my hand cutting her off.

"I'm so sorry, Rosalie. I can't do this now . . . I just needed to get them air . . ."

Rosalie grasped the back of my neck and pulled me close into a sisterly hug that I didn't even know I needed. "I know, sweetie. You did everything you could. And you defeated Allemar. Something none of us have been able to do."

"No, he defeated himself. A trap of his own making." I used the words Aura had just said to me. "But to do so, I lost someone I loved. Now I'm all alone."

"You're not alone." Rose turned to point down the side of the mountain. It was covered with hundreds of animals. Wolves, jaguars, hawks, rabbits, sheep, bears, foxes, hundreds of the lesser clans of fae all spread out in unity across the mountain.

"What are they doing here?" I murmured as Rhea took a reluctant Violet from my arms.

"They're here to pay tribute to the shifter king—er, queen. Whatever title you want to call yourself."

"But I'm not . . ."

"You are. The shifter king has always been an omni. A king by talent, not by birth right." Her stoic voice cut through the crowd of animals. I covered my eyes from the fading sun and saw Mother Eville walking up the lone path toward me, her dark hair braided in a crown on her head.

"The title goes to the one who can take the most forms. I've known ever since the first time you turned into a crow instead of your raven form. But I also knew it was best to keep that secret from you until you were older, when you were more in control of your gifts. It's the strength of your shifter blood that has made your magic all the more powerful, erratic, and hard to control." Mother Eville smiled.

"I can't trust myself. Look what happened to Atlas, the last shifter king. He went mad and murdered the queen."

"No, he didn't. He fell in love with King Alder's wife. They were going to run away together. The king found out the plan and murdered his own wife, pinning the blame on Atlas. Thousands of shifters died over the jealousy of a human king."

"How do you know this?"

Mother Eville scoffed. "It's my job to know. Atlas was your great uncle. When the shifter wars began, your parents were smuggled out and lived segregated in the mountains. They died, and you were found by that elderly couple. I'm glad you made it to my doorstep. I've never regretted it since."

Three people were walking up the mountain through the crowd of shifters, and I cried with joy when I recognized Cross, Warden, Silva, and behind them, limping along, was Brekken.

Cross reached me first. The great lion of a man was still as quiet and noble as before, bearing newly healed battle scars across his chest.

"My Queen." Cross bowed to me.

Warden winked and flashed me his most debonair smile before taking a more extravagant bow.

Silva's cheeks flushed, and he placed his hand over his heart and gave a softer bow. Everything he did was graceful. How had I not known he was a swan? It seemed so obvious now. "Thank you, Maeve, for fighting Allemar on our behalf. For saving us all." Silva's voice was like honey.

Cross coughed and stepped forward. "I would be honored if you selected me to be your honor guard. My family has always protected the ruling family for centuries. It may be unorthodox, but every royal needs an honor guard. You are *our* queen."

I chuckled at Cross's frankness.

"I'm the best assassin." Warden said, throwing his hat in.

"I would be honored to have both of you in my honor guard." Brekken looked the most nervous. He swallowed and flinched when I reached out to grasp his hand. "But it won't be the same unless I have you by my side," I said.

"I'm not brave," he said.

"You're the bravest of them all because you face your fears."

Brekken's eyes became glassy. "I mean, if you want me as your guard, I would be happy as long as I don't have to wear—"

"Pants are mandatory," I interrupted.

Brekken looked stricken. "Well, then maybe I shouldn't—" Warden elbowed him roughly, and he yelped. "Got it, okay. Must wear pants."

Cross's stoic face cracked, and he couldn't stop laughing.

"So what happened with the candidates and the

trials?" I asked Cross. "I've kind of been in a hole for the last few months . . . literally."

Cross pointed to the plaid ribbon and silver pin on his belt. "I've been knighted and given a title. In fact, everyone who fought against Hela and the sorcerer were given titles and lands. King Xander passed a title down to Torren's eldest son." Cross gestured to those beside him. "Along with Brekken, Warden, and Silva."

I started to speak when Brekken suddenly stripped off his clothes and ran into the woods, shifting into a fox.

He rolled his eyes at Cross. "Why does he forget if he does that, he's not going to have clothes when he shifts back?"

Cross chuckled. "Oh, he knows."

Warden cupped his hands to his mouth and yelled, "Go, then! Wake up with pine needles up your butt." He looked at me and hissed at his own joke.

Cross picked up Brekken's discarded clothes. "We should go after him."

"Fine." Warden pouted as they headed off after their brother.

The sun was slowly setting, and I looked west. "Walk with me?" Silva asked.

I nodded, and we slowly walked down the mountain to a clearing, away from the eyes and ears of my sisters. Silva closed his eyes and raised his face to catch the last of the sun's rays. I wanted to reach out and rub my hand along the back of his neck to see if he preened like I did.

"What now?" I asked Silva. We came to a calm lake, the wind blowing ripples across the water's surface.

"We live. We learn. We survive. Like our ancestors did

before us." His voice was filled with hope. "Look." He pointed to the sky and six black swans flying in a V cut through the air headed toward the lake.

"Are those?"

"My brothers." Silva grinned. "It took a weeks to find them, but we finally did. He kept his promise."

"Who?" I asked, noticing a man on the edge of the lake for the first time. His dark blond hair was longer than I last saw it, almost touching his shoulders. He seemed somber, but there was no mistaking. It was him.

Aspen!

The gentlest of tugs pulled at my heart, and I gasped, wondering if we were still connected somehow. He hadn't noticed me, his attention directed to the oncoming swans. Their wings flapped as they slowed their descent and then landed on the cold surface. The swans swam to him eagerly, and he bent down. As he touched them, the silver band unclasped from their legs, and one by one they stood up. Six boys stepped out of the water and donned one of the green robes laid out by the bank. Silva ran toward them and waved his hand. The youngest couldn't have been more than fourteen winters. He turned and ran through the shallows, jumping into his older brother's arms.

"Brother!"

The reunion was beautiful. As Silva hugged and cried with each one of his brothers, he turned to the man, his eyes filled with tears. "Thank you, thank you for keeping your promise."

Aspen turned, his smile reaching his eyes when he saw me.

"Am I dreaming?" I asked.

He closed the distance between us, and he pulled me into a hug. "If we are, I don't want to wake up."

"Aspen. You're alive. How is that possible? I saw you die . . ."

"No," he whispered. "I mean—yes. I should be dead, but I did something I didn't know was possible." He pulled away, and his eyes darkened with sadness and grief. "Maeve, I did a terrible thing."

"Don't say that," I snapped. "You're alive. That's all that matters."

He rubbed his chest as if it still pained him. "The answer was in his buried journals. I learned how to break the bond between servant and master."

"It required a willing sacrifice," I added. "Something you should never have done. I almost lost you."

"Yes, but if I didn't, I would have lost you. We are no match for Allemar. I knew that. The only thing I could think of was to protect you with my dying breath. I felt our connection sever, and I felt myself dying. But I saw you fighting. Not giving up, and I knew I couldn't give up either. I had to fight. In the journals, I learned that when he leaches power, it can go two ways. So at the last second, when I thought all was lost, I took back what he had stolen from me. I pulled on his life to keep me alive."

"That's what had distracted Allemar during our fight. I thought he was hallucinating."

Aspen nodded. "He caught me. I thought for sure we were all dead. But then you stepped in front of me. I forgot that spells cannot penetrate dragon skin."

"I did too," I admitted.

Aspen reached up and cupped my face. "He would

have killed me, but you saved me. Before he died, I continued to pull from Allemar. It was enough magic and energy to protect Violet until Rosalie was able to rescue and heal us."

I threw my arms around him, waiting for him to kiss me in celebration, but he didn't. He just made a strange face.

"What's the matter?" I said, feeling irritated that our reunion wasn't going as I thought it should. "Did something happen to Velora and Marco?"

He shook his head. "No, they're fine. It seems Velora has transferred her affections to Marco, and he couldn't be happier protecting her because she always gets into trouble."

He grabbed my hand, and we walked away from the fluttering swans who were dancing about half naked, still overcome with joy in their reunion. My cheeks flushed, and I had to turn away. "You broke the curse on Silva's brothers."

He nodded. "He figured it out before anyone else did. That an acolyte of Allemar could remove the spelled bands on his brothers. He didn't know how to find me since Allemar kept all of us in the dark about each other. We don't really know how many more acolytes are out there in the seven kingdoms doing his bidding. Or how far in their apprenticeship they are. Like I said, Allemar's reach was long. But Silva knew the prince of Florin was an acolyte, and that I would likely be strong enough to break the spelled bands. He also knew that Allemar's apprentice was partnered with a shifter. So he put two and two together."

"Smart."

He nodded. "He was very smart. Playing his part, holding his cards close. Watching and waiting. He came to me the night before the trials, made me promise to break the spell on his brothers. He was scared that Allemar would kill them. I told him after we made it through the last trial, I would."

"That's who you were talking to on the balcony."

"Yes." Aspen sighed and paused on the pathway, neither heading up the mountain toward my sisters, nor turning back to the lake.

"Then why the long face? What's wrong?"

"Nothing . . . and yet, everything," he fumed.

"What?"

"It's Rosalie. She's gone mad."

"Even after all this, she still won't forgive you?" I held my breath and waited for the terrible news.

"Worse." His face fell. "She went and made me king."

I snorted. "Sounds like Rosalie. She hates this country and wants nothing more than to take her family and retreat to her backward kingdom of Baist."

"I spent my whole life trying to avoid becoming an evil ruler like my father. I came back to try to make up for past mistakes, and I've found myself trapped here again. I entered the trials because I wanted to prove that I could be a good person. That I would have been a good ruler. Now it's been thrust upon me. I'm back in prison."

"But it's a very pretty prison," I said, using the same words to describe the castle when I was being held there . He frowned. "With fancy food."

He shook his head. "I've got a better idea," he said, reaching his hands around my waist and lifting me in the air. "Marry me. Be my shifter queen."

"But you hate shifters," I said warily.

He winced. "I was raised to hate shifters; told they couldn't be trusted. A long standing prejudice passed down from previous generations. But I've learned that they were wrong. Loving you and Violet is evidence that *I* was wrong. Shifters shouldn't be feared because they're different, but celebrated. We will prove that humans and shifters can live in peace without fighting and arguing with each other." He put my feet back on the ground. "We can slowly repair the distrust from the shifter wars."

My heart was happy, thudding loudly. When I looked at Aspen, I saw another broken person who was slowly healing—just like me. Someone so full of hate, that I thought it was impossible for people like us to find love. But we were both wrong.

I pushed away from him. "Oh, come on. Have you met me? I always fight and argue. It's in my very nature to be disruptive and annoying."

"Well, you can't anymore because there's no use fighting me. I will always win."

"Says who?" I said, putting my fists on my hips.

Aspen leaned forward and kissed me on the lips. "Says me because I have a secret weapon." He cupped his hands around my face and covered my mouth with his, kissing me deeper. My knees went weak, and my heart raced. When we broke apart, I was struggling to regain my train of thought.

"Wh-what's that?" I tried to ask.

"I'm just going to kiss you until you can't remember what we were fighting about," he answered.

I laughed. "Then I will make it my life goal to argue often. Daily, every candle mark even."

He gave me another kiss on my lips. "Then I look forward to all of our future arguments."

"I hate you," I teased, wrapping my hands around his neck.

"I know."

CONTINUE THE DAUGHTERS OF
EVILLE SERIES WITH

Coming December 2021

ABOUT THE AUTHOR

Chanda Hahn is a NYT & USA Today Bestselling author of The Unfortunate Fairy Tale series. She uses her experience as a children's pastor, children's librarian and bookseller to write compelling and popular fiction for teens. She was born in Seattle, WA, grew up in Nebraska, and currently resides in Waukesha, WI, with her husband and their twin children; Aiden and Ashley.

Visit Chanda Hahn's website to learn more about her other forthcoming books.
www.chandahahn.com

www.ingramcontent.com/pod-product-compliance
Lightning Source LLC
Chambersburg PA
CBHW061303190726
48288CB00002B/327